A Beautiful Day for a Wedding

Former magazine editor Charlotte Butterfield was born in Bristol in 1977. She studied English at Royal Holloway University and an MPhil in Gender and Women's Studies at Birmingham University before becoming a journalist and copywriter. She moved to Dubai in 2005, but now lives in Rome with her husband and three children.

🐦 @charliejayneb
f @charlottebutterfieldauthor
www.charlottebutterfield.com

Also by Charlotte Butterfield

Crazy Little Thing Called Love
Me, You and Tiramisu

A Beautiful Day for a Wedding

Charlotte Butterfield

A division of HarperCollins Publishers
www.harpercollins.co.uk

Harper*Impulse* an imprint of
HarperCollins*Publishers*
The News Building
1 London Bridge Street
London SE1 9GF

www.harpercollins.co.uk

This paperback edition 2018

First published in Great Britain in ebook format by
HarperCollins*Publishers* 2018

A catalogue record for this book
is available from the British Library

ISBN: 9780008302719

This novel is entirely a work of fiction.
The names, characters and incidents portrayed in it are
the work of the author's imagination. Any resemblance to
actual persons, living or dead, events or localities is
entirely coincidental.

MIX
Paper from
responsible sources
FSC™
www.fsc.org   FSC® C007454

Printed and bound by CPI Group (UK) Ltd, Croydon, CR0 4YY

To Team P: Ed, Amélie, Rafe and Theo

Prologue

*H*ow to be the perfect bridesmaid. Rule number one: Start mourning the friend you love, because once she becomes entangled in wedding planning, she doesn't exist anymore.

Gone are the easy chats about life, love and the universe, and in its place are endless one-sided monologues about whether it would be unreasonable to ask all the bridesmaids to pierce their ears so they can wear matching earrings (answer: yes). Evenings will be spent pondering the question of whether tulips are too cheap, orchids too expensive or peonies too try-hard. Who cares? They'll either end up swept up with the confetti by an Eastern European cleaner on minimum wage in the morning, or carefully preserved in an airing cupboard by the groom's granny. You know the friend that's always been very supportive about your extra curves? Well, as soon as that sparkly solitaire gets slipped on her finger she'll 'accidentally' order your bridesmaid dress a size too small forcing you to eat blended kale for a month before the wedding.

Let's talk hen dos for just a moment. What a wonderful

opportunity for some sisterhood solidarity, where dignity and self-consciousness are checked in with your coat at the door and the order of the day is friendship and fun. Wrong. Don't even think about surprising the bride with an activity, theme or outfit she hasn't approved. In writing. She may say that you have the power of attorney on this weekend, but she doesn't mean it, she's lying through her newly-whitened teeth – which brings me onto the subject of beauty. The role of a bridesmaid is to be pretty, but not too much. Save those fake eyelashes for another occasion, because God forbid you should have longer lash-action than the woman in white. By all means brush your hair, possibly even add a bit of bounce, but do not consider having an up-do that takes more than two minutes to construct. That's her arena. The only part of your grooming routine you shouldn't scrimp on is deodorant. You'll need at least half a can sprayed into your armpits at all times to counteract the iron-woman training that you'll be forced to do in the week before the big day. Fill your car with petrol, top up your oyster card, stash your heels for another day, and flex those limbs because good God are you going to be using them. Unless you are already a PA to the president of a small country, never before will you have been faced with a To Do List of the gargantuan proportions that you will soon be handed. And the best part is, you have to smile like Mary Poppins while cheerily crossing each item off. Hem curtains? Check. Polish floors? Check. Dog-sit for a fortnight? Che— Fuck. Fuck fuck fuckity fuck.

Eve had no idea that her legs could even move that fast. Weaving in and out of office workers, shoving tourists out of the way, hurdling over open drains, and banging on the sides of open-top buses, she finally made it to the front of her friend Tanya's apartment block. Steadying herself on the gate for a moment to let the burning sensation in her lungs subside, she silently offered up a little prayer that she wasn't about to walk into the rotting carcass of a pedigree pug.

The stench hit her before the key was fully turned in the lock. Covering her mouth with her sleeve and trying not to retch, Eve slowly pushed open the door and braced herself for whatever sight she might find. The flat was still. Silent. Too still and silent for an apartment with a dog in it.

'Coco, here girl, there's a good girl.' Eve wandered quickly from room to room, giving a small gasp at the doorway of each one at the carnage that assaulted her eyes. The thought crossed her mind that perhaps Tanya had been burgled, the flat ransacked and the dog stolen. It would certainly make explaining this slightly easier. But robbers wouldn't chew the sides of sofas until their filling spilled out, or wee on the expensive dhurrie rug from Peshawar. The ridiculous thing was, Eve was actually a little heartened to see the mess that Coco had made, as it meant that at some point over the last three days she'd had enough energy to create this bloodbath, rather than spend her final hours festering into a pile of bones.

The door to the bedroom was ajar, and, not having fully shaken away her intruder theory, Eve approached it cautiously. 'Coco? Coco?' A shoebox lay open at the foot of the bed, its lid chewed off. The distinctive red soles of Tanya's prized black patent Louboutin heels were thankfully unmarked by tiny teeth marks, but instead, they'd been used as a portaloo. 'Oh, sweet Jesus.'

At the sound of her voice, a sleeping Coco eagerly jumped up from the satin pillows she'd been snoozing on and gave a yelp of sheer joy. Flinging herself at Eve, in all her stinky glory, she covered her with slobbery kisses, which Eve couldn't help but tearfully return. 'Oh God Coco, I'm so sorry, please don't tell anyone,' she picked her up, snuggling her face into her fur. 'It'll be our secret.'

After giving her some water and filling her bowl with dried pellets that promised they contained organic chicken, she grabbed her lead from the back of the kitchen door. The destruction of the flat could wait, it was more important to breathe air that hadn't been contaminated by excrement.

Chapter 1

One month earlier...

'No offence Eve, but I don't like your ideas for the hen party.'

Any sentence that starts off with the words, 'No offence' could surely only ever result in the other person being immediately and instinctively offended, Eve thought. And how on earth did Tanya know what her plans even were as they were meant to be top secret? Every subject line of every email Eve had sent about the hen do had said so. In capitals. As if she had read Eve's mind, Tanya followed up with, 'Maggie forwarded me the emails.'

Maggie. Eve should have known. One of Tanya's work colleagues, who Eve had not yet had the pleasure of meeting, had Replied All to every message, finding fault with each element.

'I mean, a roller disco? What were you thinking Eve?'

'We used to love the roller disco!'

'When we were at university! I do not want to turn up to my wedding in a plaster cast!'

'So I guess that you don't want to go zorbing either?'

'No, Eve, I do not. Honestly, I thought that you of all people would be able to come up with something original, fun, and safe for us all to do. It's meant to be in three weeks' time!'

'What do you mean, *me* of all people?'

'You work for a wedding magazine, Eve! If anyone should be able to pull a fantastic hen do out of a hat, it should be you.'

'To be fair Tanya, it's taken flippin' ages to get everyone to confirm if they can come or not, then everyone had a different idea about what it was they wanted to do – you'd already vetoed any kind of cocktail-making, naked male bodies and making things.'

'How many cocktail-making hen parties have you been to?' Eve didn't say so out loud, but Tanya had a point. 'And I'm going to be looking at Luke's naked body for the rest of my life, I don't particularly want to see another one on my hen do.'

'Which is why I made the plan I did, there's not a cocktail or a penis in sight.'

Eve's colleague, Kat, the magazine's beauty director who sat at the adjacent desk to Eve's, raised a pencilled-on eyebrow at hearing Eve's last sentence.

Tanya wouldn't let up. 'So out of everything else in the world we could do, you chose roller disco and zorbing?'

'And a meal out; believe me, finding a restaurant that would cater for a vegan, a coeliac, a lactose-intolerance, a shellfish allergy and two nut allergies, was pretty bloody difficult. You have very tricky friends.'

'Yes, Maggie told me that you've booked a Lebanese place. I hate Middle Eastern food.'

'Hate's a pretty strong word Tanya, how can you hate an entire continent's cuisine? I'm sure there'll be something you'll like.'

'I doubt it.'

'That's the spirit,' Eve said, cradling the phone under her chin while she scrolled through the local dog shelter's website for photogenic mutts for a feature she was writing on Instagram engagements. She had a lovely image in her mind of two cute dogs holding up a sign saying, 'our humans are getting married'.

'Are you being sarcastic?' Tanya barked. 'This is the only hen do I'm ever going to have, Eve, and I want it to be perfect. I want a country club, a few beauty treatments, lots of champagne and sushi.'

'You said you wanted it to be a surprise.'

'Well, I don't. That's what I want.'

'You could have saved me about thirty hours of planning and phoning round if that's what you had just said in the beginning you know?'

'You're one of my best friends, you're meant to know what I'd like.'

Labelling the two of them 'best friends' was a bit of a stretch. Eve was starting to realise that being contacted by Tanya out of the blue to be asked to be her bridesmaid, a decade after they were at university together, had little to do with nostalgia or fuzzy feelings of friendship and more to do with Tanya wanting to take advantage of Eve's little black book of wedding contacts.

Eve absentmindedly pulled another paperclip out of her stationery pot and added it to a long line of clips that was now stretching across her desk. 'Fine. Leave it with me.'

'Oh, and one more thing, do you have your ears pierced?'

That was an odd question. 'No, why?'

'Could you get them done before the wedding? I've bought all the bridesmaids the same earrings to wear on the day as your gift from me.'

This took the biscuit. 'Um, not really Tanya, I've never liked the idea of it.'

Eve could sense Tanya's lips pursing over the phone line, possibly accompanied by a hint of an eye twitch too. 'Maybe you could think about it, Eve.'

'I have thought about it Tanya, and I don't want to do it. I've got long hair anyway, so you wouldn't even see them.'

'Well, I want you to wear it up, nothing fancy like mine's going to be, just a simple ponytail.'

Eve wanted to say more, to inject her friend with a hearty dose of realism and perspective right into her toned behind, but instead took a deep breath. 'A ponytail is not a problem, the ear piercing is. But I promise you it's not going to ruin your day.' Eve hung up the call and slammed it down on her desk.

Kat looked up from a row of carefully-ordered pink lipsticks that were standing sentry on her own desk for a feature called *Kiss-proof lipsticks that will stay on your lips not your groom*. 'Which one of your bridezillas was that?'

'Tanya. Taking bridezilla-dom to another level entirely. I now have to find a country hotel that can fit twelve women in for beauty treatments in three weeks' time. And a Japanese restaurant that doesn't use shellfish and delivers to the arse end of nowhere. Oh, and she wants me to mutilate my body in order to accept my present which has quite clearly come from the heart.'

Sighing, Eve turned back to her computer screen. Her *Dear Eve* inbox was heaving under the strain of the many unread emails that had come in over the weekend. As well as writing three or four features for *Your Wonderful Wedding* per month, Eve was also the magazine's resident agony aunt. But as wedding magazines were beautiful and aspirational, and not angst-ridden drama sagas like her last magazine, *What a Life!*, most of the questions were about how to stop the groom's buttonhole from drooping, rather than anything more gritty. It made a nice change to be writing about the highest point in someone's life rather than their lowest. Writing features with headlines like *Blooming lovely*, or *Love at first blush* certainly beat ones like *My nephew is also my uncle* or *Why our 50-year age gap doesn't matter.*

Hi Eve!

I'm torn between wanting a French manicure for my day or a dusky pink to match the roses in my bouquet and the bridesmaid dresses. My mum thinks that a pink will be better, but I'm worried it might chip and look more obvious? At least if a French manicure chips, you can't really see it. What should I do?

Thanks,

Helen, Staffordshire.

Eve was only meant to select the best five emails for the monthly Q&A page and to ignore the rest. Print-worthy, this one was not, but as she could sense the desperation in Helen from Staffordshire's email, Eve replied nonetheless.

> *Hi Helen,*
>
> *Firstly, congratulations on your big day, and well done for choosing such an on-trend colour for your wedding, dusky pink is a timeless choice. The best solution would be to wear the pink varnish and ask one of your brides-maids to carry a spare bottle of the matching colour in their clutch bag to solve any chipping disasters.*
>
> *Enjoy your day!*
>
> *Eve xx*

It wasn't strictly what she was paid to do, and Eve knew that her editor, Fiona, wouldn't approve of her taking time out of her working day to personally reply, but it had taken all of fifteen seconds to stop Helen from Staffordshire losing any more sleep.

Eve's phone buzzed again. It was another university friend, Ayesha, who was getting married a month after Tanya. 'Babe, where can I buy lawn flamingoes?'

Eve looked heavenward. 'Lawn what?'

'Flamingoes.'

'That's what I thought you said. What are lawn flamingoes?'

'You know, big sculptures of flamingoes that stand on your lawn. I thought it would be really nice to have one for everyone coming to the wedding and you have to find the one with your name on it and it's got your table number on it too.'

Eve had to take a deliberately slow breath in before replying in case an expletive slipped out. 'Um, Ayesha. I thought the theme for your wedding was *The Wizard of Oz*? At what point in the film were there flamingoes?'

Ayesha laughed. 'Oh, there weren't silly, I just really *really* love flamingoes, and I thought that getting lots of dwarves to stand on the lawn dressed like Munchkins might be in really poor taste. Unless you don't think so?'

Not for the first time, Eve questioned her choice in friends.

'You're too nice.' Kat remarked as soon as Eve had put down the phone. 'If I said yes every time one of my friends asked me to help them with their weddings, I'd never have time for anything else.'

'Welcome to my world,' Eve muttered.

'How many weddings do you have again this summer?'

'Five.' Eve pointed to the noticeboard that hung on the wall above her desk, which was crammed with save the dates, invitations and gift list registry cards. A couple, like Tanya's, were classically white with embossed words while others, like Ayesha's, were colourful and contemporary. Regardless of their style or size of swirly writing, all Eve could see when she glanced at them was the potential of stress and financial ruin.

'Five? That's insane.'

'But it's not just the weddings is it? It's all the hen dos and rehearsals, I literally have one free weekend between now and the end of August.'

'Eve, they're not your weddings though, you are allowed to have fun outside of being chief wedding planner you know.

Look at you, you're gorgeous, in a very English sort of way, with your long red hair and alabaster skin—'

'You can tell you're a beauty journalist,' Eve interrupted. 'I'm pale and freckly.'

'And interesting. You're young, and you're wasting the summer by being at the beck and call of people who have already found their other halves.'

'Cheers.'

'I'm serious!' Kat said, emphasising how serious she was by waving a lipstick in Eve's face. 'How long have we worked together now?'

'Two years.'

'Two years. And in those two years, how many boyfriends have you had? You're never going to find someone if you don't put yourself out there.'

What was the opposite of rose-tinted, Eve wondered, because it was exactly the same any time a friend of hers became coupled-up; they looked back on their solo days with hand-on-heart relief that they had dragged themselves out of the cesspool of single life.

'See, that's the difference Kat, it barely crosses my mind to look for a boyfriend, let alone "put myself out there!"' Eve shuddered. 'When the time is right, he'll just turn up.'

'Eve, Eve, Eve,' Kat shook her head the way you would to a child that's put their left shoe on their right foot for the fortieth time. 'Finding a partner requires a massive amount of effort, he doesn't just "turn up". Have you learnt nothing from writing about weddings?'

Kat had a point. It always amazed Eve how much effort

some of the brides, and some grooms too, had put into finding someone to marry. If she'd had the job of interviewing couples twenty or thirty years ago about how they met, the stories would have invariably included the words 'school', 'pub', or 'nightclub', but nowadays the hoops that brides jumped through to get to the altar were staggering.

'I like being single,' Eve said. 'Anyway, I am far too busy.'

'It's just that in the two years I've known you, you've never had anyone special in your life, and you're pretty cool so I just wonder why, that's all.' Kat started putting the lipsticks away in their boxes. 'You don't have to tell me if you don't want to.'

'There's no big mystery, Kat. I really liked someone once, and I'm just waiting to meet another person that I like as much, that's all.'

'So, what happened to him?'

Eve used the time it took to sweep all her paperclips into her hand and pour them back into their pot to think of an answer that was completely devoid of sentiment. There was no point getting upset about it after all this time. She settled on, 'I honestly have no idea.' Which, as it happened, was completely true.

Chapter 2

The wedding with the wizards

There weren't many instances when you could use the word puce in daily life, but as Eve lay on her back in the park looking up at the sky darkening above her, she knew that puce would be a legitimate description of her face at that moment. She'd been so disappointed when her name had been called out as the winner of a series of ten personal training sessions rather than the chocolate hampers in the raffle at her work's Christmas party. She'd tried to give the prize away, but everyone she knew either had their own gym membership already or were too much like her and couldn't think of anything worse than being shouted at while you huffed and puffed in a park after work as dog walkers sniggered by.

The personal trainer, Juan, had been in regular contact through January, February, even into March, calling her to set up her first appointment – but it wasn't until early May, when Tanya had admitted that she'd made a 'mistake' with the order of Eve's bridesmaid dress and it was 'accidentally' a size too small, that Eve thought that maybe the personal training

14

sessions might not be such a bad idea after all. The first session had been a success. She was measuring the success of it by the fact that she was still alive. And Eve was very hopeful that at some point later that evening, her face would return back to its normal shade.

'Same time on Wednesday?' Juan asked, his kit bag slung over his shoulder, casting a long shadow over the patch of grass where Eve lay. She didn't yet have the lung capacity for speech, so just weakly raised her hand and gave him a thumbs up. She thought that she'd just wait a little while longer before heading back home. It was a beautiful evening, perfect for lying back and enjoying the setting sun, and her choice had nothing at all to do with the fact that her legs felt like they were made of concrete.

The trumpet player downstairs was in full flow when Eve let herself in the front door of Becca's flat. She had to stop calling it that. It was now her apartment too, and it was an absolute palace compared to the cupboard in New York she'd called home for two years before moving back to London. Living above a live music pub was a godsend when the iPod ran out of charge, but a tad annoying when the band in question was an avant-garde experimental Cuban quartet. Which, thankfully, tonight's wasn't. Toe-tapping jazz seemed to be the soundtrack to her evening, which suited Eve just fine.

Becca had already set up camp on their tiny balcony, which overlooked the pub's beer garden, placing two beanbags next to a wine cooler that had a couple of bottles already chilling in it. Eve smiled, this was the perfect way to spend the evening.

Tonight's workout had been brutal. Juan's girlfriend had just dumped him, and his hatred of all women seemed to extend to his clients too. Forty burpees was thirty nine too many for Eve, and every inch of her was crying out for a restorative shower, a glass of something with a strong alcohol content and a night with her best friend listening to Sinatra classics.

'Evening!' Eve shouted from the hallway through the open door to the living room. 'Just going to de-sweat myself and be out in a minute. Have you got snacks out there?'

'I have the Chinese delivery menu, which is sort of the same thing,' Becca shouted back. 'And you had some post, it was heavy, a book or something. I put it on your bed.'

Eve knew what it was. She'd recently organised the delivery of sixty-five guidebooks to addresses all over the world ahead of her brother Adam and his boyfriend George's nuptials on the last weekend in August. The fifth, and final, wedding of the year. It was in the South of France and they wanted all their guests to get as excited as they were, so despite being three months away, stage one of Operation Hype Up The Wedding was the delivery of the guidebooks about the local area. There were three more deliveries planned over the coming months: a bottle of the local wine, passport holders and luggage tags. All of which Eve had dutifully sourced, ordered and, at the moment, paid for on her credit card.

Ten minutes later, wearing her pyjama bottoms with her long wet hair dampening her hooded top from university, Eve settled down onto the spare beanbag and gratefully took the glass of white wine from Becca's outstretched hand.

'Now this, this is pretty darn perfect.'

'I'll say so.' Becca agreed, stretching her legs out in front of her to poke them between the railings of the balcony, which must have looked pretty odd to anyone sitting in the garden beneath them. 'They've been practising since I got home from work,' Becca said. 'It's been great, like having a mini concert in our living room. I'm going to miss this.'

Eve knew when she'd moved in that it wasn't a long-term arrangement as Becca's wedding to military man Jack was wedding number four of the summer and Jack had been faithfully promised a family house on the base after the wedding. Whenever the thought of Becca moving out popped into her head, Eve batted it away. She and Becca had lived together all the way through university, sharing a tiny semi in one of Brighton's less salubrious back streets with Tanya, and another friend, Ben. Even though eight years lay between them sharing that semi and this flat, Eve and Becca had slotted straight back into being flatmates.

'Have you sorted your costume for Rob's wedding on Saturday?' Eve asked, trying not to wince at the word costume rather than outfit. She really didn't understand why some couples insisted on their guests joining in their theme by donning superhero capes or flapper dresses; what was wrong with a nice wrap dress?

'I'm raiding the school drama department's store cupboard tomorrow.'

'If you see something for me, can you pick it up?'

Perhaps now, Eve thought, with the chilled wine in hand and the soft jazz rising from the bar below, Becca would be open to talking about the logistics of her own wedding.

Considering that she'd been engaged for nearly three years you'd have thought she'd have been further along in the planning process. Eve remembered back to when Becca had broken the news of her engagement, calling her across the Atlantic, as she did most evenings. Their calls were Eve's favourite part of the day, which she had admitted to no one but Becca, because after all, living in New York was supposed to be fun. If you were to ask any single thirty-year old whether New York was a fun place you'd have to cover your ears with the deafening volume of the resounding yeses, which would be promptly followed by the clink of ice into gin martinis. If you were in media in New York it meant you'd made it. Hit the big time. Written your own success story. You were playing in the major league. Everyone knew that. It was only Becca who knew this wasn't really the case for Eve.

That night, almost three years ago, Eve had just carried her dinner across the tiny hallway to her windowless bedroom in a dodgy part of Brooklyn, when she had felt her phone vibrating in her back pocket. She had set the hot bowl of microwaved soup down on a pile of coffee table books that doubled up as her dining table, desk and nightstand and answered the nightly call from her best friend.

'Evening lovely, how's your day been?'

'Exhausting, soul-destroying, murderous,' Eve had replied.

'Murderous. That's a new one.'

'I think that one has staying power. Today, I've interviewed a man who lived his life dressed as a baby, a woman whose plastic surgery on her bottom went so wrong it was impossible to sit down, a couple who raised pot-bellied pigs in their

18

house instead of children, and I wrote a feature with the headline "*My boyfriend has a Spiderman mask tattooed on his face.*"' Back in the beginning, when Eve had fought off hundreds of other journalists and got the job as Features Editor for *What a Life!* in the Big Apple, she was horrified at the people knocking on the magazine's doors to share their stories for the set fifty-dollar fee. There was no way this type of magazine could ever be sustainable, Eve had thought, surely the weirdness would dry up? There must be a finite number of bizarre people around the world? It turned out there wasn't. And thanks to the page at the front of the magazine listing all the staff members and their contact details, every single weirdo had Eve's email address.

'Ask me how my day's been,' Becca had demanded.

'Becca, how has your day been?'

'Absobloodylutely fabulous. Jack and I got engaged!'

Eve's face had burst into a spontaneous smile. 'That's amazing news! I'm so happy for you, honestly that's made my day. My week! Heck, you know what? That's the best news I've heard all year. And it's the middle of December, so the year is almost up.'

'Jack was such a sweetheart. We went down to Devon to visit Mum and Dad and he took my dad for a pint and asked him, then he took me for a walk through the woods and proposed to me at exactly 3.33pm, my favourite time.'

Eve mumbled through the spoonful of tinned minestrone she'd just scooped into her mouth: 'You have a favourite time?'

'Of course I do! Doesn't everyone? Anyway, stop talking. I wanted to ask you something important. You're so amazing at planning stuff, and such an organisational fiend, and you're my best friend, so will you be my chief bridesmaid and also help me plan the wedding?'

'Yes and yes! Oh my goodness, this is so exciting! What are you thinking? A city do in a posh hotel, or a manor house in the country, or a... oh Becca, we could do it abroad!'

'I want a really low-key thing in my parent's cow field.'

Eve stopped chewing.

'Eve? Are you still there?'

'I'm sorry, for a moment I thought I heard you say that you wanted to get married in a cow field.'

'Well, not actually married, we'll do that at the local church, but I want to have the reception in the field behind my folks' farm.'

'Won't the cows mind the intrusion?'

'We'll move them silly. But I love the idea of a festival feel, with bunting and barrels and picnic baskets. Do you think we could pull it off?'

'If that's what you want, that's what you'll get. I'll start my research tomorrow. This is so exciting, and just the thing I need to take my mind off how shitty my life is.'

'You don't have to stay in New York you know, you could just come back,' Becca had reminded her, not for the first time.

Eve had pretended not to hear her, just like she did every time Becca had said it. Going back to London wasn't an option. 'So what time of year are you thinking? If it's going to be outside, I'm guessing summer?'

'Yes, not the next one though, that's too soon. Maybe the

one after that. Or the one after that.' It was typical Becca, laid-back to the point of comatose. The vague date did little to quell Eve's enthusiasm for planning though, and Becca's engagement had resulted in a new job for Eve too. The following day she'd quickly realised that there was no better antidote to the gritty seediness she usually spent her day delving into than the swirly pink and turquoise fonts of online wedding magazines that had headlines like *Super-pretty princess dresses* and *Best day ever!* Every website Eve looked at had little hearts doodled into their company logos. Each photo of couples staring adoringly at each other had a soft-focus finish that made their love seem even more magical. How could you ever be miserable writing about romance every day?

Scrolling down the page past a link to an article on bouquets called *Everything's rosy* and one on honeymoon destinations entitled *Paradise found,* Eve's eyes had rested on a little pink box on the right of the page. Above the editor's email address, were two words that had made Eve's eyes widen: *We're hiring*.

Without giving herself any time to change her mind, Eve had quickly typed out an email, attached her CV and pressed send. And Eve-the-wedding-guru was born.

She'd stayed with the American wedding magazine for a year before reluctantly moving back to London to work for its English edition when her dad had died. It had been as though the universe had aligned everything to slot into place: the job opening in London, Becca's former flatmate moving out; call it coincidence, fate, luck – whatever it was, it meant Eve's transition back into London life wasn't as awful as she had thought it might be. It didn't stop the ghosts taunting her around every corner though.

A sudden drum solo from the bar below brought Eve back to the present day, and their balcony. 'So,' Eve started gently, 'have you thought about a band for *your* wedding?'

'Jack's friends are going to bring their guitars.'

'Oh.' Eve said. This did not sound good. 'Are they, um, professional musicians?'

'No, not at all. You know Gavin, Jack's friend from work? Well, he used to play, and Jack's brothers, and a couple of other people too – we're encouraging everyone to bring whatever instruments they have and just have a mash-up.'

'A mash-up?' Eve realised that she must sound incredibly middle-aged, but she couldn't help herself. 'That might be good for the end of the night, for the people that want to stay and carry on the party, but don't you want some dancing and music that people know?'

Becca lay her head back on her beanbag. 'Eve, you're stressing me out. I'm not like Tanya, who needs everything planned to within an inch of its life. What will be will be, it's going to be fine. Now be quiet and listen to the lovely music.'

Eve refused to give up. Not when she'd just published an article about how vital good entertainment was to a wedding. 'See, that's my point. Music is really important. If you like this band so much, why don't you pop down in the next break and ask them for their card?'

'Why don't you?'

In the end, Eve did a lot better than that and paid them a fifty-pound deposit to put the date of Becca's wedding in their diaries. She would tackle the issue of what on earth Becca was intending to feed her guests in the cow field another night.

***

'So I got these.' Becca dumped two big carrier bags full of clothes and props onto the kitchen counter next to where Eve was chopping up some onions for their sausage and mash dinner.

'Oh my God Becca, I only wanted a witch's hat, not a wardrobe for the entire magic circle!'

'The invitation said to come in your wizardry finery, a witch's hat wouldn't cut it. Anyway, I spoke to a few of the other people at work that are going, and everyone is making a massive effort. Rob's even had a prosthetic nose made like Voldemort's. Can't wait to see what his fiancée's wearing – what's her name again?'

'Jackie. You're going to have to remember that tomorrow, it's very bad form to forget the bride's name, even if you do only know the groom.'

'Jackie. Got it. And do you reckon Jackie is fully on board with marrying the Dark Lord?'

Eve smiled. 'I can't say that he would be my immediate choice for a groom, come to think of it. Neither would Rob, but that's by the by.'

'They're both massive Harry Potter fans, they even got engaged at King's Cross station next to the Platform 9 ¾ sign.'

Eve's knife kept slicing. 'That's lovely. Nothing shouts I love you quite so much as the smell of tramps' urine and fourteen thousand Japanese school kids on a magic tour.'

'You are so unromantic Eve. I think it's really nice that they share a hobby. Now do you want to see what's in the bags or not?'

'Absolutely, let's have dinner first though.'

'Oh, and don't forget we need to cook the rice for tomorrow as well.'

'What are you talking about?'

'There was a note with the invitation to say that we're not allowed to throw confetti, so we have to throw rose petals or rice.'

'Oh my God Becca, they don't want you to cook it first! It's dry rice, you muppet, did you think that everyone was going to be hurling handfuls of risotto into the bride's face?'

'I did think it was a bit odd, if I'm honest.'

'I love you, I do,' Eve put her arm around her friend's shoulders. 'But I honestly don't know how you manage to get through each day alive.'

***

The next morning Becca and Eve, wearing matching black graduation gowns, waist-length grey wigs and carrying chopsticks as wands, got off a train somewhere in the middle of Sussex and boarded a waiting bus that said Hogwarts Express on the front. Becca wasn't wrong; the other guests had taken the dress code very seriously indeed, one man even sported an ankle-length white beard that looked like he'd grown it specially for the occasion. A few women seemed to have mistakenly interpreted 'wizardry finery' to mean St Trinian's tarty schoolgirl. The bus was unbearably hot and Eve's wig was itchy. She could feel beads of perspiration on the back of her neck but felt immediately better when she spotted a woman who was sweating herself into an early grave in a full-on feathery owl costume.

The vows were taken over a goblet of fire, the bride's veil was held in place with a golden snitch comb, and when the happy couple knelt down to receive their blessing, written on the sole of the bride's left shoe were the words, '*From Muggle…*' and on the right in matching writing, '*…To Mrs*'. At the point where the vicar asked for the rings the couple turned around and looked up expectantly into the sky. The congregation followed their gaze.

Nothing happened.

Then Voldemort Rob, the groom, held out his gloved arm and started shouting. 'Barney! Barney!'

Silence.

'Barney, Barney!'

Then Jackie, who had sullied the effect of a two-thousand-pound wedding dress by accessorising it with a stripy red and yellow knitted Gryffindor scarf, joined in, shrilly calling, 'Barney, Barney.'

Eve's shoulders to shake with silent laughter.

'Stop it.' Becca whispered, stifling her own giggle.

'Barney! Barney!' Jackie's father, wearing a stuck-on bushy beard like Hagrid joined in, and before too long the whole wedding party were staring up at the sky shouting at the clouds. It was too much for Eve and Becca who let themselves be taken over by uncontrollable laughter that had tears running down their faces.

Finally, after what seemed like days of waiting, a bemused looking barn owl, with the wedding rings tied to his claw, swooped in and landed with a thud on Rob's outstretched arm.

'I can't breathe,' Eve gasped.

Please don't misunderstand me, Eve wrote in her diary that night. *I love a good fancy dress party as much as the next person, actually scrap that, probably more than the next person – but would I want to marry the love of my life wearing Princess Leia style Danish pastry hair buns while my handsome groom donned a Chewbacca costume? Not really, no. It's not even about what people would say, or what the grandkids would think when they looked through the wedding album. It's because I don't really want to marry a hairy Wookiee warrior, I'd rather marry the person I fell in love with, thanks very much.*

There are times and places for costumes – the theatre, for one. Plays would be rather dull and uninteresting if everyone was just wearing normal clothes. Macbeth wouldn't seem half as loony if he was wearing Diesel jeans and a Lacoste polo shirt and there's no way that Joseph's Technicolour Dreamcoat would work if he was wearing a mac from Superdry. Bedrooms – there's another place where the odd roleplay outfit can work a treat. New Year's Eve parties, birthday parties, anniversary parties, parties for the sake of having parties. All good occasions for a raid of the old dressing up box. But when I go to a wedding I like a bit of glam; a reason to blow dust off the fascinator that's on top of the wardrobe; the chance to wear heels and perhaps carry a bag that doesn't go over both shoulders. It's very difficult to dance when you're wearing a head-to-toe owl costume. And I know this for a fact because I've seen it firsthand.

Chapter 3

It was the second month in a row that Eve had covered the rent for Becca. She understood that being a teaching assistant in a specialist autism centre was more of a vocation than a goldmine, but Eve's paltry journalist's pay was not going to pay for a two-bed flat in central London indefinitely. Not to mention, she was still paying off her credit card from her extortionate flight back to the UK from the year before, and all Adam's bits for the wedding that he hadn't paid her back for yet. And this summer was costing a fortune with the number of bridal showers, wedding presents, new outfits, and hotel stays she had to fork out for.

It didn't help that Tanya's new itinerary for her hen do this weekend had tripled the original cost. Now Eve had to pay for a facial she didn't really want (all those oils always made her skin erupt faster than Vesuvius), a night away in a hotel whose rates were far more than other hotels just because it had the word 'spa' shoe-horned into its name, and a raw fish platter that was being delivered from forty miles away due to the lack of Japanese eateries in the countryside – a potential bout of food poisoning had now been added to the list of things Eve already disliked about this weekend. But as chief party planner, it was her job to up the tempo, keep smiling, and pretend that she was loving every minute.

Plastering her 'aren't we all having so much fun' face on, she shoved her clothes in the locker, put the fluffy white towelling robe on, slipped her feet into the white slippers, trying not to wonder if they had been washed since the last person wore them, and padded down the corridor to join the rest of Tanya's friends who were lounging by the pool. Thank God Becca and Ayesha were there to keep her sane or Eve might well have crawled into the locker and stayed there all weekend.

The spa only had three therapists, so at any one time during the whole day, three of the hen party were always missing after being officiously summoned by the head therapist, who looked as though she'd been over-indulging on the non-surgical skin-smoothing treatments the spa offered. The rest of the party, and Eve used the term 'party' loosely, were left to just sit around a tepid indoor pool with overwhelming smell of chlorine and snack on cups of organic granola. This was not shaping up to be the laughter-filled weekend of silliness that Eve had had in mind, but Tanya looked like she was loving it. She'd even brought along her own sparkly tiara to wear, that she'd retrieved from her bag 'as a back up' when Eve had produced a rather more garish novelty version with flashing lights that was swiftly dismissed with a little shake of her head. Thank goodness Eve had two more hen dos on the horizon that she could re-use it for, she knew that Ayesha and Becca wouldn't be so picky.

'Shall we play some games?' Eve said, insistent on injecting a smidgen of jolliness into the proceedings. She was met with a steely silence from Tanya's work colleagues and wide-eyed horror from the bride to be.

'I don't think we have to do that, Eve. We're all having fun, aren't we?' Tanya replied, filing her nails a little quicker.

'Oh, yes, lots of fun! I just thought that not everyone knows each other yet, so it might be good to go round the group and say how everyone knows you, and maybe a funny story about you, or something?'

'Yes! That sounds great!' Ayesha said. 'I'll start. Well, I'm Ayesha, hi everyone! I first met Tanya at fresher's week at university in Brighton, when we were standing in the same queue for the Silent Dancing Club.' Eve knew this story; in fact, she'd dined out on this story many times – but looking at Tanya's stony expression, it wasn't one that she'd ever repeated to her colleagues, or indeed anyone that she'd met since that day.

'I don't think we need to—' Tanya interrupted.

'And the third years that ran the club gave us some headphones and told us to show them our moves. Bear in mind we were stone cold sober, it was the middle of the day, and me and Tanya had a running-man dance off in the crowded union.'

Becca and Eve started laughing with the memory of seeing this prim and proper Home Counties girl and a crazy short Indian girl with a black bob dance to MC Hammer in complete silence. The floor had cleared around them and people had cheered when they'd finished. Tanya had blushed almost as fiercely as she was doing now.

'You're a dark horse Tanya,' said one of the other hens.

'It was a long time ago,' Tanya sniffed.

'Oh come on, we should totally do it again for old times' sake,' Ayesha laughed. 'I bet you've still got some moves.'

'Luke and I have actually been taking dance lessons for our first dance.' Tanya said.

This didn't surprise Eve. Nothing in this wedding was being left to chance.

'Is it going to be one of those dances that starts off really slow and romantic and then the music stops and turns into *I like Big Butts and I Cannot Lie* and Luke throws you in the air, you whip off the bottom half of your dress and it turns into a stage show?' Eve asked, giggling as Ayesha and Becca roared with appreciative laughter next to her.

'No.'

'Ok then, shall I go next?' Eve said, keen to keep the momentum of the game going, despite the blank stares she was receiving from the other hens.

'Tanya and I were in next door rooms to each other in our halls of residence, and we'd never really spoken before, but at the end of the first term her boyfriend from home visited, and—'

'And after that we became friends. Ok, then shall we get the lunch menu?' Tanya said quickly, craning her neck around, making a show of looking for a member of staff.

Eve ignored Tanya's deliberate attempt to shut her up and continued. 'And we'd all gone out to the union for the Christmas party. There was a boyband there, who was it?'

'5ive,' Becca said, smiling as she knew how the story ended.

'Oh yes, 5ive! Tanya's boyfriend had gone on a bit before us back to halls and—'

'Oh look, they have smoked salmon on seeded bagels. Yum,' Tanya said, scanning the menu she'd just been given.

'But he'd obviously gone back to the wrong room because when I opened my door he was lying on my bed naked with a Santa hat covering his willy!' Eve guffawed. 'Literally no clothes on at all! And then he had to run next door with nothing on!'

The punchline to the story elicited polite smiles from the group, but that was it. Man, thought Eve, this crowd was tough. 'He never visited you again, did he Tanya?'

'No.'

A few seconds of silence followed before Becca picked up the baton. Eve could have kissed her. 'Well, I was on the same course as Eve here, and so when first year ended, we decided to live together in a dodgy house in the centre of town. You know, the kind of student house where you don't need Blu Tack to keep your posters up, the damp does that for you? And Tanya and a Kiwi guy called Ben shared with us too.'

'Speaking of Ben, has anyone heard from him lately? Is he still in New Zealand?' Ayesha interrupted.

Hearing his name spoken out loud made the hairs on Eve's arms prick up.

'He's an usher actually,' Tanya said.

'He's an usher?' Eve spluttered out her peppermint tea.

'Yes, he came back from New Zealand a couple of months ago, and now lives in Wimbledon. Luke bumped into him a few weeks ago and they went for a few beers, and he asked him to be one of his ushers.' Tanya paused, took a sip and airily added, 'Didn't you know?'

'Oh my God, I have to tell Amit! They were so close at uni, and when Ben just dropped off the radar Amit was gutted. He'll definitely want him to be in our wedding party too. Um, if that's ok with you Eve?' Ayesha added, a little apologetically. 'Sorry, I didn't think.'

'It makes no odds to me,' Eve lied.

'I didn't think it would, I mean, it's been four years,' Ayesha said. 'I hope Amit doesn't ask him to be his best man though, I dread to think what his speech would be like. He's got ammunition on all of us, and he's a right cheeky sod when he wants to be.'

The conversation then moved back to lunch options, but Eve's mind was swimming. Becca caught her eye and gave her a silent 'you ok?' stare. Out of her three uni friends, Becca was the only one who really knew how this news must be affecting Eve.

'At what point are we sacking off the herbal teas and moving onto the champagne?' Eve said brightly, with a joviality she didn't feel. 'We are on a hen do, after all!'

Despite her initial misgivings about the fun factor of the other hens, everyone seemed to like this idea, and once corks were popped – much to the chagrin of the clean-living staff – the mood lifted a little and the rest of the afternoon was passably pleasant. Passably pleasant. If ever it became Eve's turn to be the bride to be, passably pleasant was not a term she'd like associated with her last weekend of freedom. In fact, she wouldn't trust herself not to headbutt whoever described it as that. Not that a hen do in her honour seemed likely any time soon. She was a self-confessed perfectionist when it came to men, and would much rather be listening to jazz on her balcony in her pyjamas than scrolling through Tinder or attending one of those God-awful, soul-withering speed dating nights. When it was the right time for her future husband to show up in her life, he would. There was no point at all in hurrying it. Except she was thirty and her whole family thought she might be a lesbian. But that was neither here nor there.

After a quick shower and change into their black dresses, which was the standard uniform for the night, Eve and Becca locked the room they were sharing and headed down to the bar. As expected, Tanya had firmly vetoed any type of outfit for the hens, even giving a vehement shake of the head to the suggestion of badges or sash-action. Whilst Eve knew that disobeying the bride's wishes went against every type of wedding etiquette going, it hadn't stopped her from surreptitiously handing out twelve rainbow-coloured unicorn horns to the other hens on her arrival at the spa. Now, it might have been the afternoon spent drinking that made the previously stone-faced women happy to go out in public wearing horns on their heads, but whatever it was, the sight of a dozen unicorns in the bar made her burst into spontaneous laughter.

Even Tanya, who'd managed so far to maintain a concrete-like dignity, was gathering up her friends around her to take a selfie. Sometimes, Eve thought, people don't know what they want until you give it to them.

'Eve! Get in!' Tanya ordered. 'And smile!'

The sight of a herd of unicorns marching down the high street on a Saturday night was quite the spectacle. Eve guessed correctly that the most fun this Oxfordshire town had seen previously was when the local twinning association got a bit excited on cheap French wine after a boules match on the common.

Eve had already phoned ahead to the landlord of the Fox and Hounds and warned them to expect twelve lairy women, and to put a few cases of white wine in the fridges. Word had obviously got around, as the pub was packed out with the town's single male population who gave a raucous cheer as they all filed in. It didn't take long before an impromptu darts match was underway, the music turned up, and chairs and tables pushed back. Eve was seeing a side to Tanya that she hadn't glimpsed in years and certainly wasn't expecting to see tonight.

'Come on Ayesha!' Tanya shouted across the bar as the familiar start to *Can't Touch This* came on. 'You and me. Right here. Right now.' Tanya had kicked her heels off under a table and was already flexing her neck and arm muscles. Eve smiled. She'd never say so to Tanya, but this actually did beat a roller disco.

***

Eve knew that the sunlight was going to hurt her eyes before she opened them, so decided not to. She could hear Becca shift position in the seat next to her, so guessed that her friend was stirring too.

'Ow,' Eve whispered.

'Ow,' Becca replied.

They'd missed the curfew the spa manager had sternly imposed upon them as they left the previous evening, demanding that they all return before midnight as the doors would be locked then. It turned out she was true to her word. After the hens had weaved their way through the darkened town centre after a long lock-in at the pub, sometime around 3 a.m., they were faced with a dark, firmly closed hotel. Of course, all eyes fell on Eve, the chief party planner, for a solution, as though she was going to click her heels and transport them all into their cosy beds, or failing that, at least miraculously produce a master key. If Eve hadn't have been suffering the effects of an endless stream of cheap white wine being poured into her mouth for hours, she may well have come up with a solution more palatable than all of them sleeping in their cars.

'I don't think my neck works any more,' Becca moaned.

'My vertebrae seem to have fused together,' Eve added.

'I think an animal died in my mouth,' said Ayesha from the back seat. Both Becca and Eve had forgotten she was there, and they both yelped with shock at her voice, before giggling uncontrollably.

'This reminds me of that festival we went to, when our tent got waterlogged so we all kipped in Tanya's dad's Volvo,' Eve said.

'At least that was an estate car so we could all lie in the back, this is a bloody Yaris!'

'It was fun though,' Ayesha reminisced. 'Four of us squeezed into the back of it, and Ben in the front.'

Once again, Eve realised that she'd managed to rewrite history in order to forget that Ben had been there too. Of course he'd been there, he'd even queued up for the tickets for them all.

'Happy days,' Ayesha sighed.

'Happy days,' Becca agreed.

Eve stayed silent.

'Speaking of Ben,' Ayesha started gently. 'How do you feel about him coming back Eve?'

'Like you said yesterday, it's been four years, why would I care?'

'Because we both know you do.'

Eve swiftly changed the subject. 'So, how annoyed do you reckon Tanya is this morning? Do you think she'll be filled with nostalgia like us, or just pure hatred for me?'

'It's not your fault!' Becca said. 'We all forgot the time and wanted to stay longer, it's not as though she was ready to leave at half eleven, was she? It'll be fine, how could you not see the funny side to this?'

Tanya could not see the funny side to this. Waking up in a car, the sequinned black dress she'd paid an eye-watering amount for hitched around her waist, with her stuck-on eyelashes gluing her left eye shut, was not the blissful sleeping-in-a-spa experience she'd wanted. What was Eve thinking allowing them all to miss the curfew? She'd specifically made her the head hen so that situations like this didn't happen. She and Eve hadn't been particularly close in years but she had assumed that having a wedding professional in her wedding party would be extremely useful. Eve should have called time on the party, ushered them all back to the hotel, handed out the monogrammed eye masks she'd insisted on Eve ordering, and they'd all be waking up right now refreshed and invigorated ready for the hotel's fresh juice and homemade muesli. They weren't twenty years old any more.

Just then, Eve tapped on Tanya's car window that was slightly lowered to let the condensation dry out. She had the nerve smile at her, while still wearing that blasted unicorn horn. Tanya turned the engine on, closed the window, and reversed out of the car park back onto the main road and headed in the direction of London.

'Tanya's just left.' Eve announced, opening the door of Becca's Yaris.

'Left?'

'Yep.'

Ayesha and Becca started laughing again. They'd always seen the funny side to Tanya's spoiled strops. Which was helpful as they'd both been in the firing line for daring to get married in the same year as Tanya. She had actually asked them both to consider postponing their weddings until the year after, 'or at the very least autumn', as though by sending her save the dates out fractionally ahead of the other two she owned the entire summer.

'What about everyone else? Are they still here?' Ayesha asked.

Eve looked around the car park. Hens in various states of disarray were straightening up, cricking their necks and checking their limbs still functioned by stretching. 'I think everyone else is still here. We'd better go and check out, I'll get Tanya's stuff from her room.'

'You're a good friend Eve,' Becca yawned. Eve guessed, correctly, that Tanya at that particular moment didn't share that sentiment.

Chapter 4

The blonde middle-aged woman was sat opposite Eve on the train again, wearing a half-heart locket. They never failed to make Eve smile. Half a heart. Meaning that someone, somewhere had the other half. Who was it? A lover heading off on his travels? A best friend declaring their unbreakable bond? It was amazing how many people all around you at any given time were in love with someone, whether the other person knew it or not. Eve almost missed her stop again, jostling through the wall of disgruntled suits to the train's beeping doors to a soundtrack of tuts and sighs from her fellow commuters, who shifted the minimum of millimetres required for her to squeeze her body through.

'Morning gorgeous. How's my favourite redhead this morning?'

Eve smiled at the familiar greeting that the greying cockney security guard at her office building gave her every morning, before giving her standard response.

'Morning Clive, fabulous day for it.'

'You can say that again.'

'Morning Clive, fabulous day for it.'

A Beautiful Day for a Wedding

It wasn't really a fabulous day, it was grey and slightly drizzling, Eve had just forked out an exorbitant amount for a hotel room she hadn't slept in and Tanya hadn't returned any of her calls or texts, but none of that was Cockney Clive's fault. Feeling the need to cheer herself up, Eve opened up a new word document on her screen and started typing into her diary. It had become a sort of therapy for her that she'd started during those dark first few months in New York with nothing but her thoughts for company. By writing down her most cynical observations and feelings, it stopped her saying them out loud.

Hen do games. Three words to strike terror into the heart of any woman. And man. Men are not exempt from the horror of a group of inebriated women, particularly as so many of the 'fun' and 'hilarious' hen do games involve getting random things off unsuspecting men. Like underwear. What sober woman would think that running up to a strange man in a supermarket and demanding his boxers would be an acceptable form of discourse? But put a group of prosecco-sodden women together in a pub, tie some unicorn horns onto their heads and suddenly, it's 'wa-hey random bloke I've never met before, pass me your pants!'

What about the mandatory Mr and Mrs quiz? Imagine the scene. Ten or fifteen well-heeled hens, an ageing mother, the mother of the groom, a couple of aunties thrown in for good measure. 'So, bride, what's your husband's favourite position?' A couple of seconds of pensive consideration pass. 'Probably the Spork,' she replies. 'Where he positions his body at a ninety-degree angle to get a deeper thrust action.' 'Oh, good guess Enid, but that's wrong unfortunately – Jeff said CEO.'

No good can come of hen do games. Ever.

'Good weekend?' Kat asked brightly as she shook off her jacket and hung it on the back of her office chair.

'Yes and no,' Eve replied honestly, minimising her diary on the screen before Kat could see it. After the tumbleweed had blown away from around the pool and the hens started bonding over wine and unicorn horns, it had been really fun; but the radio silence from Tanya suggested she might think otherwise. 'I think I may be demoted from my bridesmaid status at some point this week.'

'Wow, that bad?' Kat chuckled.

'Let's just say that the bride is suffering from a sense of humour failure at present.'

'Don't they all?'

It was true; at some point in the lead up to every wedding the bride, even the most laid-back, fun-loving bride imaginable, would have a major meltdown over the hue of their napkins. Eve had received enough anxious letters over her two-year tenure at the magazine to vouch for that. The only bride that showed signs of getting through the run-up unfazed and unflappable was Becca, but that too could change as her date loomed closer.

Over the other side of the open-plan floor, her editor's office light was on. Fiona was always the first one in, setting a good example for everyone else, and enabling her to tut at any latecomers. Now would be the perfect chance for Eve to speak to her quietly without lots of eyes and ears around. Eve took a deep breath and headed over.

'Is now a good time for a quick chat, Fiona?' Eve said, sticking her head around her boss's door.

'Please tell me you're not resigning.'

'I'm not resigning.'

'Good. Ok then, come in.'

That was a hopeful start; asking for a pay rise after your boss had virtually called you indispensable was the stuff dreams were made of. Eve heard herself bumble around the topic, talking about the rising costs of public transport in London, rent charges, electricity costs, as reasons why she deserved more money.

'I'm sorry Eve, my hands are tied. We're on austerity orders from the powers that be; no more new hires and no pay rises. I'm hopeful that at the end of the year we may all get a small Christmas bonus, but there's no money in the pot as of now. I promise, as soon as the money tree starts shedding its leaves, you'll be the first to know. You are incredibly valued though, if that helps.'

Being valued was nice, but it didn't pay for her flat. Or her credit card. Everyone assumed that she was so much better off than she was, and no one knew that each month she was relying more and more on that little piece of plastic burning in her purse.

Eve headed back to her Dear Eve inbox which was always bursting at the seams on a Monday morning. It was mid-May, wedding season was in view just around the corner and brides up and down the country were slowly melting from the stress of it all. Eve sighed and took a large gulp of her coffee before opening the first one. The subject line said 'HELP!' In any other job, Eve would have paid more heed to this, she might even have got the authorities on standby, but being a wedding magazine agony aunt meant she knew that this type of dramatic upper case yell for assistance was probably not life-threatening.

Dear Eve

I'm at my wits' end. My fiancé is insisting on wearing a navy blue tie instead of the pale blue one that I'd picked out to match the bridesmaid dresses, and it's going to look so wrong. He just laughs at me when I cry about it, and says that it's his wedding too, but the whole theme is going to be ruined, HELP!

Sarah, Birmingham

Hi Sarah,

You are kidding, aren't you? What sort of colourblind heathen are you marrying? I'd seriously rethink because if he's happy to make this kind of monumental faux pas on your wedding day, what's he going to do in the future? You deserve to be happy, Sarah. I would reconsider whether this joker is going to last the distance.

Eve smiled to herself before pressing delete and retyping:

Hi Sarah,

Congratulations on your big day, how exciting! You have chosen the perfect colour palette for your wedding as pale blue thankfully goes with everything, and navy and light blue is a classic combination that works beautifully. Maybe think about incorporating some more navy into the scheme so that it blends in even better. How about tying your bouquets with navy ribbon? Or having touches of navy on your table place cards? Have a super day!

    Eve xx

Eve opened up a new email and started writing.

Hi Tanya,

    I'm a dick, I'm sorry. I should have been more on top of the timings and arrangements and less about the fun. I feel really bad I let you down, and want to make it up to you in any way I can. If there is any last minute arranging that you need help with for the wedding then lay it on me, I'm here to serve.

    Eve xx

That should do it. If there was one thing Tanya loved more than sulking it was writing To Do Lists. Eve busied herself for the rest of the morning researching her latest feature on registry gifts for the couple that had everything. So far, she had a tandem bike, because no one actually had one of those and it sounded fun to yomp around Hyde Park on one every Sunday morning, and a monthly subscription for a case of specialist wine. If she was going to fill three double page spreads, she'd need more than that. There was a current trend for couples asking guests to contribute towards their honeymoon by paying for different activities or meals out – a tapas meal for two; a paragliding session; a couple's massage on a beach. That was actually a great idea. Gone were the days when two people moved from their parent's homes to a shared marital home and needed everything to set them up for life. Most couples now came to a relationship with two sets of crockery, two microwaves, two irons and more furniture than could possibly fit into one house, so crowdfunding for an all-singing, all-dancing honeymoon was perhaps the future of the gift registry. It would certainly provide enough fodder for at least two of the pages.

An email from Tanya broke Eve's concentration.

Hi.

Eve noted the full stop at the end of the greeting. That wasn't a good sign.

Obviously it wasn't the hen party I'd envisioned, but there's no point wallowing about it when there's so much still to do. As you know, the wedding is twelve days away, and there are lots of loose ends that are still bothering me, so if you mean it and you do want to help, here are some things you can be getting on with:

1. Book five minibuses to take people from the church to the reception.

2. Find some of those iron-on strips that hem fabric, I need about 45 metres of it.

3. Pick up the fabric from me and hem all the fabric that will be suspended from the ceilings.

4. *Find one of those machines that polishes wooden floors. I visited the venue yesterday afternoon after getting back from the hen weekend early, and the floor is a state.*

5. *The day before the wedding, go to the venue before the rehearsal at the church and hang the fabric up and polish the floors.*

Eve stopped reading. This wasn't a list of loose ends, this was penance. She might as well fashion together a bunch of willow stems and self-flagellate for her sins. Polish the floors? Hem the curtains? Tanya had lost the plot. This wasn't even the end of the list.

6. *The day after the wedding, polish the floors again, it's bound to have stuff spilt on it and we need to get our deposit back.*

7. *Luke left it too late to book Coco in at the kennels for our honeymoon, so can you have her for the two weeks? You can stay at ours as it's probably easier than her being in your flat, and we live nearer your work than you do. Becca can come too if she likes. Don't make a mess though.*

8. *Please tell me you picked up your bridesmaid dress from the tailors and it fits?*

I think that's everything for now, but there might be more, will let you know when I think of something else. You're a star.

Tx

When I think of something else. Not if. *When*. This punishment had the potential to go on and on, Eve thought. She wished that she was the type to simply refuse, to write back that she could book the minibuses but that was it. Possibly buy the iron-on hemming stuff, once she googled what that was, but she was absolutely not going to iron them on.

Unless she had the time.

But on no account was she going to polish the floors. Who did Tanya think Eve was, Mrs bloody Mop? They did made it look so easy on *Sixty Minute Makeover* though, and it would be amazing for the biceps, she imagined, which would please her trainer Juan.

But looking after a dog for two whole weeks? She could barely keep the pot of basil next to her sink alive. But then again, it would be good to have a shorter commute for a fortnight. She could actually walk to work from Tanya's, rather than contend with the tube. And the weather was lovely at the moment. And since moving back, she hadn't made many other friends yet so really needed to hang onto the ones she already had.

Ok, she typed back. *Am on it. And yes, picked up dress, fits like a glove.*

A very tight glove that stops the blood circulating round your body.

Chapter 5

Eve's aversion to lycra meant that she insisted on pulling on shapeless tracksuit bottoms and a man's oversized T-shirt to exercise in. Kat tutted as Eve came out of the loos into the now empty office. It was just after seven and everyone had left.

'Isn't Juan single now?'

Eve grimaced. 'He's my personal trainer, Kat.'

'So? He's gorgeous, and looking for love. It might be time to invest in some gym gear that has the potential to get his pulse racing.'

'Doing laps of the park does that.'

'I'm just saying, a bit of lippy wouldn't hurt.'

'And I'm just saying, I've never thought of Juan like that, and don't intend to start now. Anyway, he spent the last three sessions talking about how women are the curse of the earth and even made a jibe about my namesake, so I don't think he's harbouring secret lustful thoughts towards me.'

'Not if you keep wearing tracksuit bottoms.'

'When my Prince Charming eventually turns up,' Eve

replied with a toss of her head, 'he'll love my tracksuit. Anyway, why are you still here?'

Kat groaned. 'Sales have sold an advertorial in the beauty section and I need to put together a storyboard to present to their clients tomorrow. So I'll be here for a while yet.'

Just then, Eve's phone buzzed. It was her brother, Adam.

'Where are you?' he started, dispensing with the customary greeting of hello.

'Just leaving the office, where are you?'

'Mum and I are waiting for you at the restaurant, how long are you going to be?'

Eve's eyes widened in horror. She'd completely forgotten her mum's birthday dinner tonight. It had been planned weeks ago, and in all the mayhem of Tanya's hen and wedding, it had slipped her mind.

'I'll be there in twenty minutes or so, buy some champagne, I'll pay.' Eve quickly got off the phone and swung round to face Kat. 'Bugger, I'm meant to be at my mum's birthday dinner now! Oh my God Kat, I have nothing to wear, I spilt coffee down my shirt earlier on, and it's really posh, and I need to cancel Juan, but he's probably already there, oh God, what shall I do?' Eve took a few deep breaths, and a plan started forming in her mind. 'Can you go to my session for me? Please? He'll seriously strike me off if I cancel again, and I need him in order to fit into that awful bridesmaid dress in twelve days' time.' Eve motioned to the long pink dress that was hanging from the filing cabinet drawer, covered in long transparent plastic. 'Bingo!'

'What?'

'My outfit for this evening! As long as I don't attempt to eat, drink, sit down or walk, it'll be fine! Yay, all sorted.' She started pulling off her tracksuit and wriggling into the dress, hoping that Fiona hadn't installed hidden cameras in the open-plan office. 'Help me do it up,' she said, turning her back to Kat.

It took a few attempts, and there was a tiny, almost inaudible, sound of a rip, but no visible sign of one, so she was good to go.

'Wait a second,' Kat said, opening the door of the beauty cupboard. As the beauty editor, Kat received more freebies from cosmetics companies than an A-lister, leaving her with a stockpile of perfumes and make-up for photoshoots, impromptu birthday presents for friends, and exactly what was needed for situations just like this.

A minute later Eve found herself waddling down Bond Street as fast as the skin-tight mermaid-style dress would allow, her face full of blusher, her lips a vibrant coral colour – since Fiona had vetoed corals in the magazine, the beauty cupboard was heaving with them – and smelling of a putrid perfume that had evidently been in the recesses of the cupboard for far too long.

'Darling!' Her mum rose to greet her, wrinkling her nose as she gave her a hug.

Her brother wasn't quite so subtle. 'What's that whiff? Eau de balsamic?'

'It's Chanel.'

'And what are you wearing?'

'My new dress.'

'Didn't they have it in your size?'

'They did, and I'm wearing it. Anything else?'

'Your lipstick. Didn't you know that no one's wearing orange any more?'

'It's coral, and yes they are, I am.'

'You two, stop it.' Eve's mum, Faye, stepped in. 'Can we please try and have a civilised dinner without you two resorting to hair pulling?'

Eve and Adam smiled. Their squabbling sibling routine was as fun as it was familiar. They were Irish twins, having been born just eleven months apart, which left them sharing the same age for one month every year. Eve had always been thankful that she was the eldest, so she came before him in the introductions, otherwise the comedy value in their names might have presented more of a problem growing up. Their dad had gone through a brief religious phase around the time of their births, but it could have been worse; Bathsheba and Moses were also contenders.

'Sorry I'm late Mum, work's been a bit crazy.' Eve took a grateful glug of the champagne that the hovering waiter poured out for her but made a silent note to convince them all to switch to house wine after the bottle was finished.

'You're here now, that's what matters. Anyway, they haven't even brought the menus yet.' Faye put her hand over her daughter's. 'It feels like I haven't seen you two in ages, what's going on in your lives?'

Eve started regaling them with stories of Tanya's hen weekend, and as she got to the part where they slept in their cars, Faye snorted wine out of her nose. 'Oh Eve.'

'I know. I know. Bad bridesmaid.'

'That's hilarious,' Adam said. 'I bet Tanya was livid.'

'Is livid. There's no past tense yet.'

'Well, I hope you perform better at my stag do.'

'Speaking of which, have you decided if you and George want a joint one, or separate ones? You've got most of the same friends, but if you want a night out flirting with male strippers for the last time without him there, then speak now or forever hold your peace.'

'I have never, or will ever, flirt with a male stripper.'

'Thank goodness for that,' Faye said in mock horror. 'The thought makes me quite queasy.'

'Says the woman who is internet dating,' Eve jibed. 'How's that going?'

Faye waited until the waiter had taken their order and was safely out of earshot before quietly replying. 'The three I've had have been very useful. Ian came to put up my shelves last weekend, Gavin works at the same hospital, so we now car share twice a week which is saving me petrol money, and Harry put me in touch with a rock choir that I now sing with every Tuesday, so not a waste of time at all.'

'You're meant to be finding a soul mate Mum, not a handyman, taxi service or a hobby.'

'I found my soul mate thirty-five years ago Eve, the chances of finding another one, are pretty slim.'

The mention of their dad made a silence fall over the table. News of his accident had come in the form of the phone call every child dreaded receiving, especially one living as far away as Eve had been. She'd packed up her life in New York the night of his crash, had boarded the next available flight from JFK and still arrived three hours after he'd taken his last breath. Their mum was a shell of what she had been before, her life shattered in one moment by a woman who'd had too many drinks at a work party and thought calling a cab was too much hassle. Eve had moved in with Faye for a while – one of them had to. It took Faye a couple of months before she felt ready to leave the house, and even then, it was only to a neighbour's for tea. Anything more taxing took a few more months. She had to be reminded to brush her hair, to eat, to answer the phone, the door. Then one day, an estate agent turned up, hammering a 'For Sale' sign up outside her house. Eve and Adam had pleaded with Faye to give herself some time, to wait. But Faye's mind was set. She didn't want to sit watching television alone in the same room she'd watched it with him for thirty-five years. She knew that one more night sleeping in their bedroom, in their marital bed where they'd made love hundreds, if not thousands of times, and conceived two children, was one night too many. Standing in front of the hob stirring a single can of soup in a pan for her evening meal, when the same hob had yielded huge family feasts in the past and countless Christmas dinners, had given her a pang in her chest so painful she had to steady herself by holding on to the counter until it had passed.

Shaving fifty thousand off the valuation meant the house sold the same day the sign was hoisted up, even before photos had been taken of it, or the estate agent had a chance to describe the garden as 'pleasantly South facing, a stone's throw from the delights of Brighton's city centre and seafront.' Eve looked at her mum across the table in this fancy London restaurant. She'd retrained as a therapist, lost a stone, had her blonde hair feathered and highlighted, and sold her trusted slow cooker on eBay. Apart from the easy humour and warmth she still exuded, there was little to recognise from the mother they'd grown up with.

'Speaking of soul mates, Eve, do you need a plus one for our wedding?' Adam asked.

'No, you're alright.'

'Come on darling,' Faye cajoled. 'It's only the middle of May now, their wedding isn't until August. Everything could change in that time, this might be the impetus you need to meet someone.'

Eve didn't want to use the same words that Faye had just done about already finding her soul mate once and the chances of meeting another one being pretty slim, but she couldn't stop herself thinking it.

'So is that a yes, you need a plus one or no?' Adam said. 'I need to know.'

'Right now?' Eve asked. 'Your wedding is in August, why do you need to know now?'

Adam tapped the table impatiently. 'Yes or no?'

'Yes,' Faye interrupted. 'Yes for both of us. Two and a half months is plenty enough time for us both to find nice companions to bring, isn't it Eve? It's good to have a goal.'

Having been single for four years Eve didn't think that ten weeks was anywhere near long enough to become coupled up again, but she didn't say so.

'Speaking of plus ones,' Faye added casually. 'Are either of you doing anything in three weekends' time, on the 25th?'

'Absolutely nothing,' replied Eve. 'Thank God. It's my only hen-free, wedding-free weekend of the whole summer.'

'Oh. Never mind then.'

'Why do you ask?'

'You know your dad's cousin, Thomas? The one that lives in Dartmouth? Well, his daughter Leila is getting married at Kew Gardens and I've got a plus one, and Ivy was going to come with me, but she's having her hip replacement then. I haven't got the nerve to tell Judy, Thomas's wife, she's quite a force to be reckoned with. But it's ok, I'll think of someone else.'

'Don't look at me,' Adam said, topping their glasses up. 'We've got a colonic detox weekend booked in the Lake District.'

'Wow, you guys have all the fun,' Eve teased. 'Look Mum, if you really need me to come, I will. It's in London, and it might actually be quite nice to be at a wedding where I don't have to do anything.'

The waiter put down their food and made a subtle retreat.

'Speaking of weddings, I posted my RSVP back to Becca earlier today,' Faye said.

'Becca invited you to her wedding?' Eve asked, a little incredulously. Her mum had kept Becca well-nourished during their three years of university and occasionally did her laundry back then, but Eve had thought Becca was trying to keep numbers down.

'Yes, I must admit I was a bit surprised that she invited me, but I was very touched.'

'Did you say yes?'

'Yes, if that's ok with you? I promise I won't cramp your style too much.'

'No, it'll be lovely having you there.' Eve turned to her brother. 'So where's George this evening?' Adam and George had been dating for nearly a decade, so it felt more like she had two brothers, except George was less rude to her.

'He's on a work dinner. Some clients are over from Tokyo and they're all out together. He'll probably stagger in at 2 a.m. after going to a karaoke bar.'

'We should join them!' Faye said. Thirty-five years of being a housewife had resulted in a volcano of pent-up enthusiasm for every activity she'd never done before.

'Mum, as much as I love the new you, and good God, do I, there is no way that I want to be singing Neil Diamond at midnight with you, my sister, my boyfriend, his boss and five strange Japanese men.'

'Put like that Mum, he has a point.' Eve laughed and picked up her wine glass, knocking the side of her soup bowl in the process and sloshing its boiling hot contents right down the front of her bridesmaid dress. The sheer surprise combined with the scalding heat froze Eve in statue-like shock for a couple of seconds. Faye pushed her chair back and stood up, waiters flocked to the table, Eve remained open-mouthed and bright red. And Adam calmly picked up his water glass and chucked the contents all over his sister's chest.

'I didn't really like that place anyway,' Faye said, as they made an embarrassed exit from the restaurant. 'Really stuffy. Literally and figuratively.'

'What the heck am I going to do about this dress? I'm meant to wear it in twelve days, and it's ruined,' Eve cried. 'This is going to send Tanya over the edge.'

'It's ok, take it to the dry cleaner's in the morning. If that doesn't work, call the tailor's and see if they can make another one.'

'It's taken four months to make this one!'

'Four months, that's crazy. Get the pattern and I'll whizz one up for you.'

'It's not from a pattern in a magazine Mum, it's from a proper bridal designer.'

'Are you sure?' Adam sneered unhelpfully.

'If there was an award for the worst bridesmaid ever, I would win it.'

'Oh, come on love, it's only soup.'

'That right there shows just how little you know about brides, Mum.'

The dry cleaner's next to work said the same thing as the dry cleaner's near her flat, who repeated exactly what the launderette said, who parroted what the internet had confirmed last night. Eve was screwed.

And the lipstick that she'd borrowed from the beauty cupboard turned out to have some long-lasting dye in it, so her lips had an unattractive orange hue to them that no amount of scrubbing in the shower would remove. At least the woman with the half-heart locket was on the train again this morning. That lifted Eve's spirits a little.

'Kat, I have a monumental problem,' Eve sighed, flopping

into her chair and swivelling round on it to face her friend. The dress lay crumpled in her lap, soup-side up.

'Oh Christ.'

'Exactly.'

'They're orange.'

'That's not the biggest problem. Look.' Eve gestured at the massive stain.

'To be fair, it wasn't very nice anyway.'

'That's spectacularly unhelpful Kat! I know you haven't met her, but Tanya is going to lose the plot over this.'

'Look, we work for a bridal magazine, I'm sure we can pull in some favours and get a new one. Where did she get it?'

'Some fancy Italian designer I think, she ordered them online.'

'Hold it up, let me take a photo of it and get our friends on the fashion desk to try and track it down.'

'See, that's why I love you.'

'I know. By the way, you were right about Juan. He's gorgeous, but boy does he hate the female species.'

'I completely forgot to ask, how did it go?'

'He almost killed me, and I'm aching in muscles I didn't know I had, but it was good. If ever you want to slack off again, I'll definitely step in.'

The fashion desk only took half an hour to find the dress in their archives, but it wasn't from a Venetian atelier, like Tanya had boasted, after all. It was from a Chinese website selling copy dresses. And the big bag of cash that Eve had handed over to Tanya to pay for it came to substantially more than it was selling for online. 'The cheeky cow!' Eve said when

Kat broke the news. She couldn't believe that Tanya had charged her more than double what she'd paid for it. 'What a crappy thing to do. Right, that's it, I'm not spending a penny more on this wedding. I'm wearing the soup dress. I'll make a feature out of it.'

Kat narrowed her eyes at Eve. 'While I love the new attitude, because you've definitely been a pushover for far too long, I'm going to have to step in and say that you can't wear the soup dress as it is.'

'I'm going to customise it.'

'That doesn't sound any better. How are you going to customise it?'

'I'm going to find some fabric in the same colour, and cut out the minestrone panel, and sew in the new panel.'

'Eve, can we take a moment to reflect on what you just said. In the time I have known you, dressmaking has never come up as one of the secret skills you have.'

'No, but I can give it a go.'

Kat just leant her head back against her chair and silently shook her head. 'Oh God Eve, I can see nothing wrong with that plan at all.'

Chapter 6

Becca had offered to give the dress to a colleague of hers that made her own clothes, but Eve refused. How difficult could it be to do a bit of darning? She'd spent years watching her mum work her way through a massive basket of mending in no time at all, and this was one small dress. Too small, but that was neither here nor there.

'Would a glass of wine make this easier?' Becca asked, standing in the doorway, looking at her friend's bent head and expression of concentration with undisguised pity. Eve resolutely shook her head. She was already unpicking the stitches she'd done the night before over one glass of wine too many. Repeating that tonight was not an option.

'I'll have one afterwards to reward myself for my brilliance. You can stick the kettle on though.'

It didn't look too bad, Eve thought, holding the dress away from her and squinting through one eye and then the other. In a flash of what she could only describe as pure genius, she'd cut out a panel from the back of the dress, in the mermaid tail bit to replace the soup panel that was centre stage at the front, and then the new fabric that she'd picked up at the market, which wasn't an *exact* colour match but was close enough, could then go on the back.

'So, talk me through the logic again of cutting out two parts of the dress when you only needed to do one.'

Eve proudly explained her inspired reasoning, ending with, '...so if it's on the back, no one will really see it.'

'That is indeed a mastermind move, Eve. Except, of course, being a bridesmaid, you'll be walking up the aisle behind the bride, so *everyone* will be able to see it.'

Eve's sudden crestfallen expression prompted Becca to uncharacteristically take control. 'I think at this point we just need to do some damage limitation. Make sure that you always hold your flowers over the front of your dress. And I'll stand really close behind you at all times so no one can see the back of you.'

'For ten hours?'

'Well, as soon as people start getting drunk no one will care anyway, so I reckon three hours tops, and then you'll have got away with it.'

Eve's eyes brightened with hope. 'Do you think so?'

'Definitely.'

In a bid to have a different sort of wedding that didn't include the words 'country' and 'hotel', Tanya and Luke were tying the knot in a warehouse. Not one of those cavernous, atmospheric warehouses that screamed potential – this was a disused, quite probably defective, former paint factory that would have building surveyors rocking back and forth in a dark corner holding their hard-hatted heads in their hands. But Tanya had

A Vision. And it was up to Eve to turn the hundreds of pinterest pins that Tanya kept bombarding her with into reality, starting with the metres upon metres of newly-hemmed fabric she was busy pulling out of the back of a taxi. The plan was to hang the swathes of white chiffon from the high pipes that ran the length of the factory, creating a 'billowing, dreamlike atmosphere' – Tanya's words, not Eve's. Eve had other words in mind that she was trying very hard not to say out loud.

Tanya had also depleted every hardware store, supermarket and most of the internet of fairy lights which were going to be stapled to every surface, be they vertical or horizontal. Thankfully this task was out of Eve's remit, and a few of Luke's friends were already up numerous ladders, trails of lights knotting themselves around the floor, steps and men's legs.

'Morning all!' Eve shrilled as she stumbled in through the factory doors, arms full with fabric. You could just about see her eyes over the mountain of chiffon. 'Where shall I put this?'

'What is it?' One of Luke's friends asked from up a ladder.

'It's the stuff for the dreamlike atmosphere,' Eve replied. 'We need to hang it from the rafters.' Or what's left of them, she thought, looking upwards and seeing a family of birds wiggle through one of the many holes in the roof.

'I'll take them off you,' said a deep voice to her side. Eve froze. She hadn't heard that voice in the four years since he'd left. 'How are you, Red?'

She'd had plenty of time to think about this moment, to plan a profound, deeply intelligent reply that would convey an overwhelming insight into how she felt. She opened her mouth to speak and all that came out was, 'Ben.' As greetings went, it wasn't great.

'You haven't changed at all.'

'Maybe not on the outside.' *Doing better Eve, doing better.* Ben seemed momentarily chastened by her reply and didn't know how to answer.

'So, do you want some help or not?'

'Not.' She added, 'Thank you though' as an afterthought. Manners never cost anything.

'Suit yourself.' Ben turned and walked over to a pile of nearby fairy lights and started unravelling them. Bugger. She really did need help, just not from him. Her arms were starting to hurt from the weight of the fabric and she had no idea how she was supposed to single-handedly hang them all up. She could hardly ask someone else for assistance now that she'd rebuffed Ben's offer.

'Ok fine,' she huffed. 'You can help.'

Ben shrugged and walked back towards her, holding his arms out for her to share the load. 'Where are they going?'

'Up there.' Eve nodded to the ceiling and piled all the fabric into his outstretched arms. 'I'm not sure how. But that's your problem now. I'm off.'

She could still hear him shouting after her as the heavy door to the factory swung shut behind her. It turned out she was right; she had changed.

Swishing out with such a dramatic exit, while insanely gratifying, did pose something of a dilemma though. She was meant to be whizzing round the factory with an electric polisher round about now. A large part of her wanted to say 'stuff it', pour a large gin and tonic and sit on her balcony for the rest of the day basking in the sun, but she had the wedding rehearsal later that afternoon, and forty years of grime to remove from the floors before tomorrow. As much as Tanya was incredibly irritating in her demands, Eve couldn't ruin her day with sticky floors.

'I need back up,' Eve said as soon as Becca answered her phone. 'I'm at the warehouse which, by the way, is a ridiculous place to have a party, and Ben's here.' Eve heard Becca's intake of breath. 'And I stormed out in a brilliant way, but I need to go back in there and do the floors, but I don't want to look like a pillock.'

'So don't. Enjoy this moment, wait until after the rehearsal and we'll go back and do it then.'

'Oh God, the rehearsal. I'm going to have to see him then.' Eve leant back against the side wall of the warehouse where she was hiding. 'Why did he have to come back from New Zealand?'

'Just ignore him, you don't need to even speak to him. I'll be there, and Ayesha, so just stay with us.'

'You're wonderful.'

'I know. What time is it again?'

'What?'

'The rehearsal.'

'Three. Do you know where the church is?'

'No. South of the river somewhere, isn't it?'

Eve smiled. She might be wonderful, but Becca was never going to win any prizes for organisation. 'I'll come by the flat and pick you up in a cab, be ready at half past two.'

'Fab. And Eve?'

'Yes?'

'Chin up.'

The only time Eve had seen it before was on nature programs. The frantic pacing, eyes flashing dangerously, a single rogue movement from the bushes and POUNCE. Whoever had said that brides were glowing with happiness, and filled with fuzziness and heart-melting romance had obviously never been to a wedding rehearsal.

'You're late,' Tanya snapped. They weren't, but Tanya tapped her watch anyway. 'We're all waiting for you.' Eve glanced around the almost empty church. Luke's parents weren't even there yet. Or Ben.

'Well, we're here now,' Eve replied brightly. 'Anything we can do?'

'Did you do the curtains ok?'

Now was not the time to get into semantics. 'All sorted.'

'And the floors?'

'Under control.'

'Well, that's something I guess.' Eve held her breath waiting for an expression of gratitude, but none came.

'So here are the keys to our flat, we're leaving for the airport straight after the wedding, so you'll have to sleep at ours tomorrow night to look after Coco. I've left out loads of water and food, but when you get in just take her once round the block. She'll have been cooped up all day and that girl poos for England.' Tanya tossed Eve a keyring and gave a big theatrical sigh, looking pointedly at her watch as Luke's parents hurried in, before turning to the waiting vicar. 'Well, we might as well make a start.'

The walk-through was almost finished when Ben came crashing into the church filled with profuse apologies. Eve held her breath, waiting for him to throw her under the bus and tell everyone exactly what had held him up, but he blamed the traffic and stood mutely as Tanya tore warm meat off his limbs.

He then demurely took his place next to Becca at the end of the aisle.

'No Ben, not there!' Tanya shrieked. 'You're walking Eve up, which you would know if you were here on time.'

As he moved next to her Eve could smell a combination of his aftershave masked with smells of manly sweat brought on, no doubt, by hanging twenty-five kilometres of bastarding chiffon. 'It's done,' he whispered.

She couldn't bring herself to thank him, so just kept her eyes resolutely resting on the statue of a crucified Jesus.

'You're welcome,' he said into the silence.

Eve just rolled her eyes. The cheek of the man. He couldn't possibly think that he could just waltz back into her life, do her a small favour and expect her to shrug, erase the past and pretend that everything was ok.

It was just after 8 p.m. when Becca and Eve managed to head back to the warehouse and start gentrifying the floors. As a surprise, Tanya had booked all the bridesmaids manicures, less as a gesture of kindness, and more to make sure that they all had rounded nails, not square, painted the same unim-aginative shade of pale pink. Personality and individuality were very much banned from this wedding. Eve promptly managed to completely ruin her nails within the first half hour of floor polishing.

'You know, you could have just said no to her,' Becca said, as she trailed behind Eve, holding the wire out of the way of the machine.

'But who else would have done it?' Eve replied, puffing her long hair out of her face as she manoeuvred the unwieldy polisher around a corner.

'She'd have found someone. Note that she didn't ask me or Ayesha as we'd have just laughed at her. You need to learn the art of saying no.'

'No.'

'Haha. I mean it though, she only tells you to do these things because she knows you will. Are you like this at work too? Do you literally do everyone else's jobs for them?'

Eve thought for a second. It wasn't that she was a control freak, or a perfectionist, or even a pushover, like Becca was insinuating; she just found it really, really difficult to let people down. But this wedding had tested even her limits of patience.

'Ok, I'll make you a deal.' Eve offered, turning the polisher off so that she didn't need to shout over its drone. 'From now on, I'm going to trial a new me. One that doesn't do anything I don't want to do.'

'That's my girl. You will still help me plan Ayesha's hen do and my own wedding though, won't you?'

'I'll make an exception for you.'

***

A Beautiful Day for a Wedding

It was proving very difficult to shield Tanya's eyes from resting on either the front or back of her dress, but Becca had been true to her word and was like Eve's shadow, standing less than a foot away from her back at any one time, and the bouquet was stuck resolutely to Eve's bodice. They hadn't yet had to navigate the complexities of either of them needing the bathroom, but that time would come. It would have been comical if Eve wasn't absolutely terrified of Tanya's wrath should she find out. They'd got through the church service, and Eve had even managed to give Ben the briefest and smallest of smiles as he offered his arm for her to hold to walk up the aisle even though inside she felt like she was going to be sick. Once upon a time she'd played this moment out in her head, albeit with a different ending.

Walking into the reception an hour later, Eve's breath was taken away by the effect of the soft white material flowing down from the ceiling, the twinkling fairy lights, and the beautiful round tables bedecked in white tablecloths and tall glass vases with white orchids cascading out of them. She had to give it to Tanya, her vision was absolutely stunning. Finding her name on the big canvas propped up on an easel at the entrance, Eve winced. She was hoping to be sat near Becca or Ayesha, but she didn't recognise anyone's names on her table at all. After all she'd done for Tanya, you'd have thought she'd have given her a fun table to sit on. As Eve approached Table Thirteen, her heart sank. She was sat on the singles table.

'Hi everyone, I'm Eve.' She gave a little wave, hoping that it fell into the friendly but not flirty camp; a quick scan of the table had already confirmed that it was unlikely her future soul mate was present. Not that she was shallow or judgmental

– one of the four men sitting around it might absolutely surprise her with their quick wit and repartee, but it seemed unlikely.

After Eve had gone round the table, politely shaking everyone's hand, one of the men took out a small bottle of antibacterial gel from his inside pocket and cleansed himself, while another started furiously vaping. The dark-haired one opposite Eve started lining up little plastic pots of lentils and homemade falafels that he'd brought with him in a mini cooler bag, and the spotty teenage nephew of the groom to her right had already started on the shots, fishing a slice of lemon out of what she was sure was *her* water and sprinkling table salt on his hand. The women were equally as welcoming.

'So, what do you do—' Eve peered at the place name of the germ-killer next to her, '—Peter?'

In the exact same nasally voice that Eve had already given him in her head, he replied, 'I'm a botanist. But you'd know that if you read your card.'

'Card?'

'In front of you.'

Eve looked down at her table setting. Four sets of cutlery were laid out, which instantly gave her a sinking feeling as to how many courses she was expected to sit through, but tucked underneath her napkin was a little card. On it in neatly typed writing it read:

Welcome to Table Thirteen (unlucky for some!) We hope you enjoy the reception, here are some introductions to your fellow guests to kickstart conversation and help you make new friends. Enjoy!

Peter – Peter is a botanist and a keen fly-fisher.

Jenny – Jenny is fluent in Welsh and can say the world's longest train station backwards.

Kevin – Kevin is a tube driver and fan of heavy metal, the heavier the better.

Anne – Anne lives in the Orkneys and breeds the North Ronaldsay sheep which mainly eats seaweed.

Bernie – Bernie is an ambidextrous vegan and has completed a marathon on a pogo stick.

Louisa – Louisa is a lexicographer and a keen trumpeter.

Jake – Jake has recently finished his A levels and hopes to become famous.

Violet – Violet is Luke's great-aunty and first started reading palms when she was seven.

'You seem very young to be a great aunty.' One of the women said to Eve.

'There must be a mix up,' Eve said. 'I'm not Violet.'

'So who are you and what do you do?'

In the same vein as an Alcoholics Anonymous meeting Eve announced, 'My name is Eve, I'm a wedding journalist and I drink ten coffees a day.'

'That amount of caffeine can be very detrimental to your health,' said the lentil man, who Eve rightly signposted as Bernie.

'You're telling me you pogo stick through a marathon on no caffeine at all?' Eve replied.

'You can't use pogo stick as a verb, it's a noun,' the woman, who Eve guessed was Louisa, said curtly.

'So, Jake.' Eve swivelled slightly in her chair to the boy to her right. 'What do you want to be famous doing? Do you sing?'

'Nah.'

'Act?'

'Nah.'

'Do you invent things?'

'Nah.'

'Might you have a Plan B for your future Jake?'

'Nah.'

Eve looked over at the table she'd hoped to be at, where Ayesha and Amit were topping up everyone's glasses, Becca was laughing at something Ben was saying and everyone was smiling and having fun. Sighing, Eve reluctantly tuned back in to the table, just in time to hear Jenny say, 'Hcogogogoilisytna llllwbordnrywhcyregogllygnywgllwpriafnall.'

'Oh, sweet Jesus,' Eve muttered under her breath, reaching into the middle of the table for a bread roll.

'I don't think we're meant to eat those yet,' Anne said, immediately singling herself out as someone who would never be Eve's friend.

Eve broke a large chunk off and popped it in her mouth. 'I don't think I got the memo about that.'

Chapter 7

'Ask me what my table's like,' Eve said to Becca and Ayesha as they met by chance in the ladies' loo in the lull before the speeches started and dessert was served.

'What's your table like?'

'Funny you should ask. The boy one side of me has propped his phone up against the bread basket and is live-streaming a football match, the bloke opposite me, Kevin, I think, has eyebrows that are alive and trying to communicate with me, one woman keeps Instagramming her food, the overweight man the other side of me, Peter, has a nasal problem that if I wasn't so goddamn hungry would be putting me off my food, and the other two women are only talking to each other. It's just fun, fun, fun.'

Ayesha pouted in the mirror redoing her lipstick. 'It's really strange though Eve, I did the table plan with Tanya, and you were definitely on our table.'

'Well, Tanya must have changed her mind and thought that I deserved punishing for the hen fiasco a little more.'

'No, I even placed all the paintbrushes on the tables this morning. Yours is lilac, like ours.' Tanya had come up with the idea of dispensing with the run of the mill paper name cards and in honour of the factory's previous life, had instructed Ayesha to write everyone's names on a hundred small paintbrushes, the ends of which were dipped in different colours denoting which table they would be seated at. Eve had noticed that hers had a purple end, while everyone else's on the Table of Doom were ironically a sunshine yellow, but she hadn't thought anything of it.

'You were between Jack and Amit,' Ayesha continued. 'But when we all sat down to eat, Great-Aunty Violet was sat there instead.'

'She's a hoot,' Becca added. 'You'll love her. She's been reading all our palms; I'm going to have twins one day and Ayesha is going to move to Africa.'

'That sounds a lot more fun than the Chelsea game or the sound of phlegm boy clearing his sinuses every few seconds.'

'Move to ours now, when we go back in,' Becca urged.

Eve opened her mouth to say that she couldn't possibly, it would seem really rude, and then remembered her new vow of woman-ing up. Reentering the room, she headed straight for her table, grabbed the bouquet under her chair, tossed it to the sheep-breeder with a smile, gave the rest of the open-mouthed guests a wide grin and said, 'It's been really fun, enjoy the rest of your day,' before heading off to the welcoming arms of the lilac table.

Amit and Great-Aunty Violet moved their chairs up so Eve could squeeze in between them. The old woman was dressed head to toe in hot pink, even her lipstick that was busy bleeding into the hundreds of fine lines around her lips was the same daring shade. How liberating it must be to be so old that people just waved away your tastes as eccentric, rather than strange, Eve thought. Violet gave Eve a big toothy smile as she sat down and immediately called a waiter over to get her an empty wine glass. There may have been nigh on sixty years between them, but Eve could tell they were kindred spirits.

Violet leaned in close to Eve, and said in a loud stage whisper: 'Speeches soon. I hope Luke doesn't rabbit on like he usually does.'

Eve tried to stifle a smile. Slagging off the groom was very poor form, especially on his wedding day, but she was inclined to agree. Luke had been in the same tutor group as Ben and often came round to their student house, their damp problem being marginally better than the one in his house. And they had cable TV, whereas he and his three rugby friends were playing roulette with no TV licence. The vans with aerials on them regularly drove around their neighbourhood trying to find and fine students playing the system. While they were all making ends meet by working in the student bars or local pizza joint, Luke was working in his uncle's stockbroking firm, and spent an inordinate amount of time recounting yawn-inducing tales of corporate high jinks to them all. It couldn't have been his chat that won Tanya over, so Eve had always assumed that either he had a large trust fund or was a demon in the bedroom department. Looking at him now at the top table, mouthing the words to his speech in a last-minute run-though, hands shaking, with his already-thinning hair brushed over an obvious bald spot, Eve gave an involuntary shudder at the thought of the latter reason.

Ben, on the other hand, was annoyingly displaying none of the signs his friends were of being a decade older; there was no visible paunch, his hair was still dark and thick, and if anything, his late twenties had ironed out the aesthetic flaws or judgments of error of his student days. Gone was the straggly excuse for a goatee that had once been long enough to plait, which bizarrely Eve used to find quite attractive. He'd always been confident, but watching him work the room now, if you'd looked up the word charming in the dictionary it would have a smouldering picture of Ben Hepworth next to it. He was currently hovering by the top table making innocuous small talk with Tanya's sister. Eve could tell by the way Cathy was curling her hair around her finger that his chat was teetering on just the right side of flirty. He looked up then and their glances met. Embarrassed, Eve quickly looked away. Out of the corner of her eye she could see Ben straighten up and start walking towards her table. She quickly turned towards Violet and said, 'I love your outfit.'

'Thank you dear, I'm going to be buried in it.'

Eve had just taken a big gulp of wine at exactly that moment, and found herself choking on it. Someone started whacking her back with a force that wasn't entirely necessary, and when she'd regained the ability to breathe again, she realised angrily it was Ben.

'Easy now, Red.'

'Jesus, Ben, you didn't need to hit me so hard.' Eve was aware that her face was an unattractive shade of purple and tried to hide behind her hair.

Ben held his hands up. 'I saved your life.'

'You did not. It just went down the wrong way.'

'You moved. Didn't you like your old table?' Ben said, his eyes taking on a familiar twinkle. 'I met Peter at Luke's stag do. Top guy. Shame about his sniffing. The curtains look lovely, don't they? It must have taken you hours.'

The penny suddenly dropped. Eve swivelled angrily round to face him. 'You? You swapped the names?'

Ben put one hand on his heart. 'I have no idea what you are talking about. Oh good, speech time.'

The tinkling of silverware against glass made everyone hurry back to their seats. Eve watched Ben merrily meander back to his own seat with an untamed rage building inside her. The last time she'd spoken to him they were arranging where exactly in Gatwick airport they were going to meet before their flight to New York. She'd said the departure lounge, he'd said check-in. It didn't matter in the end as he never turned up.

It was meant to be the adventure that marked the start of Eve and Ben the couple, and not Eve and Ben the best friends. She still didn't know if he knew that she'd been in love with him the whole way through their degrees, and for four years after that, or whether he assumed that the night they finally got together was because of a sudden change of heart, an opportunistic coupling because both of them were single and a little bit drunk. But for Eve, that night after a bad comedy club where he'd finally slept over in her bed and not on her sofa was the night everything finally slotted into place. The misty filter had been lifted off her life and everything had more colour, more vibrancy – it all just made more sense.

They were going to split the rent on a studio flat in Manhattan, and travel to work on the subway together every morning and eat slices of pizza from a neighbourhood Italian restaurant in the evenings.

When he didn't turn up at the airport, leaving her a two-line note in her passport by way of an explanation, Eve had stood there alone in the bustling departures hall, a new shiny suitcase at her feet, clutching his letter that promised her an explanation soon. Should she go to New York alone, and live the adventure that was designed to be shared, or should she stash it in the great filing cabinet of life under 'missed opportunities'? Holding back tears for every minute of the plane journey, she arrived at JFK alone, unsure and utterly heart-broken.

Without his share of the rent paid, she had to cancel the let on the studio, and live in whatever she could afford, which turned out to be a hall cupboard advertised as a 'compact bedroom'. She navigated the subway alone everyday, clutching her bag to her chest, eyes wide at the pace of life and magnitude of people, all rushing past with somewhere to go, someone to go to. Her first few dinners in her new city were eaten with just her thoughts for company. Ben hovered near the surface of everything she did, every new experience she had was tinged with sadness and then anger that he had let her down so badly. She'd managed to, if not forget about him, certainly pack up all thoughts of him into a little box in the recesses of her brain, somewhere she rarely allowed herself access to. But now this. How dare he just dance back into her perfectly ordered life, and start playing silly buggers with it.

A Beautiful Day for a Wedding

Apart from Luke's cringeworthy opening of 'That's not the first time today I've risen from a warm seat with a piece of paper in my hand', which was met with a horrified gasp from his new wife and a smattering of compatriot sniggers, the rest of the groom's speech was a roll call of thanks and protocol. Before he told everyone to 'Glaze your arses, I mean, raise your glasses,' he ended with the customary thanks to the 'stunning bridesmaids, who have all been incredibly supportive to Tanya in the run up, particularly Ayesha, with the beautiful table plan and decorations.' Cue a round of applause for Ayesha, who looked at once embarrassed and a little confused at being singled out for praise. Nothing surprised Eve about this wedding any more. The sooner she could wriggle out of the patchwork boa constrictor masquerading as her dress, climb into her own bed and put Tanya's wedding in the annals of history, the happier she'd be. But that utopia was at least six hours away.

'I'm getting some messages for you from the other side,' Violet whispered during the best man's speech.

Despite a vast amount of media training, Eve had no ready response for that. 'Um. That's nice,' she mouthed back.

'They're saying dog poo.'

'Dog poo?' Eve whispered back.

'Yes. Does that mean anything to you?' Violet's eyes were filled with expectation, perhaps that Eve would respond with, 'yes, that's my surname, Eve Dogpoo,' or 'that's my address, Number 5 Dogpoo Avenue.' She hated to disappoint her though.

'Um, we once had a golden retriever and I used to pick his business up?'

'That'll be it then.' Violet adjusted her large two-handled fuchsia handbag that was resting in her lap and settled back in her seat, smiling.

The waiters chivvied everyone outside after the meal for the band to set up and a dance floor to be laid. Eve spent most of the time in the toilet with Becca to avoid bumping into Ben again, and away from Tanya's eagle eyes fixating on her patchwork gown. Re-entering the warehouse they were stopped by the officious master of ceremonies. 'Have you got your bracelets?'

'I'm sorry?' Eve said. 'Bracelets?'

'For the evening reception,' he said, pointing to a trestle table where guests were queuing up to have colour-coded bracelets fastened around their wrists. 'Join the back of the queue, ladies.'

'What the hell's this?' hissed Becca as they shuffled their way to the front.

It transpired that despite Tanya and Luke's not inconsiderable wedding budget, their generosity did not extend to watering their guests in the evening. A little sign propped up on the table announced that Gold Bracelets were £40, Silver £25 and Bronze £15.

'I don't believe it, she hasn't!'

A rather embarrassed looking student masquerading as a server for the evening was patiently explaining to each guest that should they want to keep drinking the champagne then they needed to purchase the gold package, spirits were silver, and the house wine and beer were bronze.

'I think she has,' laughed Becca. 'Wow.'

'Wow indeed.'

'Bronze please,' Becca told the student, while Eve huffed next to her. 'You're not seriously doing this, are you?'

'What choice do we have?' Becca replied. 'We're her brides-maids.'

'Exactly! She's making us pay for the privilege of being here. Sod that, I'm going home.'

'Eve, you can't, we have to stay. Look, just go for the bronze one, we'll get absolutely plastered on plonk, and then laugh about it tomorrow. Can you lend me some cash?'

They queued up at the bar to flash their bracelets to the barman before being handed a couple of glasses of acidic white wine. Violet was next to them holding her golden bracelet up to the light admiring its shine. 'I would imagine this is what it's like being at a music festival,' she said. 'So exciting. Now I will never need to go to Glastonbury.'

The friends moved away from the bar to let similarly disgruntled guests take their places.

'I see you've gone for the cheap option,' Ben said, joining the two of them. 'You can take the girls out of the student union, but you can't take the student union out of the girls.'

'Look at you, flashing the cash with your fancy silver one,' Becca teased, while Eve stayed silent next to her, looking at the floor.

'I felt that wine or beer wasn't going to be strong enough for me to get through the rest of the evening, and I'm not really a champagne sort of guy.'

'Well, can you put it to good use and get us a round of shots?' Becca asked. 'Sambuca if they have it, tequila if not.'

As he walked back to the bar Eve hissed, 'Why did you say that? Now he's going to stay with us all night.'

'It's fine, we'll drink it then have a dance. Look, I know it must be really difficult for you, him being here after all this time, but he seems like he's making an effort to be friends, and it's nice to see him again. I know we haven't all been in love with him for over a decade like you have been—' Becca put her hand up to stop Eve from denying it. 'But that doesn't mean that we can't be civil to him. Look, here he is.'

Ben was carrying three little shot glasses which he divvied out to each of them. 'Cheers!'

Eve knocked hers back in a second and then put her empty glass on a nearby table. 'Thanks. I'll see you both later.' And she walked away, with no purpose or place to go; she just needed to not be near him.

Three hours later, Eve could hear her own voice talking to Becca, but it didn't sound like her at all. It was like one of those voice-distorters, used by someone wanting to keep their identity secret, slow and pronounced with every syllable. Also, the curtains kept moving, tall white ghosts dancing about the room. She'd managed to dart out of Ben's way whenever it looked likely their paths would cross, and in a massive open factory, with no dark corners, or indeed walls that weren't made of transparent cotton, it was a commendable feat. But a few hours spent leaping behind curtains, ducking behind chairs and even at one point sheltering inside the DJ booth had taken its toll and Eve was drunk, exhausted and on the verge of being exceedingly emotional should she not fall asleep imminently. 'I think I need to go home Becs.'

'I do too, I'm knackered. Shall we split a taxi? By split I mean you pay and I'll pay you back when I can.'

'Sure.' Eve was far too weary to even bother arguing.

'Where are you going girls? The night is still young, and so are we. Sort of.'

She'd done so well avoiding him, to fall now at the final hurdle was too much for Eve and she just burst into tired tears. The weeks and months of bridal demands, the disastrous hen do, the horrific state of her finances, the brutal To-Do List, making sure Tanya never saw her butchered dress, and avoiding Ben, it was all too much, and when you threw a few bottles of paint-stripper white wine into the mix, the result was not pretty. Becca put her arm around her best friend, gave Ben a look over Eve's head that said, 'don't ask' and gently led her away.

Weddings. Ah weddings. Joyous occasions celebrating love. Joyous occasions where the guest list is as varied as a seaside town's pick'n'mix. Imagine the venue as a massive pink and white striped paper bag, where nestling inside you have the ingredients for a massive sensory overload. You have the stars of the show, the bride and groom, the fizzy cherry cola bottles if you will. Sweet and sour little nuggets of deliciousness. Then the bride and groom's parents, the chewy fried eggs – no one questions their place at the table, they've just got to be there. There's the fudge, or the drunk uncles – everyone likes them but you can't have too many of them as they take up too much room. Gobstoppers, the boring colleagues that are a bit pointless, have no taste and go on and on. Likewise, the flying saucers, this is the vicar that you felt obliged to extend an invitation to – a bit two-dimensional and tasting vaguely of communion wafer. Dolly mixtures – these are very obviously the extended family. A hotchpotch of different flavours, sizes and shapes, mostly nice, often jelly-tot fabulous, with a pointless square one thrown in because you have no choice when they come as a package. Cue the jelly beans, the old university friends that you haven't seen for ages. These are usually sweet, you might even get a couple of fruity ones, but sometimes, just sometimes, you're the unfortunate recipient of the cinnamon one, which makes you feel incredibly sick and leaves a very bad taste in your mouth.

Chapter 8

Eve missed the hangovers of her twenties that lasted the length of time it took for a paracetamol and a can of red bull to kick in. This one was still lingering on Monday morning, despite feeding it junk food all of yesterday and staying in her pyjamas for thirty hours straight.

All eyes were on her in the weekly editorial meeting, and Eve realised that Fiona was patiently waiting for an answer to a question Eve had no recollection of being asked.

'Really, Eve, nothing? You have no column ideas at all to fill the extra page we need?'

'I'm sorry, I'm not feeling too well. I haven't had time to think, I was a bridesmaid at the weekend and it's taken its toll on me.'

'Isn't that an idea in itself?' Fiona had a whiteboard pen in her hand that whirred into action, scribbling the words 'How to be the perfect bridesmaid' on the blank canvas resting on the easel. 'Ok good, done. We're nearing deadline though, so if you can get it written today, Stephanie, you can lay it out later. Bev, stand by to sub it, ok? Then we're good for press on Wednesday.'

Eve gratefully received the outstretched Starbucks cup and full-fat blueberry muffin that was being offered by Kat, and sat down at her keyboard. Perfect bridesmaid, what an oxymoron. Well, at least where she was concerned. Despite being unsure of how to type her own name a few minutes previously, Eve's fingers started flying over the keys.

How to be the perfect bridesmaid. Rule number one: Start mourning the friend you love, because once she becomes embroiled in wedding planning she doesn't exist anymore. Eve smiled. Writing her diary was like free therapy; some people go for a run, others crack open a big tub of Ben and Jerry's, she just let her bitchiest thoughts flow through her fingers onto a keyboard.

… And the best part is, you have to smile like Mary Poppins while cheerily crossing each item off. Hem curtains? Check. Polish floors? Check. Dog-sit for a fortnight? Che— Fuck. Fuck fuck fuckity fuck.

It took two hours, and Tanya's flat was by no means ready for visitors, but at least all remnants of Coco's bodily functions had been removed, the bedsheets were spinning round in the washing machine, the rug was at the dry cleaners, and the Louboutins had been scraped, dettol-wiped and put back in the wardrobe. More importantly, Tanya's dog was alive. Eve allowed herself a smile at a job well done as she walked back to her office, considerably slower than she'd made the reverse journey.

There was a yellow post-it note stuck to Eve's screen from Fiona summoning her to her office as soon as she got back. Kat wasn't at her desk so she couldn't ask her what sort of mood their editor was in when she wrote it. Taking a deep breath and hoping that she didn't smell of abandoned dog too much, Eve hovered by the door until Fiona looked up.

'Come in, close the door.'

That was a bit unusual. Apart from when she was conducting everyone's six-monthly appraisals, where people would either leave the office close to tears or jubilant after being given a pay rise that equated to four coffees, the door was always open.

'Sit down.' This was all a bit too formal Eve thought. She racked her brains as to what misdemeanour she might have inadvertently made.

'I saw what you'd written for the column on your screen.'

Oh God.

'It's not what it looks like,' Eve blurted out. 'That's not the real column, it's my diary. I do that sometimes, write nonsense to get my creative juices flowing and then I delete it and write the proper words, it was just a bit of fun, no one would have ever seen it.'

'I guessed as much, but it's a cynical side to you that I haven't seen before. And it's not appropriate for you to be writing at work.'

Eve gulped, it sounded horribly like she was being fired. 'Of course! I've just had a difficult few weeks, my three best friends and my brother are getting married this summer, and I'm the go-to for all of them, and it's just getting pretty exhausting fielding their ridiculous demands, and all my frustration came out in my writing, but I promise you I was going to delete it.'

It was difficult to read Fiona's expression. There was definitely some confusion in there, possibly some sympathy, and if she didn't know better, Eve thought she glimpsed a smidgen of understanding on her boss's usually unreadable face.

'Don't get me wrong Eve, I know myself how difficult it is sometimes to summon up the enthusiasm to be writing about romance when your real relationships aren't quite so rosy. No one else knows this, but my divorce became final at Christmas, so I totally get the conflict between your day job and your life.' She cleared her throat. 'That's actually what I wanted to talk to you about.'

In all the possible scenarios that were running like a ticker tape through Eve's mind as to where this conversation was going, she didn't expect what came next.

'A good friend of mine is the editor of *Venus*.' Fiona paused, prompting Eve to react in the way she was evidently supposed to, with an audible 'wow' and nod of admiration, both for her friend's amazing job, and for Fiona's link to woman with said amazing job. *Venus* was a digital magazine with the tagline, *'For modern women who don't take life too seriously'*. It was a pithy, often close-to-the-bone read, dispelling the myths, standards and political correctness that print publications had to abide by. In the same vein as the Slummy Mummy blogs that had commandeered a vast proportion of the internet and filled it with humorous stories about serving up pot noodles in china bowls at dinner parties and passing it off as homemade pad thai, the site had a huge following for women who thought life was too short to be excessively well-mannered. Reading it was Eve's guilty pleasure. These writers had none of Eve's sense of propriety or convention and she felt nothing but awe and envy for them. Not that it advocated rudeness, just realism, and it was bloody funny. She still wasn't sure why this was relevant though.

'And I thought what you wrote was really good. So I sent it to my friend, and she loved it too. And she's going to run it this week, and call you about writing a regular column for them during wedding season, talking about the crazy things people get up to at weddings, bizarre requests, ridiculous stories, et cetera. They have a large budget for freelancers, which would help you out considerably, I'm sure, as you mentioned you were finding it a bit tricky making ends meet. Whatever you write for them would have to be completely anonymous though. That is vital as I couldn't have it known that our features editor who skips through life filled with the joys of love and marriage is writing a column called *The Misadventures of a Bad Bridesmaid*. And you would have to swear that you wouldn't tell anyone at all that you're doing it, let alone that I told you about it.'

Throughout this monologue Eve's eyes were growing wider, this whole conversation seemed so implausible. She'd entered the room thinking she was getting fired, and she was now being offered a potential new sideline and income stream.

'I don't think I'd be any good at that—' Eve started.

'Nonsense.'

'I just mean, it doesn't sit well with me, pulling apart the happiest day of someone's life.'

'You do it in private anyway, why not do it in public? Anyway, it's not pulling apart their day, it's more about observational humour, saying what most people are thinking. Look, what I read on your screen is exactly what they're looking for. They pay five hundred pounds a column. Bash a couple out a week and you'll be rolling in it.'

Eve gasped. That was crazy money.

'Here's Belinda's number, call her after work and go from there. But Eve, if this ever comes out that it's you, I know nothing and you're completely on your own. Understand?'

Eve understood. She understood that this was the lifeline she needed. Not just financially, but for the sake of her sanity as well. If she was going to be paid for getting all her dark thoughts off her chest, it might just be the sweetest gig that had ever existed.

Chapter 9

The Bull's Head was a throwback to the 1920s, and not in an airport-lounge themed-bar type of way. It had the original Art Deco stained glass, a heavy oak bar with leather-clad bar stools and every spare inch of wall was taken up with framed pictures of the good and great of the jazz and blues world who had graced the tiny raised platform at the far end of the pub. There were probably five hundred bars between Tanya's posh flat, where Eve and Becca were both staying, and their local underneath their own flat but to frequent one of them seemed like cheating on a faithful lover.

They'd got there early so had managed to commandeer one of the battered leather sofas near the door, which was propped open, so there was a heavenly gush of fresh air to counteract the warm muskiness of the pub.

'So, what's new?' Becca said, taking a sip of her wine and tucking her leg underneath her.

Eve could hardly tell her about the conversation with Belinda that had just taken place on her walk from the tube station. She was sworn to secrecy, and sadly, that included Becca. But the phone call could not have gone better. Belinda welcomed her on board and confirmed the fee for her columns that almost had Eve dancing on the pavement. Forget roller discos and zorbing, she was ready to suggest Vegas for the next hen do. Belinda had asked her what sort of things she was going to write about and, put completely on the spot, Eve found herself reeling off details about all the weddings she had lined up that summer: a fashionable urban wedding in a warehouse; an off-the-wall themed wedding complete with plastic birds and non-conventional aisle; a countryside village fete wedding; and a gay destination wedding. Said out loud, they sounded perfect fodder for her new column, and Belinda thankfully thought so too. As long as she changed enough details of each wedding no one would ever put two and two together.

Eve shrugged. 'I haven't been up to much, apart from being the leading character in an episode of Animal Rescue.'

Becca giggled through her hand. She was just as guilty of completely forgetting their dog-sitting duties, and when Eve had called her from Tanya's flat to describe in stomach-churning detail what she was having to deal with, she couldn't help but laugh. The part where Eve recounted scraping out the inside of Tanya's Louboutins with an anti-bacterial wipe had actually made her cry a little.

'You would have thought that we'd mature with age.'

'Like a fine wine.'

'Yes!' Becca smiled, twirling the stem of her glass. 'Or like Ben.'

Eve had wondered when Becca would bring him up. The whole way home from the wedding, and the entirety of the next day, when they'd both lain horizontally on the living room sofas for ten hours straight, his name hadn't been mentioned.

'I'd hardly say he was mature, he swapped the place cards round so I'd have a shocker of a day.'

'I meant mature as in looks. He's still quite gorgeous.'

'If you like that sort of thing.'

'Yes, you're right. Tall, dark, chiselled features, broad shoulders, it's definitely an acquired taste.'

Eve rolled her eyes. 'I didn't notice. To me he was still greasy and annoying.'

'You didn't think he was greasy and annoying four years ago.'

'I was naive and stupid back then. With appalling taste in men.'

'Did you ask him why he left in such a hurry? With no forwarding address?'

'No. And I don't care.'

'You cared enough to hide away in New York for two years.'

'I was not hiding! I was working!'

'And hiding.'

'I was not.'

'No, you're right, you were having a great time. In your windowless bedroom with your pot-smoking flatmates who didn't speak English.'

'Look, him leaving me in the lurch like that just showed his complete immaturity, as did his stunt at Tanya's wedding.'

'But you guys used to play jokes on each other the whole time, it was what you did. I bet it was just his way of building some bridges,' Becca reasoned.

'By making me have a miserable time?'

'So get him back. Come up with a prank to show him that you have the upper hand. Or just talk to him, listen to his explanation. You need some closure.'

'I'm not stooping to his level Becca, and come to that, I have zero interest in talking to him about it. Or about anything. Or even talking *about* him, so let's not. Anything new with you?'

'He's living in Wimbledon now.'

'Why are we still talking about him?'

'Which is quite close.'

'Is Jack up this weekend?'

'Just two trains and you're there.'

'It'll be nice to see Jack again, he's been on training for ages now.'

'I could get Ben's number off Ayesha?'

'If Jack's up for more than two nights, count me in for a drink.'

Becca shook her head and rolled her eyes. 'You're infuriating.'

Eve topped up both their glasses and clinked hers to Becca's. 'It takes one to know one.'

They'd called it a night around ten o'clock. Tanya's was a few stops down on the tube and it was a work day tomorrow. Letting themselves into Tanya and Luke's darkened flat the two women instinctively angled their noses up and sniffed the air.

'I swear to God I've gone through an entire Fruits of the

Forest floor bleach, half a tonne of air freshener and lit every single scented candle I could get my hands on, and it still smells like shit.'

'It's fine,' Becca said comfortingly. 'They're away for another fortnight, it can't linger that long.'

Eve was eternally thankful they were on the third floor and could sleep with the window open. She felt like she was covered in excrement and trapped inside one of the Christmas tree shaped fobs you hang from rear view mirrors.

'Oh my days, Eve, look at this!' Becca had opened the double-door American silver fridge and was standing in front of it, her face illuminated by the fridge lights. 'Did you see this earlier?'

'I was too busy fumigating the place, what is it?'

Every jar, bottle and carton inside had little post-it notes with Tanya's neatly looped handwriting on them. A half-eaten jar of pesto said 'Please finish by 25/6', a glass pot of artisan olives tied with a raffia ribbon read 'Do not touch', a cold bottle of Moët stated 'Do not drink', an M&S bottle of prosecco had the invitation to 'Help yourself' and a container of fresh coffee beans had 'Use sparingly' on the top.

'Who even uses the word sparingly?' Eve wondered out loud.

'Tanya does. Don't you remember our fridge at Stanbrook Road? Me, you and Ben all shared a massive tub of Tesco Value margarine while Tanya had her own Lurpak that we weren't allowed to use? And she was the only student in the history of students to buy avocados.'

'Do you reckon these notes are for us, or Luke?' Eve asked cheekily. 'I mean, this is no way for a grown man to live.'

Becca grinned and slammed the door shut. 'It's a miracle she found someone to marry her.'

'For so many reasons.'

'What's that? Eve Atwood being *bitchy*? Who are you and what have you done with my friend?'

It was true. Eve seemed to have experienced a seismic personality shift in the last few years. Being dumped without explanation and fending for herself in New York had sanded away some of the optimism and jolliness that had erred on the side of irritating if someone hadn't known her well, and this new incarnation was, dare she say it, cynical and a bit bolshy. And she rather liked her.

'Tanya's broken me.'

'It was bound to happen at some point,' Becca said, giving Eve's shoulder a squeeze. 'What do you say? Shall we crack open the prosecco and toast our new home for two weeks, and the new you?'

'Sod that, we're having the contraband Moët.'

It was nearly midnight and they needed to go to bed, but Becca was talking through her ideas for Ayesha's hen do. Eve knew that if she stopped her, the moment would be lost and no more plans would be made until ten women arrived on the weekend after next expecting a party and there would literally not be a single thing booked.

'So, we're agreed that the London Loo Tour sounds fun but not right for a hen do?'

'While I personally love the idea of a guided walk around the city's best toilets, no, it's not quite right,' Eve replied encouragingly. It was Becca's first attempt at event-planning and her ideas veered from the offbeat to the jaw-droppingly ludicrous. This suggestion hovered somewhere around the middle.

'What should we wear? I was thinking we could all wear Pink Ladies jackets with our names on them?'

'Let's sort out what we're doing first, how much it's costing and then see what's left over for outfits.' The Eve of old would have taken over, unearthing some new notebooks, pens and highlighters and steering Becca in the direction of hen perfection, but this Eve was letting her friend arrive at the destination by herself. However much it was killing her.

Becca suddenly ventured, 'How about a sex class where experts come and teach us all the tricks of the trade?'

'Didn't Ayesha say that she wanted her mum to be there?'

'Good point. So that rules out pole dancing, naked life drawing, Adonis cabaret, nipple-tassel making and my personal favourite, the Mermaid-a-thon where we make tails and shell bras.' Becca lay back on the sofa and closed her eyes in defeat. 'That leaves nothing.'

It was time for Eve to step in. Not in a heavy-handed, 'I've got the solution' type of way, just a gentle nudge, or they'd still be talking about nipple-tassels at dawn. Which sounded like a cracking film title for a rude western. 'Ok, let's think,' Eve said, hand on chin, pretending that the idea she was just about to voice had just that second flashed into her brain, rather than being heavily researched and wedged up her sleeve in case a back-up plan was needed. 'Ayesha is not the best cook, and she'll need a solid repertoire to impress the in-laws when they visit from India, so how about an Asian cookery class? Then we could all have dinner eating our own food we've just prepared, in a lovely Airbnb that we've hired for the weekend, maybe a funky loft apartment on the river.'

Becca sat up, her eyes wide with enthusiasm. 'Yes! That's perfect! And then after dinner we can have the séance!'

'The what?'

'It was Ayesha's idea. She was so impressed with crazy Great-Aunty Violet's fortune-telling skills, she's asked her to come as the entertainment in the evening.'

'Violet told Ayesha that she was moving to Africa, and that you were going to have twins. I'd hardly say she was on the mark.'

'But if that's in our future, you have no way of knowing it's untrue.'

Exasperatedly Eve replied, 'But you have no way of saying that it is!'

'She said dog poo to you. Can I remind you what sort of day you've had?'

Eve had completely forgotten about Violet's pronouncement until Becca reminded her. Even so, it was a tenuous coincidence. 'A séance has the potential to go horribly wrong,' Eve persisted. 'What if she tells someone they're dying and they're not? Or that their husband's cheating on them and then they get divorced, and it's all the wittering of a senile old woman.'

'I think they have to take an oath that they don't pass on bad news.'

'From where? Palm readers' college? You don't sign up to the clairvoyants' union or anything.'

'Anyway, it was Ayesha's idea and it's her hen party.'

'Well, just for the record, I think it's a ridiculous idea.'

'Is that because you didn't have it?'

'Now who's being bitchy?'

Becca picked up the two empty champagne flutes and swept her mound of olive stones into her hand. 'Forget about it, it's late, we need to go to bed, it's a work night.'

'I'm sorry,' Eve said simply. 'I don't want to argue with you, I'm just knackered from running around after her ladyship, and I'm angry at myself for agreeing to do all the stuff I did that's made me so exhausted, and for saying we'd stay here, and I want to sleep in my own bed that I know with a massive amount of certainty has never been pooed on.'

By mutual agreement they both shared the futon, which turned out to be the world's poorest excuse for a mattress. Becca was already awake, lying still and staring up at the ceiling when Eve came to.

'Do you think it's all part of a cunning plan?' Becca started. 'If you deliberately make the spare room as uncomfortable as possible then sure, your guests will moan about you behind your back, but they'll never return. Whereas if they enjoy the best night's sleep of their lives, you'll never get rid of them. It's actually very clever.'

'Will you promise to have a nice spare room when I visit

you and Jack? And then strip it back down to a prison cell when I leave?' Eve mumbled, not yet ready to open her eyes and start the day.

'Ok, but on one condition. You go and take that blasted dog out for a walk before she scratches her way through the front door.'

Chapter 10

'Are we writing for grooms now too, and no one's told me yet?' Kat asked, peering at Eve's screen. She'd been browsing stag do pranks for the first two hours of the day under the pretence of getting ideas for the feature she was writing on hen parties, but in reality she'd been wondering if Becca was possibly right and that in order to gain some sort of closure on her relationship, friendship, or whatever she had with Ben, she needed to show him that she couldn't be walked over. Again. And as she had no inclination to go near Wimbledon, or be anywhere in the same breathing space as him, Eve figured it had to be done from afar. She just needed to work out how. And what. And when.

'Long story. A friend of mine has his stag do this weekend, and I want to play a joke on the best man.'

Kat's eyes lit up with curiosity. 'Ooh, does our Eve like the best man?'

'In no way whatsoever,' Eve replied briskly. 'He's incredibly annoying and I would love to see him in a mankini.' She paused. 'That came out very wrong. I would love to see him humiliated in a mankini, not I would love to see him *in* one.'

'I'm not sure stag do pranks extend to the best man too.'

'But they do, look at this site,' Eve swivelled her screen round slightly so that Kat could get a better look at the current webpage on her screen called stitchupthestag.com. 'It seems that the best man is often included in the gags. My only issue is how to make sure that it happens.'

'What you need is someone on the inside.'

Kat was right. Eve ran through the list of possible co-conspirators which, as she didn't know any of Amit's current friends, was limited to just Luke, and she ruled him out instantly due to his humourless earnestness and the fact that every one of his movements had to be either authorised or vetoed by his wife. There *was* a way for this to happen, she knew it, it just had to come to her. Meanwhile, she should probably get back to the job she was being paid for, there were panicking brides to placate.

Hi Eve,

I'm having a massive issue with one of my bridesmaids, who is also my husband-to-be's sister. She is so much shorter than the other bridesmaids, like really short, and she's going to make my photos look really strange. I bought her five-inch heels to wear but she's refusing. Can I ask her to step down?

Jackie, Edinburgh

Hi Jackie,

Surely you want her to step up, not down? As a hater of heels myself, there's no way that I'd be able to walk around in five-inch stilettos all day without looking like a drunk Bambi, and that's not a look you want for your bridesmaid either. But you're right, a short bridesmaid is absolutely going to ruin everything, and frankly make you look like a complete fool in front of everyone you know. But I think I have the perfect solution. Find another short person, get your sister-in-law to sit on their shoulders all day and just drape her bridesmaid dress over the top. Right height and no blisters.

A little chuckle escaped from Eve as she selected all the copy she'd just written and deleted it before writing the real reply.

Hi Jackie,
As a hater of heels myself, I sympathise with your sister-in-law, but it's a tricky one, and I see it from both sides. I would have a chat to your photographer beforehand so they are aware of it, and they can choreograph shots where you're all standing on steps, or an incline, or even sat down. I promise you it's not going to be a problem.
Eve xx

Hi Eve,
You're my last hope! My parents got divorced a few years ago, and my dad says that if my mum brings her new boyfriend to the wedding, he's going to smash his face in. Should I risk it?'
Polly, Leeds

Hi Polly,

Families eh? Most weddings have some sort of family drama lurking in the background, and in your case, it's totally understandable that you're so anxious about it. Pick a quiet moment in the run up to the wedding to explain your concerns to your mum, and see if her new toyboy lover that she's purely bringing to make your dad jealous has to come. Likewise, speak to your dad and remind him that it's your day, and he's being a selfish arse if he insists on being the Hulk about it all.

Eve deleted the last two sentences. She didn't even know she was doing it now, it just slipped out. Note to self, stay in character. Your role is to relieve agony, not add to it.

... It's your day and it would mean a lot if your dad could put his grievances to one side for the day. If both do come, jiggle the seating plan around so the two men are not in each other's direct eyeline, and appoint a few people in your inside circle to make sure the two men's paths don't meet. But relax, very few weddings end in bloodshed and criminal records.

Delete. *But relax, and enjoy your day.*

Eve checked her watch, it was nearly lunchtime, and as Becca was working at the school all day, Eve had to nip back to Tanya's flat to let Coco out. If she was quick she could take her round the block, grab a sandwich and be back for the two o'clock meeting. Tanya owed her big time for this.

***

The door to Tanya's apartment wasn't double locked, and as she and Becca had left at the same time that morning, Eve knew it had been. Gingerly pushing the door open, the noise of the TV was the first thing Eve heard. She'd read about burglars taking their time over a heist, even stopping for a while to try on clothes and enjoy a beer from the fridge, but to halt a robbery to catch up on the news? That seemed unlikely. Maybe Tanya and Luke had a big bust up and had called time on their Zanzibar honeymoon early?

'Hello?'

A pair of men's shoes lay discarded by the door. They looked too big to be Luke's as he had comically small feet – she knew that after checking every shoe for more of Coco's 'presents' – but equally, why would an intruder worry about making marks on the floor?

'Hey Red.'

Eve froze. Why on earth was *Ben* here?

As if he'd read her mind, or more likely interpreted her horrified expression correctly, he added, 'The presents from their gift list are being delivered this morning, Luke called me and asked me to come as I have a spare key. He did try to call you and Becca but both your phones are switched off.'

'She's at school and I haven't turned my phone back on

after a meeting I just had.' Not that she needed to explain anything to him.

Ben shrugged. 'It's no skin off my nose, I wasn't doing anything anyway, and their TV is bigger than mine.'

'Knock yourself out. I just came back to walk Coco.'

'Already done. The delivery isn't scheduled until between one and four and I got here early, so I took her out.'

This was the point in the conversation where she should thank him. Instead she said, 'So I had a wasted trip.'

'You're welcome.'

God, that man was annoying. What had she ever seen in him?

The doorbell chimed, and they both moved to the intercom at the same time. Eve stepped in front of Ben and picked up the phone, buzzing the delivery man in. An endless stream of boxes of various sizes were carried in and unceremoniously dumped in the living room. Eve signed the paperwork and then they were left in peace, both staring at what could quite easily be the contents of a whole house.

'Bloody hell. That's a lot of presents.' Ben whistled.

'Didn't you see their gift list? It went on for sixteen pages.'

'No, I always chuck those away. Better to give a gift from the heart.'

'So what did you get them then?'

'A traditional Maori mask.'

'Which will really go with their current design scheme,' Eve said sarcastically, opening her arms wide to highlight the flat's gleaming white and steel décor.

'Ok then, what did you get them?'

'A wine oxygenator, it was on their registry.'

Ben sniggered. 'An oxygenator? What the hell's an oxygenator?'

Eve didn't want to admit that she had to Google it before she'd bought it, so quickly replied, 'It adds flavour to wines by mixing air into it.' She stopped herself from childishly adding 'Duh' to the end of the sentence, but it hung there unsaid in the air nevertheless.

'Silly me, of course. So what else was on this list apart from the incredibly useful oxygenator?'

'You know, the usual, a caviar serving set, crystal chess set, matching monogrammed velvet slippers, that sort of thing.'

'Oh, good, all the essentials then.'

Eve bit her bottom lip so that she didn't smile. 'To be honest, I stopped reading after the first half a page.'

'Once you'd spotted the oxygenator.'

'Once I'd spotted the oxygenator. I hit perfection early on, and didn't think it was worth looking for anything else.'

'I can see why you'd do that. God, after this chat, I want my own oxygenator.'

Ben's eyes then started to take on a familiar mischievous twinkle that Eve knew so well. 'We could always open a few of the boxes, see what else is in them and then seal them up again?'

'Ben Hepworth! Have you met Tanya? She would literally eat your balls for breakfast.'

'She'd never know, come on, let's just take a peek.'

'I want nothing to do with this.' Eve folded her arms across her chest.

'Yes you do. You're as curious as I am to see what's lurking inside these boxes. Come on, Red.'

'You're on your own.'

Ben took his car keys out of his pocket and deftly drew a line with them down the sticky tape holding the side of the box together. 'I'll open it on the side, not the top, so she'll never know.'

Eve covered her face with her hands. 'I can't believe you did that.'

'And hey presto. Will you look at that, we have an electric towel warmer ladies and gentlemen.'

Eve peeked through her fingers. It was indeed an electric towel warmer.

'Next up, we have a monogrammed steak branding iron for putting Luke's initials on his meat. Now that's ingenious.'

Eve shook her head. She really should put a stop to this, it could only end badly.

'Wow, a cherry pitter. That is a very useful piece of kit right there. Who likes pitting their own cherries? Not me.'

'Ben, stop it, seal it back up.'

'Come on Red, get into the spirit of this.' He threw her his keys. 'Open that one next to you.'

'One more,' Eve said holding up her index finger in the air. 'And not because you told me to, but because I genuinely want to find something to beat the cherry pitter.'

'That's my girl.'

Eve froze. It was a turn of phrase, she knew it was. But Ben had suddenly realised what he'd said too and they were trapped in an awkward impasse where the laughter of a few seconds before had been completely shattered.

Ben coughed, breaking the silence. 'Um, I brought some lunch with me, there's enough for two if you want a quick bite before heading back to work?'

There was nothing she would like less than to have lunch with his smug face, smugly chewing his smug panini. But then he said, 'You work for a wedding magazine, don't you? I'd like to pick your brains about Amit's stag do if you've got a minute?'

Gift horse. Mouth.

'Sure. But I can only stay for a few more minutes.' Eve hoisted herself up on one of the kitchen stools and tore the sandwich in half.

'Well, we're staying in London, and going paintballing in the afternoon – we're going to do the usual thing of making Amit the target for us all. Then we're out in Covent Garden at night, I've booked Rocatillos, but we want to do something else fun. Ayesha has already said that all his body hair has to remain intact on pain of death, and Amit's refusing to come if he has to wear a dress or cape, or something called a mankini, which I had to Google. I really hope my internet history never falls into the wrong hands.' Eve forgot herself for a moment and smiled, then promptly hated herself for it.

'All the pranks online seem a bit too hardcore, I don't want to hoist him up a lamppost and gaffer tape him, and in the current political climate kidnapping him with balaclavas might get us all tasered, so I've drawn a bit of a blank.'

This was perfect. Beyond perfect. This was blinkin' awesome. 'How about you force him to busk to pay for his share of the meal?' Eve suggested. 'You could steal his phone, wallet, cards, travel card, so he has no way to get home or pay for the night, and you're in Covent Garden anyway, so you could come already prepared with a tambourine or something equally hilarious. Give it to him with a cap to collect donations in, and stand there and watch him make a fool of himself.'

Ben laughed. He had the same laugh as he used to. But then he would, wouldn't he? Laughs don't suddenly change with age.

'That is genius. I love it. Thanks Red.'

He had to stop calling her that because every time he did a little frisson of something, she didn't quite know what it was, ran through her. 'You're welcome. Now, I really must go. Have fun at the weekend.'

'Will do.'

Oh, I wouldn't be so sure about that, Eve thought as she closed the door to the flat behind her and took her phone out of her bag.

'Amit? It's Eve. Look, this didn't come from me, but I've had a tip off about your stag do that I think you ought to know about so you can form a counter attack...'

Apart from the odd scratchcard, possibly a lottery ticket on a rollover week, and maybe a horse at the Grand National if it has a name the same as me, I'm not a betting woman. But right here, right now, I'm willing to put one of the new scrunchy ten-pound notes on the fact that you own a kettle. And another ten quid on the presence of a toaster on your worktop. And another fine orange specimen of the Queen's legal tender on the fact that you don't actually need another kettle or toaster, the ones you have do the job just fine thank you very much. So I get the fact that when you're getting married, you want to minimise the risk of being handed a new kettle or toaster in white wrapping paper with embossed silver bells on it. I also understand that there is a limit to how many champagne flutes one couple needs, and the same goes for vases, silver photo frames and cheeseboards. So what's the solution? Well, brides and grooms up and down the land have thought that the answer lies in having a gift list. A registry. A wishlist. A We-don't-trust-our-friends-and-family-to-come-up-with-a-nice-present-so-we're-telling-you-what-we-want List. And quite often, these are comedy gold. Tibetan Singing Bowls? I'd like three please. Hot Sauce Making Kit? Nothing bonds newlyweds together more than taking turns in the same toilet. An electronic egg-minder. Yes, this is a real thing, and if you don't already own one, then quite frankly I despair. This little gem keeps tabs on how many eggs are left in your fridge and sends an alert to your smart phone when they're nearing their expiry date or you're running low. Because using your eyes to stock take just isn't enough, and we all know how annoying it is to check the date on things. Think of all the time you've wasted over the years reading expiry dates; entire seconds of your life that you'll never get back. Monogrammed items are also enjoying their time in the spotlight. After all, a couple can't profess to be properly in love unless their initials are entwined on matching dressing gowns. So next time you're invited to a wedding, don't go off-piste and assume the happy couple need a new vase, they don't. What they really need is a Tibetan Singing Bowl. Three if you're feeling generous.

Chapter 11

A ll that was left of the bhajis, samosas and pakoras were crumbs, an indication that the ten hens were all much better at mastering Indian starters than they had first thought. Admittedly, most of Ayesha's attempts had ended up in the bin, but her mum, Asha, had stepped in and tripled her own output, ensuring the platter in the middle of their dining table was towering with spicy pastries. It was such a fun afternoon, and even Tanya, fresh from her honeymoon, seemed so much more relaxed than usual. Eve had managed to put the flavour of the entertainment to come out of her mind, until the doorbell to the loft apartment rang and a vision of turquoise stood in the doorway.

'I'll say one thing for her, she's not afraid of a bit of colour,' Eve whispered to Becca.

'Shhhh.'

Ayesha was ushering Violet in, introducing her to everyone, and showering her with compliments that Violet smilingly batted away with a wave. The other hens were jumping up and eagerly taking turns to shake her hand, but Eve hung back until Violet's eyes rested on her. 'Hello again,' Eve said.

She might be cynical about Violet's fortune-telling credentials but Violet was a sweet old lady.

They'd pushed the four pure white sofas into a square, with Violet sitting in an upright armchair between two of them. She turned down the offer of tea, and joined the hens in drinking Pimms, which she was eagerly slurping through a penis-shaped straw.

Ayesha was the first to speak. 'So how does this work?'

'I just need a moment of quiet to invite the spirits to talk to me, and then I'll start passing on their messages.' Violet closed her eyes, her palms upturned in her lap. The room fell silent. It wouldn't have surprised anyone if the candles had started to flicker, or the curtains had billowed in the double height windows. Eve suppressed the nervous giggles that were itching her throat, and turned them into a small cough instead. Nine other pairs of eyes gave her death stares.

Violet's eyes sprang open and turned her head to her right, looking directly at Asha. 'I can see you surrounded by family and friends soon, giving you lots of love and best wishes.' Eve tried so hard not to roll her eyes, as Asha was a good three decades older than everyone else there, and the only other Indian lady, it was pretty obvious she was related to Ayesha, and at weddings people rarely threw rotten fruit at the bride's mother.

'Wear the pink sari, not the other one you're thinking of,' Violet advised. In view of her sartorial choice at Tanya's wedding it wasn't a massive coincidence that she was saying this.

'And the spirits are saying biscuits, what's this?'

'I do like biscuits,' Asha admitted.

Eve raised her eyes to the sky.

Violet's gaze travelled around the room before stopping at Ayesha's pregnant colleague Trudy. 'You will need to repaint the room you've just painted in a different colour.'

Trudy gasped, and put one hadn't on her swollen belly. 'You mean it's not a boy?'

'No, it's not.'

Hang on a second, Eve thought, it was all very well telling someone that they like biscuits but you couldn't just make proclamations about the gender of a baby.

'Who is married to Mike, or Mick?'

A small blonde woman who had been nervously sat on her hands slowly raised one of them.

'He's never going to stop leaving his bike in the hallway, so you're wasting your breath nagging him about it.'

A twitter of laughter ran around the room. 'That's so true!' The woman gaped at Violet. 'How did you know?'

Violet just smiled and closed her eyes again. 'Come on spirits, keep coming through. Ok, Samantha? I have your father here, he's telling you to read through the contracts you're about to sign very carefully.'

This was ridiculous, Eve thought, anyone should heed that advice. Until Violet came up with something impressively concrete, she was right to be sceptical.

'There is a clause in there that needs to be removed.'

'My dad was a solicitor,' Samantha explained to the group, almost apologetically. 'And I'm starting a new job.' Lucky guess Violet, Eve thought.

'I think the next message is for you dear,' Violet said to

Becca. 'Your grandfather is suggesting you have hay bales instead of chairs, does that make sense? You're in a field, he's saying, no point lugging furniture through the stiles, use hay bales. He also says that he approves of your man, "thoroughly good egg" he's saying.'

Becca let go of Eve's hand that she'd been cutting the blood supply from to wipe away her tears that were running down her face. Tanya's turn was next. She was told that she needed to slow down, breathe, and enjoy her blessings. As Violet was Luke's great-aunt and had no doubt witnessed some of Tanya's pre-wedding histrionics firsthand, it wasn't as prophetic as it sounded to an uninvolved onlooker.

'I have a spirit here saying "lampposts, lampposts" – does that mean anything to anyone? No? No one?'

Eve glanced around the room at all the raptured faces hanging onto every one of Violet's words as if they were dripping with gold.

'Eve?'

Eve looked up from where she'd been stabbing her own phallic straw into bits of cucumber floating in her drink and met Violet's gaze. 'Who's Clive?'

'Clive?'

Everyone was waiting patiently for her to reply, but Eve had no idea who she was talking about. 'I don't know a Clive.' Saying the name out twice made her rethink. 'The doorman to my office is called Clive, but I don't really know him.'

'You need to tell him to get his testicular lump checked out by a doctor. This is really important.'

'Umm, ok.'

'And someone whose name begins with a B is going to play a big role in your future. I see many happy times with B.'

Becca excitedly dug her fingers into Eve's leg. 'Yay,' she whispered. Across the room Ayesha shot her an enthusiastic double thumbs up while Tanya raised her eyebrows and made a silent clapping gesture. What was with her friends tonight? They'd all lost the plot.

With Violet safely dispatched to her waiting taxi, Eve's friends crowded around her.

'It must be Ben,' Ayesha shrieked excitedly.

'It is not Ben,' Eve replied.

'But think about it Eve, he miraculously reappears again and suddenly you get a reading saying that a man called B is the one for you, it must be.'

Eve rolled her eyes. 'Seriously, it isn't. It's just as likely to be Bernie, the vegan lentil-popping pogo-sticker from your wedding Tanya.'

'No offence, but Bernie's way out of your league.'

'Cheers Tanya, that's very helpful. But it's not him, and it's not Ben, and anyway, more to the point, Violet is a lovely old lady, but I'm taking anything that comes out of her mouth with a shovel of salt.'

Ayesha sucked thoughtfully on her phallic straw. 'My mum was choosing between a pink and a turquoise sari you know. That's uncanny.'

'Not really. Didn't you say that the bride usually wears red, no one wears white, and the brighter the better? She could have quite easily said blue and you'd have assumed she meant turquoise, and you'd still think she was right.'

'You can't argue with fate,' Becca added. 'And if I was you, you know, single and everything, I know that I'd be trying to find as many Bs as possible to be having happy times with.'

'I do already, B-ecca.'

'Eve. It wouldn't hurt to just open your eyes to all the Bs around you, that's all I'm saying. Next time a bloke called B something shows a little bit of interest, and don't roll your eyes at me, you know it happens, I'm simply saying don't ignore it – see where it leads. You've been given a massive clue as to your future, don't waste it.'

'Becca's right,' Tanya chipped in. 'You can't really afford to at your stage in life.'

'Again, Tanya, very helpful. Right are we sticking with Pimms or moving onto something stronger?' Eve then wandered away from her gaggle of friends to the countertop where a range of out of date vodkas were calling for her. Now these were her kind of spirits.

Chapter 12

Eve wasn't mistaken. The heart locket lady was definitely smiling at her. After seven months of sharing the same train journey, and being caught – more than once – blatantly staring at her, she finally returned Eve's wistful smile. The sweaty mugginess of public transport in July evaporated and love, romance, and happiness filled the carriage. It was definitely a lover that gave that woman her necklace, her eyes were dancing too much and her skin too glowing, for it to be otherwise. He was probably working abroad using his niche skills to advance world medicine, or unearth dinosaur bones in Tanzania. He wrote often, of course, his own half of the necklace tarnished from the sun, but still he ticked off the days of his calendar until they would meet again.

Bollocks, Eve had completely missed her stop. She pushed her way through the throng to the door and ran off at the next station, quickly doubling back on herself and heading back up the same tube line. It was ten past nine when she finally arrived at the imposing glass revolving doors into her office, but instead of powering on through and running breathlessly and apologetically to her desk, Eve slowed down as she approached the entrance.

'Alright, Clive?'

'Morning gorgeous.'

'Everything ok, Clive?'

'Course it is. Fabulous day for it.'

Eve didn't feel like playing along today, but equally she couldn't break from convention and start talking about his intimate health. She bottled it. 'You can say that again.'

'Fabulous day for it.'

All the way up in the lift to the fourth floor she mentally beat herself up for not saying more, but apart from replaying the same four-line conversation with him every day, she knew nothing about Clive's life. She could hardly start talking testicles with him.

The meeting had already started, and Eve tried to slip in unnoticed, but Fiona made a point of pausing when the frosted glass door swung open, and stayed silent until Eve had taken her seat at the table, saying, 'Sorry, sorry.'

'I was just saying, Eve, that as per the memo I sent around last week, the sales targets are higher for the next issue, so we need editorial ideas that help generate new advertisers. As you're last in, you can be first to share what you've got planned.'

Another meeting, another completely blank mind brought about by zero preparation.

'Hen dos,' Eve blurted out, thankful that her real life was providing such rich fodder for her day job. 'Gone are the days of a simple meal out with friends, today's brides want to do something completely out of the ordinary. I was at a hen do last weekend where we had a séance.'

While the rest of the room broke out in an excited chatter at this revelation, Fiona said, 'While that's interesting, and no doubt your colleagues will be tapping you for information about it the second this meeting's over, I can't see clairvoyants with bags of cash waiting in line to advertise with us.'

'No, it was just an example of the out of box things that now happen on hen dos, I could do a round up of fun and quirky things to do in the major cities, London, Bristol, Manchester, Liverpool, Newcastle, Edinburgh, Dublin, and then tour agencies, nightclubs, adventure companies, entertainers, hotels etc, might all come in. It'd make a fun online directory too, and we can sell banners on the site, even offer discount codes. I think it'd bring in quite a bit of revenue.'

'Keep it classy though Eve, we're not out to shock like some other publications.'

Lucie, one of the junior stylists on the fashion desk said, 'Talking of which, did anyone else see that *Venus* is running a wedding column now? *Misadventures of a Bad Bridesmaid?* The first one came out a couple of weeks ago, and it's hilarious – basically all the stuff we'd love to write about if we were allowed to!'

Eve could feel the hairs prick up on her arms and tried really hard to keep her eyes from becoming saucer-like.

'No,' said Fiona curtly. 'Can't say I did. Right, yes, Eve that sounds good, remember to pass any lucrative leads onto Angie, and maybe include a Further Afield box-out on European destinations with original things to do to perhaps bring in some airlines too. Right, fashion—'

'You went to a séance?' Kat hissed as they all filed out back to their desks. 'You never said!'

'It wasn't exactly a séance, it was an old woman claiming she could talk to the dead passing on incoherent messages that were pretty vague.'

'Anything come through for you?'

The image of jolly Clive jumped to the forefront of Eve's mind, which she quickly shook away. 'Not really,' she said that I'm going to meet a bloke with a name beginning with B who was going to be important to me, but it's all a load of tosh.'

'That's so exciting!' Kat squealed. 'I'm going to keep my eyes and ears open for a Boris or a Barry I can hook you up with!'

'Stop it. Just stop it. Now leave me to my inbox.'

Dear Eve,

I have always loved elephants and really want to arrive at church on the back of one, but all the zoos I've called won't let me borrow one, can you help me?

Mia, West Sussex

Hi Mia,

Funny you should ask, I actually run a sideline special-ising in elephant hire for events, I used to do marquees but diversified last year.

Just then Eve's phone sprang into life, with Ayesha's name flashing up on the screen.

Eve answered it gratefully. 'Hey bride to be, how are you doing?'

'I'm great, thank you so much for a fab weekend.'

'Not my doing at all, it was all Becca.'

'She told me that had you not stepped in we'd have been touring toilets, having a talk by a sexpert and making bras out of shells.'

Eve laughed. 'We can do her ideas on a weekend when your mum's not with us!'

'It's a deal. Amit had a fun time too, he was telling me all about it last night. There's a brilliant video of him and Ben busking in Covent Garden. Apparently Amit had an inkling that that's what they were going to make him do, so he'd gone prepared to rope Ben in to do it with him, and even picked up a pair of men's tap shoes in a charity shop that he'd stashed in his bag, and made Ben wear those and dance while he sang Bohemian Rhapsody with a tambourine!'

This was so much better than Eve could have hoped. 'Oh my God, I bet Ben was so embarrassed.'

'He was bright red on the video. He kept asking Amit how he knew about the prank, but Amit just had a lucky guess.'

Eve sent a telepathic thank you to Amit for keeping her out of it, although she kind of wanted Ben to know that she was behind it. There was no point getting your own back if the person in question didn't know.

'And, you'll never believe it, but Trudy's just called me. First thing this morning, she went for a private scan of the baby and Violet was completely right, they'd got it wrong before, and it is a girl! She'd had three different doctors confirm a boy to her before this scan, so that's incredible isn't it?'

'Mmm, incredible.'

'And Samantha messaged me, saying that she gave her job contract to a lawyer friend, and there is a clause in there, buried on the fifth page, about having a year's probation where she can't take any holiday days! She called HR and they've agreed to reduce it to three months. Violet's amazing, isn't she?'

'Mmm, amazing. Look Ayesha, can I call you back, I just need to go and do something.'

Under the pretence of getting coffee from the cafe downstairs, Eve left her desk with a piece of paper with everyone's orders on it. There was still every likelihood that Violet had just struck lucky with Trudy and Samantha, but Eve wouldn't be able to live with herself if there was the slightest chance she might have a crystal ball where her brain should have been.

Clive sprang up from his chair just inside the front door to hold open the door for her. 'You look tired Clive, you should rest more.'

He laughed, showing yellowing teeth stained by years of cheap cigarettes, smoked strictly when he was out of uniform. 'Chance'd be a fine thing.'

'You need to take care of yourself Clive, we all do, we're not getting any younger, are we?' Eve said, smiling, trying to pitch it as a friendly talking point, rather than a direct, and quite frankly inappropriate, inquiry into his private bits.

'You're a spring chicken, love.'

'I'm thirty. But that's not the point, it's so important, isn't it Clive, to get any niggles seen to by the professionals? You know, something that might be worrying us, but we're putting off doing anything about. God knows Clive, I'm guilty of it too, but a quick check up always sets your mind at ease, wouldn't you say Clive? Sometimes, we might be too embarrassed, or maybe a bit shy about stripping off in front of a doctor, but it's what they're there for, isn't it? To feel our boobs and cup our balls.'

She'd gone from 'Fabulous day for it' to an armed assault that included the words boobs and balls. She was mortified. He was mortified. Eve fled to the nearby sanctuary of the cafe and wondered how the hell she was going to re-enter the building with seven low-fat lattes without going through the front door.

Hen dos. Chances are, your mother and grandmother didn't have one, or if they did it would have been a lovely classy affair with some cucumber sandwiches and a large teapot taking centre stage. Fast forward to the twenty-first century and hen parties have enjoyed a revolution of epic proportions. The term 'hen' was first coined in the 1620s as a slang term for women, and our friends across the pond in the US often used the phrase 'hen party' to describe any gathering of females. Even the formidable Eleanor Roosevelt was said to have hosted a Christmas hen party for cabinet wives and 'ladies of the press' in 1940 – so far, so sedate. But somewhere along the line, brides decided that grooms shouldn't have all the fun, and we jumped on the pre-wedding party bandwagon – destination: Let-your-hair-down Town. Over the next few pages are some fun ideas of how you can spend your final few nights of freedom with your friends. Flashing tiara completely optional...

Eve was boring herself. She minimised the word document and maximised a blank one.

A hen do, bachelorette party or the appallingly named stagette – just typing the word has made my fingers freeze into rigor mortis – has become an industry worth £500 million in the UK alone. That's half a billion pounds spent on phallic confetti, flammable LED-encrusted veils and strippers called Gavin who work at B&Q during the day.

A nice afternoon tea with friends in the Sixties, morphed into a meal at a Bernie Inn in the Seventies, jiggling your bits along to Wham at a disco in the Eighties, a night out wearing an L-plate and Skechers platforms in the Nineties, and now the twenty-first century has hit, we're expected to renew our passports and board a plane for Barcelona for three nights. Or worse, head into the country with ten or more women you've never met before, hole up in a self-catering house grandly, and falsely, advertised as a 'barn' and get served your dinner by a naked man in a posing pouch. No thanks Gav, put it away.

And the activities. I don't want to learn pole-dancing at 11 a.m. stone cold sober, go clay pigeon-shooting or attend a séance where a purple-rinsed clairvoyant randomly *shouts nouns into the room and fellow hens cluck that she's a genius. The foreplay and flirting workshop is so cringe-inducing I'm blushing even writing it, and model makeovers offend my feminist heckles so much I want to shake the screen until it dies a slow death. Wine tasting, I could get behind, and a nice meal out will always see me RSVP-ing in a positive way, but once the price tag goes over two digits I'm already feeling a bit pissed off before I've got there. Let's turn our attention to themes for a minute. There's nothing big or clever about middle-aged women wearing Pink Ladies jackets. Ever. Unless your first name is Olivia and your second is Newton-John, and even then most of us thought it was a cop out when she joined Rizzo's gang at the end. Be yourself Sandy, you don't need them.*

It was like free therapy, Eve thought, smiling. Except it wasn't just free, she was actually being paid by *Venus* to do it. None of this sitting on couches next to a tissue box staring into an Ikea picture of a waterfall, she was curing herself of all her woes and anxieties, and paying off her debts at the same time.

Just then her phone buzzed with an unknown number. She didn't normally answer unless she knew who it was, there'd been a couple of instances in the past of panic-stricken brides needing the calming dulcet tones of Agony Aunt Eve to quell their desperation but writing the *Venus* column had put her in the type of mood where even the most hyperventilating bride of them all could be talked back from the ledge. 'Eve speaking?'

'Eve, it's Ben.'

Eve clutched the phone so tight her knuckles whitened. 'Ben, hi.'

'I got your number from Ayesha.'

'Oh. Ok.'

'How was the hen party?'

This was very strange, Eve thought. There's no way that after four years of silence he had found her number in order to enquire after her weekend. 'Um, it was, fine.'

'It was Amit's stag do, as you know, this weekend too.'

'Yes. I heard he had a great time.'

'Did you also hear how he had "a feeling" about what his prank was going to be and made me join in too?'

Eve smiled. 'I may have heard something.'

'With tap shoes. I wore tap shoes, Red.'

Feigning surprise when all she wanted to do was burst into applause and yell 'GOTCHA' was an Oscar-worthy performance. 'Really?'

'I've been racking my brains thinking about how he could have known.'

'Oh yes?'

'It'll come to me, I'm sure. Anyway, I'll see you at their wedding in a couple of weeks. I'd better go, I've got to add in a few things to the speech, it's going to be a corker. Bye Red.'

Eve rolled her eyes. This petty tit-for-tat game playing was incredibly immature. He'd walked out of her life without even looking backwards, and now they seemed to be involved in a juvenile version of prank-tag.

Chapter 13

Hitched at Kew Gardens

Short of turning up with a megaphone announcing her marital status, Eve realised that nothing shouted 'Spinster' so loudly as being your mum's plus one to a wedding.

'Stop fidgeting, you look lovely,' Faye said, putting her arm through Eve's as their shoes crunched the gravel on the long driveway towards the Orangery where the ceremony was going to be held.

'So, the bride is called Leila, and the groom is Nick,' Eve clarified, accepting an order of service from a tall smiling usher.

'Yes, you used to play together when you were little, but you wouldn't remember that. You'd actually really get on with Leila, she wrote a blog about being single in London, it was pretty funny actually.'

They found two seats together near the back of the cavernous glass-roofed space, which was simply decorated to show off its breathtaking floor-to-ceiling windows looking out onto the gardens beyond. Delicate garlands of greenery wound their way around the backs of the white spindled chairs, with large white peonies attached to the end of every row. It was classic, and classy and even for a wedding pro like Eve, it was pretty near perfection. A small band of musicians struck up a jaunty jazz tune that Eve recognised from an old movie as the bride walked in on her father's arm. Eve could see what Faye meant about her getting on with the bride as even watching her walk up the aisle, Leila exuded a joy that quite often was missing from brides who were so hung up on every detail being right they forgot to have fun. Instead, this bride was beaming, waving hello to each familiar face she passed, doing a little shoulder jig in time to the music, and generally looking like the happiest person that ever walked the earth. Despite not seeing her since they were little, and having no real connection to her, Eve couldn't help a tear running down her face as her groom gently lifted her veil and broke into the biggest grin she'd ever seen on a groom. Eve's tears were for their unbridled joy, their happy ever after, but they were also a bit for her. For the love and passion she'd had a taste of, but was cruelly snatched away – with no explanation, no good reason, just because. The applause from the congregation snapped her back, and Eve clapped along, subtly and quickly wiping her eyes.

At the point in the ceremony where the registrar asked for the rings, two small children, who Eve assumed were the niece and nephew of the couple, threw a tennis ball up the aisle to each other, a nod to the fact the Wimbledon final was on that afternoon. As the ball reached the top, the groom split the ball open to reveal the rings. It was a fun touch that had everyone smiling.

The guests then padded across the lawn to the Princess of Wales Conservatory for drinks and canapés while the Orangery was transformed for their dinner. The vast glass-house was filled to the rafters with plants and trees, and even ponds replete with lily pads and trailing trellises of lavender. The jazz band had set up again and toes were tapping along to their music.

Eve breathed in the medley of sweet scents, and closed her eyes.

'It's beautiful, isn't it?' Faye said, handing Eve a glass of champagne she'd just taken from a passing waiter. 'Bit different to my wedding to your dad that involved a pie in a pub after the church. Is this like something you'd like for your wedding?'

Eve raised one eyebrow at her mother. 'Did you really just ask that?'

'Darling, you're thirty. I think it's possibly time you loosened up a little bit. You're hardly on the shelf yet. Have you had any joy on finding the plus one for Adam's wedding? Did you meet anyone nice at Tanya's wedding?'

A quick flashback of the table of doom made Eve shake her head with an unintended force. 'No, not at all. Except, well, Ben was there.'

Faye's head snapped round to face her daughter. 'Ben? As in Ben, your Ben?'

'He's not my Ben.'

'But Ben. *Ben* Ben?'

'He now just goes by the one name, yes.'

'And how was that? Seeing him again?'

Excruciating. Heart-wrenching. Emotional. Tormenting. 'Annoying. He was immensely irritating.'

'So there were no old feelings there at all?'

'None.'

'That's good. If it's true.'

'It is true!'

'Well that's good then. No point revisiting old wounds. Onwards and upwards. There seems to be lots of nice men here today, would you like me to circulate round the room and find one for you?'

'Oh my God Mother, absolutely not. I am more than capable of finding my own partner, if there comes a time when I want to.'

'Darling, when your father died I had no choice but to pick myself up, and believe me, it's a lot harder doing it at sixty than thirty. You and Ben were over four years ago, that is more than enough time for you to move on and find someone new.'

Eve couldn't explain it. She knew that it looked like she had spent the last four years pining for someone she'd had a six-month relationship with, but it wasn't like that at all. She'd fallen for him the moment they met in their first year of university, twelve years before. She loved the way his lip curled when he laughed, his streak of mischief and game-playing, the way his forehead got a crease in the middle of it when he concentrated, the way he made her feel as though she was his soul mate, his partner in crime, the only one that really got him. Their bond was so strong that neither of them wanted to spoil it by adding sex into the equation. A quick fumble after a night in the union could have ruined everything, and it wasn't worth the risk. Girlfriends, boyfriends, they all came in the front door and out the back for both of them, but the bar was set high, and no one measured up. The window in which both were single, living a few streets away from each other, came in their mid twenties. Fuelled by strong cider and a realisation of it being a case of now or never, they chanced it. And it worked. It really worked. Until he disappeared.

'Faye! You came, oh it's so nice to see you. You've lost weight, it really suits you, you look much better! Look Thomas, it's Faye!' The bride's father was pulled over to them by a woman Eve assumed correctly was his formidable wife Judy, who was decked out in a royal blue trouser suit with orange accessories. 'I think the last time we saw you was the funeral wasn't it? Ghastly business. And this is little Eve, oh my goodness! Thomas, look, it's Eve, don't you look like a painting, you know the ones with women with the long red hair. I must admit, we did feel a bit sorry for you when you had such bright ginger hair as a child but you've grown into it, it really suits you now.' Judy was smiling brightly, looking from Faye to Thomas to Eve, to get one of them to agree with her. The three of them just smiled back politely.

'What a lovely wedding,' Eve said, of the opinion that pretending Judy's proclamation didn't happen was the best course of action. 'Really beautiful.'

'Thank you,' Judy replied graciously, as though the whole thing was her creation. 'It really is, isn't it? But Faye tells me that you're not married yet?'

Eve smiled and gave her head a little shake.

'Oh, I wouldn't worry too much—'

Eve was sorely tempted to interrupt with 'I'm not,' but felt she couldn't stop the bride's mother in full flow.

'Just take Leila, she made a living from writing about being single, and look at her now, happily married. Your time will come, I'm sure of it.'

'That's what I've just been telling her,' Faye agreed to a chorus of middle-aged nods.

Judy and Thomas moved away after that, but not before Judy squeezed Eve's arm and gave her a wink.

'Weddings are perfect breeding grounds, excuse the wording,' Faye started, 'for new relationships. Why don't you cast your eyes around and see if there's anyone that does take your fancy? Leila's brother is over there and he must have some interesting friends, he's a solicitor I think.'

'Mum, just stop it.'

'Only saying.'

'Don't.'

'Ok then, subject closed. Anything new with you?'

'I saw a clairvoyant last weekend and she said that someone with the letter B is going to factor in my future.'

'You saw a clairvoyant? That doesn't sound like you.'

'I was forced into it. Basically it was Ayesha's hen do, do you remember Ayesha from university? And she had a séance.'

'A séance? For a hen do? I had an afternoon tea with cucumber sandwiches.'

Eve ploughed on. 'And the fortune teller, or whatever you call them, said that someone with a name beginning with B was going to factor hugely in my life, and would make me very happy. But I don't believe a word of it.'

'Don't be so quick to dismiss it my darling, I had a medium tell me twenty years ago that I'd end up finding nirvana with an incredibly handsome man with big muscles twenty years my junior, so there's hope for all of us.'

Eve shook her head resignedly. Her mother's dating status was getting less palatable by the minute. 'Anyway, I'm not taking any notice of what the medium said, it's all a load of rubbish.'

'Would it hurt though?' her mum asked. 'I mean, even if there's just a small chance she's right, it might be quite fun to seek out a B, it'd be like a treasure hunt.'

'With a human being as the prize. That's a bit odd.'

'Well you haven't had much luck with the other names. Why not give it a go, see if you can track down this elusive B that's going to make you happy? Do you think it might be Ben?'

'Not you as well! No, I don't and anyway, a few minutes ago you told me not to look back.

'B, B, B ... oh, Ann's son's single and he's called Bertie.'

'Oh good, it must be him then.'

'No need to sound so sarcastic darling, I'm only trying to help. Ooh, this is quite exciting!'

Violet must be laughing in her wingback chair watching *Countryfile* right now, Eve thought. Imagine sending people off on wild goose chases just by making a few good guesses. Right now, that pregnant lady was probably up a ladder, roller in hand repainting her nursery, Becca would be cancelling her order of proper chairs for the ceremony, Samantha, might not even take that job now because of the contract; it was crazy how much power a little old woman yielded when she spoke confidently. Of course, there was no truth in it. There couldn't be.

For the most part being single is absolutely fine with me. More than fine. I like it. I like not having to call ahead to someone to check whether it's ok if I go for a drink after work, I like the smaller grocery bills, and not having to hide the occasional splurge on a new bag or eyewateringly expensive lipstick just because the name Yum Yum appealed to my childish side. I enjoy having a whole bed to myself, to sleep in, to eat in, hell, I even like cutting my toenails on the bed – there, I said it. I like that all clothes in the laundry basket are mine and mine alone, and the same goes for the big bar of Fruit & Nut in the fridge. But do you know when's not a good time to be single? Guess. No, it's not on New Year's Eve as the clock strikes and everyone, and yes, I mean everyone, is seeing in the new year by exchanging saliva, and no, it's not even Valentine's Day, when you can't see your colleagues at their desks over the massive floral declarations of love, although as a hayfever sufferer, that's annoying for a whole heap of other reasons. No, I'll tell you when it's incredibly rubbish being single. At a wedding.

If it's not the undisguised looks of pity from your coupled-up friends and the quiet click of the tongue and head-on-the-side from well-meaning relatives, it's the fact that you've royally screwed up the table plan by coming alone so one table has to be boy-girl-girl. Or, even worse, being seated away from your family and friends and placed on the singles' table together with every other poor sod who couldn't find a plus one in time. In the past I've even been put on the kids' table and the old people's table, so unusual was my single status to the bride that she literally didn't know what to do with me. I've also been known to linger longer than is normally socially acceptable in the toilet around the time of the bride's bouquet-throwing, which, quite frankly, is an outdated custom that needs to stop. Now. Herding together all the spinsters so everyone can take a good look at the unmarried ones before expecting them all to lunge desperately for a bunch of flowers that decrees they will be the Chosen One next. Bleurgh. And you know that moment a minute or so into the first dance when the newlyweds realise that they can't sustain the slow excruciating shuffle they are doing for a second longer so they beckon all other couples onto the floor to join them? Yeah. That moment. That's definitely a crap time to be single too.

Chapter 14

Earlier that day, the glass door had been held open by a young scrawny fellow whose security uniform looked two sizes too big. He seemed friendly enough, smiling and doffing an invisible cap at Eve, but he wasn't Clive. Dawn, the receptionist, told her that Clive had asked for the day off to have some medical tests, and the agency had sent his replacement.

Half of Eve was relieved that Clive had managed to decipher what the hell she was getting at yesterday, and the other half was utterly embarrassed in case it was a complete false alarm and she'd sent him off to have his bits prodded on the advice of a batty old lady who liked bright colours. Not that she would prefer for there to be something sinister lurking just to save her discomfort. It was probably a complete coincidence that the other ladies at Ayesha's hen do had their premonitions come true, but either way, Eve was glad Clive had gone to be checked out.

'Jack's here!' Becca shrilled from the living room as soon as she heard Eve shut the front door in the hallway. Eve dropped her bag in the hall and hurried into the lounge to greet Jack. She'd only seen him a handful of times since Christmas, and he was one of those twinkly-eyed souls that lit up a room with their charm and good nature.

'Hello stranger,' Eve said, giving Jack a big hug. 'It's great to see you. Are you staying long?'

'I've got a work thing tonight, but can I treat you both to dinner tomorrow to hear all the news?'

'Oh God,' Eve batted his invite away with her hand. 'You don't want me there as a third wheel, you two lovebirds go and enjoy yourselves.'

'Well, actually there's a chap from the American base that we're working with who's in London tomorrow night, so I've invited him along too.'

Becca started jumping on the spot. 'Guess what his name is? Guess! Jack tell her! I'll tell her, Eve! It's Blake, it's flippin' Blake!'

Jack was standing with his hands in his pockets, looking bemused at his fiancée's hysterical hopping up and down. She was like a demented lemming. 'It's him, Eve, it has to be!'

'He's American.'

'Yes, so exotic,' Becca said hugging herself, mistaking Eve's sarcasm for unbridled joy. 'I can't wait for us to meet him!'

Eve turned to Jack. 'Answer honestly, on a scale of one to ten, how likely is it that this American GI Joe is going to be my soul mate?'

'I'm no good at this sort of stuff Eve, I don't know. He's a good bloke, keeps his guns really clean.'

'Oh good, because that's the main thing I'm looking for in a life partner.' Eve crossed her arms. 'I'm not coming.'

If Becca's bottom lip protruded any more they'd all trip on it. 'You have to, come on Eve, it'll be fun, and if Blake isn't *The* B it doesn't matter, although I know that he is.'

'I suppose Becca's told you then, about the ridiculous weekend we've just had?' Eve asked Jack as she slumped onto the sofa and patted the seat next to her for him to do the same.

'She has. I'm glad I've got her granddad's stamp of approval, even if I am sitting on a hay bale at my own wedding.'

Eve laughed, she'd forgotten that part. No doubt at some point in the next few weeks she'll be called upon to find, and pay for, said hay bales and arrange for their delivery. That'd be something to look forward to.

'So, Eve and Blake, Blake and Eve.'

'Don't you start Jack,' Eve said. 'I've had enough of that from this one.' She pointed to Becca who had come back in the room with three cold beers and a big bag of crisps.

'You're not a believer?'

'I don't know what I am. It all seems highly implausible, so I'm keeping an open mind.'

'So you'll come to dinner tomorrow?' Becca said hopefully.

'No, as much as I'm sure this Blake friend of yours is great, I'm still going to sit this one out.'

'You can't argue with fate Eve, I mean what are the chances of Jack being sent to London with a bloke called B just a few days after you get told you're going to marry one?'

'She didn't say I was going to marry B, just that he was going to make me happy. In my vast experiences of marriage – purely as an onlooker – marriage and happiness are rarely the same thing. Present company very much excepted. And whilst Jack, I think you're great, I don't want to marry an army man. Or an American, unless he's Jon Stewart. And as an American army man, he's not right on both counts.'

Duly chastened, Becca knew when defeat had to be conceded and reluctantly changed the subject back to hay bales.

***

'Morning Eve.'

It was the first time Clive had ever used her name.

'Morning Clive. Good to see you back.'

'I, um, told my wife about what you said,' he said quietly, motioning for Eve to stand aside to let some people behind her through. 'She made me go for some tests yesterday, and they think it might be, you know, bad, but they think they've caught it in time. We'll know more next week, but if you hadn't have said nothing the other day, I'd be none the wiser, so, cheers.'

'No problem Clive, hope it all sorts itself out.' She didn't know what else to say, so reverted to a tried and tested back up.

'Fabulous day for it.'

'You can say that again.'

'Fabulous day for it.'

Eve took the stairs so she could send a WhatsApp to Becca at the same time.

Fine, I'll come to dinner and meet Blake. What's the worst that can happen, eh? Where and when?

Blake's brutal haircut was army regulation and could in no way be held against him. But it unfortunately highlighted his head's similarity in shape to an avocado. It was tricky for Eve to look him in the eye as he was talking as her gaze kept wandering upwards to where his scalp sort of tapered into a point.

'So, what do you think of London?' Eve asked brightly. It seemed unfair to write off a potential perfect match on such flimsy criteria.

'I've only seen this restaurant and the embassy so far, but it seems, well, a bit dirty if I'm being honest with you.' Oh Blake, Eve thought. The pointy noggin she could just about overlook, but unkind words about her beloved city? He had crashed and burned, and their bruschetta starters hadn't even arrived. He was also calling her Ma'am, which, the first time he did it, Eve thought was a joke, but by the fifth time, she realised that it was just how he talked to women. It also concerned Eve how little Becca seemed to grasp his unsuitability for her, as she was still giving little shoulder jigs of excited encouragement out of the corner of Eve's eye. Were her friends so desperate to see Eve happily coupled up, that they'd accept any man with the right initial? Making her excuses the second the bill was paid, Eve left.

Are you still awake? x Eve typed into WhatsApp as she power walked to the tube station.

Adam replied straight away. *It's half past eight. We're not seven. x*

Sorry, after the evening I've had, one hour has felt like seven. x

We're out at a friend's 40ᵗʰ, at Gypsy Bar, come and join x

Mine's a double g&t. With lime. X

The bar was packed with gay men – unsurprising seeing as it was a gay man's birthday and it was being held in a gay bar. The bouncers tried to tell her that she was in the wrong place until Adam spotted her through the window, banged on it and gave the bouncers a thumbs up.

She gratefully accepted the tall glass of restorative gin and started regaling Adam and George with tales of her night.

'So you only said yes to meeting him because his name fitted the prediction?' Adam asked. 'That doesn't sound like you. This clairvoyant must have been pretty convincing.'

Eve put her head to one side, thinking about her brother's question. 'I was entirely unconvinced to be honest, but the things she said to everyone else are coming true, so I wondered if I was being a bit too quick to ignore my own reading. Turns out I wasn't and should have listened to my head.'

George, her brother's fiancé, jumped in quickly. 'But this army guy isn't the only B in the world though, is he? We know two Balthazars and a Broderick.'

'Do any of them like women?' Eve asked smiling.

'Only their mothers and sisters,' Adam replied laughing. 'But George is right, just because one B-man isn't right, ping that bell and move onto the next one.'

'It's a pity that phone books are listed alphabetically by surnames and not Christian names, it would have made my task a bit easier.' Eve lamented. It couldn't hurt to keep her ear to the ground for a single man whose name began with B, at least it narrowed down the pool of potential love interests, and Violet had been proved right for most of the others. Just then, surrounded by mirth, merriment and over a hundred homosexual men, Eve decided her mother was right, and that the hunt for the perfect B was on. What could she lose? Apart from her self-respect, but that was hanging by a thread at this point anyway.

Chapter 15

Tanya's tone of voice should have been an indication of quite how ludicrous Eve was being. Completely out of character for Tanya, she had tried to be tactful in replying to Eve's question about whether pogo-stick marathon jumping vegan Bernie was single, saying that she wasn't sure quite how compatible Eve and he might be, yet Eve was insistent on getting his number.

'We really hit it off at the wedding,' Eve heard herself say to Tanya. It wasn't a complete lie, she felt they had bonded over her excessive caffeine consumption, and now that she'd managed to jog round the 1km track at the park with Juan without stopping, completing a marathon on a pogo stick wasn't too preposterous a leap to make.

'I'm sure he'd love to hear from you,' Tanya lied smoothly. 'I can't see it myself, but you know, opposites do attract.'

Eve could see what Tanya was getting at. On the face of it, she and Bernie didn't have a lot in common: he ate lentils, she had just inhaled a hangover-remedy burger; he carried Tupperware boxes around with him with prepared organic snacks, she had the numbers of five different takeaway restaurants programmed into speed-dial; he travelled on a pogo-stick, she couldn't balance on a bike. But these were trivial differences, easily overcome by animal attraction and love. Did she fancy him? Truth be told, she couldn't really remember what he looked like. Dark-haired she thought, clean-shaven, possibly, but it was good that she wasn't instantly in lust with him. It would mean that their relationship would be based on something much more meaningful and long-lasting.

I don't think so was his curt reply, to Eve's upbeat message saying: *hello, remember me? Fancy meeting up sometime?* Undeterred – after all, no one ever said that love was an easy ride – Eve pressed on. *You don't think you remember me, or you don't think you'd like to meet up? E*

Sorry, you seem a nice girl, just don't think we'd have much to talk about. B

I'm training for a marathon. E
What? What are you writing, you ridiculous woman. Step away from the keypad, put the phone down and slap yourself a few times. She had no idea why she was being so forward, or persistent, or dishonest. She didn't even like the bloke, he just happened to have the right name. Was she going to be like this with every B? *What's that? You only wear black, sleep upside down hanging from trees and don't like the smell of garlic? That sounds right up my street, when can we have dinner?* Adam was right, there were plenty more Bs in the sea, and one of them might actually have a shared hobby and a sense of humour. She just had to find him first.

A Beautiful Day for a Wedding

***

It had been a week since Eve's columns on being single and hen parties for *Venus* had gone live on its website, and it seemed that she'd tapped into a common feeling that had women up and down the country nodding along with her. Becca had asked her as they'd walked to the restaurant together the night before if Eve had read the latest one as it was so funny that so many of the things they had talked about were in the article. Eve pretended that it was the first she'd heard about it, but would definitely look it up when she got the chance. 'I hope Ayesha doesn't read it,' Becca had said. 'It slags off séances on hen dos, and she might get the hump.'

Eve had stayed quiet. The last thing she'd want to do would be to upset her best friends, but on the other hand they were unwittingly providing rich comic material for her columns. There was no way they could link her as the author of them though, so they couldn't possibly take the content personally.

Thinking about Becca's reference to Ayesha made Eve realise that she hadn't spoken to her in a few days, and with her wedding just six days away, her nerves were probably standing on end. She thought she'd give her a quick call and see if there was anything she could help with. Typing in her number, Eve completely ignored the underlying guilt that had prompted her to pick up the phone and offer her services.

Ayesha answered on the first ring, breathless and speaking at double the speed she usually did. 'Eve! Thank goodness you called! The supplier I got the emeralds from have sent me rubies!'

Eve's brow furrowed. 'You're not making any sense Ayesha, what emeralds?'

'I ordered two hundred plastic emeralds to tie to the card for each place name, as in the emerald city, as in where Oz lives, but they've sent me red plastic gems instead!'

'But didn't Dorothy wear ruby slippers?'

'Oh my God, you're right. Oh Eve, this is brilliant. Oh thank God. I've been so stressed about it.'

'Well, you can relax now,' Eve said. 'I was just calling to see if there's anything else you need help with?'

'We can't get the flamingoes to stand up properly, the grass is really uneven, and they keep falling over.'

'Oh, so you went with flamingoes in the end?'

'Yes, I love them.' Ayesha's tone suddenly changed. 'Why, do you think they're stupid?'

Tread carefully, Eve thought to herself. Ayesha had clearly been injected with the same week-before-wedding brain-altering, anxiety-inducing hormone imbalance mandatory for all brides. 'No, I love flamingoes,' Eve replied hurriedly. 'I just didn't know that you'd definitely gone for them, that's awesome. Well, you could either weigh each down with a big stone, or maybe move them to the pathway so they're lining the pave-ment, so as each guest walks along it from the garden where they're having drinks to the reception, they can pass by the flamingoes. Would be good for photo ops too, can't imagine too many people would turn down the chance to get snapped next to a flamingo with their name on it.'

'Yes! That's a great idea. Ok, good, now I just need to sort out the DJ, we're having a bit of a nightmare with him.'

'Why, what's wrong? Anything I can help with?'

'Well, it's a bit delicate. He and his girlfriend were the DJ team, working together, but she's just left him, so he's doing it by himself. He's really depressed, and when he sent us the playlist he was intending on playing, there's a lot of songs like *Since U Been Gone* and not very many *You Make Me Feel Like Dancing*. If you get what I mean.'

'So you're worried he's going to break into a blues style "My baby just left me, duh duh duh duh duh, don't know what to do, duh duh duh duh duh, drunk a bottle of whiskey, duh duh duh duh duh."'

'A little bit.'

'Ok, here's what you do. Don't leave anything to chance, send him a playlist. I can put one together if you like, full of upbeat, dance floor fillers. Tell him to stick rigidly to it. Tell him there will be no need to MC anything, if there needs to be any announcements then I can do it, or Becca, or—' Eve's voice faltered slightly '—Ben, can do it. And on the night, I'll set up camp near his booth so that I can jump in if needed, wrestle the mic from him, and put on *Come on Eileen*. Ok?'

'That would be amazing.' There was a pause in which Eve could sense that Ayesha was practising her next sentence in her head before saying it out loud. 'Um,' Ayesha started. 'Um, and would it be ok, please say if it's not, but it would be amazing if you could, um, go with Ben the morning of the wedding to pick up the cake? The thing is that he can't go by himself as someone will need to hold it as he drives. I said to Amit that it might be weird for you, but apparently Ben's told him that there's nothing between you guys, and I know you've said the same, so I wondered whether it would be ok?'

Eve could hardly say no after that, however much the thought of being sat inches away from him in the car made her feel physically sick.

'Oh, and there's one more thing.'

A little wearily, Eve replied, 'Hit me with it.' She should be used to never-ending to-do lists from her friends by now.

'Do you know where Becca is getting her hay bales from?'

That was unexpected. 'Um, no, why?'

'I need to stuff the scarecrow that's going to stand at the gate to the hotel.'

Eve pressed her lips together as hard as they could go without drawing blood. 'Maybe a pet shop might be your best bet,' she managed to squeak before putting the phone down and resting her forehead down on the cool wood of her desk.

***

'Hey.'

'Hey.'

Ben stopped leaning against the bonnet of his car and went to the passenger side to open the door for Eve. She ignored him and went straight to the boot to put the white bag containing her bridesmaid dress on top of the suit carrier holding his wedding outfit.

'Do you know where this place is?' Ben asked.

'No, do you?'

'Somewhere in Wandsworth, Ayesha said, it shouldn't be too hard to find.'

'It'd be better if we had an address.'

'How many shops in Wandsworth are called Cute Cakes?'

'Fine, let's just go.' Eve slammed her door and buckled up, turning her body slightly away from him towards the window. She hated being this close to him. The sooner they picked up the cake and made it to the wedding venue, the better. Wandsworth was only a ten-minute car journey, and then the hotel was half an hour away, surely they could get by with minimal interaction for the next forty minutes, they'd managed alright for the last four years.

It didn't seem that Ben shared the same idea though, and as he pulled away from the kerb outside Eve's flat he cheerfully asked, 'So, how's your week been?'

'Ok.'

'Any stand out moments?'

'Not really. It was just a week.'

'There must have been something to make you laugh in it.'

'Plenty. But none that I can recall now.'

'That doesn't sound like you, you used to have loads of chat about your day.'

'That was then, wasn't it? A lot's changed since then.'

Ben looked in his rear-view mirror. 'Ok, so we're playing it like that, are we?'

'I'm not playing it like anything Ben. Can we just concentrate on finding this cake shop?'

'Well, that's me told.' Ben idly flicked the radio into action and turned it up.

As it turned out, Wandsworth wasn't as small as Google maps suggested it was, and forty-five minutes later they still hadn't found the shop.

'Can you just call Ayesha and ask where it is?' Ben asked, signaling right down a one-way street to a barrage of horns.

'I'm not calling her on her wedding day to tell her that *you* can't find her cake.'

'Me? We're in this together, Red.'

'We are not in this together, Ben, I'm here as the cake holder, you're the driver, therefore the navigator.'

'Who made that rule?'

'It's the law of driving, the one with the steering wheel in their hands is in charge of the route.'

'The division of labour in that scenario seems very weighted in one direction. Hardly seems fair. Have we been down this road before?'

'Literally or metaphorically?'

'I'm going to ignore your passive aggressiveness, and put it down to wedding nerves.'

'I'm not nervous.'

'Not even about my speech?'

'Ben, stop talking, and just find the place. Turn left here, we haven't been down that way yet.'

Tucked in between an auto repair garage and a bicycle shop was a tiny two up, two down with a little purple sign saying Cute Cakes. Ben's car skidded to a rapid halt. 'For Christ's sake don't pull a move like that when I've got the cake on my lap.' Eve rounded on him angrily.

'Er, Red, I think that's the least of our worries.' Ben pointed to the doorstep of the shop, where four white boxes had evidently once been stacked up, but the top three smaller boxes were on their sides, being pawed at by street cats.

'Shit!' Eve ran round the front of the car, shooing the cats away. A note was tacked to the top of one of the mangled boxes. *I waited nearly an hour for you to arrive, but had to leave to drop off another cake, here are Ayesha's cakes, the larger one goes on the bottom, and the Emerald City is on the top. Best, Linda.*

Eve squatted down on the pathway, and gingerly opened the boxes one by one, terrified at what sight she was going to be greeted with. Ben knelt down beside her.

'Ok, so this big one is fine, thank God.' Eve then reached for one of the boxes lying on its side, hearing its contents give a dissatisfying thud as she carefully turned it back the right way up. The medium-sized cake had crumbled on one side, and the icing was smudged all over the inside of the box. The top tier, the smallest cake had fared even worse, displaying some feline-sized teeth marks and muddy paw prints.

'Shit. Shit.'

'This is not good,' Ben added unnecessarily.

'If that's the top cake, what's in that one?' Eve said, reaching for the smallest box that had rolled to one side of the path.

Unbelievably, the cake topper, the illustrious Emerald City was intact, save for one broken turret.

'Please tell me you have a plan, Red.'

Eve was still sitting on her heels, Ben crouching next to her. 'Ssh, I'm trying to form one.'

'Can you think quicker?'

'Can you just be quiet for two minutes? Or is that impossible for you?'

'I'm just saying, we're on a tight schedule here.'

'And I'm just saying, shut the hell up, and let me come up with an idea that saves the cake and both our asses.'

'O-kay. I'll take this big box back to the car, and that ugly green castle thing.'

'It's the Emerald City.'

'Course it is. What every self-respecting wedding cake needs on top of it.'

A minute or so later Eve stood up, picked up the two battered boxes and hurried back to the car. 'Ok,' she said, through Ben's open driver's window. 'I think I have a plan. Asda's just down the road, and they do pre-iced cakes. Let's go there, get a couple of them, then use some of the decorations we can salvage to tart them up a bit. We'll stick them on top of this big one, and hopefully no one will know.'

'I love your optimism.'

The fact Ben had just said a sentence containing the words 'I love your' hadn't escaped Eve. Not one little bit.

'Just drive to the supermarket, quickly, but not over any bumps.'

'Roger that.'

***

'It could be worse. We could be coming as tin men,' Eve said pragmatically, as Becca winced at her reflection in the hotel's three-quarter length mirror. The bridesmaid dresses Ayesha had picked out for them were white with vibrant oversized red poppies printed on them in honour of the opium field Dorothy and her friends ran through to get to the Emerald City. A flower was placed conveniently, and a little crudely, Eve thought, over each breast, making her self-conscious enough to want to keep her arms folded at all times, which made holding a bouquet fairly tricky.

'These are nasty outfits.'

Eve secretly agreed, but as she'd been the sounding board for Ayesha's frankly off-the-wall ideas for months, these dresses were positively subdued compared to her other suggestions. 'At one point we were wearing stripy tights and pointy shoes, so we shouldn't complain.'

Becca pulled a face. 'Why was she so set on having a theme anyway? It's a wedding, not a New Year's Eve party.'

'You're having a theme for yours.'

'Hardly Eve, it's in a field, so it's not a giant leap to make that we'd have a country festival type feel to it. I wouldn't call it a theme as such.'

'You're having hay bales.'

'It's what my grandfather wanted.'

You couldn't argue with that logic. 'I'm just saying, a theme ties everything in neatly, but I have to admit, this one is on the wacky scale.'

Eve finished tonging the last strand of her long red hair, teasing it into a wavy tendril. 'We better go down, it's going to start soon.'

'How can you tell?' Becca asked. 'Has the tornado started swirling? Someone should go and tell Aunty Em.'

There was an incredibly narrow line between good taste and bad, and despite initial misgivings, Ayesha's vision fell for the most part on the positive side. A gently curved yellow brick road created from small painted bricks placed in a chevron design weaved its way through the middle of the rows of seats to the table at the front of the room where their ceremony was going to be held under a rainbow balloon arch. They'd hired out the whole of the country hotel, and while completely incongruous with its Sussex olde worlde charm, the Wizard of Oz theme wasn't overbearing, and added a touch of fun and colour, not eye-crossing kitsch. Apart from the bright pink flamingoes, they were as kitsch as it was possible to be. And possibly the balloon arch too.

There was an audible sigh of relief from both bridesmaids when Ayesha met them in the foyer before the service in a traditional white gown and not a blue and white checkered pinafore. Sensing their relief, Ayesha smiled and lifted her hem revealing a pair of sparkly scarlet trainers bejewelled in glitter and sequins.

'You couldn't have thought I'd be completely conventional?'

'You wouldn't be the Ayesha we know and love if you were,' Eve said, giving the bride a squeeze before the trio held hands, took deep breaths and walked in to the waiting crowded room to the tune of *You've Got a Friend in Me* from *Toy Story*.

Chapter 16

The Wizard of Oz wedding

Possibly one of the best wedding photo ideas Eve had ever seen, and God knew she'd seen a lot, involved the whole bridal party straddling fibreglass flamingoes.

'Do you need help down from there Red?'

'Thanks, but I'll manage.' She wasn't sure how, but it certainly did not involve Ben being gallant and gaining any kind of upper hand.

'Nice pair of poppies.'

Balls. In order not to slide off, her arms were clinging to the bird's neck, and not masking her flowery bosom. There was nothing else for it. Loud and proud was the only way to react. Eve gave her chest a little shimmy. 'Thanks.'

It wasn't a graceful dismount, and Eve was pretty sure she flashed her pants to most of the guests, but at least she'd got down by herself and unassisted by Ben, who was looking infuriatingly dapper in his tails.

'Have you seen the seating plan?' Eve hadn't heard Ayesha

sidle up to her, so gave a little jolt when her friend whispered in her ear.

'Not yet, why?' Eve replied, her heart sinking a little.

'Just that Amit's got some rather nice single ushers and I've put them all on your table.' Ayesha winked at her. 'You're welcome.'

Eve sighed. Her friends' definitions of 'nice single friends' had proven to be vastly different to hers in the past, so Eve braced herself for yet another afternoon of toe-curling conversation followed by excruciating silences brought on by growing mutual disdain.

When Eve was wrong, she admitted it. And boy, was she wrong. As she approached her table, four attractive men stood up, hands outstretched, and one even gave both of her cheeks a kiss, while the three women enveloped her in warm welcoming hugs. It was like a parallel universe of singleton tables, one that she had no idea existed before. And they were all already drinking and eating the bread rolls. These were her definitely more her kind of people.

Sandwiched between a paramedic called Robert and Andrew, a thirty-something political speech writer, (neither of which had halitosis which was a pleasant surprise) the banter flowed as effortlessly as the wine. One guest at a nearby table even shushed them during the main course, so loud was their laughter.

'So what's the weirdest thing you've ever written about?' Andrew asked, topping up her wine glass, while Robert looked on attentively resting his chin on his hand.

Enjoying the attention, Eve thought for a moment, selecting

the best topics that would have her audience open-mouthed and wide-eyed. 'Well, I used to work on a really trashy women's weekly, and there's quite a lot to choose from.' She started counting off headlines on her fingers. 'Why our 50-year age gap is brilliant; My husband wants to be a guinea pig and sleeps on hay; I'm pregnant with my step-father's twins; My sister's son is my daughter's half-brother; I hate my fiancé's tattooed eyeballs. Take your pick.'

'Wow. Up until this moment, I thought saving lives was an exciting job,' Robert said. 'Thanks Eve, for ruining my career for me.'

'Likewise,' agreed Andrew, shaking his head in disbelief. 'Next time I'm helping the Chancellor of the Exchequer write the budget speech, I'm going to be wondering why I'm trying to make a decrease in VAT sound like a good thing, when I could be writing about tattooed eyeballs.'

Eve held her hands up. 'Sorry guys, what can I say? It was both your faults for choosing boring jobs.'

The room hushed as the dessert plates were cleared away and a flute of champagne was placed in front of each guest ready for the speeches. Amit was effusive, and tearfully emotional when talking about his love for his new wife, so much so Ayesha had to lean close, pat his hand and say 'that's enough now, get a grip,' which had Amit's friends in stitches.

Eve hadn't had this much fun at a wedding in ages. And then Ben stood up.

'Thanks Amit. For those who don't know me, I'm Ben Hepworth, I was at university with Ayesha and Amit, and while I know it's customary for the best man to focus his ridicule purely on the groom, I'm going to cut with tradition and throw a little bit of derision to the bridal party to begin with as we take a stroll down memory lane.' A ripple of laughter echoed around the room. 'I agree with you, they all look absolutely stunning today, but that wasn't always the case.' Ben raised a clicker in his right hand and a large white screen to the left of the top table that Eve hadn't noticed before flickered into life, displaying a massive photo of nineteen-year-old incarnations of Tanya, Becca, Ayesha and Eve in all their pouffy-haired, high-waisted jeans glory before Moroccan oil was popular and Damson Plum was the only lipstick shade available.

'Please remember folks, that these pictures were taken on a disposable camera from Boots, before the era of filters, so be kind. But as you can see, Ayesha here, was always a bit of a catch.' *Click*. 'I think it's only fair if I include a photo of our leading man at this point too, so you can get the whole story.' Amiable laughter ensued as a massive still of Amit and Ben appeared on the screen, both wearing polo shirts and floppy curtains framing their faces. Their arms slung around each other's shoulders, drooping Marlboros hanging out of their mouths. *Click*.

The next photo was of the six of them in the student union, in the days where dancing involved a lot of sweaty, un-self-conscious jumping rather than any rhythmic ability. Eve's hair was plastered to her head and they all had red eyes, which was not necessarily the result of the flash. 'And this next photo was taken later that evening, at the exact moment our blushing bride and dandy groom had their first kiss.' The next photo was evidently taken in the early hours of the morning after staggering back to their house from the union. While centre stage in the photo were undeniably a lust-struck Amit and Ayesha, immediately to the right of them was the blown-up figure of a drunk Eve, fast asleep, her head lolling over the side of a beanbag dribbling, legs splayed, with half a kebab on her chest, garlic mayonnaise and shards of burnt chicken meat spilling out all over the top of her bright pink wonderbra.

Tanya, Ayesha and Becca had tears rolling down their cheeks they were laughing so hard, and Eve had no choice but to pretend to find it equally hilarious. All around her she could see people pointing over at their table. She knew it was all good-natured entertainment, but even so. She had a choice. She could do what every muscle in her body was urging her to, and climb under the table. She could roll her eyes, huff a bit and be generally quite of a poor sport about it all, or she could embrace the lunacy. With a deep breath, Eve decided to take her magnanimous attitude one step further, pushed back her chair and stood up, giving a small bow with a waving hand flourish. The room erupted in spontaneous applause and as she retook her seat, Ben caught her eye and gave her an admiring nod. She'd played that round very well.

Eve's table was one of the few that had to move to make room for the dance floor, so she and her newfound buddies all reluctantly vacated their seats, picked up their full wine glasses and headed out to the terrace allowing the waiting staff to scurry into action. Robert and Andrew hadn't left Eve's side, flanking her at all times, making Eve feel like a pop star in between two minders. Two attractive, eloquent, attentive, seemingly solvent and single minders.

Becca skipped up to them. As chief bridesmaid she had had the honour of being on the top table. Perched for the duration at the end of the oblong table next to Amit's Dad, Becca had spent most of the meal looking longingly at Eve's table of hilarity with undisguised jealousy.

'Evening all.'

Eve made the introductions, but when she said, 'This is Robert,' he quickly interrupted and said, 'I actually go by Bobby.'

Becca grinned and then spoke slowly, sounding out every syllable. 'Oh nice to meet you BOBBY with a B.'

Eve blushed and gave Becca wide 'please don't' eyes that her friend totally ignored. 'Why don't you two go and dance? I'll keep Andrew company.'

As the song filtered through to the terrace and Eve heard the recognisable Roxette lyrics *It must have been love but it's over now*, she quickly remembered her task for the evening and replied, 'Maybe later, must dash,' and hotfooted it to the DJ's booth.

The sound of a chair dragging and being placed alongside her startled Eve. She'd been true to her promise and barely left the DJ's side for the last two hours, giving him warning eyes and a slow shake of her head in between each song.

'Hi Red. Hope you weren't too annoyed at my speech?'

'Not at all, I thought it was funny.' *In no way whatsoever.*

'Like I found tap dancing in a crowded Covent Garden on a Saturday night funny?'

'Exactly the same sort of funny I would imagine,' Eve replied smoothly, a smile playing on her lips.

'Looks like we got away with the cake,' Ben said. 'I heard Ayesha's mum say that she didn't like the bottom layer much but the middle one was amazing.'

'There were some quality ingredients in that six-quid cake.'

'And it was an inspired touch wrapping the yellow brick road round it.'

'Thanks.'

They both sat side by side looking out onto the crowded dance floor.

'Why are you not jumping around the dance floor like a drunk Bambi? Legs flying in all directions and your hair whipping unsuspecting onlookers? It's not like you to sit a cheesy tune out?'

She wanted to quip back that he wouldn't have a clue what she was like now, much less have a right to guess, but the wedding had been spectacularly fun so far, and ending it in a sparring match would cancel out the fun of the day. 'I'm babysitting the DJ.'

Ben looked over at where the forlorn puppy-eyed young lad was staring at the dance floor which was filled with couples performing pre-mating rituals. 'He looks old enough to be out by himself. Just.'

'His name's Sam, he's just been dumped and his default playlist is a little suicide-inducing. So I have to sit here and give him this look—' Eve scrunched her eyes into menacing slits and slowly wagged her finger back and forth '—until he comes to his senses and puts the Spice Girls back on.'

Ben laughed. 'Wow, poor guy. Bet he's wishing he never took this gig on.'

'Him and me both, I'm desperate for a pee and I finished my drink about an hour ago.'

'I'm happy to hold the fort for ten minutes if you like?'

Saying yes meant he was doing her a favour, but saying no meant that in all likelihood there'd be a puddle on the floor soon and she'd have completely sobered up through lack of alcohol. She didn't really have a choice. 'Fine. But show me your scary face.'

'My what?'

'How is Sam the Brokenhearted going to take you seriously if you don't have a scary face?'

A pause. For a moment Eve thought he wasn't going to play along, then Ben's mouth contorted into a twist, his eyes narrowed into a sneer and he simultaneously raised his left eyebrow. The final result had Eve doubled up with laughter. 'Back in ten.' She took one step away from him, then turned back conciliatorily. 'Can I get you anything from the bar on the way back?'

If he was surprised he didn't show it, airily replying, 'A beer would be good.'

Chapter 17

'Cheers!' Their glasses clinked together, and Ben moved his chair slightly to allow Eve to squeeze through next to him. The music had been turned up a little, and their proximity to the speaker meant they had to shout to each other, and lean in a little closer than Eve felt comfortable with. It reminded her of so many nights in the student union where she'd pressed her body to him a little gratuitously under the pretence of hearing better, despite not actually needing to.

His aftershave didn't trigger any memories for her, he was wearing a scent she didn't recognise. He was more of a Lynx-sprayed-all-over-his-body man back then, and the fragrance he was now wearing was considerably more expensive and sophisticated, but it blended with his natural smell and warmth, and it was making Eve feel a little light-headed with nostalgia.

'There was a bit of a hairy moment when Sam saw you walk away and thought he'd grab his chance to line up James Blunt's *Goodbye My Lover*, but I stepped in with my menacing look and saved the day.'

'I'm pleased you're taking your role so seriously,' Eve replied.

They sat side by side in silence for a bit, both sipping their drinks and staring at the dance floor where a variety of enthusiastic dance moves were being performed. One uncle was doing the putting-up-shelves dance, miming hammering in the air and smoothing a plank, while Ayesha's mum was intent on doing the twist to every song regardless of genre or rhythm. A small circle had formed around Ayesha, who was moving her pelvis in some sort of figure-of-eight belly dance around a flamingo that someone had carried in from outside.

'So, weddings,' Ben said, making an exaggerated eyebrow raise.

'Yep. Got to love them.'

'Becca's just asked me to her wedding in a few weeks actually.'

This was news to Eve. She was sure Becca would have run the idea past her first beforehand. She could only assume the invite was extended after copious amounts of alcohol was consumed, and it was used to fill in a gap in the conversation.

'Are you going to go?' Eve asked breezily, not feeling breezy in the slightest.

'I thought I might, be good to see more of the old crowd, and I am free that weekend.'

Eve nodded, giving the impression of agreeing.

'Unless you don't want me to?'

His ability to see her thoughts lurking behind her smile caught her off guard. 'No, it's fine, it's good. It'll give me the opportunity to get you back for the photo you just embarrassed me with.'

Ben laughed. 'Oh that one was tame, I have plenty more.'

166

The thought of him keeping photos of her, lugging these photos around with him from place to place made her feel a bit strange. Had he looked at them often? What was he thinking if he had? Was there some remorse of how he'd just upped and left? Or were they merely a reminder of his youth, with no sentimentality attached to them at all? She could hardly ask him. But there were so many things she wanted to ask him.

'Why didn't you come with me to New York?' The question surprised them both. Eve wanted to pick up the words and shove them back in her mouth, and Ben's face flushed. The beat of the music was loud, too loud. It reverberated through the floor and their chairs, and when Ben replied Eve could feel his breath warm on her ear.

'I'll explain everything another time. But not now.'

'Why not now?' Eve demanded, the alcohol making her brave.

'It's an incredibly long story, and we're drunk, but I want to explain, and I—' he got cut of by an outstretched upturned hand leaning across him and stopping in front of Eve's face.

'Can I have that dance now?' Andrew asked.

There was a split second where Eve looked to Ben for, she didn't know what, his permission? He gave a shrug, and Eve took Andrew's hand, allowing him to lead her towards the revellers. Remembering her task for the evening, she turned at the periphery of the wooden dance floor and shouted back at Ben. 'Oi, Hepworth!' She pointed two fingers at her own eyes, then at his, then to Sam the DJ in the recognised gesture of 'I'm watching you, watching him'.

'You were gone for ages,' Andrew said, twirling Eve round under his arm.

'Sorry, I had to babysit the DJ. I've passed the baton over now though.'

'I'm not going to ask what that means. It's fine though, your friend Becca entertained us.'

Eve raised one eyebrow. 'Really?'

'She was telling us about how you only date blokes with names beginning with B, and that I should step aside and let Bobby ask you out.'

Oh God. In what universe did Becca think that was an acceptable topic of conversation with a couple of attractive strangers?

'Is that true?'

Eve shook her head. 'It's a ridiculous thing that was said at a séance, Becca shouldn't have said anything, ignore her.' Eve cringed – that made it sound like she wanted him to take no notice of what Becca had said and ask her out. In her embarrassment she suddenly forgot how to dance, becoming very self-aware of every step and arm movement, to the point that it looked as though she was having a choreographed fit.

Andrew was quite a good dancer; long limbs often equate to octopus-like dance moves, but he was managing what Eve wasn't, and that was dancing in time to the rhythm and talking at the same time. 'She only told me because I asked her for your number.'

Eve stopped moving. 'Really?'

'Really. And then she told me that I didn't stand a chance because I'm called Andrew. And before accepting this as possibly one of the weirdest reasons I've ever been turned down, I thought I'd go straight to the source and check.'

'That is what good writers do,' Eve retorted smiling.

'Exactly. I knew I'd score points for my due diligence, if nothing else. So, is she right?'

He was funny and capable of telling a good story, he found her interesting, laughed at her jokes, he was a few inches taller than her, he seemed to be clean in a non-OCD bacterial-hand-washing way, he didn't apparently have any dietary fetishes that involved bringing homemade falafels in Tupperware boxes to weddings, he was on the good looking side of normal and he was currently looking at her with one eyebrow flirtily raised waiting for her answer.

Part of her was drunk enough to say yes, and possibly lunge in to seal the deal; seeing Ben again had made her realise that wasting any more time pining for him was such a waste and she needed to move on once and for all, like he clearly had.

'Um, I'm very flattered,' she began.

'Don't say no, let me take you to dinner,' he persisted. 'We both live in London, we can meet after work one night this week?'

'I really don't want to waste your time,' she said, biting her lip. He was extraordinarily nice, and if she'd never met Violet she'd be shouting 'hell to the yes' round about now. Damn that little old lady in turquoise. And damn the fact that Eve was even considering that what Violet had said was remotely true.

They'd done a 360-degree turn on the dance floor, shuffling

round so Eve was back facing Ben. Over Andrew's shoulder she could see him texting on his phone, no doubt messaging the woman he'd left her for.

'If it helps, my middle name is Bartholomew.'

'Is it really?' Eve asked incredulously, her eyes swinging back to Andrew's. If that was true, it could be the connection that Violet was talking about, it was too much of a coincidence otherwise. 'Ok,' Eve said decisively. She was seizing the day. 'Why don't you buy me a G&T and we'll talk about it.'

Andrew smiled appreciatively. 'That's a little forward.'

'I thought I'd start as I mean to go on,' Eve replied cheekily.

'This just gets better and better. Back in a minute. Don't move.'

Eve stood at the edge of the dance floor studying Andrew's back as he waited in line at the bar. His white shirt sleeves were rolled up, showing his tanned forearm as he raised it to run his hand through his dark blond hair that was damp from dancing. He must have sensed her eyes on him. He turned, locking eyes with hers and gave her a smile before turning back around. This could be him, Eve thought excitedly, it really could be. Their children would be strawberry blonde with freckles, she imagined. She'd probably go freelance, while he continued writing speeches that millions would watch. They'd always have to live around London, due to him needing to be near Westminster, but they'd probably move out to a family-friendly suburb like Barnet. It would be good for the kids to have a garden, but they'd probably spend weekends visiting the V&A or the Science Museum, so would need to be on a tube line.

'Penny for them,' Bobby's dark brown eyes twinkled at her. 'You were miles away.'

'Sorry, daydreaming, it's a bit of a habit.'

'Where did you get to? I was looking for you.'

Ordinarily this sentence from a handsome tall dark paramedic would have rendered a much more positive response, but Eve was conscious that any moment now Bobby's best friend would be arriving back, gin in hand for her. 'I had to stop the DJ slitting his wrists, and then I fancied a bit of a dance.' *And your friend.*

'Great idea, come on,' Bobby grabbed Eve's hand and pulled her onto the dance floor. He'd loosened his tie, had his top button undone and Eve could glimpse a few dark chest hairs poking out of the top of his shirt, which made her insides do a little dance of their own. She stood still, swaying her hips and moving her shoulders enough to be considered dancing, while craning her neck to see if Andrew had returned. He was standing on the edge of the crowd, two glasses in hand, looking around him, a little bewildered at her absence. Just behind him was Ben, unmoved from the seat where she'd left him, his phone mutely in his hand, nursing an empty beer in the other hand, moodily staring right at her. Good. He'd put her life on pause for the last four years, made her question every moment of intimacy they'd shared before that – she owed him nothing.

Bobby was enthusiastically jiggling away in front of her with his enticing chest hair that she suddenly wanting to twirl in her fingers and her charming potential soul mate Andrew was ready with refreshments to her side. A trio of choices laid out in a three-square metre patch of floor.

'I'd really like to see you again,' Bobby shouted over One Direction's cover of *One Way or Another*. 'I think we really clicked.'

Eve wriggled about a bit more, then leant in, just as the song changed to a Lionel Richie classic. What the hell, she literally had nothing to lose.

'I'd love to go out with you some time.'

'Brilliant, I'll look at the roster for next week and make a plan.' He then placed his hand strongly in the hollow of her back and dipped her, while suggestively mouthing the words to the song.

Eve was saved from actually swooning in an eighteenth-century-needing-smelling-salts type way by a loud yell and scream from the dancing crowd just next to them. The floor cleared enough for Eve to glimpse a bleeding groom lying spread-eagled on the raised stage having attempted to recreate his famous caterpillar dance from university, and in the process concussing himself and breaking his nose on the floor.

'Shit! Amit!' Bobby rushed to his friend's aid, his medical training put into practice with various barked orders and a masterful plan of action that had Eve incredibly turned on. Within seconds Amit was awake and propped up, his bleeding stemmed by Bobby's tie. Andrew had sidled up to Eve, handed her her drink and was watching the scene with a similar undisguised awe. 'It's good to have a paramedic in the house.'

You couldn't argue with that. Particularly when the man in question was incredibly attractive and knew all the words to *All Night Long* which, when he had sang it to her, sounded remarkably like a promise.

Chapter 18

A huddle consisting of Ben, Bobby, Andrew and the other two ushers stood next to the revving taxi, where a very serious game of Rock Paper Scissors was underway to see who was going to accompany Amit. Ayesha was the obvious choice, but she'd immediately vetoed herself on the grounds of 'needing to stay with her guests.' It was a selfless proclamation that only her very good friends knew really meant, 'I'm having far too much fun to spend the rest of my wedding night with the town's drunks and my childish groom in the emergency room.' Ayesha's initial bout of giggles at seeing her new husband lifeless on the dance floor had subsided when Bobby had stepped in and it all became rather more serious, but once she'd been convinced that she wasn't about to become a wife and a widow on the same day, she'd calmed down.

From where Eve was standing in the car park, next to Becca, Tanya and Luke, it looked like Ben had lost the game as he had now opened the back door to the car and was climbing in amid much cheering from the rest of the men who banged on the car with their hands as it began to drive away.

'There is no way I'd ever have done something so stupid,' Luke said.

'There is no way I would have let you,' Tanya tutted, her arms folded across her chest.

'There is no way you could ever have done the caterpillar in the first place,' Eve replied, stone-faced, before running towards the taxi which had stopped a few metres down the driveway for Amit to open his door and be sick.

'Are you ok?'

'Are you talking to me or the third chuckle brother here?' Ben replied, his head out of the other back window like a terrier.

'Him, but sort of you too. I remember how crap you are with blood.'

'Put it this way, it's going to be touch and go which one of us is sick next.'

'Would you like me to come too? You can sit in the front, I'll go in the back with Mr. Breakdance.'

'Would you do that? Are you sure? Your admirers over there will be a bit pissed off.'

Eve looked back at the hotel where Bobby and Andrew were stood shoulder to shoulder on the front step, their hands in their pockets looking at the taxi. 'Just get in the front seat, Ben.'

It wasn't the ending to this wedding Eve had envisioned, but she also knew that Amit would have a greater chance of getting to the hospital and not a casino if she chaperoned him and Ben.

'Eve, wait!'

Becca was running up the driveway. Bobby and Andrew had breathlessly jogged to join Becca. 'What do you think we should do now? It's only ten o clock, it's too early to call time on the party isn't it? But then would it be in poor taste to continue?' Becca said.

'Why are you asking me?' Eve asked.

'Aren't you the guru of all things weddings?'

'I can honestly say that this situation has never popped up before. I'm in unchartered territory.' Eve closed her door and said out of the window. 'Right, Bobby, go and change your shirt,' Eve said, gesturing at his blood-soaked chest, where another button had opened, revealing even more dark curled hair. 'You look like you've committed a murder.' There were less than four seconds between Bobby disappearing inside, and Andrew taking out his phone and saying, 'Before I forget, can I get your number now?'

Eve couldn't fault his opportunism, his eagerness, or his timing, with Ben being in gratifying earshot. But before she could reply, Ben did. 'It's not really the best time mate, maybe ask her later.' He then told the driver to start driving.

'That was a bit rude.' Eve said as the car revved away.

'But he wasn't? Asking for your number while our friend is dying?'

Amit groaned next to Eve. 'He's not dying Ben. Well, maybe of embarrassment, but a broken nose is not life-threatening. Reputation-threatening yes, but life-threatening, no.'

'He seems a bit of a twat.'

'Don't be mean about Amit, he's sat right here.'

'I meant your fancy man, as you well know.'

'He's not my fancy man, and anyway, even if he was, it's none of your business.'

'Fine.'

'Fine.'

The rest of the journey to hospital was undertaken in silence, Eve rubbed Amit's back from time to time and changed his bloodied hotel towel for a new one at one point too, while Ben stared resolutely ahead out of the windscreen. Eve didn't know whether it was because of the blood in the back or their heated exchange.

After checking Amit in with the triage nurse, Eve and Ben were left alone in the waiting room of A&E.

'Red?'

'What?'

'I'm not feeling so good.'

Ben's face had taken on a greenish tinge, no doubt brought on by the sight of a pair of brawling teenagers who were sat opposite them with oozing open cuts on their faces and hands.

'Do you want some air?'

'I'm aware this sounds extremely undignified, but can you help me walk as I think I'm about to keel over.'

Eve helped Ben to his feet, and across the bleached white tiles to the door. They sat on a bench overlooking the dark car park.

'Better?'

'Much.'

'Why didn't you just say to the other ushers that you couldn't bring him because you're scared of blood?'

'I am not *scared* of blood. I have haemophobia, it's a legitimate phobia.'

'Giving it a fancy Latin name doesn't make it better, Ben.'

'Excuse me Red, but you're scared of snow.'

'A-hem. Chionophobia if you don't mind.'

Ben laughed. 'Oh sorry, Chionophobia. Because that's a real thing.'

'It is absolutely a real thing! Much like zemmiphobia, which is the fear of the great mole rat.'

'Now that one I can understand, they're vicious buggers. But snow? Everyone loves snow.'

'Look, my fear incapacitates me for what? Three days a year? You have the potential to throw up if you get a paper cut.'

'That's what I've always loved about you, Red, your endless capacity for empathy and compassion.'

What he's always loved about me.

'What about slushies? Can you have them?' Ben asked.

'I can indeed have slushies. Should the mood for processed ice and food colouring take me. I think you're mocking my affliction.'

'You're mocking mine.'

'I am not! I offered to come here with you to save you from yours. You should be thanking me.'

'Thank you. To show my appreciation, I may well buy you an advocaat and lemonade cocktail, otherwise known as a Snowball.'

'And I'll get you a Bloody Mary. Then we'll be quits.'

'So I'm done,' Amit announced, standing in the doorway

of A&E with three wide white stripes of tape across his nose. 'Now I need another drink.'

As the trio walked across the carpeted floor of the hotel's hallway back towards the wedding reception, Bobby was coming down the stairs. Ben and Amit went on ahead, while Eve waited at the bottom of the stairs for him. He'd changed his shirt and evidently showered and spritzed himself with some deodorant and aftershave – which gave him the upper hand over Eve, who, after a couple of hours of enthusiastic dancing, taxi-ing and sitting in casualty had become a little fragrant.

'That was quick,' Bobby said.

'Didn't want to miss any more of the party.'

'Is Amit ok?'

Eve smiled. 'I can't comment on his state of mind, considering the humiliation, but his nose will be fine. It was pretty impressive stuff you did back there, springing into paramedic mode.'

'It was almost as if I planned it,' Bobby smiled.

Eve gasped. 'You didn't?'

'Of course not! Amit's a good mate, but even he wouldn't break his nose on his wedding day in order to help me impress a girl I liked.'

A smile played on Eve's lips. 'A girl you liked?'

Bobby grinned back. 'Yes, there's a small brunette in there that I had my eye on.'

'Oh, bad news, I think she left already. But you can buy *me* a drink if you'd like to?' Eve had no idea what had got into her, she was never normally this flirty or forward.

'I'd love to,' Bobby said.

The second they walked into the small ballroom they sensed the mood had changed, and not just because of the groom's maiming incident. Left to his own devices, Brokenhearted Sam had lined up a playlist so depressing he'd blanketed the whole room in misery, forcing everyone out onto the terrace.

'Looks like the party's over,' Bobby said.

'Let's find Ayesha, and see what the plan is.'

Ayesha's plan was seemingly to get as trolleyed as possible. They found her lying across her cousins' knees on an outside sofa. Her eyes were open but glassy, and she even had a cigarette in hand, which Eve guessed was her first since leaving university.

'Hey Ayesha.' Eve squatted down next to the sofa. 'We're back, it's half eleven, most of the guests are still here, and the DJ's booked until one, what do you want to do? I can tell everyone to shuffle off home, or we can get the party started again, your call.'

Ayesha sat up, aided a little bit by one of her cousins tugging at her, while another one pushed. 'Party started. Definitely party started. Drink?' She offered Eve her glass, which had a dead fly and a crouton in it.

'No, you're ok. Let me take that. Ok, party started, no problem.' Eve dispatched Becca to go and sweet-talk the barman into making jugs of cocktails, and to also get Ayesha a tonic water masquerading as something more potent. Eve and Bobby headed for the DJ desk to curtail the melancholy and find some Wham!.

'Can I do anything to help?' Tanya asked sweetly, popping

up from nowhere. 'What a disaster this is.' She made no attempt to make the words convey an aura of tragedy, more gleeful amusement.

'As soon as we've got the music started, you can start to usher people back in from outside if you like.'

'That's what I love about you Eve, your optimism in the face of catastrophe. You can change the song to whatever you want, but there's no saving this wedding. We might as well all go home.'

'I disagree,' Eve replied through gritted teeth, desperately scanning Sam's laptop for upbeat tunes. 'Ayesha and Amit are our friends, and we owe it to them to help them make the best of it.'

Tanya inspected her perfect manicure. 'Just give up Eve, you're flogging a dead horse. I know you all laughed at my level of preparation for my wedding, but this is exactly what happens when you leave things to chance.'

'See, that's where we differ Tanya, I don't think that you can orchestrate things like fun. But don't let me stop you leaving if you really want to.'

'A friend of yours?' Bobby asked as Tanya walked stiffly away.

'Do you have friends from way back when, who if you met now there's no way on God's green earth that you'd be friends? Well, that's me and Tanya.'

It took four jugs of cosmopolitans, five flamingoes, the cheesiest tunes she could find, and some forceful coercing for the guests to leave the tranquility of the terrace, but finally, finally, the party was resuscitated.

'I didn't realise weddings were such hard work,' Andrew said, a couple of hours later, as he and Eve helped load the last of the DJ's equipment into his little Toyota. 'I just came for the free booze and sparkling company, and now I'm knackered.'

They were standing outside, just in front of the ivy-covered hotel. The village beyond the gates was in darkness, the air was cold and crisp. Not for the first time that day Eve wished she had a shawl or a cardigan – earlier to cover up her ridiculous breast poppies, and now for warmth.

'I think we can be very proud of ourselves,' Eve said, folding her arms and rubbing them. 'I'm sure there's a market for this type of service, party planning for when your party fails.'

'We could call it Plan B Parties and show up in a car that instead of having a siren on top has a disco ball,' Andrew added.

Eve laughed. 'I like that.'

'I've had a good time though.'

Eve had to agree; despite running around putting out fires, it had been a really fun day. Fun and utterly exhausting.

'Do you want my jacket? You're shivering.'

She shook her head. There was something a bit too high-school prom about accepting a man's suit jacket after a dance. 'I'm fine, honestly, it's nice to get some air.'

'The party doesn't need to end if you don't want it to,' Andrew said. 'Bobby and I were just saying that we'd both be up for staying awake a while longer, if you were to keep us company. Come on, let's have a party of our own.'

'It's very tempting, but the only party I'm going to be having is in my bed.'

As she walked away, leaving Andrew standing there, Eve replayed her last sentence and gave a shudder. That sounded far too rude. Thankfully Andrew didn't seem to notice.

The doors to Eve's lift had barely shut before Andrew came bounding into the nearly empty bar and shouted, 'Bobby, we're game on!'

Ben was also one of the last stragglers in the bar and looked up from the brandy he was nursing at the interruption. He downed the remnants of his drink and headed for the lift at exactly the same time as Andrew, who was carrying an ice bucket filled with expensive champagne, and Bobby, who held three glasses.

'After you,' Ben said, holding the lift doors open for the duo.

The doors closed and Bobby leaned into Andrew. 'I can't believe Eve's up for it, what a way to end a wedding, is this your first threesome?'

Ben's ears pricked up.

'No, third. You?'

'First for me, mate. Can we keep the lights on though so we don't touch each other by mistake?'

'Yeah, definitely.'

Ben's head stayed bowed, eyes firmly on his feet during this whole exchange. They must be talking about another Eve, there's no way that his Eve would do something like this.

'She'll be my first redhead as well.' Bobby said. 'I wonder if it's natural?'

'Well, we're about to find out.'

182

The lift shuddered to a stop and the doors noisily opened. The three men got out, two of them walking quicker and jauntier than the third. Ben's room was next to the lift. He resignedly put his key into the lock as he silently watched the pair stroll confidently down the corridor, and Ben felt his shoulders drop.

Chapter 19

It was one of the first weddings Eve had been to where she was sober enough to remove her eye make up before going to bed. Dragging the wet cotton pad slowly across her eyes she realised that it wasn't just an excuse when she told Andrew she needed her bed. Exhaustion had suddenly crept up on her and every part of her brain and body ached with over-use. Padding back into the bedroom Eve lay on the bed in the hotel's white bathrobe, her long red curls spilling over her pillow as she looked up at the ceiling. Having lived above a live music venue for two years, Eve was normally adept at getting to sleep with the soft thump of bass from the floor below, but tonight the incessant beat was a constant reminder that only floorboards lay between her, her past and her future.

She was trying to understand why she'd instinctively turned Andrew's invitation for another drink down when she was single, he was single, and it would have been a fun end to a fun day. He and Bobby were good-looking, funny, interesting, and one of them could even be a potential boyfriend. Yet here she was, in a posh hotel room, by herself. And actually, that was just the way she liked it. She opened her laptop and began writing.

I've never been to a school reunion, and I never want to. All those faces, familiar yet unfamiliar, all assessing the success you've had in life by what you're wearing, whether you've turned up with a partner and the amount of dog-hair/baby-sick/unidentifiable food stains on your clothes. No one goes to a school reunion to see their friends. If they were your friends you'd see them all the time anyway. You certainly wouldn't choose your next night out to be in the draughty assembly hall of your old school. No, you go to show off and be nosy. Let's call it like it is. But weddings on the other hand, they're the tombola of reunions. Unless you're in the bride's inner circle where you have access to the guest list, knowing who else is going to turn up at the church is a lottery. Chances are, your friend, the bride, has also stayed in touch with Esther, the mean girl from the year above, possibly Harriet, the siren who stole your first love with her flicky hair and ability to steal spirits from her dad's drinks cabinet. You may even bump into your first love himself, now hopefully fat, bald, and sporting a facial tattoo or two, but my point is, at a school reunion you expect this, and can avoid it. At a wedding, where everyone in the couple's past and present are crammed together in a room for ten hours or more, you have no choice about who you're going to be stood next to at the mojito station. No choice at all.

A soft knock on her door surprised her. Eve pulled her robe tighter around her, and opened the door. A silver ice bucket with a bottle of Moët in it was thrust into her face held by a smiling Andrew, while Bobby, just behind him, held up three glasses. They looked excited, expectant.

'So, we brought the party to you, just like you asked.'

'Um,' Eve was confused. 'I'm actually going to sleep, it's really late.'

'Which is why we should all go to bed,' Andrew added, his left eyebrow suggestively curling up.

'It's nearly three.'

'You say three, we say threesome.'

Eve's eyes widened in horror. Flustered, she shoved the ice bucket back at Andrew, with a firm 'Good night!' and slammed the door in their faces. Leaning against the back of the door with all her weight as though she expected them to shoulder-barge it open, Eve tilted her head back and looked up at the ceiling and laughed. What a day, what a ridiculous day, start to finish.

Someone softly knocked on the door, jolting Eve into action. Those two were incredibly persistent.

'What now?' Eve hissed through the door. 'No means no. Bugger off.'

'It's us, Ayesha and Becca,' came the whispered reply.

Eve opened the door, to find her two best friends there. Ayesha had taken her veil off, and her short black bob was a little dishevelled showing signs of being swished back and forth on the dance floor for hours. 'We were just going up and thought we'd say goodnight. Is this yours?' Ayesha was pointing at the unopened bottle of champagne and trio of flutes that were propped up on the carpet outside Eve's door.

'A present from the ushers for me.' Eve said. 'You don't want to know why.'

'Well, it'd be rude to let it go to waste. What with today being my wedding day and everything.'

'Speaking of which,' Eve said, holding open the door for them, 'shouldn't you be with your groom?'

'The cocktail of drugs he's on, mixed with the brandy he insisted on buying everyone has rendered him good for nothing apart from sleeping. Thank goodness I hadn't saved myself for my wedding night, I'd be well disappointed!'

'Poor Amit,' Becca added, giving a wry smile.

'Poor Amit, my foot. What a div, thinking he can still do the caterpillar. I have no sympathy for him whatsoever.'

'Careful Ayesha, you sound a bit like Tanya,' Eve warned.

Ayesha gave a theatrical shudder. 'Why are we friends with her again?'

'It's called nostalgia,' Eve said.

'It's called masochism,' disagreed Ayesha. 'She told me that having a rainbow balloon arch made it look like a gay pride parade.'

'It's good to be inclusive,' Eve retorted, handing each of her friends a full champagne flute.

'And she said that she was very surprised not to see dead fake legs with stripy tights poking out of tables, but that might be a step too far even for me. What does that mean, *even for me?*'

'She's just jealous that she didn't have the imagination or personality to pull something like this off,' Becca said.

'Do you think so?' Ayesha cocked her head on the side. 'I have pulled it off, haven't I? It wasn't too weird and out there?'

Eve shook her head. 'It was unique. That's very different to out there.'

'I couldn't have done it without you two though, nor would I have wanted to.'

'It was honestly the best wedding I've been to in a long time,' Eve said. 'Becca's going to have to pull out some serious stops to compete with today.'

'Oi,' Becca said, pointing her glass at Eve. 'I'll have you know, there are some elements to my wedding even you don't know about.'

'Don't forget to give Eve a plus one, or two, judging from today.' Ayesha winked.

'How are the dastardly duo? Which one's inching ahead?' Becca asked Eve, who sighed in response.

'Neither.' Eve hesitated before saying. 'The champagne you're drinking was bought to be poured all over my body and ceremoniously licked off by both of them.' Laughing at her friends' horrified expressions, Eve added, 'But don't worry, I got rid of them before that could happen.'

'Is it so wrong that I'm a bit jealous?' Ayesha whined. 'Here I am, a married woman, and never again will I get proposi-tioned by two men in the same night.'

'Me neither,' Becca chimed in.

'You make it sound like it happened all the time before today!' Eve laughed.

'Well,' Ayesha smiled. 'Not all the time.'

'Well it's a first for me, having two blokes vying for my attention.'

'Three.' Ayesha said. 'Ben asked Amit if you were married now.'

Eve rolled her eyes while simultaneously feeling her belly flop.

'What did he say?'

'He said the truth, that you were single.'

'Why did he ask?'

'I don't know, you know what blokes are like. Amit would hardly have asked him his feelings behind the question. Why? Would you be looking to rekindle anything?'

'Of course not! That was eons ago, another lifetime. I can categorically say that I have no feelings towards him of any kind, apart from mild irritation at all these jokes he keeps playing on me.'

'Phew,' Becca said. 'Because I kind of found myself inviting him to my wedding. We were chatting about old times, and he was asking if I was still in touch with different people and then I said yes, and that a lot of our uni friends were coming to my wedding, and then I heard myself invite him. Sorry Eve, are you sure it's ok?'

'It couldn't be more ok, it's fine, I'm totally over him.'

'That's good,' Ayesha said. 'Because that man has more baggage than a footballer's wife travelling to the world cup. Top up?'

Eve couldn't ask her what she meant without it sounding like she cared, and she was doing a sterling performance of pretending that she didn't. The three of them finished the bottle while recounting funny stories about the day, who said what, who danced with whom, but all the while Eve's mind was a million miles and a few years away.

Chapter 20

L ater that same day, after getting the train back to their flat, Becca and Eve lay in their living room listening to the Sunday afternoon jazz session from downstairs winding its melodic way up to them. The set list included some Nina Simone classics that had kept the two friends tapping their toes and humming along from their respective sofas. Eve had set Becca the task of going through all her RSVPs to her wedding and writing a definitive list of everyone that was coming. Becca had started the challenge so well, but now, less than six minutes into it, she'd fallen asleep. Eve carefully removed the pen from her friend's fingers, and replaced the lid, before lying back down on her own sofa and opening up her laptop to write the week's *Misadventures of a Bad Bridesmaid* column.

Despite being a professional writer for ten years, Eve was finding it really hard to find a replacement noun for fibreglass flamingoes. There was so much comedy to be had recounting the trials and tribulations of Ayesha's wedding verbatim, from the outlandish theme, to the broken nose, it was comedy gold for Eve's new column – but she just couldn't do it to her friend. So Eve was trying to disguise every detail of the wedding by using alternative descriptions. The flamingoes had become swans, the broken bone was no longer on the face, but on the foot and the lonesome DJ was called Larry. As she wrote, Eve couldn't help laughing out loud at the lunacy of the day. Even if she'd tried to concoct a completely fictional account of a drama-studded wedding, she wouldn't have been able to come up with anything as funny as the original.

'Why are you grinning?' Becca asked yawning. 'And how long was I asleep for?'

'Only twenty minutes or so, and it's nothing, just work stuff.' Eve shut her laptop.

'I never had your job down as being particularly funny. Heartwarming, yes, but laugh-out-loud funny, not so much.'

'Well you know, it has its moments. How are the RSVPs looking?'

'Not great. We sent out about sixty I think, but I've had two hundred and eighty-two back, which is a bit strange.'

'When you say, you sent out about sixty *you think,* what does that actually mean? Where's your list?'

'I didn't make one. I just kept writing them, whenever I thought of a new person I'd like to invite.'

'Well how many invitations did you order in the first place?'

'That's the thing, don't you remember, my cousin Janine did the design of it? So whenever I thought of more people I just printed some more off. I didn't really keep track of who or how many.'

'Right.'

Becca sat up. 'Right what? What does that mean?'

'It means, right, well, we've got to make a list now of everyone that you remember sending an invite to and then tally that up against the RSVPs you've got, and then chase the ones that haven't replied.'

Becca groaned and leant her head back against the sofa. 'But that's the thing. I can't remember, I keep inviting people I meet, like I did with Ben, and I gave Jack, my mum and sisters a few to hand out to their friends—'

'And you invited randoms like my mum.' Eve interrupted.

'Your mum isn't a random, she's your mum, but I sort of did an open invite at work as well, tacking one of the invites up on the notice board in the staff room.'

'We're not talking about flyers for a car boot sale Becca! This is your wedding, you have to stop asking everyone you come across!'

'I know. I just got a bit carried away.'

'Ok, give me the list of everyone you have invited, and their email addresses and I'll get in touch with them all to confirm. Worst case scenario, how many people do you think might come?' Eve asked.

'Is the worst case the biggest number or smallest?'

'Depends on your outlook. For me, the worst case would be six hundred people rocking up expecting free food and drink.'

'That's also a lot of hay bales,' Becca said.

Eve didn't reply, she was too busy counting to ten in her head. Becca took the silence to mean that the conversation was over and everything was resolved, so she closed her eyes again and drifted off into a dreamless nap.

Later that afternoon the two friends were standing amiably next to each other preparing the salad for their early dinner. Just as Eve reached over Becca for the punnet of cherry tomatoes both their phones that were charging next to each other on the counter lit up with life and buzzed simultaneously.

The videographer just sent the video of our wedding! It premieres tomorrow night at ours – come at 7.30, screening at 8, dress up!

'I'm guessing yours was from Tanya too?' Eve said.

'Yep. Summoning us to her *premiere*.'

The two women looked at each other and exchanged the same thought, *what a dick*.

'Shall we go?' Becca asked, scrunching up her nose to signal how distasteful she found the text message.

'There are many other things that I'd like to do instead,' Eve admitted. 'But I haven't got anything on tomorrow.'

'So shall we say yes?'

'Yes, but I'm going to tell her that I'm coming straight from my training session as the park is pretty much opposite their house, so she can take me in my tracksuit bottoms or not at all.'

'In that case, I'll say the same so you're not the only one in sweatpants while everyone else is in black tie.'

'She can't seriously expect everyone to come in evening dresses?'

'Tanya can do whatever she wants.'

'Ain't that the truth,' Eve said. 'Well look, if you're going to be wearing the gear anyway, why don't you meet me after work and join the training? Juan won't mind, I think he's getting a bit bored of my chat.'

'Could do. I guess I should do at least one exercise class before I get married, isn't that what brides are supposed to do?'

Eve didn't want to tell her that most of the brides she'd ever come across would have been having inch-loss slimming wraps twice a week for the last six months, and purely existing on ice cubes.

***

Juan had one muscly lycra-clad leg up on the railings at a right angle, creating a perfect square with the ground.

'Is that him?' Becca whispered as they approached the part of the park where he'd already set up little cones and a variety of torture instruments masquerading as skipping ropes and barbells.

'Yep.'

'You didn't tell me he was that good looking.'

'Is he?'

'Eve, even you can't be totally immune.'

'I can see he's alright looking, but he's so bossy.'

'That's what you pay him for. I bet he's not in real life.'

'Just wait, you'll see.'

Within ten minutes Juan had the two women doing prisoner squats and diagonal lunges. Their T-shirts had matching sweat patches, and despite Eve piling her long hair up on her head in a massive top knot, damp tendrils had come loose and she had to keep blowing them out of her reddened face.

'This isn't fun,' puffed Becca.

Eve panted back, 'I did try to tell you'.

'Ladies. Less talking, more squatting,' Juan barked. 'Right, time to sprint to the markers, ready? Go!'

'I don't think I like him very much,' Becca told Eve, rubbing her small hand towel under her arms and around her neck as Juan collected the bollards ten metres away.

'See? I told you that.'

'Well, not for the first time, you're right.'

Juan approached them, and Becca stuck out her hand. 'Thanks Juan, that was, brilliant.'

'You're welcome. Please come any time you like.'

'I might well try and get another couple of sessions in before my wedding in a few weeks time.'

'Oh, you're getting married?'

'Yes. On August 6th. Do you want to come?'

Eve rolled her eyes and muttered some choice words under her breath as she turned away.

'I didn't anticipate being so smelly,' Becca said, giving her armpits a sniff before wincing. 'Tanya's going to freak out.'

'We did warn her that we weren't going to come in sequinned gowns,' Eve replied, stopping just outside the steps to Tanya's apartment to retie her laces.

'Yes, but I don't think she's expecting a couple of sweaty tramps turning up on her doorstep either, not for her premiere.'

'It's not a bloody premiere Becca, it's a wedding video. Stop believing her hype. If she wants us there, she has to take us as we are.'

'Amen.'

'Evening girls. Are you lost?' Tanya's friend Maggie, the one that sabotaged the hen do roller disco was getting out of a cab. A thigh-high slit in her black evening dress showed a beautifully tanned leg. It reminded Eve to buy a new razor.

Eve gave her a pinched smile. 'We're here for probably the same reason you are, for the grand unveiling of the wedding video.'

'Oh, this is embarrassing. Tanya stipulated a dress code, you obviously didn't know.' Maggie's bottom lip extended into an exaggerated pout as if to say, 'you poor things, prepare for ritual humiliation'.

'Oh, we knew,' Becca jumped in. 'We just chose to ignore it.'

Their childish giggles accompanied the squeaky sound of their trainers on the polished parquet flooring leading to Tanya's front door. Maggie remained open-mouthed standing next to the taxi driver who was still waiting patiently to be paid.

The doorbell chimed inside the flat. It sounded more like a gong than an everyday doorbell that you'd pick up at a DIY store. Knowing Tanya she'd probably ordered it from the 1920s and had it teleported to 2018. The door swung open, to reveal Luke standing in a tuxedo.

'Eve, Becca, come in.' Then suddenly the penny dropped,

as did Luke's face. 'No, don't, wait. You can't come in wearing that, Tanya will go mad.'

'She knew we were coming straight from training, I messaged her.'

He still hadn't let them in, so this exchange was conducted on a monogrammed doormat that Eve had seen on their gift list and wondered, at the time, who on earth would ever buy it for them.

'Can we come in Luke? I need the loo,' Becca said.

'I don't know.' He looked nervous. 'She's put a lot of effort into tonight, and this would ruin it.'

'This being us coming?' Eve asked, one eyebrow raised.

'Can't you go home and change and then come back?' Luke said quietly, closing the door a little bit, so the gap narrowed.

'Hi Luke,' came a plummy voice from behind them. 'Sorry girls, can I just squeeze through between you to join the party?' Maggie slithered through the doorway, air kissing Luke on her way through.

'Luke, stop being an arse,' Eve said, her patience fast evaporating. 'Open the door, and let us through, give us some wine, some snacks, we'll watch your stupid video and then we'll leave you in peace and we can all get on with our lives.'

No one had ever spoken to Luke like that before, well, apart from Tanya, and he had been so scared he'd married her. He was completely at sea about what to do next, stuck between two feisty women, and he wished that he hadn't been the person nearest the door when it rang.

'What's going on?' Ben appeared in the background in the

198

hallway behind Luke. From what Eve could see, he was wearing a DJ as well. 'Eve? Is that you?'

'Yes, but the doorman says that our name's not on the list.'

'Luke? Why won't you let them in?'

Luke opened the door wide enough for Ben to see Eve and Becca in all their sweaty glory, hair scraped back, holey tracksuit bottoms, faded oversized T-shirts with wet patches clearly visible under their arms, and across their chests.

'Ah.'

'But it's ok,' Eve insisted. 'I messaged Tanya that we'd be coming straight from training, so she knew.'

'Well if that's the case, let them in Luke. You wouldn't want to get on Tanya's bad side so early into your marriage would you?'

As Luke stood aside to let them in, Eve saw to her delight that Ben was actually wearing cargo shorts and battered converse on the bottom half, and a tuxedo with black bow tie on the top. 'Nice get up,' she said.

'Thanks, Tanya didn't think so.' He followed them into the living room singing in a nah-nah-nah-nah-nah tune, 'you're going to get it, you're going to get it.'

The chairs were set up in a semi-circular design around a large projector screen, and in the centre of the room was a low level coffee table heaving with cute individual popcorn tubs and a silver tray with already-filled champagne flutes. Tanya had her back to them as they entered, but it was clear she'd modelled herself on Audrey Hepburn for the night. Her shoulder-length brown hair was twisted into a chignon, and she was wearing a tight black dress with above-the-elbow black gloves. She was talking to a man Eve didn't recognise, but Tanya saw his jaw drop at their entrance, followed his gaze and swivelled round to face them. She took a sharp intake of breath and rushed over, shooing them out of the room like you would a stray cat that had accidentally wandered in.

'What the hell are you two wearing?'

'I told you we had a training session in the park opposite you, so we'd be coming straight from there.'

'I thought that you were merely telling me about your whereabouts before my party, I had no idea that you were proposing to turn up in this get up! There's no way I would have allowed it!'

Eve snapped. 'Ok, do you know what Tanya, it's fine. I'm sure I speak for Becca too when I say that we're not that fussed about staying, we're knackered, we'll just go on home and leave you to enjoy your *premiere* in peace.' She didn't mean to say the word premiere in such an obviously disparaging voice. She just about stopped her fingers from making air quotes around the words.

'Absolutely not. You two are my bridesmaids. How would it look if my bridesmaids—' Tanya was practically spitting now '—couldn't be bothered to come.'

There was a moment while Tanya was talking where Eve was tempted to pick her up on her use of the present tense when saying 'you two *are* my bridesmaids' as though their duty to her would be ongoing for the rest of their lives, rather than just a temporary subservience on one day. Clearly Tanya disagreed, and thought that by conferring his status onto them, she owned them. Forever.

'Eve's right,' Becca said. 'There's clearly been a misunderstanding, we thought it would be ok to come like this. Now we know it isn't, we'll just be on our way.'

'That isn't an option. I have carefully counted out everyone, there is the exact number of chairs, snacks and glasses. Can you imagine how embarrassing it would be to have empty seats and surplus refreshments? Come with me, and you can wear something of mine.'

As Tanya sashayed down the corridor in front of them, Eve leant in to whisper to Becca. 'Now I would never say, be more like Tanya, but in light of the conversation we had yesterday about your RSVPs, can you please be more like Tanya?'

Becca punched Eve in the arm.

Chapter 21

At five foot ten, Eve towered over petite Tanya normally, and yet as Tanya stood in front of Eve handing her dresses from her wardrobe, they seemed to be at eye level. Eve looked down and saw to her horror Tanya was wearing the five-inch Louboutins that Coco had relieved herself in. Eve made a strange strangulated giggle that had Becca and Tanya peering at her in concern. Eve shook her head as if to say 'don't mind me' and turned it into a cough.

Becca, being around the same size as Tanya, found a suitable dress straight away, and Tanya was getting increasingly impatient with Eve's dithering. 'The screening was meant to start at eight,' she said, tapping her watch. 'It's now ten past. Choose one. I'm going to get everyone seated in the right places.' Eve blindly grabbed a dark green wrap dress. She was sure she'd read in one of Kat's beauty columns that redheads should wear more green. Or maybe she was confusing that with leprechauns. Either way, when she'd put it on, the colour wasn't the issue, the length was. Designed to be a mini dress on Tanya, it was nigh on gusset-skimming on Eve. Thankfully, the ultra revealing bust line took part of the attention away from the bottom half, but only momentarily. Even Becca, who was so heterosexual she was marrying an army man in a matter of weeks, had eyes that were playing vertical tennis going from Eve's bulging bosoms to her indecent hemline and back again.

'Wow.'

'Not helping Becs.'

'Wow.'

'Shut up, and find me something else.'

Tanya shouted from the corridor. 'Eve. Becca. Now.'

'It's fine, come on, the sooner it starts the sooner we can leave.'

Luke was standing at the door of the living room wearing an old-fashioned usherette tray around his neck. The mini popcorn cartons were neatly stacked in rows on the tray, and as Eve and Becca entered the room he handed them each a small tub. 'Enjoy the show,' he said with a rehearsed smile that Tanya had pre-approved as being in character. Next time Eve felt bad about her life, she would count her blessings that she wasn't Luke.

There were two empty seats, one next to Maggie, the other next to Ben. Eve sighed. Rock and hard place. Begrudgingly she started moving towards Maggie.

'No Eve,' Tanya shrieked, from her chair in the centre of the semi-circle. 'That's Becca's seat, you're by Ben.'

There was no point arguing. Eve would wait until after the 'show' before deleting Tanya from her friends' list, life was too short to be bossed around so much. It was almost as though Tanya was doing it on purpose, constantly pushing her next to Ben at every opportunity, knowing how difficult it was for her.

'Ooo, spiky,' Ben said as Eve's bare leg brushed against his.

'Shut up,' Eve replied sulkily.

Luke took his seat beside Tanya and the screen flickered into action. It became immediately apparent that a large chunk of the wedding budget was now nestling in the videographer's bank account as this was no ordinary wedding video, it was a Hollywood production. Close-ups, wide-angles, out-of-focus, in-focus, soft-focus, this film had it all, and set to a suitably jazzy sound-track that made the wedding seem a lot more enjoyable than it actually was. One smiling face replaced a laughing one on the screen, a conveyor belt of happy people having the Best Day Ever. If you hadn't been there, after watching this, you definitely would've wished you were.

The dancing sequence was shot in black and white, and with the backdrop of the long white curtains suspended from the ceiling pipes, the effect was beautiful. While the guests were jumping up and down in the centre of the screen, to the right stood Ben, beer in hand watching the dancers. Behind him was a billowing curtain, which blew to one side revealing Eve, who was clearly hiding. The videographer must have thought it a sweet shot as they had zoomed in on Eve peering round the curtain at Ben, then darting back behind her screen. Eve could feel her cheeks growing hot and hoped that no one, particularly the man next to her, would realise what she was doing. What she'd spent the wedding doing. Another minute into the video, and Eve appeared again, this time ducking under a table as Ben passed by.

'Whatever are you doing Eve?' Tanya asked.

'Um, I think I dropped something.'

'I think I'll ask Bridget to edit that bit out, it looks like you spent my wedding playing hide and seek.'

Another close up. Not of a face this time, but of a patch of lurid fuchsia pink fabric haphazardly sewn into the tail of a pale pink bridesmaid dress. Eve winced and sank a little into her chair. Out of the corner of her eye she tried to gauge Tanya's reaction but it was too dark to see. The level of light in the room had no effect however on the ability to hear Tanya's unladylike expletive followed by 'What the hell was that?' Tanya had pressed the pause button on the video and ordered Luke to turn on the light.

'Eve? Was that your dress?'

'Um, it's difficult to tell.'

Tanya swivelled to face Becca, who was squirming in her seat too. 'Becca?'

Becca shrugged. 'Beats me.'

Tanya's eyes became slits. 'So, it must have been Ayesha. Well it's a good job she's on her honeymoon because when I get hold of her, she's going to know about it.'

'It was me, it was my dress,' Eve said. 'Nothing to do with Ayesha or Becca. I spilt soup down my dress—'

'We didn't have soup,' Tanya interrupted.

'No, a few days before, when I wore it out to dinner.'

'You wore it out to dinner? My bridesmaid dress? Do you have any idea how much it cost?' Tanya spat.

That was too much. 'Yes, actually, I know exactly how much it cost, and it was far less than what you made us all pay for them!' Eve stood up, her rage making sitting difficult. 'You conned all of us into forking out for expensive designer dresses, but you'd actually got them from a knock-off Chinese website.'

There was a sharp exaggerated intake of horror from Maggie, and a snigger from a couple of Luke's ushers, but nothing from Ben.

'So you can understand why I didn't feel like spending too much money on patching up the dress after I'd stained it. No one was any the wiser, it didn't ruin your day, everyone is still alive, the world is still bloody turning. I'm going to go now.'

'I think that's probably for the best.' Tanya said, pointedly turning her head away from Eve as she stormed past her, grabbing her carrier bag of exercise clothes on the way out.

'One more thing Tanya,' Eve shouted from the doorway. 'You know the shoes you're wearing? Coco pooed in them'

It felt good. And very bad. A complete mixture of elation and mortification, if that was possible. Eve slammed the door to Tanya's apartment block, startling an elderly neighbour in the process, and rested against the railings for a second. If Eve smoked, now would be the ideal time for a restorative puff of nicotine, but she didn't. No one could blame Eve for her outburst. Well, no one except Tanya. Even Luke looked like he wanted to punch the air and yell 'you go gal!' but the prospect of having a lifetime of paying for it stopped him. It was a miracle it hadn't happened sooner; it wasn't just a build up of two months that had led to it, but a build up of twelve years. They'd all swept their differences at university under the carpet as though the tension back then had never existed, but Tanya had never had an easy relationship with any of them. Eve always put this down to Tanya's sense of superiority – in monetary terms she was head and shoulders above the rest of them, with a healthy trust fund and a father who bore more likeness to an ATM than a dad. But it was more than that. Tanya had always drawn them into her dramas, expecting so much from her friends, and giving very little back in return.

The only time when Eve found any solace in their friendship was directly after Ben left and Eve was in a state of panic. Tanya was almost kind, watching Eve cry and deliberate on what path her future was now going to take. It came as a surprise at the time as Tanya had never hidden her scepticism at Eve and Ben's travel plans, calling them 'pipe dreams,' and a 'deluded fantasy.' Becca always put this down to jealousy that Tanya didn't have the nerve to leave the comfort of England and go it alone in New York, seeing in Eve a strength of character and streak of adventure that Tanya quite simply didn't possess. Eve even wondered whether Tanya was afraid of being left alone, and that her cynicism about New York stemmed from not wanting to lose her friend. *Friend*. What an oxymoron.

'Red, wait!' Ben jumped down the final two steps onto the pavement next to her. 'Are you ok?'

Eve gave a shrug. 'I'm fine, sorry about the show I put on up there.'

'Tanya was totally out of order.'

'But I shouldn't have said all that I did.'

'No, it was all her, which I told her.'

'You don't need to fight my battles for me Ben.'

'I would have done the same for Becca, Tanya was out of line.'

'What happened after I left?'

'She threw her shoes in the bin.'

Eve laughed. 'Did she really? That's hilarious.'

'And that frosty blonde one, I don't know her name,'

'Maggie?'

'Yeah, well she fished them out when no one was looking and put them in her handbag.'

Eve grimaced. 'I wasn't making that up, you know. I wasn't making any of it up.'

'I know. But look on the bright side,'

'What's the bright side?' Eve asked.

'Tanya still doesn't know that you butchered the front of the dress too.'

Eve couldn't stop a giggle escaping. 'And how did you know?'

'I saw it when you weren't trying to dodge me, by lunging under tables or hurling yourself behind curtains.'

Eve's smile faded, and embarrassment took over. 'You noticed that too.'

'Look Eve, I'm really sorry if me moving back here has put you in a difficult position. I thought that maybe enough water had passed under the bridge for none of what happened back then to matter any more, and for what it's worth, I'm sorry if I misjudged it and you're still angry at me.'

She wasn't angry. She hadn't been angry after the first couple of months had passed in New York. She was reflective. She was wistful, for what might have been had he stuck to the plan and they'd have started their new life together. She felt a lot of different emotions towards Ben. But she wasn't angry.

'Don't be daft, I'm not cross at you, it's really good to see you. I just didn't know that you were back, and it brought up some old feelings, and I managed those feelings by acting like a complete div and commando rolling under a table every time I saw you.'

Ben smiled. 'Some of those moves were pretty impressive.'

'Thanks.'

Ben ran his toe along the riser of the first step. He'd said what he rushed after her to say, and now a whole book of unspoken words hung in the air.

'Why did you move back, Ben?'

'It's complicated.'

'I would have been surprised if it wasn't.'

'Do you have time for a drink?'

'Yes. But can I get changed back into my gym gear? I'm feeling a bit, um, exposed, in this get up.'

'Sure, although we're going to be the weirdest dressed couple in the pub, with you in a sweaty tracksuit and me in a tuxedo jacket and shorts.'

Eve looked down at herself, then at him and laughed. He was right. 'Ok fine, I'll stay as I am, but try and keep your eyes on my face.'

Ben threw his head back and laughed. 'Say what you really mean Eve.'

After a quick deliberation over which way they should walk, they set off. Despite Ben having said that he would open up about what happened to make him run off back then, as they walked they talked about everything but. They chatted about how the summer evenings in London made the rest of the year's rain worth it, they commented on all the blue plaques they passed, the amount of cyclists on the road and they took a picture for a Japanese couple. But it wasn't until they'd found a table outside the pub on the pavement, Eve had a large white wine in front of her and Ben had taken a larger than average gulp of his pint that they started the conversation that she'd waited four years to have.

'I'm really pleased you went to New York,' he said.

'I wasn't going to,' Eve said truthfully. 'I'd barely left Brighton before, let alone lived by myself in a huge, new city.'

'What was it like?'

'Honestly? It was really hard to begin with, I was terrified. I thought everyone around me was a drug dealer or going to stab me. But then I started work at the magazine and it got a bit better.'

'How long did you stay?'

'Two years. I moved back Christmas before last, family stuff—'

'Oh no, are your folks ok?' Ben asked, concern making his brow wrinkle. He'd spent a lot of time in her mum and dad's kitchen having a tea or beer while his washing spun round in their machine, so Eve knew that it wasn't just a polite enquiry, he genuinely meant it.

'Mum is, Dad's not. He was hit by a drunk driver, and didn't make it.'

'Oh God Eve, I'm so sorry. I genuinely had a lot of time for your dad.'

'Thanks, but I seem to remember you calling him a bit of a bore.'

'Only when we all went camping together and he lectured us for hours about camping etiquette, and always tying a flag to the top of your tent so you can find it easier, to pack your matches in a plastic waterproof container, to take into account the wind direction when building your campfire so it doesn't blow into your tent.'

'All vital survival skills,' Eve said defensively.

'Absolutely. How many times have you been camping since then?'

'Um, that would be none.'

'Me too.'

'Well, we'll be fully prepared next time we do.' *Not together, obviously* Eve wanted to add, but didn't.

'But I'm really sorry to hear that Eve. So that's when you moved back?'

'Yes, I came straight back, with the intention of going back to New York a month or so later, but Mum was in such a bad way, and so I had to stay. There was a job opening on the English edition of the bridal magazine I worked for in New York, Becca needed a new flatmate and everything seemed to stack up for me to stay in London. Anyway, I thought we were here to talk about you?' Eve took a sip of her drink and sat back on the bench, making it clear that her turn with the mic was over.

'What do you want to know?' Ben asked.

'Why didn't you come to America with me?'

'To answer that I need to go back a bit.'

Chapter 22

The last few rays of sun were dappling their table in a warm light, and they both instinctively turned their heads appreciatively to it. Within half an hour the sun would set, and the magic would be gone.

'Are you hungry?' Ben asked Eve. 'We could order something?'

She was. And she desperately wanted to say yes, share a platter of something, pretend that he hadn't monumentally let her down, and spend an evening catching up, but Eve was also very aware that she probably wasn't going to like what Ben was about to say, and didn't want to be stuck eating a plate of cured meats with him before going home.

'No, I had a lot of popcorn at Tanya's.'

'Poor Luke and his usherette tray,' Ben said, giving a rueful smile at the fate of his friend.

'Poor Luke nothing. He knew what he was signing up for. Tanya hasn't changed a bit since uni.'

'Neither's Becca,' Ben said. 'She's still as free-spirited as ever.'

Eve smiled. 'You say free-spirited, I say lovably disorganised.'

'And you two share a place?'

'Yes, in Clapham. We live above a jazz pub. You're in Wimbledon?'

'For the moment, it's all still very new being back after four years in New Zealand. I'm not sure where I'll settle.'

Him mentioning New Zealand was the perfect lead-in for her to offer a prompt. 'So, are you going to start this long and complicated story then or what?'

Ben took another long gulp of his beer and said, 'Do you remember the girlfriend I grew up with back home who I split up with when I moved to England?'

'Kate?' Eve said.

'Yes, Kate. How did you remember that?'

Eve didn't want to say how she'd withered inside each time her name had come up, even though Ben was adamant Kate was a family friend and nothing else. A couple of months into their first year of uni Kate had travelled all the way from New Zealand to see Ben, and she'd stayed for a couple of days in their house, sleeping in his room. What made it worse was quite how lovely Kate was. She had an infectious laugh that had everyone giggling along, no matter how bad the joke was. Kate was so upbeat, so optimistic, so, jolly, but in a quiet, unassuming way that made women really want to be her friend. But she was gone as quickly as she'd arrived and they had never really spoken about her again.

'Well, just as we were about to move to New York together, I got a letter.'

'From Kate?'

'From her parents.'

'Saying how she was totally bereft when you two broke up and that you had to leave straight away to mend her broken heart?'

'Asking me to come back as soon as possible.'

'So you left me for her? She snapped her fingers and you went.'

'It wasn't like that Eve,' Ben said quietly.

'But you did cancel our trip and pack up your flat in the night and disappear to go to her?'

'Yes but—'

'And you never came back, or wrote to explain, or gave a second thought about New York.'

'It was complicated.'

'So you said. It's not sounding particularly complicated to me. It sounds like a simple choice. Eve or Kate. Heads says Eve, tails Kate, oh will you look at that, its tails. Best pack up my stuff in the middle of the night and run straight to her.'

'There's no point trying to explain to you if you're going to be like this.'

'I have tried to give you the benefit of the doubt Ben, I have concocted so many reasons in my head as to why you might leave me like that, walk away from all our plans, but they were always far more dramatic and easier to swallow than you just dumping me for your ex-girlfriend. You're really not the man I thought you were.'

'Well, you've gone massively down in my estimation too, now we're talking about it.'

'What the hell does that mean? I have done nothing wrong!'

'No, nothing wrong, just a bit sordid and cheap. I saw them

Eve, I saw those two bolshy ushers go to your room after the wedding last weekend. And then I saw the empty champagne bottle and glasses outside your room the next morning. The Eve I used to know wouldn't have done that.'

Eve stood up, downed her wine, and said, 'Goodnight Ben.'

She thought he might run after her. If it was a movie he would have done. But there were no pounding footsteps behind her, no panting declarations of regret, no hug of reconciliation. Eve had reached the steps down into the tube station, and she had no choice but to go down them. Alone.

Becca was already at home and in her stripy pyjamas when Eve came back.

'I was getting worried,' Becca said. 'Where did you get to?'

Eve slumped down on the sofa next to her. 'I went for a quick drink with Ben.'

'I thought you might have done, after he dashed out after you.'

'What happened after I left?'

'I left pretty soon after you. Tanya was like a woman possessed, and I didn't want to be around such negativity so I came to find you. You were completely within your rights to say what you did though, she was well out of order.'

'That's what Ben said too.'

Becca nudged Eve's foot with her own. 'Did you two kiss and make up?'

'In no way whatsoever.' Eve sighed, she was exhausted and felt on the verge of tears that she'd much rather shed in her room alone. 'He told me that he left me to go back to Kate, his ex-girlfriend in New Zealand.'

'The pretty girl who laughed a lot?'

'That's the one.'

Becca looked confused. 'But when I asked Ayesha why he came back, she said that it was complicated. So there must be more to the story.'

'Complicated, complicated, everything's bloody complicated. Is that all Ayesha said?'

'She was very secretive, she said that it wasn't her story to tell. But he's obviously not with her now if he's here and she's not.'

Eve shook her head. 'I don't know Becs, it's nothing to do with me anymore is it, Ben Hepworth's life decisions. He can come and go as he pleases, it's none of my business.'

'Is that all he said, that he left you for her? Bastard.'

'Yep. But then I didn't really give him a chance to say more, the last thing I want to hear is more details about their great love that he couldn't be without.'

The best friends sat in companionable silence. 'I wish I hadn't invited him to my wedding now,' Becca ventured finally.

Eve nodded. 'You and me both.'

'Maybe he won't come after tonight.'

'That'll be one less hay bale.'

'I invited the pub landlord downstairs today, and gave him a plus one.'

'For fuck's sake Becca.'

'I know.'

Chapter 23

Uncharacteristically Becca was awake before Eve the next morning, sitting at their fold out table in the corner of their living room. 'Have you seen this?' she said, as Eve stumbled bleary-eyed into the room clutching a mug of tea.

'Your laptop?'

'This.' Becca swivelled the screen around for Eve to see it. Eve winced at the brightness of it before allowing her eyes to focus on the words. It was her latest column on the *Venus* website. The one which she'd loosely based on Ayesha's wedding, but carefully shrouded the details in disguise.

'No,' Eve replied nonchalantly, with her heart in her mouth. 'What is it?'

'This new wedding column that everyone's talking about. It's quite funny, but this one sounds just like Ayesha's wedding.'

'Let me see,' said Eve, scanning the words to make sure her eyes moved left to right, to give the impression to Becca that she was reading it for the first time. 'No, look, it says this couple had swans, no mention of flamingoes or scarecrows.'

'But look, the best man broke his foot, that's like Amit breaking his nose.'

217

'That's hardly the same thing.'

'The bride wore cowboy boots, and Ayesha wore sparkly trainers.'

'Most brides have unconventional elements to their day.'

'It's more than that though, it reads just like Ayesha's. I bet the writer of this column was a guest at Ayesha's, or even snuck in uninvited to take notes on it in order to make fun of it.'

It was too early for Eve to create an eloquent response that would convince Becca that this was ridiculous. Try as she did, the words just weren't forming in her brain, so she just said, 'Nah, that's crazy talk.'

'Hmm ... I'm not convinced. Maybe I'll send it to Ayesha when she's back from honeymoon and see what she thinks.'

'No, don't do that, honestly Becs, you're reading way too much into it. Think about how many people get married every Saturday in July, loads and loads. Ayesha's wedding was a little odd, but so are loads of weddings, and I should know.' As soon as the last few words were out of her mouth Eve wanted to swallow them again. Now was not the time to be setting herself up as the guru of all weddings, she was trying to distance herself from the *Venus* column, not draw attention to the fact that writing about weddings was how she paid the rent. 'I'd better get a move on, or I'm going to be late.'

All the way into work the argument she'd had with Ben kept circling around Eve's mind. In the first few months after moving to New York, she'd had the desire to find solace in the new, the unexplored, just to save herself the misery of walking familiar footsteps without him. Eve knew that back home, drinking in the same cafes and bars she'd been to with Ben, sitting in the same cinema she'd shared popcorn with him in, wandering alone through the same parks they'd ambled hand in hand through, everything would be tinged with a little sadness. And Ben was still alive, would it have been different had he died? She certainly didn't feel that she had the same right to grieve as a widow, but his absence was just as keenly felt. Just knowing that he was out there in the world, drinking in a bar, seeing a movie, walking in a park, doing all of those things without her by his side used to give her a sharp stab of pain. Now that Eve knew that his leaving wasn't because of some massive tragic incident, and that he'd simply had enough of her – it made all her months, years, of wondering 'what if' seem like such a sham, such a monumental waste of time. He chose Kate and didn't look back, while she was still rebuilding her life, four years later, one brick at a time.

Eve was waiting in the downstairs café for her morning latte when her phone buzzed.

'Don't say no straight away.'

'Morning Amit, no.'

'I said don't say no straight away!'

'I didn't, I said Morning Amit first.'

'Open your mind, then your mouth.'

'I should have that as a tattoo.'

'Eve, be quiet. Ayesha told me about your incident with Andrew and Bobby, I'm sorry they were such losers. We were old school friends, but they get a bit drunk and lose all common sense and propriety.'

'No need to apologise, I'm flattered, in an odd way. Anyway, aren't you on your honeymoon, can't this wait?'

'Ayesha and I were just talking about it in the pool and I want to make it up to you. I have another friend, Bryn, who couldn't make it to the wedding as he was on duty, he's a doctor at the children's hospital, and I think you and he would really hit it off. He's single, and I'd really like to hook you guys up.'

'No.'

'Eve! I said, don't say no.'

'Look, I think it's lovely that you think you need to fix me up and get me married off, but I am genuinely very happy just being me.'

'We all know you are, but would it hurt to have an evening of fun with an attractive man who saves children's lives, whose name begins with B?'

'Oh my God Amit, not you too!'

'What? I'm not a believer in all this psychic crap at all, but it's very strange how all that woman's fortune telling is coming true.'

'Really? And how is your move to Africa coming along?' Eve jibed.

'I got an offer to launch an office in Nairobi. I'm thinking about it.'

'Are you kidding me?'

'Ayesha doesn't know yet, I'm telling her tonight. So look, Eve, go out with Bryn. What's the worst that can happen? You have a crappy date that you can turn into a book one day or that you can talk about at dinner parties.'

***

Becca pulled her hair back into a ponytail in the hall mirror and pulled her cyclist's reflective vest over her head. 'If I don't see you later before your date with Bryn the dashing doctor, have an awesome time and let me know if you're staying away,'

That was impossible. Aside from the fact that Eve had forgotten to buy a new razor, there was no way that she was going to sleep with Bryn on the first date. She'd had a one-night stand once before in New York and it was an unmitigated disaster involving bald private parts (his), a glass eye (his) and tears (hers), so she wouldn't be doing that again in a hurry.

'I know now's not really the time to ask as we're both running late—'

Here it is, thought Eve, here's the moment when Becca would ask her outright if she was behind the columns. And there was no way she'd be able to deny it. Not to Becca.

'But how are you feeling about seeing Ben all the time?'

It was a reprieve on one hand, but another confrontation that she was equally uncomfortable about. Eve mumbled an incoherent reply that was completely noncommittal.

'Because it's ok to feel awkward, or pissed off you know. You've had zero answers or closure on what you thought was the big love of your life and now you're expected to just pretend everything's normal and resolved.'

'Amit said that Bryn is very emotionally connected,' Eve said, changing the subject. Becca didn't have a clue what being emotionally connected entailed, but it sounded painful. 'Where's he taking you tonight?'

'I don't know, it's a surprise, except he said in his message

I have to wear comfortable shoes, bring a cardigan and a bottle of water.' Spoken like a true doctor, Eve had thought when she received his instructions. Not many other men would be able to reduce the risk of bunions, hypothermia and dehydration in one text message. Eve added, 'If it's the walking tour of London's loos I may cry.'

Eve felt really nervous walking to the prearranged meet-up spot. Now that she'd decided to draw a thick line under her time with Ben and move on, this date had far more significance than any other date that she'd been on because previously Ben was always lurking in the background whispering 'what if?' from the shadows. And now he wasn't. He'd taken up too much of her past, and he had no place in her future.

Bryn was already at the corner in Chelsea they'd agreed to meet at. Casually dressed in chinos, a pink shirt with the sleeves rolled up, and a pale grey jumper slung around his shoulders and tied in a knot on his chest, he looked like he'd just stepped out of the Boden catalogue. He was also wearing slip on brown boat shoes with no socks. It wasn't a look that she usually went for, but then that hadn't worked out too well for her, so maybe it was time for a change.

'Hi,' Eve said brightly, noting the double cheek kiss that made him seem terribly debonair and cultured.

'Did you bring water?'

Eve patted her little drawstring bag. 'Yep.'

'Good. Can you guess what we're going to be doing?'

'Does it involve toilets?'

Being ignorant of the back story, her question sounded a

lot ruder than it was meant to. Eve quickly followed it up with, 'There's a company that does a guided tour round the toilets of London. My friend Becca wanted to do it for Ayesha's hen do until I overruled it.'

'That doesn't sound very hygienic.'

'Well no, I don't think you have to touch them or anything. I think they might be famous ones, or ones with historical significance.'

'It doesn't sound like a fun way to spend your time,' Bryn said, wrinkling his nose in distaste.

'No, no it doesn't,' Eve agreed. 'So what are we doing then?'

'We are doing a walking tour, but it's a blue plaque spotting tour around Chelsea and Kensington.'

That was ... nice. It wouldn't have been Eve's first choice of dates, she normally preferred some level of alcohol consumption to be involved, but thinking about it, it was perfect. They'd be able to talk all the way round the tour, finding out a lot more about each other, and she wouldn't need to feel guilty about cancelling Juan for tonight as she'd be doing exercise. So multiple box ticking at the same time.

She assumed that Bryn had a map or an app that they would follow, taking it at their own pace, maybe even curtailing it a little early to sneak off to a neighbourhood pub, should the mood take them, but as they rounded the next corner a massive gaggle of Spanish tourists and about thirty pensioners were all crowding around someone who had a stick with a flag attached to the top of it clipped onto their belt.

'Here we are.' Bryn said. 'Let me fight my way through. Do

you want to go halves on the tickets or are you quite traditional?'

The question threw her; if she said that she was quite traditional, she would sound like she was a money grabber who expected him to pay, but if she said they'd go halves she worried that would make her seem ungrateful. She took the middle road, and shrugged smiling, saying, 'I don't mind, whatever you want to do.'

'Ok, well I'll get this, and then if we go for some food after, you can get that.'

'That sounds like a plan.' It did, there was nothing wrong with that at all, Eve thought, watching him squeeze through the blue rinses and bald heads. It *might* have been nice for him to pay for her without asking, just to be a bit chivalrous, but then again, it wasn't the 1950s – maybe he thought she'd be offended by him paying for her, which was why he hadn't straight away. Yes, it was actually very thoughtful of him.

'Got them,' Bryn waved two tickets in front of him a few minutes later. 'I'll keep them both safe, shall I? In case you lose yours. My ex, Caroline, was always losing things, I think she went through about ten Oyster cards a month as she kept leaving them places.'

'Good idea.' Eve didn't often lose things, but it was probably good to be on the safe side.

'Oh look, we're off,' Bryn said, tagging on behind two Chinese students. They walked for about fifty metres in silence before Eve couldn't stand it anymore.

'So, what hobbies do you have?'

'Cricket.'

The world's dullest game. Closely followed by motor racing. 'And Formula 1.'

'Oh that's good. Did you see the rugby game at the weekend?' Eve said.

'I'm more of a football fan myself. Follow the foxes.'

'Heh?'

'The foxes, Filbert the fox? I'm a Leicester City supporter.'

'How come? Aren't you from London?'

'I used to support Spurs, but my ex, Caroline, is from Leicester, and her dad used to take us both to home games whenever we visited, so they sort of became my team.'

'Isn't that a bit frowned upon in the footballing world?' Eve asked light-heartedly. 'Switching allegiances to a different team? I thought it was a "one team till I die" sort of thing.'

'Leicester has a lot of happy memories for me, so it's more of an emotional bond really. I still go up for home games from time to time with Keith, my ex, Caroline's, Dad, which is nice.'

This must be what Amit meant about Bryn's emotional connections. It was quite refreshing really, to hear a man talk about a deep and meaningful reason for supporting a football team rather than a childhood home's proximity to a stadium.

'What else do you like doing Bryn?'

'Well, I'm afraid that life is pretty much my work, being a doctor in a hospital doesn't really give me much time for anything else.' He gave a little chuckle. 'My ex, Caroline, used to say that there was no point me owning proper clothes when all I wore was scrubs.'

Eve smiled to lessen the seriousness of her next question,

the answer of which her future happiness was riding on. 'When did you and Caroline break up Bryn?'

'Oh God, ages ago. Three years, five months to be precise.'

Eve gave a sigh of relief, that was ok, it was a very decent amount of time between then and now. She was fully expecting him to give a response including the words 'days' or 'weeks', but three and a half years was just fine. She'd been single for almost the same amount of time, so they had that in common, the only difference was that she wasn't aware that she'd mentioned Ben yet.

The group had stopped outside their first blue plaque, mounted on the wall of a tall grey brick terraced townhouse. It read *Thomas Wakely 1795–1862 REFORMER and founder of 'The Lancet' lived here.*

'I wonder what "The Lancet" was?' Eve murmured. 'I bet it was a den of vice and iniquity.'

'It's a medical journal,' Bryn replied straight-faced. 'I know an interesting fact about Thomas Wakely actually. Before he became a surgeon, he was an amateur boxer and used to fight bare-fisted in pubs.'

'That is interesting.' On a scale of one to ten it was around two on the scale of interesting things to know, but you never knew when a fact like that was going to come up on pub quizzes. Eve firmly believed in things happening for a reason, and that little nugget of information might one day come in very handy.

'What are your hobbies, Eve?' Bryn said as the group shuffled onwards.

'Writing, although that's my job, so it's not really a hobby.'

'Caroline used to write poetry. I read some of it, and it was really very good.'

Eve didn't really know what to say to that. 'Um, that's nice for her. I also like going out for a drink, I live above a jazz pub, you see.'

'That sounds loud.'

'Sometimes, but it's mostly really good fun. They all know me and my flatmate Becca in there, and it's really handy having your local literally on your doorstep.'

'How many units do you think you drink a week?'

Oh God, Eve thought, a night of difficult questions. She had wanted to apply the honesty is the best policy approach to this date, but the truth was absolutely going to result in a lecture she didn't want to receive. She was starting to realise that Bryn was perhaps not her soul mate. He was still waiting for a reply to his question, and Eve couldn't for the life of her remember the recommended alcohol limits, so was just going to estimate the real number, then halve it.

'Um, not many, twenty?' she said uncertainly.

'Twenty? In one week? Are you joking?'

Should she have gone higher or lower? Was his incredulity due to how little she drank or was he getting ready to fast-dial a rehab unit for her to dry out in?

'Oh look,' Eve said quickly, looking up at a tall white townhouse sandwiched between two grey ones. 'Dame Millicent Garrett Fawcett.'

'Who?' Bryn said, looking at his watch.

'Dame Millicent Garrett Fawcett.'

'I can see what it says, but who is she?'

'A pioneer of women's suffrage.'

'You're just reading that from the plaque.'

'I'll have you know, I'm a bit of a closet feminist and Dame Millicent here is a heroine of mine. She was the leader of the National Union of Women's Suffrage Societies, she co-founded the first women's college at Cambridge, and because of her, six million women got the vote. You're not the only one with interesting facts up their sleeves Bryn.'

Bryn didn't appear to be listening, instead he was watching one of the pensioners from the tour group who had splintered off and was leaning against a rubbish bin. The woman's pale skin was shining in the evening sun and her friend was fanning her with a discarded copy of the *Evening Standard*.

'Bryn?' Eve waved her hand in front of his face to get his attention.

'Sorry,' he said, not taking his eyes off the two elderly women. 'I'm just concerned that lady is suffering from heat prostration.'

'Heat what?'

'Prostration. Hyperthermia, not to be confused with hypothermia. Wait here.'

He barked the last two words like an order, not a suggestion, and it raised Eve's hackles. She wasn't used to being told what to do, and she didn't like it. In fact, as she watched a group of pensioners gather round her blind date, she was coming to the realisation that she didn't like Bryn very much either. So far, every male with the letter B had been a monumental idiot. Or, just maybe, she was the idiot for humouring the prediction in the first place.

Chapter 24

Eve slipped away while Bryn was administering water, fashioning a cold compress for the old lady's neck and generally basking in effusive praise from the woman's flirty white-haired friends. She had sent him a message once she was far enough away for him not to follow her, saying, *Thanks for a really interesting night, you looked like you had your hands full, so thought I'd leave you to it. All the best, Ex*

Eve had a little smirk to herself when she realised for the first time that her initial next to a kiss looked like the word Ex, which seeing as she'd just spent the evening listening to Bryn genuflect to his former girlfriend as she sat on her golden pedestal was very fitting. She only added the kiss at the end of the message as it seemed a little abrupt with just an E, but Eve hoped he didn't read into the kiss any emotion she absolutely wasn't feeling. She wasn't mistaken, she knew she wasn't; it was a rubbish date.

Becca was at a parents' evening when Eve got in after the date, and was still in bed when she left for the location shoot the next morning, so Eve hadn't had a chance to workshop the date with her yet. Eve guessed correctly that the topic would come up that evening as she and Becca were meeting Amit and Ayesha for dinner, who, fresh from their two-week honeymoon in Kerala, were desperate to catch up on wedding gossip with their friends. It was a common gripe of brides, that they had to head off on holiday straight after their wedding, leaving everyone else to exchange tales about the wedding, who spoke to whom, who danced with whom, who insulted whom, and by the time they returned, everyone was bored of talking about it. Eve reckoned that Ayesha must have messaged her from the luggage carousel at Heathrow asking about her dinner plans, so eager was she to meet up.

The final shot of the day on the magazine's photoshoot in a studio in South London, was of an over-the-top arrangement of tall-stemmed exotic orange flowers, which didn't look dissimilar to the beaks of Atlantic puffins. They were deeply unattractive and incredibly antisocial, as guests wouldn't be able to see, let alone converse with, the people opposite them on the table. Eve said as much to the stylist, who flicked her ponytail and muttered a few choice words about 'leaving it to the professionals.' Eve thought about fighting her corner, rationally laying out her reasoning of why these flowers looked rubbish for a wedding, but instead she flipped open her notebook and wrote down 'puffin beaks' ready to recall for her next column for *Venus*.

They were due to all meet at seven-thirty that evening. Eve got there just before seven, and had a moment of indecision as she found the pub quicker than she had anticipated. She wondered whether to keep walking up and down the street until nearer the allotted meeting time, enjoying the last few hours of sunshine, smiling smugly at the lost tourists and feeling at one with London, or whether to be brave and go in and have her first drink alone. After the week she'd had, it was a no-brainer.

'Double gin and tonic please,' Eve asked the barman.

'If you have a fresh lime, can she have that instead of lemon?' said a familiar male voice behind her. He followed it up with, 'Hello Red.'

This couldn't be Becca's doing, Eve thought. Becca knew how Eve and Ben had left things, there was no way she would have set her up like this. It must have been Ayesha or Amit who invited him along.

'Amit messaged me from the airport earlier and asked if I fancied drinks and dinner,' said Ben, reading her mind. 'By the look on your face, that's not ok. If I'd known you'd be here I wouldn't have come.'

Eve shrugged as she handed over the money to the waiting barman. 'It's a free world.'

'You ran off pretty quickly the other night.'

'Do you blame me?'

'Look, who you want to sleep with is none of my business.'

'It really isn't.' Eve knew that her reply only confirmed what he thought she'd done and did nothing to dispel it, but she was just really fed up of them tiptoeing round each other.

'I know. Look, I wanted to explain, to try to make you understand why I did what I did back then, and then you just left.'

'Excuse me for not wanting to hang around to hear how

amazing your life has been with Kate since you dumped me for her.'

'It hasn't actually been that amazing.'

Eve stuck out her bottom lip. 'Aw, did ickle Ben get his heart broken after breaking mine?'

'Kate died.'

A stab of horror passed through Eve's chest. 'Oh God, Ben, I'm so sorry, I would never have said that if I knew, I'm so sorry, shit, I'm such an arsehole.'

'Hello! Hello! We're back!' Ayesha bounded up between the two of them and gave Eve a bear hug, breaking off to bestow Ben with the same honour.

'Hello, you two, you look serious, looks like we arrived in just the nick of time to liven things up!' Amit slapped Ben on the back and kissed Eve's cheek. The bruising on his nose and under his eyes had gone down, and the Keralan sun had given them both healthy tans.

'Becca not here yet?'

'No,' Eve said quietly, looking at Ben. She felt like such an idiot for storming off on Sunday, and being so juvenile about what was obviously a really serious situation. He wouldn't meet her eye, obviously thinking her to be a shallow, unfeeling imbecile, which was exactly how she felt. 'She shouldn't be too long.'

'Shall we go to the table?' Amit suggested. 'They give it away if you're fifteen minutes past the booking time.'

The four of them weaved their way through the crowded restaurant at the back of the pub. No two tables or chairs matched, each being sourced from local markets or junk shops, and either painted white or left untreated and natural. Glass jam jars held flickering tea lights on each table, and the daily specials were written on little chalkboards propped up on easels dotted around the room. The atmosphere was casual, inviting, and judging by the noise of chatter and laughter at every table around them, perfect for a night out with friends.

'Great place,' Ben said, pulling out Eve's seat for her to sit down before him. She hesitated for a micro-second in case he was going to revert to being the joker and pull it out completely, leaving her sprawling on the floor like he used to, but he didn't.

'We brought Tanya and Luke here once, but she hated it.' Ayesha said.

At the mention of Tanya's name Eve stiffened. Ben must have sensed this because he spoke up quickly. 'We had a bit of a run-in with Tanya actually a few days ago, I don't think any of us will be seeing too much more of her.'

'Too much more of who?' Becca said, dumping her bag down at the empty seat at the end of the table and giving the returning newlyweds big hugs. To Eve's relief Becca looked very surprised that Ben was at the table too, proving that she wasn't privy to his invitation to join the party. 'Sorry I'm late.'

'I was just saying how we fell out with Tanya at the weekend.' Ben's use of the term 'we' pleased Eve, it united them, and showed that maybe he didn't think she was an imbecile.

'It was bound to happen though, I don't know why we persisted in being friends with her for so long. She's like a viper,' Becca said, opening out the menu.

'You should hear some of the things she said to me at the

wedding,' Ayesha said, pulling a face. 'She basically made fun of everything.'

Becca suddenly took a sharp intake of breath. 'You don't think it's her, do you Eve?'

Eve had no idea what she was talking about. 'Is what her?'

'The writer! Of the wedding column! Oh my God, it totally makes sense now.'

'Unlike you,' Ayesha said. 'What are you on about?'

'Eve said that I shouldn't mention it to you, but the day after your wedding this column came out on the website *Venus*, and it was basically a really sarcastic article all about the zany things brides do at weddings, and the similarities to your wedding were too much for it to be a coincidence.'

'It was entirely a coincidence, take no notice of Becca,' Eve gushed quickly. 'I read it, and it bears no resemblance to your wedding at all.'

'It does! Look,' Becca got out her phone and tapped in the URL. Eve's column filled the screen. Becca read out loud:

Is there an unspoken contest going on that I don't know about, one where brides compete to outdo each other in the ludicrous stakes? This weekend's nuptials were held in a country hotel. So far, so normal, I hear you cry, but what came next was anything but. The bride entered to a Disney song, the aisle was made of mirrors that made it look like everyone was walking on water (not very practical for the short-skirted), and plastic life-size swans on the lawn denoted which table everyone was sat at – they scared the bejeezus out of the little people (children, not dwarves).

'See?' Becca shrieked. The rest of the table stared at her. 'It must be Tanya, she must have written this. She was so scathing about everything, and it sounds just like the poisonous clap-trap she spouts.'

Poisonous claptrap? It was fiction, Eve thought, completely fabricated, made-up, untrue. Her eyes darted around to her friends to gauge their responses. Without exception, their foreheads were furrowed, as if deep in thought.

Eve started counting off her points on her fingers. 'You came in to a Pixar song, not Disney, you had the yellow brick road as an aisle, not a river, and you had flamingoes, not swans. It's entirely different, I did try and tell Becca this.'

'I'll send you the link so you can read all of it,' Becca said. 'But I'm convinced this is the work of Tanya. And if it is, she's even more spiteful and vindictive than we thought.'

'What a bitch,' Ben said. 'I really hope you're not right Becca, but it sounds too similar to just be a freaky coincidence. Particularly the timing of it. I mean, we all love your quirki-ness Ayesha, but there can't be too many brides to have the same wedding date with your level of uniqueness.'

Eve remained silent. She couldn't really protest any more without anyone asking why she was defending Tanya, but equally, she didn't want Ayesha's feelings to be hurt that her wedding had been the inspiration for so much ridicule. That wasn't her intention at all in writing it. Ben was right, Ayesha's brand of quirky was the reason they all adored her, and the idea that nothing but spite and malice was behind this column was completely wrong. In wanting to entertain people she had never met, was Eve losing sight of her allegiance to the people that were important to her?

Ayesha topped up everyone's wine glasses while saying, 'I think Eve's right, it's similar, but doesn't mention any exact details that are the same. Thank you for being so insulted on behalf of me guys, but it's actually made me like my wedding more, that it wasn't cookie-cutter and showed off our personalities. Even if it was based on our wedding, then I take that as a compliment that it was so different it was worthy of someone writing about it.'

'Even if that person was Tanya?' Becca asked.

'Even then. Although I don't think it was, because I don't think she's that eloquent. I think it was probably a proper journalist or writer that did this.'

If Eve could sink any lower in her seat she would have done. She'd been thoroughly put in her place, without anyone even realising it. Like a gift from the gods their food arrived at exactly that moment, amid much bustling and shuffling of condiments and space-making on the crowded table.

A few mouthfuls in, Becca suddenly said, 'So Eve, are you going to tell us how your date with Dr McDreamy went?'

'What's this?' Ben asked.

'Amit set Eve up with a doctor friend of his to say sorry for the way his two friends tried to have a threesome with Eve.'

'Tried?' Ben asked.

'Yes Ben, tried. I slammed the door in their faces then drank their champagne with Becca and Ayesha. Although to be honest, part of me regrets not inviting them in now.' That wasn't true, but Eve really wanted to see Ben's reaction. He remained poker-faced, not taking her bait. God, he was annoying.

'So?' Becca asked. 'How'd it go?'

'Not great.'

'Let me guess,' Amit said. 'Bryn took you to a museum or an art gallery to show you how cultured he is, asked you what your BMI was, and gave you a bottle of multivitamins to take home?'

Eve laughed. 'That's amazingly spot on, I thought you were in Kerala, not following me around spying on me?'

'Let's just say, he's got form,' Amit said smiling. 'But it was worth a go.'

'And his name began with B,' Ayesha added.

Eve flashed a look at Ayesha that told her to be quiet. Ben knew nothing about the premonition, and annoyingly it was his initial too.

Ben helped himself to a big chunk of bread from the basket in the middle of the table. 'What does B have to do with anything?'

'Eve's only dating men with names beginning with B.'

'You're only what?' Ben said, jumping in, cupping his ear for added effect.

Eve ignored him. Explaining Violet's prediction out loud would make it seem as ludicrous as Eve was starting to realise it was. She had recently lost all sense, common or otherwise and she didn't really know why. She wasn't unhappy being single, so why had she been swept along by her friends' desire to see her coupled up?

'It wasn't an entirely wasted night, I got to see where Millicent Garrett Fawcett had lived, so culturally it was a good date, even if it ranked as disastrous romantically.'

Becca ruffled Eve's hair. 'Cheer up love, could be worse, I could have invited him to my wedding.'

Eve sat up in horror. 'You didn't, did you?'

'Of course not! I don't even know the bloke. Although that has never stopped me before.'

Becca then started yawning, and excused herself before their desserts had even arrived. Eve noted that she didn't leave any money for her share of the food and wine, but she knew that it was less to do with being stingy and more to do with being absolutely broke.

'So, now that she's gone, we can talk about her hen do,' Ayesha said, leaning in across the table and nearly setting her hair alight on the candle. 'We've had the date in the diary for months, but what are we going to do?'

Eve had gone back and forth about this very issue ever since Becca asked her to be her maid of honour. Becca was gregarious, loved parties, enjoyed having a good time with her seemingly endless roll call of friends, but then on the other hand, she also thrived on one-on-one times, and in-depth chats and intimate settings. A hen do like Tanya's or Ayesha's wouldn't suit her. But she'd never be able to whittle the numbers down for fear of offending anyone, hence why her wedding had grown to the numbers of a small country. Becca once referred to her approach to friendship as being like a fried egg, having Eve and Ayesha in the yolk with her, and a cast of hundreds around them as the white.

'I wanted to chat to you about that actually. Depending on your cash flow, I was thinking of organising a weekend away just the three of us. She's got the mother of all parties planned for her wedding, and I thought it would be really great if you, me and her went away for the weekend, and just hung out together like we used to.'

'When the three of you used to hang out together, I was always there too, so do I get an invite?' Ben said cheekily. Thankfully Eve could tell that he was joking. A weekend away with Ben when she seemed to keep putting her foot in it with him was not going to be a sensible prospect.

'Not a chance,' Ayesha said. 'Anyway, I need you to stay here and keep an eye on my new husband, I've read Eve's trashy mags, I know what happens when wives are away.' She turned back to Eve, 'Great, a weekend away sounds perfect, but it can't be too expensive, this wedding has wiped us out, and I know you and Becca probably haven't got much at the moment either.'

'No, not at all.' Eve could hardly let on that thanks to her *Venus* columns her life wasn't quite so hand-to-mouth anymore. 'Right, I'll form a plan in the next couple of days.'

'Wouldn't it be fun to have one last blowout: me, you and Becca going clubbing like we used to?' Ayesha said.

'Leave it with me, I'll come up with a plan.'

As Amit and Ayesha walked ahead of them out of the restaurant, Eve tugged on Ben's sleeve. 'Can you stay back and walk home with me? Please?'

Eve blamed her bladder for needing to run back into the restaurant, and Ben gallantly offered to stay behind to walk her to the tube, insisting that the newlyweds should go home. As soon as Amit and Ayesha had rounded the corner out of sight Eve started, 'I just wanted to apologise about earlier. I would never have made fun of you, or Kate, had I known she'd, you know, died.'

'It's ok, I know you didn't know. I did a really bad job of wording things when we had the drink on Sunday. It wasn't your fault that you took offence at what I was saying, you have every right to be angry when you don't actually know what happened.'

They stopped on the pavement to wait for a gap in the traffic to cross the road, Ben took Eve's elbow to guide her through the cars. 'And once you do know what happened, you have every right to be angry then too. But I don't want you to think that I ever dumped you for her, it wasn't like that at all. Like I said, it was—'

'Complicated,' Eve finished.

'Yes, have I said that before?'

'Once or twice.'

'The thing is, I got a letter from Kate's parents—'

'You said.'

With a lot more patience than many men would have shown in the circumstances Ben said, 'Yes, like I said, but they weren't asking me to come back because she wanted me back, she'd just found out that she had cancer, and she was asking for me to say goodbye. She meant a lot to me Eve, we'd known each other since we were born. I thought that I'd go back for a couple of weeks and that would be it. I wasn't expecting for all these old feelings to resurface and to feel this need to be with her when she died.' He paused. 'And I owe you an apology too, about the usher-threesome-thing. I should have known you wouldn't do that. But then again, what you do in your own time is really nothing to do with me.'

I wasn't expecting for all these old feelings to resurface and to feel this need to be with her when she died. What you do is nothing to do with me. Well, thought Eve, if I didn't know before how Ben felt about me, I've just been served it up on a platter with a massive flashing neon sign stuck in it.

***

A couple of days away from work, her *Venus* column, Tanya, her search for the elusive B and her constant misunderstandings with Ben was just what Eve desperately needed. She wanted some time out, and although she'd never plan Becca's hen do purely on her own needs, the idea of spending the weekend with four hundred randoms in a raucous basement nightclub doing the Macarena was as far from therapeutic as it was possible to be, so a quiet weekend away with her best friends sounded perfect.

'Wake up,' George, her soon to be brother-in-law, teased. 'We're never going to get all these luggage tags labelled if you keep drifting off to goodness knows where every two minutes.'

Eve shook her head. 'Sorry, I don't know what's wrong with me, I've just got a lot on my plate.'

'You should have said, Adam would have understood.'

'Adam? My brother? Your beloved? He'd have understood

that his sister has priorities that are not his forthcoming wedding that is set to rival a royal one?'

'You're right. My mistake. As you were.'

The two of them were sat opposite each other at George and Adam's eye-wateringly expensive transparent Perspex dining table using their neatest handwriting to label every guest's name onto a luggage tag, which would be sent to them tomorrow. It was Stage Two in getting everyone excited about their destination wedding. Eve thought it was very disconcerting to be able to see her legs through the table, so kept moving the paper directly over where her bare skin was. It was one of the hottest days of the year so far, so she was wearing shorts, which were even shorter than she remembered them being last year. Maybe it was her old age making her more self-conscious, but she was quite glad that her catty brother wasn't there to pass judgment. At his request she'd hooked him up with Juan for a few last-minute attempts to tone up pre-wedding, so he was at his first training session. 'He's a hot Argentinian, but he's straight, I promise,' Eve had said to a nonplussed George, who was so secure in his relationship with Adam that even if Juan turned out to be the founder of Grindr he'd have waved Adam off just as cheerily as he did that lunchtime.

'So, anything you want to talk about?' George said, studiously looping a name, then holding the card up and flapping it dry.

'Not really, just stuff.'

'Men stuff?'

'Sort of. Do you remember Ben? The guy that dumped me just before we were meant to go to New York together?'

'Yes, handsome fella.'

'If you say so. Anyway, I didn't realise how much of a grudge I held against Ben, until I saw him again a month or so ago at a wedding. And I've run into him a few times since that too and each time managed to come out of each meeting looking like a prize idiot.'

'I'm sure you're being hard on yourself.'

'George. I saw him last night and said in a stupid baby voice something like, "ooo, did ickle Ben get his heart broken," and he told me that he left me because he found out that his ex-girlfriend was dying from cancer.'

'Oh.'

'Yes, oh. So anyway, that's making me feel pretty rubbish about myself, and then I've gone on a wild goose chase trying to find a B to marry.'

'Oh yes, the Desperately Seeking B saga. How's that going?'

'It's not. I met that one American army guy I told you about, then I tried to date a vegan pogo-stick marathon jumper, who turned me down, can you believe it?'

'What an arse.'

'I know. Then I almost had a threesome with a Bobby and his mate whose middle name was Bartholomew. And this week I've had a date with a bloke called Bryn,'

'All very sexy names.'

'I'm ignoring you. But anyway, turns out there's no happy ever after with Bryn because he was incredibly dull.'

'Arses, all of them.'

'And I massively fell out with my friend Tanya last weekend.'

'The one that was making you jumps through hoops of fire in the lead up to her wedding?'

'The very same.'

'Well she's an arse too.'

'I know. Arsey McArseface. And I've got some work stuff going on that's making me question my integrity—'

'Eve, you have the strongest moral principles of anyone I've ever met.'

'I used to. Now, I'm not so sure. So basically, I've screwed up. Quite a lot.'

George pointed at her pen that was hovering in mid air. 'Keep writing the labels while you talk, they're not going to write themselves.'

'Sir, yes sir. So anyway, I need a break from it all, so after I finish here I'm going to go on the internet for a few hours and book Becca's hen weekend away somewhere, and it's just going to be me, Ayesha and Becca, completely cut off from the ridiculousness that has become my life.'

'Ooh, where are you going to go?' George said, flapping a card in each hand.

'Don't know, I was thinking somewhere quiet, in the country, nothing flash – just a lovely hotel in a gorgeous town, lots of cheap wine and lovely food, but we're all on a tight budget, so probably a little place close to home.'

'O-M-G. I have just had *the* best idea.' George had put down the cards, and now his hands were flapping with nothing in them. 'You know the hilltop village in France we're getting married in?'

'The one with the address I've just written out thirty-five times on these luggage tags?'

'Yes that one. Well, we had really wanted to visit there before the wedding to taste the wines at the vineyard and do a food run-through with the caterers, but work is crazy busy at the moment, and because I'm taking three weeks off for the wedding and the honeymoon I can't take any more days off. So we were just going to blindly pick the food and drink, cross our fingers and hope for the best, but you could do the trip for us! It would be my shout as you'd be doing us a huge favour and it would be such a relief knowing that someone we trust has actually gone there and chosen it in person.'

Eve thought that now would be the wrong time to mention her penchant for cheap-as-chips paint-stripper wines, so instead she launched herself across the table into her soon to be brother-in-law's lap scattering the neat pile of drying luggage labels all over the floor.

George smiled, returned her hug, patted her back and said, 'You're an arse too.'

Chapter 25

The minutes were ticking by on the tiny clock in the corner of Eve's computer screen, taunting her every time another five, ten, fifteen minutes went by. She'd never suffered from writer's block before, smugly assuming it to be a fictional affliction before it happened to her. She had two deadlines hovering menacingly over her. She had to submit the next column for *Venus* in just under an hour, and she had three blank pages in the magazine that had the sub editors breaking into cold sweats, and Eve's fingers were literally frozen. For the magazine feature Eve didn't feel remotely romantic; love was over-rated, elusive and like the Monkees song, she thought love was meant for someone else and not for her. Writing about how glorious it was to be in love made her feel like a fraud. And for the *Venus* article Eve was so anxious about accidentally offending one of her friends, or writing something that could be linked to Tanya, or even herself, that she couldn't think of a single thing to say. Pointing out what she thought was the comedy in situations had spectacularly backfired and had been interpreted instead as something driven by spitefulness and malice. How could she now regain the lighthearted humour her earlier columns had, without making any reference to anything that had happened in real life? She suddenly knew what she had to do to make things right.

The more outlandish the wedding, the more likely it is to stick in our minds, and creating memories is the name of the game when it comes to tying the knot. So what if Great-Aunt Edna frowns at your cactus centrepieces and your Union Jack bustle is the talk of Table Three; quirky is the new classic. Re-reading last week's column, it hit me that my appreciation for the ingenious, and my respect for the innovative may have been mistaken for derision, but this is grossly untrue. Creative touches of jaw-dropping brilliance will never be a bad thing, and a personality-less event would be worthy of nothing but yawns. Sequinned cowboy boots instead of white kitten heels? Bring it on. A song that actually means something to you as you take your first steps towards your new spouse? Absobloodylutely. Forget the naysayers, the critics and the downright curmudgeonly, they'll be the ones with boring old bagpipes as their first dance not Monty Python's Always Look on the Bright Side of Life.

Do you really want to walk down the aisle of a hotel's function room on the same swirly carpet that 150 delegates from the local gas board just had their conference on? Not likely. So why not have a two-foot wide strip of green AstroTurf running up to the top to fit your country theme? A red carpet, Turkish rugs, heck, why not tile the whole thing like a chocolate river and have twenty-five bridesmaids dressed as oompa-loompas following you, orange faces and green wigs and everything?

Life is too short to do what is expected of you. And weddings are filled with traditions, customs and conventions of how things should be done, but maybe it's time for that rulebook to be torn up, shredded and burnt on a sacrificial pyre made up of bridal garters, sugared almonds and buttonholes.

This is your day. Make it yours, not a Pinterest board of someone else's.

'Eve, can I have a word?' Gemma, the chief sub editor was casting a shadow over Eve's desk. Eve quickly minimised her document so her screen displayed the work of her day job.

'Sure. But I know what you're going to say, I'm late on the copy, and I know, it's on its way I promise.'

'It's just that we can't leave tonight until it's done, and the design team will take a good couple of hours to lay it out – I'm presuming you've got images already?'

'Er ... of course I do.'

'At least that's one thing, but after they're done with it, we'll need at least two hours to check it, and peer-sub, which means that already we're going to have to stay late.'

'I'm so sorry, it's literally minutes away, honestly, grab a coffee and a biscuit and by the time you've finished them it'll be with you.'

She was so convincing that Eve herself almost believed that she had already written it and it was ready to be sent over to the subs desk. In reality, she hadn't got a bastarding clue what she was going to write about and she could see through the glass doors to the canteen that Gemma and her team were already gathered around the boiling kettle.

It was a shame that she couldn't tone down the *Venus* piece and run that in both, but that would well and truly blow her cover. Eve had a sudden flash of inspiration. Becca had asked her to help create a moodboard for her wedding, a sort of checklist of different ideas she could implement to transform a one-acre field into a beautiful village fete wedding. She'd already started brainstorming it, it wouldn't be too tricky to turn it into a feature. Eve fired off an email to Rosie on the picture desk, begging her to drop whatever else they were doing and try and source as many pretty images as possible. *Think fairy lights strung through trees, bunting, close ups of wild flower bouquets and lavender in jam jars, barrels used as bar tables, lawn games like jenga, bridesmaids wearing wellies, dried rose petal confetti in colourful paper cones, large glass jars of pick n mix and pink and white striped candy bags, a stage lit with fairy lights with musicians in checked shirts playing guitars and ukuleles, a white marquee tent, but not a posh one, one that's open on all sides, decorated with bunting. Sorry for the long list, but as much of this as poss would be fab. And can I have it in about 20 mins? Eek. I know. I'll owe you big time. And if Gemma asks, you sourced these images for me last week, not 18 hours before we go to print. Big love Ex*

Again, it wasn't a piece of journalism she'd ever win prizes for, but it was fun and would look good on a page and totally killed two birds with one stone as she had lots of words and pictures to impress Becca with.

Keeping busy was at least stopping Eve from driving herself mad with unanswered questions after her drink with Ben. One side of Eve's brain was saying to her, *Text Ben, you know you want to.* The other side was completely against this idea. So far the reluctant side was winning. There were so many questions that Eve wanted to ask. When did Kate die? Had they got back together before she did? It was very noble of him to race back for a final moment with Kate, but then, why stay there for four more years? Clear the air, say your goodbyes, fly to New York and start the life he'd planned to share with Eve. What had stopped him? Eve knew that she wasn't going to find out any of the answers if she never got in touch with him, and yet she didn't know if she wanted to hear his story either.

Walking into work that morning, Eve had been pleased to see Clive back at work after his surgery. They'd given him a chair inside the office's front door, so he was taking it a bit easier. He'd signalled for Eve to stand to one side when she arrived, and led her slightly away from other ears.

'I want to thank you so much Eve,' he started. 'I don't know why you said what you said to me that day, but you're the reason I went to the doc, and got myself sorted out. They said if I'd have left it another six months I might not have been so lucky. It's like you had a sixth sense my love. My wife thinks it's well spooky.'

Eve smiled and patted Clive's arm. 'I'm so glad you're up and about, you need to take it easy though, make sure you rest a lot.'

'Will do. My wife, Cath, she'll make sure of it.

Eve hesitated. She was about to go and then said, 'I hope you don't mind me asking Clive, but how long have you and Cath been together now?'

Clive puffed out his chest like a proud pigeon. 'Thirty-two years.'

'And how did you meet?'

'I was nineteen, she was a year older, and she always took the same bus as me in the mornings. At first we ignored each other, then smiled at each other, then we started talking, and one day I plucked up the courage to ask her to the flicks and six months later we were married. Four kids we have. Not a cross word.'

Writing about marriage and relationships had increasingly made Eve feel that fate threw people together for a reason. What if Clive had taken a later bus every day, would he have married someone else? Would he have been as happy? How could it be so easy, and yet so difficult to meet someone you want to share your life with?

As she tore herself away from daydreaming about Clive and his wife and back to the present, she saw there was an email waiting in her private Gmail account from Belinda at *Venus*. She'd received Eve's latest column and was 'disappointingly underwhelmed'. As Eve read on, her heart began to sink. Belinda's accusation of Eve using her latest column to apologise for her previous one was unfortunately spot on. 'You have basically contradicted everything you said in last week's opinion piece, and completely backtracked,' Belinda wrote. 'I don't understand why you had such a change of heart in just one week, and it's very confusing for the readers. This latest article wouldn't be out of place in *My Wonderful Wedding* and that's not the point of *Venus*. We're spiky, sassy and honest. We say the things that others feel but don't voice, and you were absolutely on the right track before this latest column. I really hope that this was a one-off Eve, and that you can find that funny frankness inside you again as I do want to retain you as a writer. You mentioned in our first conversation that you have a country festival type wedding coming up and a gay wedding, these are absolutely perfect breeding grounds for comedic observations, so focus on those for your next articles, and don't hold back.'

Don't hold back on making fun of your best friend and your brother, Eve thought. Well, that wasn't an option, but then, losing the *Venus* job wasn't either. Eve was barely making ends meet before it came along, and it had given her a financial lifeline she desperately needed. She had thought she'd been quite clever at disguising Ayesha's wedding in her previous column, but evidently not, so if she was going to do the same for Becca's and Adam's she'd have to be a lot smarter about it.

Chapter 26

'Which one did we say we liked again?' Ayesha slurred, reaching across Becca to taste test a punchy sauvignon. The bowls that they'd each been given to spit out the wine they'd been sampling for the last two hours into were still clean and dry, and the three friends were well on their way to being skunk drunk.

'I do not like this one,' Eve announced, taking another big sip. 'Oh, hang on,' she furrowed her brow. 'Actually, I do, that's lovely.'

'Let me try that one,' Becca said, grabbing the glass from Eve. 'No, it's got undercurrents of lemon.'

'Hahaha, you sound such a ponce!' Ayesha laughed. 'Next you'll be talking about bouquets and noses.'

They laughed, Eve clutching onto Ayesha for support as she wobbled on the bar stool. The French vineyard owner looked on with good-natured bemusement. They weren't the first group of English visitors to turn a wine tasting into a piss-up, and at least these three women were young and attractive, not the senior citizen coach trips or stag dos he'd had to host in the past.

'Mademoiselle,' he said, approaching the table and directing his question to Eve as she seemed to be the one in charge. 'I assume you will be tasting the rose, vin rouge and the champagne as well?'

'Oh my God,' Eve burst out. 'I forgot about the other colours! I hate red wine, so these two will do those, you can load me up with the pink and bubbles though.'

As he walked away, shaking his head smiling, Becca said, 'He seems nice. No wedding ring either.'

'Stop it,' Eve said. 'Just stop it. I'm not in any hurry to go on another date, with anyone.'

'Unless it's with Ben.' Ayesha hiccupped and ignored Becca shushing her. 'Why do you think we invited him along to the dinner last week?'

'What do you mean?' Eve asked. 'He was Amit's best man, so I just assumed that that's why he came.'

'A bit, but mainly because when we were on honeymoon we kept saying how you two should get back together. Amit told me he'd set you up with Bryn, but then we both said that Ben's a much better match for you.'

Eve rolled her eyes. 'It's a bit late for that, too much has gone on.'

'Has he told you then?' Ayesha said.

'About Kate?' Eve said, knowing that her response was vague enough to hopefully prompt Ayesha into divulging more information that Eve didn't yet have.

'It was so tragic, finding each other again just as she was dying, and the sacrifice he made afterwards, staying there for the good of the family, it was just heartbreaking. I'm sorry

Eve, I know it must be hard to see him all the time now,'
Ayesha said, reaching across the table to put her hand over
Eve's. 'But he's been through a lot and doesn't have any other
friends in London, we're all he has.'

'I wouldn't call myself a friend of his,' Eve replied, a little
sadly.

'I think he would.' Ayesha stuck her bottom lip out. 'I'm
sorry, I shouldn't have mentioned him. I've ruined the mood.'

Eve shook her head. 'Not at all, don't be silly, it's not as
though I'm still in love with him or anything. It's fine.'

'His name does begin with B though,' Becca pointed out,
and Ayesha solemnly nodded.

'Oh my God, stop it, both of you! Enough of the B-talk. It
was the ludicrous announcement of a senile pensioner, it is
not a real thing. I'm banning any more blind dates or set ups,
or even mention of any name beginning with B. Done. Finito.'

Just then the French sommelier approached the table
pushing a small bar trolley with half a dozen bottles of red
wine and champagne on it. 'Mademoiselles, here is the vin
rouge and the champagne. Might I make a suggestion that
you don't swallow these ones?' he said with a smile.

'I'm sorry, are we being really loud and unruly?'

'Unruly?' the vineyard owner looked confused at the unfamiliar word.

'Unruly, it means out of control,' Eve explained. 'Disruptive,
rowdy.'

The young man laughed displaying a perfect set of pearly
whites. 'Not at all, you are very fun, it is a pleasure for me to
have you here. You are much nicer than most of the people

that come here, it is amazing how many people think themselves to be connoisseurs. Can I explain a bit about the grape varieties of these wines before you taste them?' he said.

'Of course, why don't you take a seat and join us? No one else is here at the moment,' Eve replied. 'Sorry, what's your name?'

'Bruno.' He was a little confused as to why his name resulted in howls of laughter from these strange English women.

Chapter 27

Ayesha was drunk, Becca felt ill, and Eve was wide awake and surprisingly sober. So when Bruno asked her if she wanted to go out for dinner with him when the other two started talking about heading back to the hotel, Eve could see no reason to say no. It had absolutely nothing to do with his name, so she kept telling herself, and a lot to do with the fact that he was very charming, rather persistent and her two friends had bullied her into it. Eve watched Ayesha and Becca link arms to weave back down the cobbled street to their small family run hotel, throwing Eve knowing smiles and winks over their shoulders. Eve stood outside the darkened, locked-up vineyard shop and for a split second wished she was going back with them.

'My cousin runs a little bistro a few minutes' walk away, we could go there?' Bruno suggested, holding his arm out for Eve to take. She hadn't really paid him much attention before he'd asked her out, but he was very easy on the eye, with dark hair perfectly styled, his shirt crisply ironed with a crease down both sleeves, a cashmere jumper casually resting on both shoulders. He was smooth, continental, and his accent was incredibly sexy.

'Your English is very good,' Eve said. 'Much better than my French.' Although that wasn't saying much.

'Thank you, I worked in London at a top hotel for three years after leaving university, so I, how you say, picked it up, then.'

As they walked through the small medieval town, everyone they passed raised their hand to greet Bruno, either silently or with a friendly exchange of pleasantries.

'You seem to know everyone.'

'My family have lived here for five generations,' he explained. 'Most people here have history going back hundreds of years. You see that woman there—' he pointed to an attractive brunette woman wearing a little white apron over a miniskirt serving a table of old men their aperitifs outside a bar '—her great-grandfather was mine too. And that lady there—' he gestured to an elderly grumpy-looking woman sitting on a bench holding a small white terrier on her lap '—had a big argument with my grandmother when they were at school together and to this day has never said hello to me or my sister.'

'It's like a soap opera,' Eve said laughing.

'A what?'

'You know, a television drama.'

Bruno laughed along with her. 'Yes, it is exactly that. And soon the whole town will be talking about Bruno Dupont being seen with a beautiful red-haired woman that nobody knows.'

Batting away the compliment he'd casually thrown her way, Eve replied, 'I can't imagine I'm the first strange woman that you've been seen with.'

'Like I said, it is quite unusual for my customers to be so attractive. I don't really like taking fat old men on coach trips for dinner.'

Eve laughed. It was refreshing to be in the company of someone so disarmingly charming, and for the evening at least, she was going to enjoy it. She knew no one in this small hilltop Provencal town and had nothing to lose.

'Here we are.' They had stopped outside a small restaurant with colourful floral baskets overhanging the doorway. Through the window Eve could see the small interior was glowing with candlelight. Bruno held open the door for Eve to walk through first and followed her in, greeting the staff with enthusiastic handshakes and double kisses. He'd obviously phoned ahead when Eve wasn't aware of it as they were immediately shown to a prime table for two in the window, its reserved sign discreetly removed. Bruno pulled out Eve's chair for her, making Eve remember a time when Ben had done that in the university canteen and she'd fallen on her bottom. This time though, the act was chivalrous, not mischievous.

'White wine?' Bruno asked. 'Are you sure you would not like to try an excellent red? Perhaps you've just never tasted the best reds before, which is why you think you don't like them?'

Despite having a day of drinking little else, Eve still found herself saying, 'I'll stick with white, and I think I'll let you choose it if you don't mind, even though I am now an expert of course.'

'Of course,' Bruno smiled as he read down the wine list

before ordering in spine-tinglingly seductive French. Eve had scraped a C in GCSE French and while she couldn't quite remember how to reserve a bedroom in a hotel or say that her tyre needed changing, both of which she clearly remembered writing out countless times on little white index cards, she was pretty sure that Bruno had also said the words for prawns and duck while he was ordering the wine.

'Are you too cold, Eve?' he said her name like it was made of syrup.

'I'm fine, it's warm out. What a lovely place.'

They both looked around at their surroundings then, Eve for the first time and Bruno seeing the familiar setting through Eve's eyes. 'My uncle runs it as a creperie during the day, and my cousin as a bistro in the evenings. It has a cellar where my great-grandfather hid many of the town's families during the occupation.'

Not for the first time Eve was in awe at how so many of France's historical villages and towns had such sad histories attached to them, yet seemed places of purity and beauty just a few decades on.

Their wine arrived, and Bruno underwent the formal protocol of label checking, swilling around the bottom of the glass and tasting, before he shared it out between their two glasses. 'So, tell me what brought you and your friends here today,' Bruno asked. 'I was expecting two men, and then got a lovely surprise.'

'It's my brother's wedding to his boyfriend at the end of August, up at the chateau, and they were planning on coming out here to sample the food and wine choices, but couldn't get away, so I stepped in with my friends. The short brown-haired one is getting married in a couple of weeks and so it's sort of a hen weekend for her.'

If Eve noticed Bruno's blink-and-you-miss-it eyebrow-raise of surprise at the mention of a gay wedding she didn't mention it.

'And you? You are not married? At least, I hope you are not, he might be angry with me, if you are.'

'God no. I'll leave that to my friends and family.'

'You do not want to get married?'

On all the dates Eve had been on, though admittedly none of them had been with French men before, not one had started off talking about Eve's thoughts on marriage. Bruno didn't even know her surname, her hometown, her hobbies or political persuasion, but he was asking about her marital intentions.

'I'm not against marriage per se, I think it can be lovely for some people, not so much for others.' Her mum and dad flitted into her mind, Tanya and Luke, but then so did Becca and Jack, Ayesha and Amit.

'I will get married in the next two years,' Bruno announced with a certainty most people reserve for meal choices. *I will be having a roast dinner on Sunday. I will be ordering chips with my burger.* Speaking of which, Eve thought, why hadn't they been given menus or placed their orders yet? She wasn't particularly hungry, but after the mountain of bread and cheese they'd been given with the wine, she wouldn't say no to a nice salad.

'Do you have a lucky lady in mind?' Eve said, visibly wincing

261

at how overt and flirty that sounded when it was meant to be just a question.

'It depends how tonight goes,' Bruno replied, very much being intentionally overt and flirty.

The candlelight was casting shadows over his face in exactly the right places to highlight his cheekbones, his dark long eyelashes, his smooth tanned neck – there would be many worse sights to wake up to every morning for the rest of her life. Eve hoped the flickering flame was having the same effect on her own looks.

'Do you believe in God, Eve?'

Crikey, Eve thought, he was pulling out all the big gun questions early on. 'Um,' she stammered. 'I don't disbelieve. Is that the same thing? I mean, I don't go to church or anything, except for the huge amounts of weddings I seem to go to, but I think it would be a bit sad if this is all there is in life.'

'This? Aren't you having a good time?' Bruno smiled, poking fun at her flustered embarrassment.

'I didn't mean this, as in this,' Eve made a sweeping gesture with her arms, almost knocking over the waitress who was approaching behind her with a big bowl of pink king prawns in her hands. 'I meant this life, earth, you know, *this*.'

'I know what you mean, I am just teasing you. I hope you like prawns.'

Thankfully she did, but it irritated her fleetingly that he didn't check with her before ordering them. On the plus side, at least her recollection of GCSE French food was up to par.

'What would you have done if I didn't?'

'Excuse me?'

'If I didn't like prawns, or had an allergy to them?'

'I'm sorry,' Bruno shrugged, his turn to look a bit embarrassed. 'Most women like it if the men take charge.'

'I'm not sure that's the case any more,' Eve said. 'But I am teasing you a little bit. But next time, I think I'd like to choose my own food.'

'Next time?'

'Yes,' Eve said decisively, locking smiling eyes with Bruno. 'Next time.'

Before Eve had broken even one tail off the end of a langoustine, Bruno had motioned for the waitress to come back with a menu, which he handed immediately to Eve. 'I ordered us both the duck salad, but you might want something else.'

Annoyingly, after a cursory scan of the main courses the duck salad was the dish that Eve would have chosen herself given the option. Which left her in a bit of a quandary, order something else just to prove her now heavily laboured point, or go with his suggestion, which diluted her feminist stance somewhat. A date was no place for politics, thought Eve, handing the menu back to the hovering waitress with a smile. 'The duck sounds lovely, thank you.'

'So,' Eve continued. 'God.'

'You can call me Bruno.'

She'd heard that the French sense of humour was questionable but Bruno clearly was the exception. Eve now added funny to his growing list of glowing attributes.

'So, like the Monkees say, are you a believer?'

'Monkeys?'

A sense of humour he may have, a knowledge of bizarrely-named Sixties bands maybe not. 'Doesn't matter. So, *you* asked the question, God, oui or non?'

'Oui. There has to be a purpose for everything. Everything learned, every person in our lives, every sadness, every happiness, every achievement, it is all for a reason. It has to be. There are too many coincidences in life, too many crossed paths for it to mean nothing.'

Eve chewed thoughtfully, that was what she thought too, or at least used to think; now she didn't really know. One thing was for sure, she much preferred Bruno's chat to Blake's or Bryn's.

'Like you being here instead of your brother. That did not happen by chance.'

'Maybe not.'

'How are your prawns?'

'Annoyingly delicious.' Eve and Bruno shared a smile. They both reached for the bottle of wine at the same time to top up their glasses and their fingertips brushed each other's. It was like an electric shock that made them both recoil and lock eyes. It was *him*. He was the B.

Chapter 28

The bistro had shut to the public an hour ago, but still Eve and Bruno sat in their cosy window table, large amber brandies in front of both of them. Bruno's uncle and two male cousins had joined them from the kitchen, all still wearing their distinctive chef's checkered trousers. Eve was getting a lesson in French male chivalry firsthand, and she'd never felt so beautiful or interesting. Bruno was the designated translator, so whatever he was saying she had said was eliciting loud guffaws and very obvious adulation.

They'd already ascertained that yes, she was a natural redhead, and yes, that was a little unusual, particularly when teamed with bright green eyes; no, she wasn't married, yes she did want to be, maybe; she *was* a little concerned at the rise of the National Front in both their countries; yes, Bruno was indeed a lovely man. If she hadn't started making noises about the lateness of the night, Eve knew that they would have also got out of her her thoughts on climate change, gender selection and the long-lasting appeal of Edith Piaf.

'I'll walk you back to your hotel.' Bruno said, rising from his seat, before going round the table to pull Eve's chair gently out too. A flurry of kisses and promises to return to say hello when she came back for Adam's wedding followed, and then Eve found herself and Bruno on the deserted street, empty except for a few teenagers sitting on the bench where the cantankerous old woman had been a few hours before.

Bruno manoeuvered her to the inside of the pavement, so he walked on the outside, closest to the road. He then took her hand, threading her fingers through his, and they fitted perfectly, as Eve knew they would.

'I've had a lovely evening,' Eve began. 'Thank you for asking me.'

'Thank you for saying yes.'

'I don't usually go out for dinner with complete strangers.' It wasn't strictly true, she'd been out the previous week with a man she'd never met before too, but Bruno didn't need to know that. And actually, if it was a question of semantics, Eve thought, justifying her fib to herself, she only went for a walk with Bryn, so no dinner was had by anyone.

'I am very pleased to hear that. I hope that remains the case.'

And you? Eve wanted to ask. *Are you in the habit of finishing off a wine tasting session with a romantic dinner a deux?* But she never got the chance to ask. They'd stopped in front of her hotel. An unassuming double fronted townhouse, the only indication that it wasn't a private house was a discreet plaque by the front door with three little stars on it.

'We're here.' Bruno announced, bringing their joined hands up to his lips and kissing hers. As he brought their hands down, still locked together, his dark brown eyes stayed firmly on hers. His intention was clear, and whether it was the combination of wine, brandy, being in France, being heart-broken, being lust-struck and being lonely ... well, she didn't know what it was, but she found her mouth moving slowly towards his.

His lips were soft, and his tongue gentle as it circled hers, and his other hand reached around her back and pulled her into him more. Very few dates of Eve's had got to this stage since Ben, and she had forgotten the rush of adrenaline a kiss like this gave you.

'Monsieur Dupont,' came a disapproving female voice from the porch behind them. 'I was just locking up and wondering about the location of my guest.'

'Madame Villeneueve, I apologise.' Bruno then swiftly swapped to French to say the next few sentences, the rapid-ness of his delivery making it impossible for Eve to follow. Whatever he said made the formidable landlady disappear back inside, saying 'deux minutes' as she left.

'Where were we?' he murmured, locking his hands behind Eve's back.

'What did you say to her? It's rude to speak a language not everyone involved in the conversation understands.'

'The way you get angry with me is funny.'

'It's not meant to be funny.'

'I like it. You are fiery. Is that the right word? You have fire inside you. It is, sweet.'

He didn't mean sweet, Eve thought. He meant enchanting. Captivating even. She couldn't expect him to understand the nuances of the English language, but regardless he was still

267

streets ahead of her in the language department. She was still chuffed that she remembered that canard meant duck.

'I should go,' she said.

'Can I see you tomorrow?'

'We leave in the afternoon,' Eve said. 'And we have lunch at the caterers, but I am free before that if you are?' She felt a pang of guilt at planning to spend the last morning of the friend-bonding mini break with a man, but also knew that Becca would be squealing with excitement for her.

'Bon. I will come and meet you for a coffee in the morning, around eleven? Good night, Eve.'

'Good night, Bruno.'

Eve took the front steps two at a time, and even the reproachful look and cluck of condemnation the stern hotel owner gave her as she breezed past her in the hallway couldn't change the width or brightness of Eve's smile. First kisses were awesome. Much more so than last kisses because you rarely knew when a kiss was to be the last. First kisses were filled with expectation, newness, novelty. They had none of the weight of experience and history, they held nothing but potential and promise. And Bruno's kiss had both in spades.

The corridor was quiet. She, Ayesha and Becca all had adjacent rooms in the eaves of the tall house, and Eve was desperate to shake them both awake for a post-date workshop like they used to do at university. She paused, pressing her ear to each of their locked doors, confirming that her friends were sleeping and would probably be unreceptive to Eve bouncing on their beds. She'd have to settle for bouncing on her own bed. By herself. Had the landlady cum headmistress not been lurking downstairs, Eve may well have acted entirely out of character and smuggled Bruno in, and as she thought about it, Eve didn't know if she was disappointed she hadn't.

She'd even had a leg and bikini wax a few days before coming away to France, so her body was prepared though she had no idea if her mind was. She didn't have a bad body, Eve knew that. She was long and lean and thanks to Juan's bossiness had turned at least half her wobbles to muscle, so it wasn't prudishness that had stopped her stripping off and throwing her bra round her head like a lasso. She'd just rarely met anyone that made her feel inclined to do that. Not since Ben. But tonight, tonight she really had.

***

'I think I love him,' Eve confided, leaning in over her croissant. 'Well ok, not love, not yet, but I really like him.' Eve broke the end off her pastry, smothered it in jam and popped it in her mouth.

Completely true to expectation, this declaration prompted girlish screams and much bottom-hopping on the dining room chairs from her two breakfast companions who were sat facing her. 'Eve's got a boyfriend, Eve's got a boyfriend,' Ayesha sang.

'So will you be needing a plus one for my wedding now?' Becca asked with a wink.

'Don't be daft.'

'Why not? It's perfect! Ask him, it's a cheap flight away, and it's not as though I'm being strict with numbers is it?'

'I wish you were being, but that's a different story.'

'Think of it for a second Eve, your first time doing it with him could be under canvas.'

'I am not sleeping with Bruno in a tent.'

'Oh, it's so romantic,' Ayesha said, with one hand on her heart. 'Weddings bring out the best in people.'

'Except brides.' Eve said sarcastically, before adding, 'present company very much excepted.'

'I have sex camping all the time,' Becca said. 'As long as you're quiet, and don't have any interior lights on in the tent, it's actually really fun.'

'I'm not sure Bruno's the camping type,' Eve admitted. 'His shoes were patent leather.'

'My favourite shoes from childhood were black patent leather,' Ayesha said.

'The difference is, he's a heterosexual male in his thirties,' Becca replied.

'He's French,' Eve retorted a little more haughtily than she'd planned to. 'That means that ordinary clothing rules don't apply to him.'

'What about ordinary dating rules?' Becca said, nodding over Eve's shoulder making her turn around. Bruno was an hour and a half early for their coffee date. Eve offered up a silent prayer of thanks to the gods that she'd decided to get properly dressed and brush her hair before coming down to breakfast – she'd been so close to coming down in her zebra print pyjama bottoms and a sweatshirt.

'Hey Bruno,' she greeted him with a much more nonchalant tone than she was feeling.

'Bonjour Eve, ladies,' he replied. 'I hope you don't mind me interrupting your breakfast, but we have a late booking for a wine tasting session at eleven. I did not want to miss my chance to see you this morning, and I realised that I do not have your number.'

He didn't want to miss his chance. 'It's no problem, will you join us?' Eve said, motioning to the empty seat beside her.

'As long as you're sure it's ok?' He gestured for the young waitress to bring him a small coffee.

Becca and Ayesha said 'of course' in tandem and then proceeded to kick Eve under the table.

'Eve was just telling us what a great evening you had last night,' Ayesha said, fluttering her eyelashes. If Eve didn't know better, she'd say that she wasn't the only one to be charmed by the wiles of the handsome Frenchman.

'And I said to Eve that she should ask you to be her date for my wedding in a couple of weeks,' Becca said, choosing to ignore the wide-eyed look of horror Eve had on her face. 'It's on August 6th. In Devon. In England. You'd have to sleep in a tent though. Is that ok? Do you like camping?'

Now it was Bruno's turn to look horrified, which he deftly changed to a blasé expression. 'A tent?'

'Yes,' Becca replied. 'Is that ok?'

'You don't have to say yes, think about it,' Eve said.

'If Eve would like me there with her, then I think it sounds fun.'

Eve wondered why he was talking about her in the third

271

person when their shoulders were touching, but then again, maybe it was a language thing. She'd have to learn to be more forgiving on the grammatical front if they had any chance of a future. She suddenly realised that three pairs of eyes were looking directly at her.

'Oh, yes, of course, Eve, that is, I, would love you there. With me. In a tent.'

'Well, that's settled then. You'd better give me your number now so that I can get all the details from you.'

Eve tapped her number into his outstretched phone, and handed it back to him. He promptly called her so she had his number too. There didn't seem to be any dating etiquette dodging where Bruno was concerned, none of this 'he has my number, but I don't have his,' or 'you have to wait three days between dates'. The fact that this time yesterday Eve hadn't even met him and Bruno was somehow now her plus one to her best friend's wedding defied all dating logic.

An hour later when the least hospitable innkeeper in the history of innkeepers had made it quite clear that breakfast was over, the four of them reluctantly left the dining room. Ayesha and Becca said they needed to pack, and bid a hasty retreat leaving Eve and Bruno standing awkwardly in the hallway of the hotel.

'You are just as beautiful in the daylight,' Bruno said.

'Hardly,' Eve blushed.

'You are like a pre-Raphaelite painting, with your white skin and long orange hair.'

'Auburn,' Eve immediately wished she hadn't been so pedantic.

'I am very happy you invited me to your friend's wedding.'
I didn't. Eve thought, but then realised that once again, semantics didn't matter. Without Becca's heavy-handed nudging, Bruno definitely wouldn't be coming to Devon and sharing a hay bale with her, let alone a sleeping bag. Becca had merely fast-tracked what Eve wanted. As he leaned in to kiss her again, Eve closed her eyes and gave an involuntary shiver of excitement at the thought that the next time they did this, they might be naked in the middle of a field.

Chapter 29

Most people would admit to having 'a type'. Some of the celebrities Eve used to write about would move from one cookie-cutter model to the next, with only their names being different: same height, same build, same hair style, same faraway expression. Eve never thought that she prescribed to that, and had never favoured one attribute over another when it came to men. If you'd caught her in a moment of honesty, she'd admit that Ben's abrupt departure in her life had stopped her seeing other men that way, not really paying attention to what strangers looked like, or if she liked how they looked. But if she ever allowed herself to picture her soul mate, a slip-on-shoe-wearing, charismatic Frenchman probably wasn't it. That wasn't to say that she wasn't open to widening the boundaries of what she found attractive, but Eve had assumed that a more casual and slightly dishevelled man might be the one. A joker that didn't take life, or themselves, too seriously.

Someone not unlike Ben.

Ben. Once upon a time, she and he had planned the family they would one day have. They even had names picked out: Rosie and Stella for girls, Harry and Oliver for boys. Knowing that he'd said all those things, instigated conversations about their future, Eve sadly realised that she'd wasted the last four years pining for a man that clearly wasn't worth it.

Eve's phone pinged, signalling a new message. She assumed it was from Adam or George. Eve had been waiting for them in the cafe they were supposed to be having lunch in for over half an hour, but they were running late.

It wasn't them though, it was Bruno.

I can't stop thinking about you.

Eve was unsure of the next step. Should she immediately tap back a similar message, wait a while and then write back echoing his sentiments, or ignore it, and play hard to get? A complete novice at relationships, Eve was at sea. Thankfully back-up arrived at that moment in the form of her brother and George. The pair were laden with distinctive yellow bags from Selfridges. Eve's irritation at them choosing shopping over her passed as soon as George reached into one of the bags and brought out a pair of oversize clip-on gold earrings shaped like feathers, just for her.

'We saw these and thought of you,' he explained. 'They'd look amazing with your hair down. And they look like quills.'

'Thanks guys, I love them.' Eve attached the new earrings on straightaway.

'So, how was France? Did you choose the wines and taste the food?'

'Yes, and yes. And I met a man.'

George started flapping while Adam yawned, pretending to play the disinterested younger brother while itching to show the same enthusiasm as his boyfriend.

'Tell us everything.'

'Well, the guy that runs the vineyard you sent me to—'

'Oh my God, you mean Bruno?' Adam suddenly said, sitting forward in his seat. 'He is gorgeous!'

George nodded. 'We met him when we found the chateau and they recommended we get the wines through him, and we were both like, "wow."'

'Yes, so we went for the tasting, and Ayesha and Becca got a bit pissed and went back to the hotel, and he took me out to dinner.'

'Squeal!' George chose to say the word rather than make the sound.

'And then we kissed.'

'And his name's Bruno. Which begins with a B!' Adam suddenly shouted, the penny dropping. 'You're going to have French children!'

'Steady on, it's just one kiss. Well, two, but then Becca invited him to come over for her wedding, and he said yes, and now I'm freaking out a bit.'

'Yay! So we'll meet him again then!'

Eve looked confused. 'You're going to Becca's wedding?'

'Yes, we've already got our outfits.'

Becca was a lost cause. It was totally possible literally thousands of people were packing their rucksacks ready to descend on a Devon field next weekend. Eve was secretly pleased Becca had invited Adam and George though, at least it meant she'd have friendly faces around her should it all get a bit too much.

'You know Mum's coming too?' Eve said.

276

'Yeah, we went tent shopping with her last weekend.'

'There's a sentence I never thought I'd hear my brother say,' Eve laughed.

'I'm looking forward to it. I mean, I wouldn't want to do it for more than one night at a time or anything, but now we've got all the kit, we might make it a regular thing.'

'We better bloody had do!' George spluttered. 'It cost more than a long weekend at Hotel du Vin to buy all the camping stuff, we're going to use it all the time.'

'I bet you've bought proper beds and everything,' Eve teased. 'No roll up foam mats for you two.'

Adam shuddered. 'Baby steps little sis, baby steps. Why people pay good money to pretend to be homeless is still baffling me.'

'But we went camping all the time when we were young, you liked it then.'

'That was before I got a taste of the good life.'

'I know what you mean though' Eve said. 'The whole point of holidays is to have a better life than your normal one isn't it?'

George and Adam exchanged a look.

'And how is *your* normal one?' George asked, in the same voice a therapist might use when catching up with a client.

The last time she saw George Eve recalled unloading all her angst on him, so his question was understandable, if not exactly welcome.

'It's fine. It's good. I kissed a man, and I liked it.'

'Not just any man either,' Adam reminded her. '*The* Man.'

'Perhaps.' Eve shrugged. 'So my love life is potentially

looking up, work is ok, and I just have Becca's wedding and yours left this summer, and wedding season is over.'

George reached for a biscuit and had his outstretched hand slapped by Adam. 'Saving the best for last, obviously.'

'Obviously.'

'Which reminds me, we need your help putting together the wedding newspaper,' Adam said, getting a big folder, note-book and a new pack of pens out of his bag. He handed a pen and notebook to Eve. 'For you. Ok, so we want a mini magazine to be handed to each guest when they check in. Nothing too long, only about ten, fifteen pages or so. It should have an itinerary of the weekend, a map of the local area, a guide to things people can do in their down-time, some inter-esting facts about the chateau and village, some essential French phrases, a bit about us and how we met, and also a Who's Who of everyone at the wedding.'

'O-kay. And where do I come in?' Eve asked.

'We thought you could help us put it together,' her brother said.

'Yes. But I don't work for the local tourist office.'

'But it's easy for you. It'd take us ages, we're not writers. You can just knock out something like this in an evening.'

The penny dropped. 'Hang on, you want me to put together a whole magazine for your wedding?'

George squirmed a little. 'It's more of a pamphlet really.'

'Fifteen pages is not a pamphlet George.'

'I honestly thought you'd want to help us Eve, especially since we just gave you and your friends an all-expenses paid trip to France, and hooked you up with the love of your life,'

Adam said, moving his chair slightly away from Eve to high-light how irritated he was with her. It was a tactic he'd perfected when they were young. By turning his back slightly to her and sticking his nose a few centimetres in the air Eve would normally have handed over the last piece of cake or coveted piece of Lego.

'This is more than an evening's work though, Adam. You must see that George?' Eve swivelled her attention to George, who could usually be relied upon to be slightly less demanding.

'It would be helping us out so much, Eve. We still have so much to do, and this is such an important thing that means so much to us, and we just couldn't do it justice like you could.'

'Say I do this—' Eve held her hand up to stop the prema-ture jubilation '—say I do this, who is going to lay it out and print it?'

Once again, the two grooms looked shifty.

'So let me get this straight, you want me to write it, design it and print it?'

George replied first. 'You work in magazines, you have all the knowledge.'

'And the contacts,' Adam added.

'And we'll give you lots of the information, you just need to make it better.'

'And wittier.'

'Oh ok, no pressure then. Better and wittier. Jeez guys, thanks for commandeering every minute of free time I have between now and your wedding,' Eve said sulkily.

279

'Those earrings really suit you.'

'Shut up Adam.'

***

'Ben's here.'

Becca's yell from the living room made Eve stop dead in the hallway. Eve could tell by Becca's airy shout that it was a warning more than an announcement of fact. Eve was wearing a bright purple pacamac raincoat that she'd hurriedly bought from the pound shop on her way home as the heavens opened. Her long wet hair was dripping onto the carpet and her mascara was no doubt running in two narrow rivers down her face. How did Ben even know where they lived? She stood frozen to the spot frantically wondering how to stop time so that she could change, dry her hair and redo her make up before going into the living room.

He suddenly appeared in the doorway to the lounge. 'Hey Red. Becca's address was on the bottom of the wedding invite as an RSVP, and I was in the area. It was pouring down so I thought I'd pop in, say hi and wait for the storm to pass. Nice mac.'

'Bugger off.'

'No, really, what would one call that colour? Puce? Magenta?'

'Crimson, I'd say,' Becca chimed in, joining Ben in the doorway.

Ben shook his head. 'It's more plum than crimson, although you could argue that it's got a touch of fuchsia.'

'It's purple.' Eve rolled her eyes. 'It's sodding purple. And yes, I know I look ridiculous but it's bloody pouring out there and it's all the pound shop had.'

'Pound shop? Well in that case, it's a steal.'

'You'll be pleased to know that the rain's easing off, so you can go now Ben,' Eve said haughtily.

'Becca's invited me to have a pie at the pub downstairs with you two, so you've got the pleasure of my company for a bit longer. I need to go by eight though.'

'I'm not hungry, so you guys go ahead. I need a bath anyway. Have fun without me.' And with that Eve turned her back on them both and stamped down the corridor to the bathroom and slammed the door noisily locking it. She was livid. How could Becca invite Ben into their flat for a start, and then ask him to join them for dinner? Eve stood there in silence for a few minutes staring at the grout between the tiles above the basin before moving to the bath and angrily turning on the taps so Ben and Becca could hear the running water. Eve realised that her towel was in her room, and didn't want to dilute the effect of her storming off by creeping out to retrieve it. She'd just have to wait until they went out before getting it.

Scowling at the purple monstrosity that was the cheap raincoat in a heap on the floor, Eve eased herself into the boiling water, wincing at its heat. She lay back in the bath with her eyes closed and forced her mind to go blank. Ben had no right to magically appear back in her life and disrupt it like this. No right at all. He'd made his decision back then and they both had to live with it. Turning up, making jokes, teasing her, pretending that everything was now fine was not cool. Not cool at all. Thank goodness Eve had Bruno now. Oh God, she'd forgotten to text him back after he messaged at lunchtime. Oh well, she'd do that as soon as she heard Ben and Becca leave the flat and could go and get her towel.

Right on cue Eve heard voices in the hallway and the front door slammed shut.

Clambering out of the scalding water, Eve looked down and saw that her body was bright red. She drip-dried on the bathmat as much as she could so that when she sprinted across the hallway to her bedroom she wouldn't get the carpet too wet. She opened the door to check that the coast was clear and once making sure that it was, Eve made a run for it.

Flinging open her bedroom door Eve inhaled sharply, Ben was in the middle of her bedroom and looked as shocked as she did seeing her standing stark naked in the doorway.

'Bath water a bit too hot?' he said finally with a smile.

One of Eve's hands flew to cover her breasts and the other one a bit lower. Her face, despite not getting wet, was as scarlet as the rest of her body. 'Oh my God Ben, what are you doing here?' She took her hand away from her chest to grab her dressing gown that was hanging on the back of the door, and quickly tied it tight around her middle.

'I was leaving you this letter,' he said, gesturing to an envelope with her name on that was propped up on her pillow. 'We keep getting interrupted as I'm trying to explain why I left so suddenly, and I wanted to tell you everything.'

'Ben, you don't need to,' Eve said, her embarrassment turning into blind rage at the sight of him in her private space. 'Can you get out of my room now?'

'Just read it,' he replied, moving towards the door. 'Then you'll understand.'

'I really don't think I will Ben, and anyway, I said I'm not interested. You said it yourself, you fell in love with her again after ditching me at the airport. End of story. Take it with you.'

'Eve, I—'

'Here.' Eve picked up the envelope from the bed and held it out to Ben. It was heavier than she had anticipated, it felt like many sheets. 'Take it.'

'Please Eve, just—'

She shook it at him. 'Take it.'

He reluctantly took the letter from her and thrust it deep in his jacket pocket. 'Fine. If that's what you want.'

'No, Ben, its not what I want. It's far from what I want. What I wanted was for us to be married, probably have a couple of cute little kids, and be living out our dreams in upstate New York. We might have been able to afford a brown-stone by now, which we'd have decorated with amazing artwork we'd buy from art students, and furniture we'd have picked up at weekend flea markets and painted ourselves while listening to your old vinyl records. You'd be head of photography or creative director at a top agency, maybe teaching photography at New York Film Academy. I'd be writing my own novels that topped the bestseller charts. We'd hire a motorhome for our holidays and drive across Canada or maybe rent a little cottage on a lake or something. But you know, you can't have everything can you?'

'No,' Ben said sadly, turning to leave. 'You can't.'

Chapter 30

The country wedding

The likes of Bruno didn't belong on budget airlines. Eve thought so, most of the other passengers on his flight thought so, and it was quite clear by his wrinkled nose and the way he wheeled his expensive suitcase behind him as he emerged from Exeter airport that Bruno himself thought so too.

'How was your flight?' Eve asked cheerily. It was more of a rhetorical question. He'd arrived in one piece, and that was all that mattered. He clearly agreed as he chose to ignore what she'd said completely and instead kiss her with such force she had to take a step back. So that was the way it going to be, Eve thought with a smile. O-kay then.

They held hands all the way back to Eve's rental car, a small two-door city motor, that again looked completely at odds with Bruno, who, in his designer jeans, crisp salmon-colour shirt and cream V-neck sweater should have been putting one long leg into an Aston Martin rather than a Fiat Panda.

'Sorry,' Eve said. 'It was the only choice that was left, can you fit in?'

'I'm sure I'll manage,' Bruno replied, pushing the passenger seat back as far as it would go.

They drove the first twenty of the seventy-mile journey in complete silence. Eve kept opening her mouth to fill the car with banal information about the weekend ahead or random facts about the villages they were passing through, before thinking better of it and then closing her mouth.

'So,' Bruno said finally. 'Your friend Becca, the bride.'

'Yes.'

'She is your best friend?'

'Yes. We were at university together. Most of the people you'll meet today are from university.'

'And the groom?'

'Jack. He's lovely. He's in the army. He wasn't at university with us, Becca met him a few years ago in a pub.'

'Who else will I meet?'

'Oh God, literally everyone and his wife is going to be at the wedding,' Eve said, then wondered if that phrase made any sense at all to Bruno, but decided to press on regardless. 'My mum, Faye, will be there, and my brother Adam and his fiancé George, you've met both of them before I think.'

'Yes, they are nice, but it is strange they are getting married.'

'Strange how?'

'It's just a bit, I don't know, bizarre.'

'Because they are both men?'

'Do you not think so?'

Eve couldn't believe she was hearing this. 'In no way whatsoever. Love is love. I'm all for anyone getting married if they want to. Do you honestly think it's wrong?'

'I didn't say it was wrong. I said it was strange.'

Eve had an overwhelming urge to childishly reply, 'Well I think *you're* strange for thinking that.' But didn't. 'And then there's my personal trainer Juan, you'll recognise him as he'll be drinking mineral water and bench-pressing the bridesmaids.'

'You have a personal trainer called Juan?' There was no mistaking the steely tone in Bruno's question.

'Yes. He's Argentinian.'

'Is he homosexual, like your brother?'

Eve was still unused to such bluntness, so the question took her aback a bit. 'Um, no.'

'Married?'

'No.'

'I think perhaps we can find you a more suitable personal trainer, n'est ce pas?'

'I think I'd like to stick to Juan,' Eve muttered back before continuing her monologue leaving no pause for Bruno to interject further. 'And there's an annoying girl called Tanya coming—'

Unfortunately, the invitations had gone out before Eve's bust up with Tanya, and there was no way to retract Tanya's invitation, as much as Becca would have wanted to. Particularly as a few days previously Tanya had emailed, not even called, Becca to say that Luke was called away on a last minute business trip to Spain, and so she was flying solo for the wedding. Becca's wedding breakfast consisted of picnic baskets in the meadow, so a no-show was no great catastrophe, but even so, if the shoe was on the other foot, Tanya would have gone apoplectic if two became one only days before her wedding.

'Why is she annoying?' Bruno asked, his interest piqued.

'She's been annoying since we shared a house at university, but she's one of those people that if you met them now you wouldn't be friends with, but because it's been so long, you sort of still are. Although we had a big fight a few weeks ago and haven't spoken since, so ... sorry, can you just lean your head back so I can see if something's coming? Thanks. Where was I?'

'Annoying friend.'

'Yes.' Eve hesitated. She wasn't going to mention Ben, but felt that she had to as they were now just fifteen minutes away from arriving, and sod's law being what it was, Ben was bound to be the first person they would see.

'Speaking of annoying, there's a guy called Ben, who is meant to be coming. He shared a house with us too at university.'

'One man and three women?'

'Yes.'

'And this annoying Ben, he was with annoying Tanya?'

The very idea made Eve want to simultaneously retch and laugh out loud. 'No, not at all. He wasn't annoying back then. Only now.' Eve knew that if Bruno was in fact The One, she would have to tell him how important Ben once was to her, and at least now they were sitting side by side so she couldn't see his reaction when she did.

'Um, the thing is, Ben and I were sort of best friends the whole way through university, and afterwards. We dated for a while and we had planned to go to New York together, then he changed his mind, never turned up at the airport and went back to his ex-girlfriend, Kate, in New Zealand.' Eve paused, waiting a few seconds for Bruno to comment, but he didn't, so she carried on, recounting the facts but none of the feelings, it was better that way. 'So I went to New York by myself, and stayed there for two years, forgot about him, moved back to England a couple of years ago and saw Ben again for the first time two months ago at Tanya's wedding. So that's that. Oh look, a thatched cottage. There's an interesting fact about thatched houses – do you know the water reed can last for up to seventy years?' Eve picked up her water bottle, one hand still on the steering wheel.

'Do you still love him?'

Luckily his question came before she'd taken a sip or they'd both be covered in water.

'No! Of course not! He's incredibly annoying, and has more baggage than a Kardashian on a trip to Paris Fashion Week. I'm literally just giving you a rundown on who you're going to meet. If you look to the right now, you'll see a sign to Westward Ho! which, interestingly, is the only place name in the British Isles with an exclamation mark.'

'Is he still with Kate?'

'Is who still with Kate?' As soon as the words were out of her mouth Eve wished they weren't. She was being deliberately obtuse, of course she knew who Bruno was referring to, and by pretending she didn't, she was making a big deal over something that really wasn't that important. She risked a quick side-glance at Bruno who had folded his arms across his chest and was looking out of the window.

'Kate died,' Eve said quickly.

'Oh great. So, it is not just this Juan I need to worry about then.'

If Bruno had said this with a light-hearted tone of voice, even a sarcastic one, it might have been a funny way to break the tension, but he delivered it instead in a deadpan monotone that gave nothing away. Eve was upset that there was none of the easy banter they'd had at dinner in France. His intensity that was so passionate and refreshing back then just came across now as serious and sombre. He was probably just tired, he'd been travelling since 4 a.m., and it was now eleven-thirty. Plus, they had the added barrier of language, which she kept forgetting. She could barely string a sentence together in another language let alone get the nuances and intonation right to crack jokes.

The gravel on the driveway crackled under their tyres as they veered to the left of Becca's parents' large farmhouse and ventured down a narrow dirt track. Tall, lush green trees ran alongside them, bending their branches over the lane. They had only driven a hundred or so metres before the path stopped at a metal gate. Eve jumped out to push it open. Beyond it a field had been made into a makeshift car park. One of Becca's cousins was sat in a deckchair and briefly looked up from his phone to point to a space Eve should manoeuvre her Fiat into between a campervan and a Mini Cooper.

'Is this a festival or a wedding?' Bruno was only saying what Eve had said to Becca, but somehow when he did it, it annoyed her.

'Just wait until you see where the wedding is, it's beautiful.'

Putting together the moodboards and scheme for Becca's wedding had almost, almost, made Eve consider being a wedding planner as she'd loved it so much, but that was probably due to how laid-back the bride was. Eve knew she wouldn't be able to last five minutes with a perfectionist bride like Tanya, or even one like lovely Ayesha whose madcap ideas would have her reaching for the gin bottle. Becca had given Eve complete carte blanche to turn her 'village fete' wedding into reality, and it had been really fun. She'd used the column she'd written as a blueprint for the plan, and followed it to the letter.

'You might want to carry your bag, not wheel it, it's bit muddy down the path,' Eve advised Bruno, getting out of the car and seeing him pull up the suitcase handle and prepare to drag it behind him. To his credit he didn't say anything as he calmly pushed the handle down and picked up the bag.

'This way.' Eve pointed to a little opening in the hedgerow at the side of the car park field, and like the tiny door in Alice's wonderland, the garden it led into was beyond breathtaking. There was still an hour to go before the wedding started and people were bustling back and forth carrying flowers, rolling the big barrels into position and setting up the bar with pitchers of Pimms and elderflower cocktails. The field was small by farmer's standards, but huge as a wedding venue. Wildflower arches and trellises zoned off the dancing area – with a stage formed from pallets and planks where the blues band had already set up their instruments – from the more chilled picnic area that had the all-important hay bales and blankets laid out on the ground. Becca and Jack hadn't wanted a traditional meal or buffet, so had opted instead for woven baskets overflowing with salads, cold meats, cheeses, and antipasti to accompany the Cornish pasties and pies that a local company would be serving from their bunting-festooned food van that was already parked up. A lady was busy diligently writing today's offerings on a blackboard that she had positioned outside the van.

The ceremony was going to be held at the parish church down a small lane running alongside the field, and Becca was to be married by the same vicar that had christened her thirty years before. As Eve and Bruno stood under the first archway looking at the scene in front of them, at all the villagers and neighbours pitching in to help string up the fairy lights, lay out the last jam jar lanterns and adorn the blankets with cushions and beanbags, Eve suddenly understood the reason why Becca had flung open the doors of her wedding and announced it a free-for-all. Why wouldn't you want to share this moment of such magic with as many people as possible? Her parents had lived on this farm all their married lives, and Becca's maternal grandparents before that. They were part of a community who were just as excited about this wedding as the bride and groom.

'I have never seen anything like this,' Bruno gasped.

'I know,' Eve replied, bursting with happiness and pride at the small part she'd played in it. It would be impossible to conceive of a more romantic setting unless you crawled inside a packet of lovehearts. She knew all Bruno's misconceptions would evaporate as soon as he saw it.

The enigmatic Frenchman smiled, reached for Eve's hand

then wrinkled his nose. 'It looks pretty, but smells like cow dung.'

***

'He came! He actually came!' Ayesha squealed, grabbing Eve's hand by the posh portaloos just after everyone came back from the ceremony to find their spots on the picnic blankets. 'And he's even more gorgeous than I remembered! How's the big reunion going? Have you sneaked off to your tent yet and done the deed?'

'No! We haven't been to the tent yet, he wanted to iron his shirt again, so we got changed in the farmhouse – in separate rooms.'

'This is so exciting, I'm so envious of you, having a first time again. It's been years since I saw a new naked body.'

Eve played along, smiling in all the right places, but the truth was that she didn't feel the same connection to Bruno as she had in France, and so was already dreading the end of the evening when they both had to sleep with their bodies pretty much on top of each other in her small two-man tent. She knew that she didn't have to go through with what Ayesha was politely calling 'the deed' tonight, but she did have to share the space of a coffin with him regardless of whether anything rude happened.

Eve had just left him in the very capable, and embarrassingly fawning, hands of Adam and George, who were busy complimenting Bruno on the flattering cut of his suit as she'd slipped away. She hadn't seen Ben yet, but as she'd arrived at the church with Becca, Eve had missed the pre-ceremony drinks with everyone at the pub next to the church, so hadn't had a proper chance to see all the other guests yet. She looked around the field trying to spot her mum, or woman-hating Juan, who didn't know anyone else. Possibly a wedding wasn't the best place for him right now either, which would explain why he was nowhere to be seen. Eve had glimpsed Tanya, although Tanya pretended not to see her, quickly looking away and laughing extra loudly at whatever the group she was attached to were saying.

Walking back to the party Eve saw Juan leaning against the side of the pie van. Ironic, Eve thought as he was probably the only guest not to partake in one.

'Hey Juan,' she said, walking up to him. 'Thank you for helping me fit into my dress,' she gave a little twirl in her floaty knee-length pale green dress as if to prove the point that the zipper had gone all the way up to the top.

'You look great,' he said, giving her a lopsided smile. 'And it was all your hard work, not mine.'

'Believe me Juan, if I wasn't absolutely terrified of you screaming at me three times a week for the last few months I wouldn't look any different to the way I did at Christmas.'

'I'm not that scary, am I?'

Eve considered this for a moment. 'You know when Bruce Banner turns into the Hulk? Well...'

They both laughed. 'I think I've been a bit grumpy lately,' he admitted. 'Thank you for putting up with me.'

Eve shook her head. 'Nonsense, it's fine. You had a lot going on. Is it ok, you know, being here, or is it a bit weird?'

'It's not weird because it's a wedding, I like it, everyone is so happy – but it's a bit strange because I only know you, and your brother a little bit.'

'Ok, come with me and I'll introduce you to everyone.'

Eve brought Juan into the Bruno, George and Adam group, that had grown to include Faye as well.

'Everyone, this is Juan. You already know Adam, this is George, his husband to be, my mum Faye, and my, erm, this is Bruno.'

Adam and George greeted the new addition with a flurry of hugs and back pats, Faye blushed as Juan kissed her hand, and Bruno hung back. He had a look of disinterest mixed with pure hatred on his face. She should probably have sidled up to the Frenchman, staked her claim, batted his concerns away with a seductive kiss or coquettish cuddle, but she really didn't feel like it. She remembered some advice from the dog trainer she once took the family retriever to when she was a teen: make clear what you find acceptable and what you don't early on, that way he'll know the rules from the beginning. Don't reward behaviour you don't like by giving them attention, save that for when they do something good.

Eve knew Bruno wasn't a mutt from a rescue centre, but she felt the same guidelines might still apply.

Chapter 31

Ben looked aloof and pensive all through the picnic, after finally making an appearance. The thought had crossed Eve's mind that this might be the wedding that he turned up with a plus one. He'd made it quite clear that they had no claims on each other's affections any more. But thankfully he seemed to be alone today. Eve didn't know why she might have been uneasy about seeing him with another woman – like she said to Bruno in the car, the idea that she was still in love with him was preposterous. The only feelings she had towards him now was sadness that a decade-long friendship had ended up like this.

Ben had given a cursory nod to Eve as he sat down moodily on the blanket a few metres away from her. She didn't know if he'd clocked that the good-looking man next to her was her date for the weekend. For some reason, she hoped he had.

Tanya certainly had, which was immensely gratifying. Bruno may be a closet homophobic, and an antisocial, jealous zealot but he was incredibly nice to look at, which, when it came to Tanya, was all that mattered. Tanya kept looking over at them, correction, Bruno, in a cartoon-character-type way

295

where her jaw was comically trailing on the floor while bright red love hearts had replaced her pupils. Barely married for two months, Tanya certainly seemed to be out of the lust-struck honeymoon period – well, with her new husband anyway.

'Your mother is a very attractive woman,' Bruno was saying to Eve, opening a pot of olives from the basket and popping one in his mouth. 'It is good for me to see what you might look like in twenty years.'

Eve was not sure that this relationship was necessarily going to last twenty days, let alone twenty years, but smiled politely, shaking her head at the proffered olive pot.

'You don't like olives?' Bruno asked.

'No, never have.'

'But that's crazy, they are delicious. Have one.' He jiggled the pot in front of her.

Eve shook her head again. 'No thanks, I really don't like them.'

'I have never met anyone that does not like olives.'

'Well, now you have.'

A shadow cast across them, and Eve turned around to find Tanya standing just behind them. 'I thought I'd come over and say hello. To show you that I don't have any hard feelings.' Tanya stretched her hand out to Bruno. 'I don't think we've met.'

Bruno, ever the gent, scrambled to his feet to shake her hand, while Eve stayed sat down silently seething at Tanya's magnanimous greeting. Was Eve supposed to be grateful that Tanya was so forgiving when it was clearly her that was in the wrong? Life really was too short to spend it getting the positivity sucked out of her by someone like Tanya.

While Bruno and Tanya talked, standing up so that she was sat next to their legs, Eve glimpsed out of the corner of her eye that Faye had run up to Ben and was giving him a hug. There was nothing unusual about that; he wasn't just her daughter's ex, he was also the cheeky friend that had made one of Faye's kitchen chairs his own, stretching his long legs under her table and scoffing down whatever home-cooked meal Faye had put in front of him. When Ben and Eve had started dating years later, it seemed like the most natural progression in the world. Her mum and dad, Adam, Becca, Ayesha, they'd all said that it was just a matter of time before Eve and Ben knew what everyone around them had known for years.

'Eve?'

Bruno bent down. 'I just asked if you wanted more Pimms, I am getting Tanya one.'

'That'd be great, thank you.' Eve really hoped that Tanya was going to go with Bruno to the bar, but instead Tanya made a big show of folding her skirt between her legs and attempting to sit down alongside Eve as elegantly as possible, stretching out her tanned legs in front of her, while Eve was keeping her pale pasty legs tucked underneath her.

'It is absolutely ridiculous that we're expected to sit on the floor at a wedding.'

'There are hay bales if you prefer.'

Tanya just looked at Eve with one eyebrow raised and pursed lips. 'A hay bale?'

'It's the countryside Tanya, not a five-star hotel.'

'Weddings are not supposed to be in fields Eve.'

'They're not supposed to be in dilapidated warehouses either, but you managed it.' It was bitchy, Eve knew it, but she couldn't help herself.

'I put a lot of effort into my wedding, I'll have you know.'

'You didn't actually Tanya. I did. Becca did. Ayesha did. All Luke's friends did. Ben did.'

'Saint Ben, don't you mean?'

Eve rolled her eyes. 'I didn't say that, and I don't know why you'd say that.'

'Just that he can do no wrong, can he?' Tanya said meanly. 'He dumped you, did a runner to the other side of the world to shack up with his dying ex-girlfriend, be a virtual monk for four years grieving for her, then reappear as though none of it had happened, and you're taken in by him. You're a complete doormat, Eve.'

Adam and George had now joined the Faye and Ben reunion, all joking and laughing like the old friends Eve supposed they were. Tanya followed her glance.

'It must hurt you a lot seeing him with your family, you're probably thinking about what might have been.'

Enough was enough. 'No, not at all, I've moved on and Bruno's my future now. As I'm sure you saw for yourself, he's quite a catch.' Eve stood up, brushed the grass off her skirt and walked away, not turning around once.

Bruno had just been served the three Pimms he'd ordered. Eve took a few massive gulps of one of them, reducing the liquid by more than half, then poured the rest of Tanya's drink into her own glass.

'Tanya changed her mind,' Eve explained.

'I hope you are not going to get too drunk,' Bruno said. 'I want you to remember tonight.' It was a cheesy line that suited a bad movie, and if a man had said it on one of Eve and Becca's much-loved reality shows then they'd have both stuck their fingers in their mouths and made retching noises. But this wasn't TV or fiction, this was Eve's life, and she suddenly didn't like it very much.

The band Eve had hired from their local pub were clambering up on stage and picking up their instruments. It was a welcome distraction, and meant that Eve could legitimately turn away from Bruno's intense gaze and look elsewhere. Becca and Jack were walking onto the dance floor, which was much too grand a term for the square patch of mown grass in front of the stage, cordoned off by a U-shape of hay bales. Becca was wearing a knee-length, white, flapper-style dress in lace, with delicate beading showcasing her small frame. Her hair was set in tousled waves, tucked behind her ears by a clip attached to a beautiful white peony. Jack was sporting a look not unlike a '30s farm hand, with linen trousers held up with braces over a white shirt and bow tie, and a flat cap on his head. Their first dance wasn't the heavily choreographed numbered steps of Tanya's and Luke's, nor was it the madcap free-for-all that was Ayesha's and Amit's, it was more of an improv blend of twisting, hugging, turning and laughing. A lot of laughing.

Halfway through the song Becca turned and waved everyone onto the dance floor to join them. Ayesha ran on, dragging an unwilling Amit behind her; after his breakdancing debacle at his own wedding he was strictly forbidden from attempting anything other than shuffling demurely round the floor. Becca's parents were the next on. Her dad, who should have been looking uncomfortable in proper shoes rather than wellies, had consumed enough cider not to worry about it, and her mum seemed naturally high on life wearing a pale peach outfit that she'd travelled to Bristol to buy.

The floor was soon full. Eve smiled to see George and Adam jiving together, each insisting on leading, culminating in much giggling and hand slapping. Even Faye and Juan were dancing, Juan's muscles straining underneath his slim-fit shirt, and Faye looking happier and younger than Eve had ever seen her. Eve couldn't remember her parents ever dancing together, they weren't party people. A big night out would have included the words Harvester or Fondue, and there was no way that her dad would have had the rhythm, or the stamina, to twirl Faye round as enthusiastically as Juan was doing now. Eve made a silent note to thank him afterwards for hanging out with her mum. She knew that he was used to spending time with clients that weren't necessarily his cup of tea, but it was sweet of him to make sure she had a good time. It was sweet of Juan to come at all actually, after a bad break up the last thing he probably wanted to do was be engulfed in a sea of couples. Every corner of this field seemed to be an advert for love, and it was really starting to annoy Eve.

'Let's dance.' Bruno held out his hand for her to take, as though they were at a 1940s tea party.

'I'm not really feeling it actually.'

'Come on,' Bruno whined. 'I am a good dancer. I want to show you.'

'I have no doubt of that at all, but I'd much prefer to just keep drinking.'

'This is the trouble with you English,' Bruno said, shaking his head. 'You think fun begin and ends in a bottle of alcohol.'

His casual xenophobia set Eve's teeth on edge. 'That's completely untrue, but right now, I want another drink, and don't want to dance.'

'I'll dance with you, Bruno,' a keen voice suddenly piped up. 'That's if you don't mind Eve?'

If Tanya's eyelids fluttered any faster she might well take off, Eve thought.

'I don't mind, but your husband might?' It was catty of her, but Eve felt Tanya needed reminding of her marital status.

'Oh, what he doesn't know won't kill him. Come on then Bruno, show me what you've got.'

Eve watched their backs disappear into the crowds that had grown so much the hay bale perimeter had to be moved back a couple of metres. Teachers were having fun with Jack's army mates, the boys from the dairy farm were dancing with Becca's schoolfriends. This wedding had all the right ingredients for a good time, yet it just left Eve feeling flat. Why wasn't she having fun? She should have been bursting with pride at it all coming together so well, at seeing her best friend so happy, at watching three or four hundred people from all walks of life dancing and laughing together, but the merriment just reminded Eve that she was alone. Not alone. She was never alone. She was lonely. Really bloody lonely.

Chapter 32

The band had packed up, leaving the stage empty, which Jack's friends saw as an open invitation to invade it. They lugged their own guitars up there, one bloke even had a harmonica, and they swiftly set about murdering *Hey Jude*.

'Are we ever going to talk about why you're still so angry at me?'

Eve looked up from where she was sitting on the hay bale, bits of straw scratching the backs of her bare legs. Ben took her unresponsiveness as an invitation to sit down next to her. It was almost a carbon copy of when they'd sat side by side at Ayesha and Amit's wedding, the two of them sat on the periphery of the action, starring in their own silent movie while the noise and bustle just a metre away from them blurred into the background.

'I don't think we need to do that,' Eve replied.

'I think we do.'

The Pimms had made her brave. 'I don't want you to think that I've wasted my life pining for you Ben, because I haven't.'

'Um, that's good to know.'

'I mean it. Was I totally heartbroken when you left? Of

course I was. Was I absolutely devastated when you never got in touch? Yes. Am I bothered by any of that in the slightest now? No, not a bit.'

'Excellent. That's great news. I do still want to explain everything, but now's not – stay still, you've got a bee in your hair.'

The cool, calm and collected Eve that was doing such a great job being casual and nonchalant instantly evaporated and she jumped up, yelling, pulling her hair out of its up-do, shaking it like a wet sheepdog while hopping from foot to foot.

'Shit! It's stung me, Ben, help me, it's stung me on my head!'

'Is now the wrong time to say that you shouldn't have moved?'

'Ben! My head is on fire, it fucking hurts, help me!'

'It's too dark, come with me near a light.'

'What if its poison goes through to my brain?'

'You do know how crazy you sound.'

'You have no idea how much this hurts Ben, it's like I've been stabbed in the skull.'

They stopped near a lantern that had been staked into the ground.

'Ok, now tilt your head so that I can see it.'

Eve did as he said, and he gently parted her hair to get a better look. 'I can see the stinger, stay still, I'll try to get it out.'

'It hurts so much,' Eve whined.

'I know, I know, hold still. Dammit, I can't grip it properly, come with me, I have tweezers in my toilet bag.'

Eve didn't even try to argue. Her head was throbbing and she was starting to feel a bit sick. She gratefully accepted Ben's proffered arm as he led her away from the party and towards the adjacent field where all the tents stood. Ben weaved them swiftly through the sea of brightly coloured canvas triangles, then stopped dead.

'What's wrong?' Eve asked.

'I can't find my tent. I was sure it was right here.'

'What colour is it?'

'I can't remember really, it's new. Um, green, I think.'

'Didn't you tie a flag to the top of it so you could spot it easier? I thought you remembered my dad telling you that?'

They wandered around the field for a few more minutes, Ben helping Eve narrowly avoid tripping over guy ropes, before Ben gave a sigh of relief. 'There, I'm pretty sure that's the one.' He unzipped the tent and held the canvas flap to one side for Eve to clamber through first.

'Hang on a second,' she said, reaching into her bra.

'Steady on, Red.'

'I'm merely helping you out, repaying your kindness.'

'I'm flattered, but we should probably talk first,' came Ben's jokey reply.

Eve stuck her tongue out at him and retrieved the clean handkerchief she'd placed inside her bra in case of emotional emergencies, shook it out of its neat little square and tied it to the tent pole sticking out above the tent's door. 'There. That's better.'

'Thank you. Now let me de-sting you.' He ushered Eve through the open door flap and bunched up his sleeping bag that he'd already laid out so it made a comfier seat for her to sit on. 'Come in here and relax a sec.'

He then started rummaging through his toilet bag using the light from the torch on his phone. 'Aha, got them. Ok, let's get this bad boy.'

Eve once again tilted her head towards him. The tweezers felt cold against her scalp and she winced as he pulled the stinger out.

'It's a little bit swollen around it, I think we need to put some toothpaste on it.'

'Toothpaste?' Eve asked surprised.

'Yes, it's meant to help soothe it.'

'Is this another one of your jokes? I'm really not in the mood.'

'While I will never tire of stitching you up Red, I promise you I'm not making this up, toothpaste really helps.'

'What's your source?'

Ben smiled. 'Ever the journo. Um, not sure, the internet?'

'Do you remember when we were about twenty-one and we were at the beach and I got stung by a jellyfish and you suggested that you wee on me to stop it stinging?'

'That was a proven scientific theory, I'll have you know.'

'It was not! Or the time that you convinced me that jam soothes sunburn and then I was surrounded by flies and wasps for the rest of the day. Or when I had hiccups and you made me drink neat whisky from my dad's drinks cabinet.'

'Look, at this point Red, you should be grateful that it's just toothpaste I'm suggesting. There's some in my toilet bag, stop procrastinating and just get it out for me while I keep my fingers parting your hair.'

They hadn't shared this easy banter in years, and Eve realised quite how much she'd missed it. Missed him.

Eve's fingers closed around the toothpaste tube and as she brought it out of the bag a long chain was wrapped around its lid. Attached to the end of it was a gold locket. Eve knew what it was, what it represented, before she even asked. 'What's this?'

Ben answered quietly. 'It was Kate's.'

'Oh.'

'She was wearing it when she died.'

'Oh. That's nice.' Flustered, Eve added, 'Not that she died, that's not nice. That you kept it.' The pain in Eve's chest was a stark stab of realisation that she was in love with Ben, she always had been, and the tragic reality was that he was, and probably always would be, in love with someone else.

Eve quickly unscrewed the cap of the toothpaste, desperate to get this over with before her tears started forming, dabbed a little dot on her finger and rubbed it on the spot where Ben's fingers were.

'Let me do it,' Ben said. 'I can see where it needs to go.'

'No, I'll do it, it's fine. Thanks for this, I'm ok now.'

'It still looks pretty angry, you might need to take some paracetamol.'

'I'm fine, I'd better be getting back.'

'You're pissed off. Is it the locket?'

'No, of course not. Right, I'm going back. Bruno, my, er, boyfriend, will be wondering where I got to.' Eve started inelegantly scrambling to her feet.

'The Cashmere King?'

'He's French,' Eve realised that she was using his nationality as an excuse for pretty much everything Bruno was doing.

'I didn't realise there was a national rule about wardrobe choices.'

'You're so rude.'

'I'm observant.'

'Offensive.'

'Vigilant.'

They were tramping across the field, while lots of people were weaving through the long grass the other way. Eve's hair was in complete disarray and smelling of mint, her face was flushed from a medley of embarrassment and anger. Ben hurried a step or two behind her calling for her to slow down, when Bruno appeared in front of them like Heathcliff walking across the moors, if Heathcliff had ever worn pressed linen and carried designer luggage.

'There you are,' Bruno announced frostily, and a little unnecessarily. 'I have been looking for you for ages. I see that you've enjoyed a reunion with your ex-boyfriend.'

'Enjoyed is the wrong word,' Eve said back.

'Perhaps consummated would be better?' Bruno replied bitchily.

'Now hang on a second,' Ben stepped forward. 'Eve got stung by a bee and—'

Bruno threw his head back and laughed sarcastically. 'Stung by a bee? Really? Surely you can do better than that?'

'Look!' Eve put her head down so her long hair fell over

307

her face, it was a completely redundant gesture as the field was dark and Bruno was completely uninterested.

'I have come halfway across the world—'

'You came from France,' said Ben. 'People from the Midlands had a longer journey than you did.'

'Not helping, Ben. Why don't you go back to the party?' Eve said, trying to use her telepathy to get him to go.

'No, I think I'll stay. Why don't we all walk back to the party together?'

'The party is over, that is why I was coming to find you.'

The silence of the field beyond the hedge proved that Bruno was speaking the truth. Eve looked at her watch. It was 1.30 a.m., far later than she'd thought.

'I got my suitcase from the farmhouse,' Bruno said. 'Where is our tent? I am tired now.'

'Did you get my bag too?' Eve asked confused, as he seemed to only be carrying his and a bottle of champagne in the other hand.

'No, I forgot.'

'What a gent,' Ben muttered under his breath.

'Shut up Ben,' Eve hissed. 'Right, ok Bruno, let's go and find our tent. Goodnight Ben.'

After Bruno assured her that her brother and his 'friend' had taken care of Faye and deposited her safely back into her own tent, Eve crawled into her own two-man tent of hostility and prepared for a sleepless night.

Bruno was in a complete mood with her, refusing to speak to Eve, lying on top of his sleeping bag in his clothes, playing with his phone. Because Eve didn't have a change of clothes, she too was forced to lie down in her bridesmaid dress, silently seething while her head still throbbed from the bee sting.

Eve guessed that about half an hour had passed when Bruno whispered into the darkness. 'Eve? Are you asleep?' Just in case he'd calmed down and wanted to drink the champagne with her and get amorous, Eve remained still and silent. The last thing she wanted was a frisky, tipsy Frenchman on her hands, regardless of what letter his name might begin with. Taking her muteness as a yes, he gently eased himself out of the tent, slowly zipping it shut behind him. Eve's eyes flew open.

He'd left his case, so he couldn't be making a run for it in the middle of the night. *Like Ben had done.* He was probably just going to the row of portaloos at the entrance to the field. As that thought entered her head Eve realised that her own bladder felt like a water balloon.

She edged her way gingerly through the sleeping tents, reminiscent of so many campsites she'd been to with Ben. A giggle punctured the silent sky. Eve stopped and listened. There it was again.

Eve crouched lower and darted between the canvas triangles, mindful of the zigzagging guide ropes. The sudden sound of a zip opening made Eve quickly duck behind a red tent, cautiously peering out round the side of it. Eve took a sharp intake of breath, and instinctively put her hand over her mouth to stop it making more noise.

Juan had crawled out of the tent and was hungrily kissing Eve's mum, who was crouched just inside the tent, her face and naked shoulders illuminated by the dim moonlight.

Another girlish giggle and the zip closed, and Juan walked off, back to his own tent.

Eve sat back on her heels a little unsteadily. Of all the sights she was expecting to see, that was not one of them.

Eve had completely lost her bearings, and now she was still a little drunk, disorientated and absolutely desperate for a pee. There was nothing else for it. Once she was sure that she was the only person awake in the field, she headed for the edge of it where it backed onto woodland. She walked less than a metre into it, ducked behind a tree and squatted down. The relief was unreal, until she lost her balance a little, a bit of wee went on her foot, which startled her and made her fall backwards into a bush of nettles. Jumping up, her back on fire with fresh stings, she danced around, arms flaying desperately trying to scratch areas she couldn't reach. Eve couldn't help the fat tears from falling down her face, and she took big gulps of air, trying to calm herself down. There was no point looking for dock leaves to help soothe the itching, it was too dark and with sod's law being well and truly against Eve, she might end up with her hand in a rat trap.

Ben would probably tell her to bathe herself with the blood of a bat or something equally disgusting. The thought of Ben made her tears fall faster. Knowing that he still carried Kate's locket around within him cemented the fact for Eve that she would always be in second place. Tanya was right, she was a complete doormat. A weak-willed doormat, whose complete self-worth had become dependent on finding and keeping a man.

Eve knew she couldn't stay in the woods all night, as much

as she wanted to just hide there away from the world until it was time to go home, back to her bedroom, which she had already decided she wasn't leaving ever again.

A noise to Eve's right startled her. This wasn't the playful giggle she'd heard between Faye and Juan – this was animalistic, frantic love-making, with huffing and deep breathing providing the nighttime chorus. Eve felt an immediate sigh of relief that it wasn't coming from her mum's tent again, that may have just finished her off. But to her horror it seemed to be coming from a little green tent with a distinctive white handkerchief fluttering in the breeze on the top of it.

Chapter 33

That huffing and puffing didn't sound like Ben. But then the last time Eve had heard him make anything like those noises was four and a half years ago, and he must have evolved his technique since then. Edging closer to his tent, Eve was in two minds. She desperately didn't want to know who he was with, and what he was doing for the shrieks to be so plentiful and loud. But then, she couldn't go back to her own tent, slip into her sleeping bag alongside a snoring Bruno and never know.

'What in God's name is all that noise? Is someone ill?'

Eve swivelled round. Ben was walking up behind her, her small overnight bag in his hand.

'Ben!' Eve whispered, her body flooding with relief.

'Jesus, is that what I think it is? Where's it coming from?' Ben held out the battered holdall to Eve. 'Here's your bag, I went and got it from the farmhouse, I thought you might need it.'

The kindness of his gesture threw Eve. She thanked him, then said, 'The noise seems to be coming from your tent.'

'Mine?'

'I thought it was you making that noise.'

'Chance'd be a fine thing. It must be Tanya,' he said striding towards the tent.

'Tanya?' Eve replied, hurrying after him.

'She came to my tent when she heard me and your French boyfriend arguing,' he said over his shoulder.

'Bruno? Why were you arguing with Bruno?' Eve replied, hurrying to keep up with him.

'He came to my tent and accused me of sleeping with you, and told me to keep my hands to myself. I put him right, and then Tanya butted in and I'd just had enough. I told them both to go back to their own tents and I went to the farmhouse.'

They'd reached the tent and Ben yanked the zip up before Eve could tell him not to. Bruno's naked bottom was rising up and down in the semi-darkness and Tanya's recognisable Home Counties voice haughtily shrieked under him for 'whoever that is to bugger off.'

'I think it's you two that need to bugger off actually.' Ben said, opening the tent door wider. 'Off you go. And you can take my sleeping bag with you, you owe me a new one.'

Bruno and Tanya scrambled out of Ben's tent, clutching their clothes to their chests, Bruno wrapping the sleeping bag around his waist, while running off into the darkness.

'Sorry about your boyfriend,' Ben whispered finally, once silence had once again descended on the field.

'Don't be. Turns out he was a bit of an arse. And believe it or not, it's actually not the worst thing to happen to me today.' Exhaustion pricked at Eve's eyes again and she needed to be alone. 'I'm going back to mine now. Thanks for, you know.'

Ben shrugged. 'Don't be daft, it was nothing. See you tomorrow.'

He wouldn't, Eve thought. She was planning to get up before everyone else and go back to London before small talk had to happen and she had to pretend to be upbeat and cheerful. She raised her hand as a farewell, even speaking out loud was alluding her.

Eve spotted the orange flag that she'd tied on the top of her tent easily, and was only a few steps away from the door of her tent when she felt a squelch underfoot and gasped in horror to see brown sludge oozing between her toes. She laughed. Big silent belly laughs that turned into big silent sobs.

She reached into the tent and upended her bottle of water all over her foot, washing the manure and her own urine off as best she could, then plonked Bruno's suitcase violently outside the tent, keeping his bottle of champagne for herself. Popping the cork open, Eve looked around for a receptacle she could use to drink from, and realising there was none, brought the bottle to her lips and took a long, satisfying swig.

What a God-awful day.

Eve then did the only thing she knew would make her feel better. She got her laptop out of her bag and started writing.

I'm not one to complain, but … the stench of dung is over-whelming; my back is covered in itchy red bumps from nettle stings and I have a festering sore on my head from a vicious insect bite. My legs are covered in a crisscross pattern of scratches from the hay bales we were forced to sit on all day, and if the incessant itching is anything to go by, there's a good chance I may have fleas. I smell of my own bodily fluids and animal excrement. I'm dishevelled, bedraggled, desolate. You'd be forgiven for assuming I'm on a reality show in the jungle, or perhaps the sole survivor of a tragic air accident that resulted in me wandering for days in a tropical rainforest. The reality is much more depressing. I've been at a wedding in the countryside.

It's not the bride's fault for thinking that a jolly village fete would make a good theme for her nuptials. It would. In theory. I love a nice toffee apple stand as much as the next person, and don't get me started on gingham bunting, it's beautiful. You know who else likes toffee apples? Wasps. Bloody hundreds of them. And you know the cute bunting fluttering in the breeze? Once the sugar from the toffee apples has kicked in, the kids will try to strangle each other with it. What about a jovial, well-mannered game of cricket? Those are always jolly good fun, aren't they? Well, turns out they're not. Not when some bright spark suggests pitting the bride's side against the groom's and introducing some strong scrumpy to the proceedings. And you don't need chairs when you're in a field do you? Hay bales, that's the answer to a countryside seating dilemma. Hay bales are all the rage, particularly with the Straw Itch Mite, or the Pyemotes Ventricosus if you will, a tiny predator that loves nothing more than chomping down on human flesh.

It's the casual air of country weddings that makes them so unique, don't you think? There's nothing like old friends getting together, bringing their guitars and harmonicas, and bonding over a shared love of playing songs that bear little or no resemblance to the original. There's putting your own stamp on a song and then there's stamping all over a song. Tonight's rendition of Mustang Sally *even had the Pyemotes Ventricosus jumping out of their hay bales and running for the silence of Stinging Nettle Wood.*

Do you know where's good for a wedding? A hotel. Do you know why? My bedroom normally has a lock on it. And a bed. And a toilet. And walls. Oh, how I miss walls as I sit here in my tiny excuse for a tent that I picked up at Tesco for twenty quid. I feel I've taken walls for granted up until now, not thinking beyond their structural abilities to hold up roofs. But there's so much more to them than that, I feel like I owe them an apology. I don't know what it is about camping, maybe it brings out the instinctive mammal in us, where we're reduced to fulfilling our basic needs. Maybe we're more like our animal counterparts than we like to think. Once you have a field full of tents and there's only fabric between our naked bodies, primal urges to reproduce take over. Walls stop you sniffing out a potential partner, canvas doesn't. Walking around this field after dark, once the bar had been drunk dry and all the families had left for their expensive guest houses, was like a nature documentary. The only thing lacking from the noises of pre-, during, and post-coital fun and games, was the dulcet tones of Sir David Attenborough telling us about the mating habits of the lesser known homo sapiens.

So there we have it. A wedding like no other. A wedding to remember. A wedding it's going to take a lot of time, calamine lotion and gin to get over. Oh good. It's started to rain.

The champagne bottle was empty, signalling that it was time for Eve to turn in for the night. It was now almost four, and the non-existent lining on this cheap-as-chips tent meant that as the sun woke up, Eve probably would too, although she was pretty drunk so she was hoping she might sleep through the dawn chorus.

Grabbing her phone to switch on the alarm, Eve saw that she had a few emails marked urgent. Sighing as she opened her inbox her heart sank when she read an angry message from Belinda at *Venus*, saying that her last column was well overdue and that they would be terminating her contract with them unless she provided them the copy by 9 a.m. the following day. *And save the pussy-footing niceties for your day job.*

Eve couldn't lose this gig, she just couldn't. It wasn't just supplementing her income, it was tripling it, there was no way that she could keep up the credit card repayments without it. And she couldn't go back to just writing about hearts and flowers and happy endings, she'd go mad. But to craft a pithy, cynical column out of thin air now would be nigh on impossible. She was drunk, exhausted, and completely spent. Eve doubted she was capable of writing a good text message at that point in time, let alone a 700-word opinion piece.

The solution was staring Eve in the face. Literally staring her in the face from the screen of her laptop. Without thinking, Eve copied and pasted her latest diary entry into the body of an email, wrote *Hi Belinda, Sorry it's late, here's my latest column, hope you like it, Eve* at the top of it and pressed send.

She then opened up a new email and typed in Fiona's address.

Hey Fiona,

It's Eve. Well, you know that because it's come from my email. Sorry, I'm a bit drunk. Which should in no way dilute what I'm about to say because I'm thinking very clearly. Well, not very clearly, but on this particular topic, I'm very clear. Crystal, in fact. The thing is, I hate weddings. Like REALLY hate weddings. I hate everything about them, the fact the industry is worth about two billion pounds, I've just made that up, but it's something like that, two billion pounds that could have been spent on schools or hospitals or something better than weddings that in all likelihood will end in divorce, then there's the fake nails, fake eyelashes, fake friends. Orchids flown in from the Far East that are adding to the carbon footprint, that makes me very sad. If I could add a crying emoji here I would, but I can't because it's an email. Dresses that are only bits of fabric sewn together but the fact they're white they cost ten times what they would if they were purple. The fact that no one really wears purple wedding dresses. I hate gift registers, kitten-heel shoes, tiaras (no one should wear tiaras except princesses or prom queens, and I hate prom queens, so just princesses. They're fine.) Anyway, you get the picture. Which is why I'm resigning. I feel a fraud for writing about true love when I really don't believe that it exists.

Yours, Eve

It sent. Then she slept.

***

'I brought you this,' Becca stuck a thermos of tea through the opening in the tent.

Eve murmured back a reply that was noncommittal. Even the thought of reaching for the flask was too much effort.

'Everyone's up and the bacon butty van has arrived.' That was another one of Eve's flashes of inspiration – what would hungover campers like more than anything the morning after? A greasy bacon bap served on their doorstep. Except the thought of it now made her want to throw up.

Becca climbed inside the tent, and sat cross-legged on the end of Eve's sleeping bag. 'I just ran into Ben. He told me about your shitty Frenchman.'

'He's not mine,' Eve muttered, her head still resolutely refusing to peek out of the top of the bag.

'I'm sorry if you didn't enjoy the wedding,' Becca said sadly.

Eve poked her head up. 'I did enjoy it, Becs. I could have done without seeing my kind of boyfriend's bare bum for the very first time in the way that I did, but that's not your fault.'

'I don't know if having it in a field was necessarily a good idea now,' Becca admitted a little sadly. 'You'd be surprised the amount of people that have come out in little bites from the hay bales, apparently there's a type of insect that live inside them.'

Eve shook her head. 'Wow. Who knew?' Last night's keyboard tirade suddenly came flooding back to Eve, and she felt the colour drain from her face.

'Are you ok?' Becca said. 'You look really pale. Are you going to be sick?'

'No, I'm ok. What time is it?' Eve was hoping beyond hope

that it was before 9 a.m. and that she could fix this mess before it became a massive mine that exploded everything she held dear into millions of pieces.

'Eleven.'

Fuck.

'Look, you go ahead, I'll just pull on some clothes and I'll be right behind you.' As soon as Becca left Eve grabbed her phone and called Belinda's mobile. It rang once and went to voicemail. 'Belinda, it's Eve, look, I sent the wrong column last night, it's not meant for *Venus*, I'm sorry, please ignore it, I'll send over another one in an hour, please just delete the last one, it's all a load of rubbish anyway. Can you call me when you've got this.? It's really important. Thanks, cheers, bye.'

Eve then threw her head out of the open zip and vomited all over Bruno's bag that was still outside the door of the tent.

***

Eve left countless voice messages, texts and emails tearfully begging Belinda to delete her column, but none of them were answered. She needed to get back to London as fast as she could, to try to implore to Belinda's good nature in person. This could all still be salvaged if the post didn't go live. Then Becca would never know how close Eve had come to ruining everything. Eve rammed her holdall full of her things and ran from the tent back towards the car park. She had to pass through the party field where the fry-up van was still being mobbed by hungry campers, but Eve kept her head down and stuck to the edge of the field so she wouldn't be seen.

A Beautiful Day for a Wedding

There wasn't a traffic light or roundabout that Eve remembered from the journey back to Clapham, the last two hours passed by in a foggy blur. How she didn't crash was a miracle as her sight was clouded by tears the whole way from Devon to London, and her hands shook as they gripped the steering wheel. She felt sick with guilt. Physically nauseous. Letting herself into the flat, remnants of her last girly night with Becca littered every surface. The last bottle of wine they'd shared lay at the top of the recycling bucket; their trainers lined up next to each other just inside the front door; Becca and Eve's clothes scattered like confetti over the living room as Becca had packed her suitcase for her honeymoon, cherry-picking the best things from both their wardrobes. A photo montage of the two of them punched her in the face when she went to the kitchen. Their young arms wrapped around each other in one photo from when they were freshers at university, others were taken on holidays abroad, one of them both leaning against a yellow New York taxi when Becca had visited, another of them jubilantly holding up matching keys to their flat when she had first moved in. It seemed like a catalogue of happy memories that now didn't deserve to be in a nice frame. The glass should be smashed into pieces, just like their friendship was about to be.

Chapter 34

Eve went through the motions of filling the kettle up from the tap, flicking the switch on at the side, retrieving a mug from the cupboard – all part of the same routine she had done thousands of times, but never before with such a feeling of dread and foreboding. How could she have turned into the type of monster that would throw her best friend under the bus for some cheap laughs and a fat fee, was she really that person? Eve sank down onto the kitchen floor, her back against the units, her legs bent up to her chest. She used to be a nice person, she knew she did, but how did she turn into someone so blinkered and self-obsessed? The catastrophic hunt for B, the sarcasm she spouted in the *Venus* columns, this wasn't her, and if it was, this wasn't who she wanted to be.

Eve heard her phone buzzing from her bag in the hallway where she'd dumped it on the way in. Praying it was Belinda, Eve scrambled to her feet to answer it.

It was Faye. Eve held the vibrating phone in her hand and didn't know whether to answer it or not. The drama that had happened after seeing Juan climb out of Faye's tent last night meant that Eve hadn't had any time to process how she felt about her mum and her personal trainer getting it on. Her instinctive reaction was to be disgusted, but this was quickly replaced with a feeling that people should enjoy happiness where they could find it. Eve didn't really want to think too long or hard about the ins and outs of their burgeoning relationship if she could help it, but it wasn't a union she was going to be against.

Eve let the call go to voicemail.

Darling, it's Mum. I'm worried about you, can you call me? You just disappeared this morning and I want to check you're ok. Love you, bye.

She also had loads of unread WhatsApp messages, and Eve was gutted to see that none of them were from Belinda. Adam had sent her one with the same sentiment as their mum's yet with different language *Yo. Where u at?* Three of the messages were from Bruno blaming the emotion and jealousy he felt on seeing Eve with Ben for the reason he took his trousers off and lay on top of Tanya. Then there was one from Tanya saying *No hard feelings, let's keep this between ourselves.* Becca and Ayesha were wondering where she was, and then there was one from Ben.

Red, I need to talk to you. It's really urgent.

It was sweet of him to check up on her like this but she wasn't ready to talk to him either. Not now she'd seen the locket in his wash bag. Kate must have been incredibly special for his reunion with her to rival the ten years he'd known Eve. And Eve couldn't compete with that. Nor did she have any strength left in her to try.

While she had her phone out, she tried Belinda's mobile

again and it went straight to her answerphone. Again. Eve left yet another heartfelt impassioned plea for Belinda not to read her email and to call her straightaway. She then spent the next couple of hours wandering from room to room, carefully folding up Becca's clothes and placing them in her chest of drawers, taking the recycling downstairs, wiping down the kitchen counters, basically anything she could do to keep her body and mind active and not dwell on the swinging wrecking ball that was just about to smash everything into pieces.

The doorbell made Eve jump. Everyone she knew was enjoying a barbecue in a field in Devon so she ignored it, assuming it would be someone trying to sell something or a wrong address. The shrill bell rang again. Eve sighed, put the toilet brush back in its holder and padded over to the intercom in the hall.

'Yes?'

'It's me.'

'Ben?'

'It's started to rain. Are you opening the door or what?'

If this surprise visit had happened a day ago Eve would have instinctively pulled out her ponytail and fluffed up her hair and pinched her cheeks to give them some colour. Today, however, she didn't even think to remove the yellow rubber gloves she had been wearing to clean the bathroom.

As he reached the top step Eve anticipated a comment like, 'that's a good look,' or something equally Ben-like but none came.

'Can you take your gloves off and come into the lounge, I need to talk to you.'

He'd never been that serious with Eve before and it worried her. 'Is Mum ok? Has something happened?'

He walked ahead of her into the living room and sat on one of the sofas. Eve sat on the other facing him.

'Look, I'm really worried about you, Eve,' he started.

'Me?' Eve replied. She was worried about her too, but she didn't know why he was.

'I think you've lost your way a bit, and I think it's all my fault.'

Eve stared at him. He had no idea quite how much she'd lost her way.

'Look at me. Eve, look at me. You always had a heart of gold, doing anything for anyone and that was always your problem You couldn't say no to people and as long as it made people happy, you would do it. They say that even the nicest people have a tipping point, and I can tell you've reached yours.'

It was like he had an uncanny ability to peel back her skin and skull, peer into her brain and see exactly what was going on. But what he said next had Eve gasping.

'Please tell me that you haven't sent the column to this Belinda woman?'

'What?' Eve spluttered.

'The piece about how rubbish Becca's wedding was, did you send it to her as well?'

Eve looked horrified, and completely confused. 'As well as what?'

'As well as me,' Ben said.

'You?'

'At 4 a.m. this morning I got an email from you saying something like "Hi Belinda, here's my column," and then it went on and on about what a shitty wedding it was. Please tell me that it's not going to be printed anywhere.'

Eve closed her eyes and sank back against the sofa's cushions. She must have started typing *Be* in the empty To box on the email, and it came up with Ben's address and not Belinda's.

'Eve?'

Her head fell back with the purest sense of relief that coursed through her veins and her entire body.

'Thank you,' she whispered finally. 'Thank you.'

Ben didn't know what she meant by that, but he knew Eve. He moved across to her sofa, put his arm around her shoulder and pulled her into his chest. Great heaving sobs escaped from her exhausted body. She couldn't explain what had happened, she just cried until there were no more tears left. He felt her relax and go limp after a while. The medley of emotion and heartbreak and longing and guilt had been too much for her to bear, and she was back in her safe place where none of that mattered anymore.

Ben gently kissed the top of her head and told her that it was going to be ok. That whatever had been going on with her, with them, was going to be ok.

'I've been such an idiot Ben,' Eve gasped. 'I've lost all perspective on everything, and nearly ruined everything.'

'But you didn't. And I deleted the email immediately, so no one except you and I are ever going to know about this.'

Eve didn't want to move her head from the warmth of his

chest, or for him to stop stroking her hair. Eve couldn't tell, but he didn't want to break the spell either. But he knew he needed to.

'This is the first time I've hugged a woman in years.'

Eve tilted her head to meet his eyes and wiped her eyes on her sleeve. 'So, is this the moment where you tell me why you actually left me for Kate?'

'Are you sure you want to talk about that now?'

It wasn't a conversation Eve particularly wanted to have any time but she'd been putting it off, skirting the issue, making every excuse possible for why this inevitable talk should never take place. But they both knew it had to.

'Do you remember the first time we met each other?' Ben asked.

'Of course I do.'

'When was it?'

'Are you asking me to answer first because you don't know?' Eve countered.

'No! I'm just wondering if you remember it as clearly as I do.'

'Well I do.'

Ben smiled. 'What was I wearing?'

'What was *I* wearing?'

'Your navy drawstring trousers, a black vest top, those embroidered flip flops you insisted on wearing with every outfit and your hair was loose and longer than you have now. You'd let it dry naturally so it was all wavy and you had a jade beaded necklace on.'

'Wow. Even I didn't remember that.' If he'd pushed her,

she'd be able to recount what he was wearing too, right down to the black leather plaited bracelet. But she had no idea that she'd had that much of an impact on him on that first day.

'Do you know why I knew all that?'

Eve shook her head.

'Because that was the moment I fell in love with you.'

The room was still. Ben didn't speak again for another few seconds, to let what he'd just said have time to sink in. Eve shifted on the sofa slightly, bringing one knee up under her, and turning her body towards him. He did the same.

'I'd never met anyone like you before. Everyone else seemed so shy, or so obvious, but you were so self-assured, so confident.'

'So bossy?'

'No, not bossy, you were just you. You made me laugh the first time we spoke, do you know what you said?'

'Did I make fun of your accent?'

'Almost. You asked me where I was from, I said I was a kiwi, and you said that my costume was rubbish, and that I should make more of an effort.'

Eve laughed. 'It sounds like something I'd say.'

'Didn't you guess that I had a massive crush on you during university and all the years afterwards until that night in Clapham?'

'You did a pretty good job of hiding your feelings by parading an endless stream of leggy blondes through our front door and up the stairs to your room.'

'You noticed?'

'How could I not?' Eve wavered before saying anything else.

Ben was being completely honest with her – if she was to open up too, now was the time. But it was so hard.

'If I tell you about my life since the day I should have come to New York, can you not storm out or interrupt or say anything until I'm finished? Please Red? I need you to hear me.'

Eve didn't say anything, just nodded, her face pale. Their knees were touching and neither of them moved.

'When we became friends, I told you about Kate. I told you that I had a teenage romance with someone back home in New Zealand, but that she didn't mean anything to me.'

Eve nodded.

'Well, that was a bit of a lie.' Ben took a deep breath. 'She was my very first friend. Our mums had beds next to each other in the maternity ward, so I think I was born in the morning and Kate was born in the afternoon on the same day. Our parents joked that one day we would marry each other, and then as we got older, it wasn't a joke any more, it was an expectation, not just from them, for us too. We were inseparable, we walked to school together every day, sat next to each other in lessons, celebrated every single birthday, each milestone together. But she'd always been adamant that she never wanted to leave New Zealand. Her family were there, her life was there – but with my mum being British, I'd always wanted to come here for university. It was horrible leaving Kate, but we promised it was only for three years, and that she'd visit, and I'd go home in the holidays. But then life sort of took over. I got a holiday job—'

'In the drinks kiosk in the zoo—'

'Yes, the salubrious zoo kiosk. And I met you. You were sparky, hilarious, beautiful, fun, mad, and it wasn't until Kate visited me a few months into the first term and stayed over a few days, do you remember...?'

Eve nodded. Of course she remembered.

'I didn't know she was coming, and it was great to see her, but I didn't feel anything romantic for her at all. I realised that I loved Kate, but I wasn't *in* love with her anymore. She was lovely, and kind and sweet, but she wasn't you. She didn't guess what I was about to say, she didn't laugh at my jokes, she didn't make me laugh until my stomach hurt like you did. I told her that it wasn't going to work, she got really upset, and she left on an earlier flight.'

Ben blinked a few times, his eyes looking watery. 'And I never heard from her again until the day that I got the letter from her parents just before we were going to New York. You have to believe me how excited I was about our future Red; you and me, our plans to conquer America, to do it all together. Our future was so obvious to me. You know a few weeks ago when you got mad with me and shouted about the brownstone and the kids, and the travelling round in a camper van ... I'd had those thoughts too, all the time. Then this letter arrived from New Zealand, telling me that Kate had been diagnosed with leukaemia, and she only had a few months to live. She didn't want to die without making peace with me. The letter was so sad Eve, some of her mum's words were smudged where she'd obviously been crying writing them, it was heartbreaking. I can't imagine what it must have been like knowing that your child was about to die, that nothing you could do would give you an extra day with them, that you would never see them laugh again, or dance, or have a family of their own.

Tears were rolling down both their faces. It was Eve's turn to pull him close, to stroke his head, to tell him that it was alright, to let it out.

'I couldn't tell you, Eve,' Ben said, pulling his head up and looking at her as intensely as he ever had done. 'Not then. I needed to go there, do what needed to be done, and then I could bring you into it. I knew you would want to help, to share the burden, but I couldn't let you do that. I owed it to Kate to be there at the end, to let her die knowing that I cared, and I needed you to follow your dreams, to go to America and carve out an incredible career for yourself that you couldn't have done if you were helping me grieve for another woman. And then I thought that if fate existed, then life would bring us back together, that we'd find each other again. But when I got to New Zealand all these old feelings I had for Kate bubbled to the surface and I knew I couldn't just say goodbye and leave again. I needed to stay with her, to show her how much she meant to me. When Kate died, I didn't anticipate the weight of grief that came with it. She was so brave Red, so brave. She knew the morning that she passed away that it was to be that day, can you believe it? She said it. "Today's the day I'm going to die." Then she told her mum what she wanted to be wearing, it was a knee-length blue dress with little spots on it, and she asked for us all to have a picnic in the garden.'

Eve remembered how solemn Ben looked at Becca's picnic

reception, and realised he wasn't being moody, he was reliving this moment, this tragic memory.

'She hadn't been outside in weeks, but we took her. We spread out a blanket, and I carried her out and sat her resting back on a beanbag. And we all began to eat and laugh together, but she just watched us. She looked so peaceful, her hair was fanned out, and her mouth even looked like it was smiling, but we knew she'd gone. I'm sorry, I don't know why I'm crying. I never loved her the way that I love you, but I did love her Eve, I really did. And in that moment, watching her parents break their hearts over her body, I knew that my life had changed. I couldn't just pack up and join you in New York, and I couldn't imagine coming back to London without you being here. I felt so guilty for making her so unhappy, for making her family, and mine, so sad when I cast her off like that after a whole lifetime of preparing to spend it together.'

Eve wasn't expecting to ever feel sorry for Ben, to pity the decisions he made, but she did. In finishing with Kate, he'd made Eve happy, and in ending it with Eve, he'd made peace with Kate.

'I thought about you all the time, and read everything you ever wrote online. I was so proud of you for going to New York by yourself, and for making a success of yourself. But I just couldn't get in touch with you, I felt so guilty.'

'But why did you never tell me Ben? You knew exactly where I was and I had no clue where you were, not a clue. You're not on social media, you didn't reply to my emails, you just disappeared off the face of the earth. You know I would never have let you face this by yourself. You didn't need to do this alone.'

'I did though Eve, don't you see that? You would have given it all up, your dreams your life, your family, to come to the other end of the world and help me get over another woman. Even if I had come to you, I was a mess, Red. I could never have let you see me like that.'

'But it's not the '50s, Ben, keeping a stiff upper lip doesn't make you a social pariah, grieving for someone you loved is nothing to be ashamed of.'

'It wasn't like that. Kate's parents were in a really bad way, she was their only child. They'd waited years to have her, and then for her to be taken away from them when she was twenty-six? I felt that I needed to make their path as smooth as possible. They welcomed me into their family without question, and I became really close with them after Kate's death. I didn't feel that I could introduce my girlfriend into the equation, I felt that would be disrespecting them, and Kate. Although, funnily enough, in Kate's last few weeks she spoke about you quite a few times. She told me she really liked you when she'd visited and that we would be really good together.'

'Don't you think that was her way of saying that she wanted you to be happy with me?'

'Maybe, looking back on it now, yes, perhaps it was. But it was all so raw then, it was difficult to know what to do for the best so I literally just shut down all my own needs and wants and focused entirely on doing right by her memory.'

'So why come back now?' It was a question Eve had been

asking herself for months. 'Why wait four years before reappearing?'

'I didn't know what else to do, I'd become part of the community in Wellington, but it never felt like home, not somewhere where I'd be happy forever, and although some of my old friends were there, it seemed strange being there without Kate. So I decided to move back, to make a home here. It was horrible at first, everywhere I went had a memory of you attached to it.'

'Why do you think I stayed in New York for two years?' Eve replied.

'I wanted to contact you so badly, but this isn't the sort of story you can tell over the phone, or email and so I wanted to talk to you in person, and then, as you know, it's just never been the right time. And anyway, Tanya said that you'd moved on, that you were pleased I didn't come with you to New York, that you never wanted me to come, but didn't know how to let me down.'

'She said *what*? When?'

'After I'd been in Wellington for almost a year I was missing you so much, and so I got in touch with Luke to see if he had an address for you, and Tanya replied to my email, saying that you wouldn't be interested in hearing from me. That you were having an amazing life in New York and had met someone special. I didn't want to spoil things for you, so I didn't try again.'

'That woman is evil.'

'So it's not true?'

'The opposite is true Ben. I had a miserable time in New

York, I barely saw sunlight, couldn't afford to eat anything that wasn't in a tin or frozen, the cleanliness of my flatmates made the prospect of contracting legionnaires, salmonella, listeria or the bubonic plague a daily reality, and I missed you. Every single day I wondered what you were doing, who you were with, where you were. If you were thinking of me. My life has pretty much been on pause since the moment you left.'

'So what now?' Ben asked, still holding her hand, stroking her thumb with his.

'Well first I want to blow my nose, and then...' *Then I want to kiss you.* 'Then ... I think we should order some food.'

Chapter 35

'So, here's a question for you,' Ben said, prising the lid off the chicken chow mein and setting it down on top of the other lids on the lounge coffee table. He handed her a plate and a pair of chopsticks. 'Dig in.'

Eve braced herself for a personal enquiry into her love life. 'Yes?'

'When did you have your ears pierced?'

Her hand instinctively went to her ear lobe and felt the long feather earring that Adam had bought her that she'd worn for the wedding the day before but hadn't yet taken off.

'That's very strange question, what made you think that?'

'Just that I remember you didn't have them done, and now you do. I want to catch up on everything that's happened to you over the last few years.'

'Starting with when did I pierce my ears?'

'That's a good a place as any.'

Eve smiled. 'The answer is, I haven't, as much as Tanya wanted me to. They're clip-on. Now I have a question. Have you had the Chinese tattoo removed from your back yet that should have said "Freedom" but actually said "Free of Charge?"'

336

Ben burst out laughing and almost spat his rice all over the table. 'I completely forgot that you knew that, I have never told anyone else that!'

'I don't think you'd have told me either had I not been with you when that Chinese girl made fun of you on that beach in Worthing.'

'I haven't had it verified from another source though, so she could have just been teasing me.'

'Ben, she had tears of laughter running down her face, she wasn't joking.'

'She may have been laughing at her own gag. I've done that plenty of times. Take Tanya's wedding for instance. Seeing you sat with nasally Peter, that lentil-loving dark-haired bloke and the woman that breeds her own sheep had me chuckling for hours.'

'Funny you should say that because the idea of you tap dancing your way through Covent Garden on Amit's stag do made me laugh pretty hard too.'

It wasn't hard to fall back into the trade of easy banter they'd perfected over the previous decade. Quick quips flew back and forth, and the natural warmth and affection that was the hallmark of their friendship made two hours seem like thirty minutes. As their laughs faded they listened to the clanks and crashes of the band in the pub below packing up for the night, the musicians keen to get home to their families. Car doors slamming, shouts of farewells and finally the sound of the heavy bolt being dragged across the pub's front door signalled that the evening, at least for the people on the street below, was over.

'I should go,' Ben said, not moving from his patch of floor.

This was the part where Eve was meant to ask him to stay for one more drink. To stay to finish up the food. To stay for dessert. To just stay. They'd read the script, they knew what was supposed to come next. But she couldn't.

'You're right,' she said quietly. 'It's late, and we've got work tomorrow.' Eve gathered up the foil boxes and started throwing them into the brown paper takeaway bag that was stained with some soy sauce that had leaked through. He read her signal and stood up stretching, clinking together their wine glasses in one hand, and picking up the empty bottle in the other.

They tangoed around each other in the small galley kitchen. He pulled the full rubbish bag out of the bin and tied it together.

'You don't need to do that,' Eve said, making a move to take it off him. 'The man doesn't always need to take the rubbish out while the little lady washes up.'

'No thank goodness, because you wouldn't know a scourer if it came up and introduced itself,' Ben teased. 'Don't forget I've lived with you.'

'I'll have you know that I cleaned this place from top to bottom before you came around, I even bleached the plug.'

'Bleach the plug? Have you ever, in the your entire life, used those three words in the same sentence before?'

'I'm not sure anyone has, to be honest.'

'Oh, I don't know,' Ben said with a smile. 'I'd put money on it being on Luke's weekend to-do list from Tanya.'

At the mention of Tanya's name, Eve pulled a face. 'Can we not say her name again without pretending to spit?'

'She may be a despicable human being, but she did get us

338

back together.' Ben looked instantly uncomfortable with his choice of phrasing, and Eve busied herself putting away the dry cups from the draining board. 'I didn't mean like that, I just meant—'

'It's ok, I know what you meant.'

'You know, with her wedding, and the curtains, then the gifts and the tent-sex thing, we were sort of thrown together a lot. I didn't mean—'

'Ben, it's fine. Look, leave the bin bag, I'll take it down on my way to work in the morning.'

'It's no problem, I'll do it now on my way out.'

Eve followed him to the front door and unlocked it for him. 'I, um, look, thanks for coming round.'

They both stood next to the open door. In one hand Ben held the bin bag, and he brought the other hand up to tuck a loose curl behind Eve's ear. 'You haven't changed, you know Eve. I know you think you have, that you've lost all perspective and that you've become cynical and hard, but you haven't. You're still you.'

'I don't know that anymore.'

'Well I can see it, even if you can't.'

He then ducked his head slowly until his lips brushed hers and Eve's eyes instinctively closed.

And then he was gone. Again.

***

'I'm surprised to see you here.'

Fiona's frosty greeting stopped Eve in her tracks. It was a

Monday, why would Eve being at her desk be an odd thing? She said as much.

'I just thought with the email you sent me at 4 a.m. on Sunday morning I'd be recruiting for a new features editor.'

Eve's stomach lurched. The drama of the column had completely erased from her memory the drunken message she'd angrily typed to her boss.

'Oh God Fiona, I'm so sorry, I didn't mean it, I—'

'Shall we talk in my office?' It wasn't a request that needed a response as Fiona was already striding away, fully expecting Eve to scuttle behind her. Fiona accepted the resignation that Eve didn't really remember submitting, giving her no opportunity to explain, or backtrack. As her editor read out bits from the barely coherent email she'd sent her, Eve winced – it was as bad as it was possible to be.

'So, I'll go and pack up my desk shall I?' Eve said, fully aware of the pleading tone in her voice imploring her boss to reconsider, to just forget about it.

'I think that's probably for the best.'

Eve stood on the street grasping a carrier bag. It was filled with photos with drawing pin holes in the top of them that had been tacked up around her desk, a Tupperware box containing her lunch, her notebooks with feature ideas that would never get written and her diary with meetings that she'd never attend. The bright sunshine was incongruous with her mood. The clouds should have been gathering, a clap of thunder, some rain at least, but the pavement was warm, the people who passed her were basking in the summer sun with their sleeveless tops and carefree smiles. It wasn't supposed to be like this.

If it was a movie she'd head to an open-all-day pub, settle in for the day and drink away her worries. She'd sit on a bench in a park and gaze at people with agendas, things to do, places to go, people to meet. But she wasn't in a movie. This was her life, and she knew that at the moment she was making a giant hash of it.

Chapter 36

Faye was refusing to fly to Adam and George's wedding. No amount of acupuncture, hypnosis or alcohol could get her to board the fast shuttle that would have got them from London to Marseille in under two hours. Instead Eve had agreed to hire a car, and drive them on the thirteen-hour journey to Provence.

It seemed like so much more than just a week had passed since Becca's wedding. Six days since Eve's evening with Ben, five days since leaving the magazine. When you had nothing to get up for, no reason to shower, iron creases out of work clothes, or get dressed at all, the hours seemed agonisingly long. Becca and Jack had jetted off on their honeymoon straight after the wedding, and so Eve hadn't needed to contend with Becca's clucks of disapproval at her daytime TV marathon sessions, or the fact that she hadn't changed out of her pyjamas for four days straight. If Eve had thought about it she may have linked Faye's sudden phobia of airplanes with Eve's sudden phobia of the outside world, but she was too wrapped up in a cloud of self-pity and self-doubt to connect the two.

'This is nice, isn't it? Us girls taking a road trip.'

Eve decided to let her mother have her *Thelma and Louise* moment, even allowing the reference to them both as 'girls' go unchecked.

'We don't do this enough, do we?' Faye continued.

'Drive through the Channel Tunnel?'

'No silly, spend time together.'

Eve's eyes flitted to the navigation system. It was a pretty easy route down to Provence, through the French countryside, skirting the Alps. They were breaking their journey in Dijon, about halfway down, and they should be there within five hours if the traffic was light. Eve murmured so. If it was up to her she'd have wanted to press on, to not stop at a random French city where Faye would no doubt insist on them having lunch together, to spend a couple of hours having small talk when what she really wanted to do was to ask her daughter what the hell was going on.

Eve was making sure that the volume on the French rock radio station obliterated the opportunity for conversation, and for the first three hours of the journey her plan worked well. Until, after an unscheduled loo stop, Faye abruptly flicked off the radio as Eve started the engine.

'I liked that, Mum.'

'We can put it on again in a bit. I fancied a bit of a chat.'

There wasn't a daughter alive that couldn't hear the badly-concealed agenda behind the words 'bit of a chat' from their mother, and Eve was no different.

'What do you want to chat about?' she asked airily.

'Why don't you start by telling me why you left Becca's wedding in such a hurry and then refused to answer your phone, why Ben rushed after you, and why you haven't been at work all week.'

'Oh good. For a minute I thought you were going to be subtle about it.' Eve indicated and moved into the fast lane to overtake a tiny old Fiat, then moved back into the outside lane once passing it. 'Why don't you start by telling me about your evening with my personal trainer?'

Even though she couldn't see her mum's face, Eve knew that she was blushing. It was a bit cruel to deflect her mum's questions back onto her. Faye would tell her about Juan when she was ready, but they both knew that Eve was stalling for time.

'Juan is a lovely chap. Kind, attentive—' Faye's voice dipped a little, adding a little conspiratorially '—and very attractive.'

'Are you going to see him again?'

Faye smiled. 'I hope so. I was toying with the idea of asking him to be my plus one for this wedding, but didn't have the nerve in the end.'

'Oh Mum, you should have done, you deserve a bit of fun and happiness. It's not too late, the wedding's not for another two days, he can fly in tomorrow or Saturday morning.'

'I wouldn't know what to say. Anyway, he's probably having huge regrets over what happened. I'm twenty years older than him for goodness sake.'

'Well I actually think you two make a lovely couple. And anyway, it doesn't need to be anything serious, just have some fun, you've deserved it.'

'You deserve some fun too you know.'

Eve kept her eyes on the road. 'I do have fun.'

344

'No, you don't. You make sure that you're far too busy to have fun. When is it going to be your turn Eve?'

'My turn for what? If you say my turn to get married you can walk the rest of the way.'

'Your turn to have people do something for you. You're always the first to put your hand up to help, the first to get stuck in organising, or sorting things out for people, and you don't let anyone do the same for you. It's like if you accept help or support then you're somehow weaker in some way.'

'I don't need any help.'

'We all need help from time to time.'

'Well I don't.'

'How's work going?'

Eve faltered. She could lie, say something like 'same old same old' that would have a fifty-fifty chance of being believed, or she could take advantage of the fact that her mum could only see the side of her face and not the whole of it and tell the truth.

'To be honest, Mum, I've messed everything up.' Eve blinked away tears that were threatening to form and her knuckles whitened on the steering wheel where she was gripping it too hard. 'It's all going horribly wrong.'

They pulled off the motorway and into a roadside café. Once the matronly café owner had left a couple of strong coffees on the table, Faye reached over and put her hand over her daughter's. 'Begin at the beginning, the King said, very gravely, and go on till you come to the end: then stop.'

Faye's reference to *Alice in Wonderland*, one of Eve's favourite stories from when she was young made her eyes watery again.

345

'I miss Dad, Mum.'

'Oh darling, we all do.'

'How long does grief take to heal?'

'Oh God Eve, I don't know, there's no set rule about grief. It's not a case of waking up one morning to find the mist has suddenly lifted. Sometimes you can have weeks of clear skies and then bam, there it is, fog so thick you can't walk through it. Why are you asking this? Is this just about Dad?'

Eve shook her head. 'You know when Ben never showed up at the airport? He left me to go back to New Zealand and see his ex-girlfriend that was dying.' Eve's tone was a lot more matter of fact than she felt. It had to be or she would never get the story out. 'And while he was there, with her, Kate, in those final few months, he fell in love with her again. When she died, he felt so guilty for once choosing me over her, and coming to England, that he stayed there, with her family, and his, all of them grieving together.'

'But now he's back.'

'And now he's back.'

'And you two are getting close again?'

Eve's fingers closed around the sugar sachets in the little china pot on the table. 'We could be. But I'm so scared Mum. It's taken me four years to get over him, and I don't know if I have it in me to try again.'

'So what's the alternative? You find someone you don't like as much to be with, or you resign yourself to being your ageing mum's plus one to every party?'

Eve smiled weakly. 'I love being your plus one.'

'Well, if my luck has changed you might need to fight a

muscly Argentinian for that honour in the future,' Faye laughed. 'But seriously Eve, you can't build a little wall around your heart so it never gets broken.'

'Why not?'

'Because that would make me extremely sad. If I knew when I married Dad that I'd be a widow before I was sixty, would I have still done it? Of course I would. If I knew I was to be a widow at fifty, forty, I still would. Did it feel like my universe had shattered into tiny shards of glass when he died, you bet it did, but that pain was worth the love, and I'd do it again in a heartbeat.'

'That's the thing Mum, you talk of love like it's this amazing thing, but my experience of it is that it's only ever temporary. And I'm not just talking about me and Ben before you jump on me and tell me I'm wrong, but my job is...' Eve paused at her use of the present tense, but didn't correct herself, she needed to tackle one topic of conversation at a time. 'My job is about love, about the supposedly happiest day in a couple's life, and more often than not, it doesn't work out. In some of the brides' cases, the flowers last longer than the marriages do.'

'I think those years on that horrible reality magazine has skewed your view of normality. When you only meet and write about the strangest sort of people, of course you start to think the world is full of people that will sleep with their brother's parrot.'

Eve burst out laughing. 'I think that's actually impossible Mum.'

'You know what I mean. You had years of writing about

the world's weirdos, and then years writing about brides, who, lets be fair, are not the sanest of people. Then you had all your friends' weddings this summer, it's no wonder that you're viewing love as a bit of a chore. Do you still have feelings for Ben?'

'It's not my feelings I'm worried about, it's Ben's. He still carries Kate's locket around in his wash bag you know.'

'Did you ask him about it?'

Eve looked sheepish. 'No.'

'There's nothing wrong with him keeping a part of her close. I still have loads of your dad's things, that doesn't mean that I can't like or love anyone else ever again.'

'I know, I know that, but how can I compete with her? She's like this perfect person, who I'll never measure up to.'

'This Kate was incredibly important to him obviously, and if you want to be important to him again, then you can't ignore her.'

Faye was saying everything that Eve had already thought. In fact, after Ben left last Sunday night, Eve had barely thought about anything else. She'd lain in bed staring up at the ceiling, going over and over everything that he'd said. She understood his thinking entirely because she understood him. And keeping Eve out of his life for her own good was also so like Ben. He was right, if he'd told her the real reason, she would never have boarded that plane to New York. As the hours and days ticked by in the last week she had ricocheted between anger that Ben made the decision for her, and absolute pride that he'd stepped up and been the friend Kate and her family needed.

'Ok, so while you're dishing out free therapy Mum, I got fired on Monday.'

'Oh, Eve.'

She didn't need to tell her mum that actually she got fired twice on the same day. Once, twice, who's counting? After standing solitary on the street, her sad little carrier bag in her hand, Eve had answered a call from Belinda at *Venus* who'd been on a hiking weekend in Snowdonia. When she'd got back to civilisation and reliable mobile service she'd received a never-ending stream of garbled messages from Eve begging her not to run a column that she'd never even received.

'I'm not sure what's going on with you Eve,' Belinda had said. 'But I'm giving you one last chance to redeem yourself with a column about the gay destination wedding you're going to. And I want you to camp it up. Big time.'

Eve told her that she wasn't going to write about that anymore, that she wanted to write about something other than weddings. When she'd said she couldn't write about the gay wedding of her brother, Belinda had told her that it was that or nothing. So Eve chose nothing.

'So what are you going to do for money?' Faye asked, entirely reasonably. Principles were great but they didn't pay the rent.

'I'm not entirely sure,' Eve replied. 'But I have enough saved up to buy us another round of coffees before we hit the road again if you fancy it?'

Chapter 37

The 'lets get married abroad so all our loved ones have to use up their annual leave allocation and get a bank loan to attend' wedding

'Are you serious?' Adam shrieked as soon as Faye and Eve walked into the grand hallway of the chateau where the wedding was to be held in two days' time.

Eve plonked her suitcase down on the chequerboard floor. 'I think what you meant to say was, "Hi Mum, sis, how was the thirteen-hour journey, you must be shattered, it's this way to a glass of wine."'

'Where are your partners?'

'Our what?'

'You told me, no, you *promised* me, that you'd both be bringing plus ones to the wedding. Please tell me they're arriving separately.'

'They're arriving separately.'

'Are they really?'

'No. You just told me to say that.'

'Eve, look at me, do I look as though I'm in the mood for your sarcasm?'

Eve studied her brother for a minute. His cheeks were flushed, his hair a little disheveled from his hand constantly running through it, his shirt was uncharacteristically creased. 'No, you don't. You look like a groom that's lost all perspective on life. Come on Adam, lighten up, you're getting married!'

'The table plans are ruined.'

'Look, if it's that important, Mum and I will go out in Avignon tonight on the pull and find a couple of nice local men we can bring along.'

'Would you really do that, for me?' Adam asked, his hand on his chest.

A horrified Faye swivelled to her daughter, who just laughed, shaking her head. 'Of course not! Get a grip Adam, then open a bottle of wine, give me a list of things that need doing and we'll all get on with our lives.'

'I thought I heard voices, hello, hello,' George came bounding down the stairs into the hallway and engulfed his soon to be mother- and sister-in-law in big bear hugs. 'You must be shattered, do you want tea or wine?'

Eve grinned, and pointed at George. 'See Adam, that's the welcome we wanted.'

'Bugger off.' Adam replied sulkily.

'He's annoyed because Eve and I are both single.'

George gave Faye a wink. 'That's not what I heard. How is the gorgeous Latin American?'

Faye blushed. 'Gorgeous. And slightly out of my league.'

'Oh hush. He looked completely smitten last weekend,' George teased. 'And what about Ben? He rushed after you after you left early, didn't he Eve? Something to tell us there?'

'Something and nothing,' Eve shrugged. 'As usual.'

She wasn't quite telling the truth to them all. Ben had phoned her countless times over the last week, and each time Eve saw his name come up on her screen she'd muted the call. If it was possible to be in eerily familiar and yet entirely unfamiliar territory at the same time, then she was in it. She wasn't sure now whether she'd imagined the look that passed between them when Ben had suggested it was time for him to leave her flat. Whether, if she had asked him to stay, he would have done. And if she had, would it have been because he really wanted to stay, with her, or just his loneliness talking. She guessed she'd never know now.

***

With all her clothes upended in the chest of drawers in her round turret bedroom, and her empty suitcase stowed under the bed, Eve splashed some water on her face and peered into the tiny square mirror over the basin. She looked exhausted. After a snatched dinner of bread, cheese and ham with her mum, Adam and George, she had tumbled into her room and was willing herself to fall into a dreamless sleep. She'd spent the day turning the ancient chateau into the vision of loveliness that jumped out from the pages of the scrapbook that Adam had reverently presented her with at breakfast that morning announcing, 'This is the blueprint for how we want it to look.'

'No pressure there then,' Eve had replied. Extravagant displays of white flowers burst from every page, and there was even one picture depicting a tower of pastel-pretty macaroons. Eve wasn't entirely sure whether these were just inspirational or whether her brother actually expected her to source, pay for and construct said tower of sugary splendour. After his meltdown the evening before about the lack of plus-ones, Eve couldn't be sure. It was just as well she had turn up solo because the gargantuan size of her job-list meant that the hypothetical plus-one wouldn't have seen her. Between helping the florist loop greenery through the bannisters, popping thousands of tea lights into little glass jars, carrying bay trees out to the terrace, tying ribbons onto chairs, and putting a copy of the wedding newsletter she'd written into every one of the chateau's bedrooms, by the time the antique grandfather clock in the salon struck five in the afternoon, Eve was absolutely knackered and the wedding part of the weekend hadn't even started yet.

She was woken the next morning by an incessant hammering on the door and a jubilant 'I'm getting married today!' being shouted through the keyhole. Eve lay back on her pillow and smiled at her brother's wake up call. Shards of sunlight poked through the warped wood of the old shutters on her window, giving her room a soft morning glow. Obviously expecting Eve to turn up with a man, Adam had given her a double room, and as Eve stretched her limbs awake, she made a snow angel in the middle of the big bed, moving her legs and arms up and down and side to side, laughing as she did so. Today was a new day. A good day.

A few of Adam and George's friends were starting to filter up the driveway and according to the itinerary Eve had written and propped up on the easel, they all had an hour 'at leisure' before pre-ceremony drinks on the terrace. Eve slipped into the ankle-length jade-green wrap dress that Adam had picked out for her. She clipped on her feather earrings, fluffing her hair out as she ran down the corridor to Adam's room to continue her Best Woman duties.

The terrace was heaving with glamorous people wearing what the fashion team on her old magazine could only describe as 'Riviera chic'. The women sported swirling kaftans or clinging minidresses, the men wore a uniform of linen shorts with open-necked shirts and designer sunglasses. A steel drum band were playing at one end of the pool and a few women were already sashaying in front of them. Eve weaved her way through the laughter, chatter and clinking glasses, to the familiar sight of Faye. Her mum looked gorgeous in an ever so slightly see-through silk evening dress in a riot of blues and greens, her short blonde hair was slicked back and a brown muscly forearm was draped across her shoulder. It was nice when a plan came together.

Eve smiled as she approached them. 'Hi Juan, fancy seeing you here.'

'Juan told me you called him yesterday and told him to come, you naughty girl,' Faye laughed.

Seeing her mum so happy proved to Eve that she'd done

the right thing. An unlikely couple they may well be, but you couldn't argue with the width of their grins and obvious chemistry.

'Sorry to drag you away from each other,' Eve said, 'but Adam's ready for us now Mum.'

Everyone had taken their seats on the terrace, the tealights had been lit, the flowers were giving off a heady scent in the sun, and the steel band started playing Bob Marley's *One Love* as Eve and Faye walked a beaming Adam up the wide aisle alongside George flanked by his parents. The joy surrounding them was completely contagious and everyone started clapping along to the jubilant beat of the drums and by the time they'd reached the registrar all their friends were out of their seats dancing and cheering.

It was Eve's sixth wedding of the summer. The sixth trading of vows and rings, the sixth couple who stared into each other's eyes and made promises of lifelong love, fidelity and truth. Watching Adam and George tearfully work their way through their pledges, seeing the way George's thumb kept reassuringly stroking Adam's, witnessing their intense happiness as the registrar proclaimed them married, Eve couldn't help but share in their joy. It would be a pretty sad world if love like this didn't exist.

'Thank you again,' Faye whispered to Eve as the ceremony ended. 'For calling Juan and making him come here.'

'You're welcome. I know he's not Dad, but I thought about what you said, and life's too short to keep grieving for the past. Anyway, we couldn't have Adam hyperventilating over two empty spaces at the dinner table, could we?'

'No, we couldn't,' Faye agreed. 'Which is why I found you a plus one too.' Faye glanced over Eve's shoulder as she said this.

'Hello Red.'

Eve spun round, her eyes wide. 'Oh my God, Ben, what are you doing here?'

'Apparently making up numbers.'

There was suddenly and conveniently someone very important Faye wanted to introduce Juan to, and she slipped away, leaving the two of them alone.

'Say something.'

Eve opened her mouth but nothing came out. For a woman who worked with words, she literally couldn't find any.

'Ok, I'll go first then, shall I?' Ben said, taking a deep breath before all his words gushed out at once. 'You and me Eve, we're meant to be together. I know it. You know it. We've wasted too much time pretending otherwise and so here's the plan. You jack in your job, I quit mine, we take three months off, hire a camper van, travel the length and breadth of Canada and fall in love with each other all over again.'

Eve was still open-mouthed. The noise from the band, the laughter of everyone around her, the smell from the flowers, it was all so real, and yet this conversation wasn't.

'Ben, I—'

'Don't overthink it Eve. You plan everything to the nth degree, but just let go. Forget about all the baggage, the past. Just say yes, and let us start again. Let's do it, let's go away from here and everything and spend some real time together and see what happens.'

It was everything Eve wanted to hear – but it wasn't realistic, too much had happened. 'It sounds lovely Ben, but I've changed, we've both changed, and we're not the same people that we were.'

'I know that. So why don't we pretend we're strangers meeting for the first time?'

'What?'

'Just that. Imagine that we've never seen each before, and we've spotted each other across a crowded party, and we quite like the look of each other. I've come up to you, you're a bit irritated at the interruption, but intrigued, so I say, "Hi, nice to meet you."'

Eve shook her head. 'This is silly.'

'Humour me Red. What have you got to lose?'

He was right. She had less to lose than even he knew about. Ben pounced on her pause as a sign of her willingness to play along, so he followed it up with, 'Hello, I don't think we've met before, do you come here often?'

Eve sighed, and couldn't help a hint of a smile playing on her lips. 'Not that often no, you?'

'It's my first time.'

'I'm Eve.' She held out her hand for him to shake.

'Ben.' He took her hand and held it in his, then broke into a big grin. 'With a B.'

Acknowledgements

This novel was conceived during a phone call with my fabulous editor Charlotte Ledger who asked what I loved writing about, and I replied 'funny women and weddings' and she told me that sounded like a good place to start. I've said it before, but I think it needs repeating: the whole team at HarperImpulse is, quite frankly, extraordinary. Thanks especially to Charlotte Ledger, Kim Young, Kate Bradley, Dushi Horti and Sahina Bibi. To my fellow HI authors, it's fantastic being part of such a supportive community – lots of love particularly to Eve Devon and Christie Barlow for their pep talks and offers of metaphorical gin.

I am ever grateful to my wonderful agent Luigi Bonomi and the beautiful team at LBA – Alison and Dani – thank you for your words of wisdom and inspiration.

I wrote this novel during our first year living in Rome, and we had a steady stream of visitors that summer, each of whom contributed in some way to this novel being written – Alex and Jasmine Collin thank you for your plot tips and for keeping the kids amused for 47 hours straight, Lisa and Joe Stratford for pouring Chianti into my mouth every evening,

Rachel and Jodie Hamilton for reading bits of the first draft and for being well housetrained, Anya White, Dan and Matt Lomax, thank you for bringing your Antipodean humour with you, some of which may have found its way into this book. Big love and huge amounts of grateful thanks to Anna, Claire, Kate, Kerry and Rachel, my new gang in Italy, for telling me all your stories and for making the transition of being a Roman expat much more fun.

To my family, the Butterfields, the Coopers, the Harpers, the Poulains, the Denfords, the H-Ms, the Harveys, the Poultneys, you're all magnificent human beings. And to my own little tribe, Ed, Amélie, Rafe and Theo, Je t'aime, Ti amo, I love you.